PRAISE FOR *WESTERLY*

"Spanning three generations, from the windswept shores of Ireland to the craggy coastline of Maine, Bernhard weaves an unforgettable tale of identity, loss, and love. Featuring an indelible sisterhood of characters, *Westerly* is about what we avoid and what we run toward in our quest to discover who we really are. A masterwork of storytelling. I loved every page."

—Katherine A. Sherbrooke, author of *Leaving Coy's Hill* and *The Hidden Life of Aster Kelly*

"*Westerly* is a sweeping portrait of how one woman's lie multiplies through time. Mother to daughter, secrets beget secrets in a spiraling cascade destined to unravel. Each family member must question who they are—and find the courage to become their true selves. Written in Bernhard's luminous prose, *Westerly* will live in your heart long after the final page."

—Tess Callahan, author of *Dawnland* and *April & Oliver*

"What if the secrets that kept us safe also kept us apart? In this luminous novel, Susan Bernhard traces the echoes of an unspoken trauma from the wild Irish coast to a secluded inlet in Maine, where three generations of women strive to build new lives among old silences. *Westerly* is a portrait of family in all its fragility and grace—a story that will break your heart, then leave it wiser."

—Janet Rich Edwards, author of *Canticle*

"Powerful and immersive, *Westerly* is an extraordinary novel about the secrets we carry, the burdens they cause, and the redeeming power of love. As Faye and her daughters make choices that are complicated and have profound consequences, Bernhard reveals with stunning prose why we strive to endure, to change, and ultimately to heal. An utterly beautiful achievement."

—Marjan Kamali, *New York Times* bestselling author of *The Lion Women of Tehran*

"A sweeping novel carrying the reader from one edge of the Atlantic to the other, from one generation to the next, at an extraordinary time in world history—alive with all the secrets, beautiful landscape, and depth of character a reader could want."

—Ben Shattuck, author of *The History of Sound*

"In a story packed with as much secrecy as love, *Westerly* follows two generations of women as they move from war-torn Germany to an Irish village to mid-coast Maine across five decades. But the larger journey is one of learning to share our lives—our past and present truths—with those who are supposed to know us best, and trusting that they will still love us. An absolutely beautiful story of choosing honesty and forgiveness over secrets and shame."

—Heather Aimee O'Neill, bestselling author of *The Irish Goodbye*

"An utterly beautiful achievement."

—Marjan Kamali, *New York Times* bestselling author

Westerly

OTHER TITLES BY SUSAN DONOVAN BERNHARD

Winter Loon

Westerly

a novel

SUSAN DONOVAN BERNHARD

Little
a

This is a work of fiction. Names, characters, organizations, places, events, and incidents are either products of the author's imagination or are used fictitiously. Otherwise, any resemblance to actual persons, living or dead, is purely coincidental.

Published by Little A, Seattle

www.apub.com

EU product safety contact:
Amazon Media EU S. à r.l.
38, avenue John F. Kennedy, L-1855 Luxembourg
amazonpublishing-gpsr@amazon.com

ISBN-13: 9781662537905 (hardcover)
ISBN-13: 9781662537882 (paperback)
ISBN-13: 9781662537899 (digital)

Cover design by Tree Abraham
Cover image: © Rebecca Aldernet; © Henrik Dønnestad / Unsplash

Printed in the United States of America

First edition

For my immigrant grandparents—Elizabeth Flacker,
Robert Sonntag, Anna Sullivan, and John Donovan—
and for all the Tomorrows.

west•er•ly

adj: moving toward or belonging to the west

n: a wind blowing from the west

Come away, O human child!
To the waters and the wild
With a faery, hand in hand,
For the world's more full of weeping than you can understand.

From "The Stolen Child" by William Butler Yeats

PROLOGUE

1995: Mid-Coast Maine

Faye puts the pies in the oven and turns on the timer, her hands quivering. She hears William in the living room reading picture books to their granddaughter, Nola Wren, the murmur of his voice, the kerplink, kerplank, kerplunk of blueberries hitting Sal's pail. The child giggles, a joy-filled chirp, like birdsong from the yard. *The Irish Times* sits heavy as an anvil on the table, though the photo there billows like ash above the newsprint, an apparition, the past come to life. Faye wonders how she might lash herself to this kitchen, to William, to the life they've built—anything to keep from being swept away by what that newspaper could unleash.

This is her favorite time of year, the season turning from summer to fall, the way sunlight becomes shimmery and golden. Already, squirrels bustle about with green nuts from the oak tree. Already, robins congregate in friendly flocks. Yet some storm gathers. She feels it in her bones. It broods there on the table, black and white. She remembers a line, something from a Millay sonnet. *My sky is black with small birds bearing south.*

William gasps, and she knows he has moved on to the theatrics of *Miss Spider's Tea Party*.

That damned newspaper.

"Take a look," he'd said earlier when he came in from the barn. "Are these your German girls? The ones from the boat?" When Nola Wren interrupted, tugged on his pant leg, William abandoned the paper as if it contained nothing but a human-interest story and not the story of lives tangled and lost and resurrected. And on this, of all days. Molly's homecoming.

Faye grips the kitchen shears like a weapon, gingerly steps toward the table as if she might slay, with quick stabs, this beast that stalks her. The headline is bold and dark as a crow.

OFFICIALS, FAMILIES TO CELEBRATE

OPERATION SHAMROCK 50TH ANNIVERSARY

Beneath the headline is a photograph, a group of children, thirty or more, alive with ribbing and pushing and horseplay. She can almost recall the pop of flashbulbs. The boys perch in back; some hold archer's bows and single arrows. The girls sit on a concrete barrier, arms draped around shoulders, scraped knees and slouched socks dangling lazily over the edge. They are happy and fed. Oranges and chocolate, milk and butter and bread. Faye's stomach aches with memory. She is there, her younger self, peering past the camera and into the future. Her accusing stare gives Faye the shivers. Another girl, her face as familiar to Faye as her own, turned slightly, head tilted in laughter. Like a herding dog keeping sheep in line, a nun in black, her white wimple flapped like donkey ears, has corralled the group along with yet another woman, younger, hair spun up like sugar on a paper cone.

Faye sets the shears down, holds the picture to her ear. She bows her head, hoping to hear their voices, if even for the briefest moment, before she must quiet them again.

PART ONE

1946–1968

CHAPTER ONE

1959: Mid-Coast Maine

Faye pulled together a bouquet from the flower shop's discarded stems. She laid out her choices on the rustic pine workbench behind the cash register and trimmed away the worst of the browning and dry petals. Her mother, Jean, had requested flowers to take to dinner at the home of William Sullivan, the widower son of Faye's father's friend Kevin, who'd died the year before. Faye remembered that funeral not only because Kevin Sullivan had been the man who'd welcomed them to America, who'd gotten her father, Thomas, his job at Bath Iron Works, but because one of Sullivans' Boston daughters had specifically asked that there be no lilies, not one—an unusual request. So, they had made the family arrangements with daisies and stock and deterred mourners from lilies as well.

This dinner invitation, a bit out of the blue, was not a formal occasion but a thank-you, according to her father, for help he'd given William earlier that spring at the Sullivans' rambling farmhouse. The day's discards would be good enough for the bouquet. Likely, this William wouldn't know the difference.

Faye could hardly tolerate the cinnamon smell of carnations, yet they were, by far, the flower she handled most. She had started working for the florist when she was still in high school, snipping thorns from roses, wiring tulip and daisy stems to keep them from going limp, making sweetheart corsages and boutonnieres for dances she herself didn't attend. When she graduated high school, the stooped flower man, Aldo, offered her a full-time job, told her she'd gained a woman's eye for the new free-form style. She took it as a compliment, though rarely did either of them have much opportunity to be creative. Most of the roses were red or white. Occasionally, Aldo would order pink or yellow for variety. The shop had a standing account with Saint Catherine's for oversize altar arrangements every two weeks, with an extra refresh during Easter and Christmas. They tended to split weddings and funerals with the florist on the other side of the bridge, and those flowers were almost always white—the Sullivans' dreaded lilies, roses, white carnations. Little imagination was called for when it came to affairs of the church.

Now that Faye was in the shop full-time, Aldo would often linger in his greenhouse or sit on the stool by the door with his beloved spaniel, Emily, who slept the days away in moving beams of sunlight. Honestly, it didn't bother her, having him around while she worked. He would point a long finger at the flowers in the cooler, tell her when she'd chosen right or wrong, tell stories of his children who'd long moved away, a wife with legs like flower stems who left him for another man years ago.

Faye woke each day to the tang of fish, seaweed, and algae in the greening air. Even in town, the sea clung to the bricks and steel and iron. Everything here was about the ocean, the fish coming in on the day boats that cruised up to the docks and the bigger trawlers that would go out for weeks at a time. When she was a little girl, she would taste icicles and snowmen, certain that even winter was made of fish and salt.

In the shop, Faye was surrounded by flowers, a shelter of petals, a garden where she felt safe. Even the carnations were welcome sentinels. She liked flower names and would often whisper them to herself when she worked, the satisfying sounds and repeating consonants rumbling off her tongue. Rudbeckia and ranunculus, zinnia and cosmos, snapdragon and dahlia.

Words had not come easy to her, especially not important ones. It had been more than a decade since she'd spoken her first words in America. On the voyage from Ireland across a mercifully calm Atlantic, her father had turned two cane chairs so they could face one another in the tiny cabin. He would hold her hands in his while her mother Jean wept on the bunk, her back turned. "I know this is difficult. But we've done it now. You must say it." Thomas had begged over and over. "Please. You must answer the question. For all our sakes. What is your name?"

She had felt the warmth of Thomas's hands holding hers. "Fee. Ah," she whispered, four days into their journey, five since the same sea had nearly taken her life.

"Yes, that's a good girl," Thomas said, exhaling his relief. "And? What else?"

"I am ten."

Jean let out a wail, rolled back into her stupor.

On the long docks in County Cork, Jean had tried to turn them back. "What if we're caught? They'll send us to the jail."

Thomas insisted. "What's done is done. That's all."

"She's tricked us."

"The child? Nonsense," Thomas rebuked. He lifted his chin skyward. "'What could she have done, being what she is?'"

"Ack," Jean scoffed. "Enough with your Yeats."

"Besides," he'd said. "This is on us all now."

The leaving had been swift and stealth, by dark of night, away from eyes who would recognize the ruse afoot. On deck for air, as they had watched Ireland slip away at Fastnet Light, Thomas had held Faye close while Jean had stared as if some grim spell had been broken and the curse upon her was clear.

When they'd disembarked in America, the magnificent green woman and her torch welcoming them to this foreign place, Faye spoke little except her name, "Fiadh," and her age, "I am ten." Yet every time she said it, Jean let out a cry until she could not tolerate the name aloud.

"Call her anything. But not that. Not anymore."

"Faye then," Thomas said.

It was settled.

The men who came to the shop to buy flowers for wives and girlfriends would ask Faye to write endearments on the card. *Honey, sweetheart, dearest, darling.* She was no one's dearest except maybe her father's. She could tell when flowers were a romantic gesture because the men seemed eager for her approval. "What would you choose? What do you like?" She tried to keep those bouquets sweet and simple, to meet the shy gesture. But there were other types, too, sheepish, careless men who came in looking for a peace offering after a late-night bender or a missed anniversary. "Nothing's too good for my gal," they'd say. Or "Do you have something to get me out of the doghouse?" She was often able to upsell them, and Aldo would wink when she moved the offender off carnations onto something more exotic. Cads never wanted to keep a receipt as evidence and paid in cash since the woman who would receive the flowers often kept the checkbook. If Aldo wasn't in the shop, Faye would overcharge by a dollar and stuff the bill into her pocket. She had heard the phrase "sin tax" and thought of the stolen money that way. She kept these dollar bills in a coffee can in her bedroom under the eaves in the house on the cove. Each time she added one, she counted them all, beads on a rosary. *Forgive me, Father, for I have sinned.* She told herself that someday she might use the money to right wrongs, though she was never sure where one would begin to reconcile a past like hers. When she replaced the lid, she hoped the squirreling away might be enough to prove to some watching god that she was not all bad, that intention mattered even if no action came of it.

As far as she could recall, she'd never seen William Sullivan in the flower shop. But that would make sense, him being a widower. She'd heard the story of it, something about a young wife who'd died in childbirth along with the baby. That morning over breakfast, the blueberry pie she baked already out of the oven and cooling on the sill, her father had said William didn't discuss that tragedy so there would be no bringing it up at dinner. "Leave the past in the past," he'd said. "His and ours."

Her mother had pushed away from the table with a sigh so deep it felt like the whole cottage sunk a foot into the ground. "Yes," she'd said and climbed the stairs to her sewing room.

Now, Faye locked the door to the flower shop, the shabby bouquet wrapped and tucked into the crook of her arm. She hoped her mother wasn't still doleful. Bad enough they were having dinner with a dour widower. They didn't need to bring their own family ghosts.

That evening, Faye and her parents drove inland, the Buick turning and twisting past apple orchards and turnip fields, family farm stands where, in this buzzy, late-summer heat, they would sometimes stop for fresh produce and honey. The blueberry pie rested on her mother's lap, its crusty sweetness slathering the air around them, thick as jam.

When they pulled into the long drive up to the house, a man stepped out from the porch shadow into the lowering sun, his hand visoring his eyes. This was a widower? His hair was high and red, and it swooped like a character's in the funnies. He wore a white shirt, black pants, suspenders. When Jean opened the car door, he raised his hand in a casual wave and walked to greet them. He was tall, over six feet, with a trim waist and the muscular forearms and biceps of a man who, like her father, did not work with his arms by his sides.

Thomas extended his hand to the man. "Will, thanks for having us. I think you remember my wife, Jean?"

"Of course, yes ma'am. Thanks for coming." His voice was higher than Faye might have guessed, almost nasally.

"Our pleasure," Jean said. "So nice to be on a farm again."

"And this is our Faye. Probably you haven't seen her since she was a girl. All grown up now," Thomas added.

Faye's neck flushed to her cheekbones. The way he said it—"our Faye"—as if he were presenting her for judging at the county fair. "Papa," she chided, trying to gather her wits. "Nice to see you." Even to her own ear, her voice sounded weak and childish.

Now it was Jean's turn. "Faye baked a pie." She handed it to William, who put his nose to the crust and sniffed.

"My favorite. Well, and apple. Come fall, of course."

"Yes, apple season," Faye added awkwardly.

A musk of barn hay and manure stuck to the air like a sweaty shirt. Faye noticed sweet peas climbing a trellis by the porch. She snapped her fingers. The flowers. She practically skipped to the car to retrieve the bouquet. "These are for you. They're from the shop where I work, but I see you have plenty you can cut yourself."

"It's only me here. I'm not much for picking flowers." William grinned, ducked his head, a shy gesture, boyish even.

Faye, disarmed, smoothed her slacks then her hair before realizing she was preening. *Ridiculous. You're a child, and this is a man. Clearly a man.* She tried to hand William the flowers when his hands were full with the pie. He made a quick attempt at juggling before Thomas rescued them. "How about we drop these off and you give the girls a tour? We can show them my handiwork on those window pulleys."

"Good idea. After you," he said to Faye, gesturing for her to head inside.

Faye rested the bouquet in her arms like a pageant queen and glanced over her shoulder. William was behind her, and her parents, side by side, behind him with their heads bowed. All she could think about was her shape as William saw it. She wished she'd worn a skirt like her mother had suggested. She could have worn something more flattering, been more thorough when she'd brushed and restyled her hair. Why was she thinking this way? Thinking about this man, this *widower*? In the kitchen she paused as William held the screen door for Thomas and Jean. Strapping. Was that the word? She might as well topple on the ground and writhe around right there, she was making such a fool of herself.

William set the pie on the table next to a metal napkin stand and salt and pepper shakers shaped like lighthouses. The kitchen was a mess, onion skins and potato peels on the counter, carrot tops dropped on the floor. Burned caramel of roasted vegetables scorched the air. "Irish stew," William said. "I'm sure you have it all the time, but it was my mum's favorite so we—well, my dad and me, when he was still alive—we make it when we can. The lamb's from a neighbor, but the vegetables I grew myself. Carrots and potatoes are not so hard."

Faye knew it must be killing her fastidious mother to see the untidy kitchen.

"Sorry about the mess. Should have had you come in through the front door proper."

"Never mind that," Jean said. "Where do you keep the aprons?" She pulled out drawers, rattling utensils and pot lids before she found William's mother's aprons. She took a wrinkled yellow one with an orange ruffle and started tying it around her middle.

"Can't have that. I'll be fine getting this all cleaned. Let's go into the dining room, and you let me get this food on the table." He took the apron from her and set it on the countertop.

The table was set for four, two across from two. Faye sat next to Thomas and across from William, who, along with Jean, had his back to the sideboard and mirror. It was disconcerting to look at her own reflection perched over his shoulder. She focused on clusters of photographs in tarnished silver frames instead.

"Are those photos of your family?" she asked.

William set his fork down and twisted in his chair. "Yes," he said. "This is my mother and father when they were married. And then there's one of my whole family together. I was only a boy, as you can see. Both of my sisters married and moved away. Before the war. And, of course, this." He took a photograph, considered it, then handed it across the table to Faye. "You're what? Twenty-two?"

Faye nodded, the frame cold in her hand.

"I was younger then than you are now," he said. "I convinced my dad to sign the papers."

His face in the photo was fresh and stern, the uniform so crisp, Faye could practically smell the starch. "So. You're a soldier?"

One of her earliest memories of America was traveling on a northbound train, heading to Maine. Faye had watched the grimy city of New York give way, stop by stop, to a marine countryside. When soldiers boarded the train in Connecticut, she had cowered into Thomas. He stroked her head and back as if she were a trembling kitten, nodding to the men as they maneuvered down the aisle, the stomp of boots on metal like the drums of war. She nestled closer and dared to look at the soldiers who smiled wearily. *The war is over for you,* she thought. *You've killed all the Germans and you've won and now we smile and hope to not provoke your anger.* She wanted to say to them, to everyone on the train, "We are all so tired, aren't we?" Instead, she turned to the window, rested her head against her own dim reflection, and watched the shoreline streak by.

At William's dinner table, she shook herself slightly, shattering the memory. "I'm sorry?" she said, handing William his framed picture, careful not to drop it, though her hands were quite clammy. "What did you say?"

He put the photo back with the others. "Was. I *was* a soldier. Yes. I was lucky the Nazis didn't kill me. Came back in one piece for the most part."

Jean excoriated them both with a clap. "No talk of war. Let's talk of more pleasant things. Tell us about your place here all alone. What else do you grow in your garden?"

The stew was good, though too salty. The biscuits, dry. Faye felt eyes on her the whole time, each pair hungry, as if she must add something about building boats or slaughtering lambs. As the table was cleared to make way for pie, talk turned to Ireland. "You were so young when you came over," William said, stacking plates. "Do you remember much?"

Faye was used to the question. "Not much." The wooden punt, the dirt road, the O'Kanes' donkey braying every time it broke the fence. Fog rolling into Dunmanus Bay. Three girls holding hands; three girls scattered.

Behind her, Jean let out a sigh.

William pressed. "You must miss it. Ireland."

Faye dared a tender glance at Thomas, who was plating the pie. "I miss who I was there."

William looked at her, puzzled.

Something about his open face, the downward slope of his neck, strong arms poised to rise, like a robin protecting a nest. Being next to him felt safe. She wanted to tell William everything, blurt out what she bottled up.

As if she sensed Faye coming unglued, Jean jostled into the conversation. "What can a girl remember? A child. She has no idea what it was like for us there, laboring and pinching."

"You went around to the neighbors to say goodbye," Faye said. "I remember that." There was a wake—tradition for Irish heading to America, like they were sailing west to their deaths. They had gone door to door, bristling child in tow.

Thomas touched Faye's arm lightly. The gentlest warning. *Steady, child.*

Jean quivered. "Said goodbye is right." She raised her hand and turned her head as if she'd left nothing at all behind.

"And so, you've been happy in America. That's wonderful to hear. I've told Thomas. I've never been to Ireland, though my father, God rest his soul, he always talked of returning to Galway. I was in France and Germany. Not sure I would want to go overseas again. I'm fine right here at the farmhouse. Could be I've seen enough of this world for a lifetime."

"Still, you must get lonely in this big place," Thomas offered, glancing at Faye. She slanted her eyes at her father. *I see what you're up to with your matchmaking.*

A dollop of sauce soiled the edge of William's shirt. He made a tsking sound with his teeth and tongue. "I probably should have an apron. I'm not much for laundry, and these slacks are clean." He looped the strap of the crumpled apron over his bent head then fumbled with the strings. "Faye, would you mind?"

He turned his back. Faye took up the dangling strings and tied them in a bow. Up close, she could smell his woodsy aftershave, his hair, his person. It was all she could do to stop herself from pressing against him.

She stepped back, fidgeted with the neckline of her top. "All set!"

William swiped his fingers through that swoop of hair, then delicately held out the ruffled hem and curtsied deeply, never taking his eyes off hers.

Faye put the back of her hand to her mouth and bit her knuckle gently, pushing laughter into her quivering shoulders.

"Well, aren't you lovely?" she said.

He batted his lashes. "Stop," he said. "You'll make me blush."

On the drive home, Faye replayed the evening, ignoring her parents, who chattered like grackles in the front seat. All of it—the messy kitchen, the dining room with wallpaper beginning to peel, the living room with the lumpy davenport and matching chairs, the way William had asked if he might keep a slice of pie to have with his coffee the next morning. She had been certain her fate was to be alone. She had sealed it herself. She was too quiet, too selfish, too suspicious, too lost inside for companionship. And yet something had shifted in her, some closed-off space had opened a crack. *That William!* He was golden, like sunlight might follow him into the bleakest of places. Faye let her head fall back. She couldn't help but smile.

CHAPTER TWO

1959

It had been almost two weeks since the dinner, and Faye hadn't been able to get William Sullivan off her mind. She imagined him walking into the shop every time the bell above the door chimed. She had practiced how she'd keep her eyes down, demure and coy, how she'd toss her hair, fiddle with the buttons on her blouse just so. For days, she'd chosen skirts instead of her regular trousers, which she preferred. But every day the door chimed and chimed, and it was never William. She'd given up skirts after a week but not the daydream. She'd even asked Thomas, as casually as she could muster, whether he thought William had enjoyed their company.

Her father had considered her over his paper, one brow raised, and told her that, yes, William had thanked them for coming and thanked Thomas again for his help.

"Nothing else?" she asked, sipping her morning coffee.

"What were you expecting?" he'd replied, a hint of mischief in his voice.

The weather had turned to a bluster that week, the dragon's tail of a hurricane whipping through, and the store that Saturday morning was quiet. When the bell sounded, Faye startled, pricking herself on a thorn. "Shoot!" She stuck her finger in her mouth absentmindedly and looked up. There was William Sullivan, larger than a man ought to be in a small store. He wore a barn-style raincoat with patch pockets, where he buried his hands.

"Oh, God," Faye said. "Oh, I mean hello. Hello. William." She spread her hand on her chest, wondered if she should remind him of who she was. *Thomas and Jean's daughter, you remember. We had dinner at your house.*

"Hello, Faye. It's nice to see you. Are you okay? Did you cut yourself?"

She wiped her bleeding finger on her pants. Drat. She had been dabbling with her watercolors earlier, a distraction she likened to doodling. That would have been such a better image than this one, the bleeding shopgirl. "This? No. Job hazard. I'm fine." She shook her head, loosened the stardust. "How can I help you?"

He pulled his hands from his pockets and undid the button of his coat while he looked around the shop. Faye followed his gaze. Strictly for decoration, Aldo lined high wood shelves with his favorite ironstone pitchers, depression and milk glass candy dishes, ruby and cobalt and golden goblets and birdlike vases. "The owner is from Venice, in Italy," Faye offered. "The colored glass is from there."

"It's nice in here," William said, crouching to pet the spaniel who lay quietly on her little bed in the corner. "And who's this?"

Faye smiled at the old girl, who shifted to accept William's rubbing. "That's Emily, the owner's guard dog."

William gave the dog a final pat. "Not very threatening."

Faye took a breath between her teeth. "Suppose not."

She worried her pounding heart might rattle the shelves, but she could think of nothing else to say.

William broke the silence. "I'm in need of flowers. I'm afraid I've been a bit neglectful."

So, he was one of those. There was a girl already, someone he hadn't mentioned to Thomas, someone he wasn't close enough to yet perhaps, but ready to take the plunge. Or, he said he'd been neglectful. How neglectful exactly? Hurtful maybe. Or too many beers after work, and he'd missed a date. Faye had heard it all. She wanted to ask him what he'd done wrong.

But it was not her business. He was her father's coworker, and too old, as she looked at him, for her to have wasted a moment of thought. "What flowers does she like? Carnations?"

William turned up his nose. "Can't stand the smell. You?"

Faye shook her head. "We have them in all colors. But they're not for me. I prefer daisies personally, something a bit wilder."

The gesture that had so charmed her, he made again. A tilt of the head, fingers running through red hair. That grin. "So, we're in agreement. Would you mind putting together something you would be happy to receive, something that would put a smile on your face? I'm certain that would be perfect."

Faye tightened her lips into an accommodating smile. "Of course."

"And big," he said. "I really want to make a statement."

They'd gotten a delivery that morning from Boston. Fresh and fleeting. She chose her favorite flowers, the most expensive ones in the store. She added the sums in her head as she selected stems. Aldo was in his greenhouse, so she would charge William extra for preoccupying her thoughts. She imagined the woman who would receive this beautiful bouquet—tall certainly, blond of course, with an hourglass figure and breasts siloed in the latest foundations. Faye licked her own lips, imagining the woman's lipstick—fire engine red, no doubt. Too bad William had the good taste to eschew the carnations. Otherwise, she would have bombarded him with them, which any woman with half a mind would know was a cheapskate's way out.

It was beautiful, even Faye admitted. Pink and yellow daisies, delphinium and freesia, branches from a second flush of wisteria Aldo had cut from his own stock. "Make sure she puts it in water right away," she said, setting the bouquet on the counter next to the register. "I assume you'll be paying in cash?"

"Oh, yes," William said. "Of course."

"And a receipt?"

"Not necessary," he said.

Faye made the sum, her take included, and gave William the total, expecting him to gasp.

"Worth every penny. Absolutely gorgeous. And perfectly fitting."

He took his wallet from his pocket and counted out the bills to the exact amount. Faye cashed out the register and put the money inside, expecting William to walk out of the shop and out of her life into his own. Despite herself, she let a disappointed sigh escape.

But William didn't move. He stood there, smiling and staring.

"Is there something else?" Faye asked, annoyed. *Go on. Go find your woman.*

"Faye," he said, presenting the bouquet back to her with both hands. "I'm sorry it's taken me so long to do this. I was unsure whether it was the right thing, and I had to think so hard about it, then work up the courage to ask Thomas if he would approve, considering our age difference. And then more days to get here after work and before the shop closed. Maybe I should have called your house or come by. But I wanted to ask you without your mother and father around in case you felt pressured by them. Or me."

"What's this?" Faye had never been asked out on a proper date, not by a man worth his salt, someone who wasn't being a silly flirt teasing a shopgirl. But she knew what he was trying to say. And she knew how she'd answer by the beat of her heart, the pulsing in her body.

"I was hoping you might have dinner with me."

That night, Faye put the three extra dollars she'd charged William into her coffee can with the rest of her getaway money. Through a window left ajar, she heard the tide lap the granite rocks, the buoy bells clang in the harbor. The bouquet on her dresser overwhelmed the room, but she didn't care a bit.

She had a date with William Sullivan.

Over the next month they had dinner together twice, then attended a matinee about a teenage boy who turned into a sheepdog. Every kid in town was there, and the wild guffawing made the movie nearly impossible to hear. At one point, William joined the popcorn throwing, beaning a particularly obnoxious kid in the back of the head before slouching in his seat, pulling Faye down with him. They laughed, foreheads together, and William pecked her on the lips. She leaned back in the seat, fireworks bursting like they were on the screen. Her first kiss. William took her hand, laced her fingers in his. They turned their attention back to the screen, but Faye stole a glance. William beamed.

They didn't talk about the kiss on the ride home, but William held her hand walking to the car. When they arrived, the sun was setting, casting long fall shadows across the front lawn of the house on the cove. William opened the car door for Faye and walked her to the porch. Usually Thomas or Jean was outside to greet them, but not this time. Faye welcomed the reprieve from their brazen curiosity and hopeful grins.

"Thanks," she said, her mind on the kiss, her lips wanting more. "That was fun."

"Those kids, though."

"More like hyenas," Faye added. She ran her fingertips down the grainy door frame, searching. She smiled at William. "Old habit."

"What's that?" He put his hands in his pockets, leaned against the porch rail.

"When we first arrived. There was a story about Papa's brother."

"Your uncle," William added. "My father knew him."

"Yes. My uncle. I was in a bit of a shock when we arrived. It was all new, of course. And to come from a place so different from all of this." She waved her hand around. "Their house," she stuttered, "*our* house, in Ireland, was quite rustic. Stone and dirt and sea. Here, everything was white and wood. It's always had this same green trim. Very Irish," she said, her nerves on edge, trying to keep the story right as she told it.

She could not tell him about how certain she was that war would have wiped out America too, like it had wiped out so much of Europe. It had taken her years to understand that the war had never come to American cities and towns, not like it had come to Germany and France and England. Not like it had come to Japan. No, America shipped her men overseas—men like William—to fight. How surprised she'd been that soldiers came out for local parades, that guns of war stayed in armories and on military bases and on warplanes and ships at sea. Tanks didn't plod down the streets of Maine, America, the way they did in movie reels. Instead, the roads were lined with bushes and flowers and berries, waterways and estuaries.

"The house was full of this uncle's things. My father hadn't seen his brother in years. I would come across the strangest items—a watch, a bookmark, coins, matches. I wondered about them and this man living alone in this sort of house when the space in Ireland was so small. Jean swept so many of his things away. With her hand even." Faye made the motion of clearing a table. "Right into a box. I was very quiet then. But I watched everyone. I think it was our first spring here. Winter had been hard. So much snow!" *And so much sorrow!* "And the wind! It took getting used to. We were there, by the fence, and a neighbor woman comes by and tells my mother that this uncle had planned to marry a woman with two sons. He had given her a ring." Faye turned away from William's gaze, embarrassed that she'd brought up marriage. "Anyway," she continued, "he bought this house with a life of savings so they would all have a place to live. She was to meet him at the courthouse and he'd waited but she never showed. My mother was shocked by this. 'Up and left. Just a note tacked to the door,' the woman said. For the longest time, I looked for the hole where the thumbtack would have been. I could imagine the note and his heartbreak, having invested so much, given so much, only to have someone you love up and leave you with nothing but a piece of paper blowing in the wind and a tiny hole in your house." She closed her eyes, traced her fingers along the woodgrain, feeling around for the tack mark. She could not tell him how she left Ireland without a single word. "But then I would think, what was that woman to do if she truly thought she had a chance for a better life somewhere else, with someone else? And so I feel for it. Like I said, old habit." She smiled and crossed her arms.

"You never found it?" William asked.

"No. I imagine it's been painted over. But it's still there. Beneath the surface."

"Hm. Big losses do leave big holes," William said, his mouth tightening into a line of resolve. "At least in my experience."

"Mine too." Faye knew she was pressing unhealed wounds. "Maybe you'll tell me about it sometime. What's missing in your life."

William pushed himself from the railing and took Faye's hand. A strand of hair fell into his eyes, and Faye brushed it away, surprising herself with her own tenderness. They stood for a notable moment, eyes locked. The door opened, and Faye and William stepped apart.

"William," Jean said, her voice light and friendly. "I've taken a meat loaf out of the oven. Would you join us for dinner?"

Faye marveled at this change that had come over Jean since William Sullivan had taken Faye on that first date. She was almost pleasant. Faye could only guess she was hoping to finally be rid of her. It was okay. Faye understood.

"Not tonight, ma'am. It smells delicious, but I've got chores to attend to before it's dark. But another time." He turned his attention to Faye. "We'll talk soon, I hope."

"Yes," she said. "Yes, absolutely."

Faye lay awake that night, touching the tips of her fingers together, remembering the roughness of peeling paint in her search for the tack hole. William had said big losses leave big holes, and she'd felt the puncture of his words.

As a little girl, new to America, she'd had nightmares she could never remember beyond the terror of them. Little girls spinning endless circles, ashes and ashes, a door bolted shut, the churning green sea. Thomas would come running when the screaming started, kneel beside her, shush her gently. Five hushes in a row—shh, shh, shh, shh, shh. Faye tapped her fingertips, thinking of William, thinking of that uncle's lost bride, of loss and of her own aching loneliness. Shh, shh, shh, shh, shh.

She burrowed under the covers, let her mind wander around that hazy dreamscape, a childhood riddled with holes. No, that was too sad to think about! Think instead about William's lips. Would there be more kisses? She imagined making snowmen with William, ice skating with William, sipping cocoa by a fire. She pulled the quilt to her chin. She had no need to cry like she had as a child, drawing company to her bedside for a few hushed moments. She was in love with William. Of that, she was sure. She dimmed her eyes, imagined his face golden with stubble on a pillow facing hers, his hands the ones that tapped her yearning body beneath the covers, delicate and tickling like wings of white moths, until she fell into a dreamless sleep.

It was late autumn, the leaves past peak, the sky jay blue and feathered with clouds, pumpkins on porches and stoops when William showed up unannounced on a Sunday morning, dressed for a day outdoors—dungarees, a chunky fisherman's sweater the color of oatmeal, and a green plaid overshirt. "Come take a ride with me."

They drove up the coast road, along Penobscot Bay through harbor towns to the state park outside Camden. There, they walked the carriage road hand in hand to the top of Mount Battie that looked over rust and gold hills to the blue harbor and distant islands below.

"This view! It's breathtaking! Like an oil painting!" Faye laid her hand over her heart, which fluttered from the short climb and more. Her stomach was in knots too.

William spread a Pendleton blanket on a flat of granite. He stood behind Faye, one hand on her shoulder as he gestured with the other.

"That's Acadia," he said, pointing north. "And Owl Head just there. Such a clear day. We got lucky. Hot cider?" William asked, pulling a moss-colored thermos from his knapsack.

She'd known from the moment her father opened the front door that he'd expected William that morning. She had run up the stairs to change in a hurry, heeding William's advice to wear slacks and a sweater and comfortable shoes and to grab an overcoat. She'd brushed her hair behind her ears, tucked it in with long pins. She applied a quick dab of lipstick and pinched her cheeks into color. It would have to be good enough. Her nerves had silenced her most of the way up, though she was able to express to William in the touch of her hand, with a smile, that she was listening to him, that she was happy to be with him.

"Cider sounds perfect," she said now, rubbing her hands together for warmth.

William handed her a cup and poured one for himself. "Let's sit," he said.

She sat, twisted herself into a comfortable position, then reached up and took William's cup so he could sit too. The sun turned his hair copper as an oak leaf. He was meant for this season and this spot. She sipped her cider, wishing she could think of something to say besides the obvious—how nice it was to be with William, how lucky she was that he was her boyfriend. *Boyfriend.* She couldn't believe how easily that had happened despite how unlikely it had seemed to her. And yet here she was, completely taken with him.

William set his cup on a rock. "I want to tell you some things about me."

Faye saw that William was trembling. "I'd like that," she whispered, trying not to say the wrong thing.

"I was young when I enlisted. Not quite eighteen. Too young, but my father was loyal to this country, and he signed the papers. My mother was angry. She said I should wait. But after the Japs bombed

Pearl Harbor, I ached to join the fight. I thought I'd go to the South Pacific, but they sent me to Germany."

Faye's spirit crumpled, and she had to look away.

"I don't think I understood, but my unit, well . . ." William faltered. "Listen, I've seen terrible things. I've done terrible things. For my country. But what those Nazis did to the Jews. People forget. But we were there. My unit was at one of the camps, Faye. There was a child. I don't know if it was a boy or a girl. This child was so thin. I thought it must be a ghost. Imagine that! I asked my buddy if he saw it, and he could only nod. Our COs made civilians go in and see what was done in their name. I still hear their voices. I would be happy to never hear another word of German."

"I know, William. You don't have to tell me more."

"No, I need to tell you. Please, let me. And then I would like to never speak of it again. I don't want you to be afraid of me."

"I understand that. Believe me," Faye said. What else could she say? While William spoke of guns and tanks, fields and streets and mud and bullets, the rubble of German buildings and of German bodies and German victims, of his nightmares and his dreams of returning home to Maine, to his parents and a quiet life, to the sweetheart he left behind, Faye's dread mounted. She'd unclenched her fist of a heart, had allowed herself to love William, to want something as simple as a peace-filled life with him and the safety he might provide if he truly loved her in return. He was still in mourning. This thing between them was not meant to be. How had she allowed herself to believe otherwise? Her chest tightened as he continued.

"Pauline and I wrote to each other and, when I returned, we got married. I was happy. Happy the war was over, happy the Nazis were defeated and the Japs too. Happy to come home to Pauline. I had been so full of myself going in. Like I said, I was a kid after all. Then I got home, and all I wanted was to forget. I still do—want to forget," he said. "Who wants to talk about war?"

Faye flattened her palms against the granite, grounding herself. He was right. She did not want to talk about it. Over the years, she had come to understand the war the way Americans did: through grainy photographs and newsreels and documentaries. What the Germans had done, their cruelty.

William looked down as if gathering memories or courage. He sighed. "Pauline got pregnant right away. She was strong and healthy, but when the baby came—we picked out names ahead of time so I knew what she wanted. I knew we would call a boy Sterling." At the mention of the child's name, William faltered again. Faye wished she could stop this, make his pain go away. She knew what he was trying to tell her. There could be no one else for him. "There was a tear, you see. In Pauline's uterus. In the artery. They couldn't stop the bleeding. And Sterling, the cord was around his neck. I lost them both in one day."

"Oh, William!" Faye tilted her head back as she squeezed his hand, though she was certain he was slipping away. "I understand. She was the love of your life."

"Yes," William said. "My heart has been broken. But that silver maple out past the barn? The one you said last week looked like it was on fire, the colors were so beautiful? I planted that for Pauline and Sterling. But Faye." William reached into his shirt pocket, then shifted to bend on his knee in front of her. "You've helped me find something I didn't think I'd feel again. A tree and memories are not enough. I don't want to live in the past. You've mended my heart, Faye. And now I want a life with you, if you'll have me. I love you and will love the life we can make together." He held up a simple gold ring with the tiniest of diamonds. "Marry me?"

Together. Faye gasped, pummeled by waves of emotion. *Was this possible? Was it real?* Maybe she'd been thinking about it all wrong. Maybe her heart *was* a fist. Not clenched shut, though. No. Strong and ready. She could see it. This husband, the children they would have. A beautiful life. "Yes, William. To all of it." Relief welled in her. She and

William would choose the future, and the heavy door would shut on the past. For both of them.

William put the ring on her finger, and they kissed. William rolled onto her, and they kissed more, the rock beneath Faye cold and hard, the skies above her cloudless and shimmering.

CHAPTER THREE

1946: Ireland

A fight broke out in the gymnasium of the old barracks moments before the doors would open for Irish families to begin the weekly process of choosing their very own German orphan to take home. It was always this way—the boys, sick with adrenaline, off-gassing their excitement and fears on each other with jabs and pokes and shoves. Gisela was exhausted by anticipation, by hope rising only to be dashed. She and her younger sister Elisabeth, both nine years old, had been mistaken for twins, both with bobbed hair the color of molasses, button-brown eyes to match. They wore their traveling clothes—ill-fitting boots, brown wool dresses over sagging wool tights, and floppy orphan jackets hastily crafted from German army uniforms—so they would be ready to leave immediately if a foster family chose them. Gisela could not understand why the boys continued to fight after all they'd seen and endured. But then again, she thought, maybe they would always have to fight for scraps of food and love and attention. When the doors opened and sets of men and women entered, Gisela dragged Elisabeth to a quiet corner, away from the fray of their fellow orphans desperate to be the right child to milk Irish cows, to clean Irish pots or cut Irish turf. Surely some of the families were good and charitable, Elisabeth had told her. That's what the children, and what was left of their families, had been promised, after all. Operation Shamrock, they called it. A reprieve for

Was Ireland that heaven?

Elisabeth poked and pointed and fidgeted next to her as the gruff man, Hugh Flanagan, coaxed the car down the rutted township roads like he was driving a plow mule. Hannie put a doughy palm on her husband's arm in a way meant to calm him. His shoulders dropped, and his breathful cursing ceased. Gisela smiled tightly when this Hannie glanced over her shoulder to check again on her little German charges. "Almost home," she said. This word Gisela knew.

Hugh maneuvered down a twisting dirt path carved from sea-swept sedge and low trees. The car jolted to a halt at a farmhouse. "We'll walk the rest of the way," Hannie said, motioning dramatically for the girls to get out of the car.

From the well at her feet, Gisela grabbed a cloth bag the size of a cabbage that held all their possessions. She scooted out behind Elisabeth, who shaded her eyes with her hand, squinting and blinking as if she'd been kept in a box. Gisela tilted her head back, stuck out her tongue like she was catching snowflakes. Sweetness and damp, soil and manure, no trace of metal or gunpowder. No trace of war.

"It's green here," Gisela whispered into Elisabeth's ear. "It tastes good."

"We are good girls in a green place," Elisabeth replied. "God will care for us now."

Gisela pulled back sharply and pressed three fingers into her own forehead, a gesture of worry and annoyance she inherited from their beleaguered father.

"You are doing it again," Elisabeth said, careful not to attract Hannie's attention. "I know what you're thinking."

Gisela flicked her eyebrows at her sister, pursed her lips. Elisabeth was correct. It was something their father would say, reading news of that monster Hitler's rise.

"No," Elisabeth said before Gisela could speak. "We can't afford more despair." She grabbed Gisela's hand, squeezed it tight. "We're together here. That's what matters."

I don't know what matters anymore. "Gott ist tot." Vati said so.

Hugh shook a man's hand in the doorway as a gaggle of red-haired children pushed around to stare. Gisela played nice, though she wanted to stick out her tongue, to make devil horns with her fingers to ward off whatever ill will might be directed at her or her sister.

"The Dalys," Hannie said. "Good family."

"Good family," Elisabeth repeated.

Hannie looked pleased. "Yes! Though—" And she tapped her head. "Not so bright."

"*Dummkopfs*," Elisabeth offered.

"Sounds about right," Hannie said. "And they've got the only car around."

Elisabeth's ingratiating eagerness made Gisela flutter her eyes. Her sister. So quick to please. It was the reason Gisela had chosen to sleep between Elisabeth and their bilious cousin Herbert back in Germany—she was afraid Elisabeth wouldn't know how or when to fight back. Who was to say what these Irish people might do if they understood that the girls had nothing?

The sun had gone, and there was little light save for a rising moon. The girls walked on either side of Hannie behind Hugh, who led the way down a mud path with a berm of grass raised in the middle. Gisela hopped puddles and manure pies, jerking Hannie's hand.

"Pssst," Elisabeth hissed. "Pay attention to where we're going!"

Gisela looked ahead, then back at Elisabeth and down to the path. "I am paying attention to where I am. These are the only shoes we own. And you've stepped in shit."

They arrived at a settlement of seven stone cottages—some with slate roofs, some with thatch—and made their way to the farthest one. Hugh swung the door open and lit a lamp. A cozy room emerged from the darkness and took on a glow. Hannie sat on a wooden bench to remove her shoes, and the girls sat on the floor next to her. Hannie wrinkled her nose. "Dear. Elisabeth." She gestured to the child's boots. She plugged her nose and told Elisabeth to leave them on the stoop.

Gisela set hers, clean, next to Hannie's and smirked at her sister. She, too, could play eager if it suited her.

"This is your home now," Hannie said, gesturing awkwardly around the room.

Gisela thought of their father, their Vati, his calloused hands, the twisted mustache, his muscular thighs, how he would bounce the girls on his lap, a wild pony galloping away with them. He'd been forced to don the Nazi's uniform and had never returned home. She shook her head to shoo the memories.

Hugh lit more lamps, revealing a kitchen with a cooker and fireplace under a ceiling timbered with high trusses. Along the back wall was an open stair to a low attic. "Hugh and I sleep there," Hannie said, pointing to a room beyond an open door. "And you girls will be there," she said, pointing into the beams. "Don't worry. It's snug and plenty for the two of you."

"*Die Fledermäuse*," Gisela whispered to Elisabeth, imagining the two of them hanging by their toes like bats.

"The nuns told us to encourage English. So, please, Gisela. Again, but in English this time," Hannie scolded.

"We thank you . . . miss," Gisela said carefully, a reminder to her sister that she could speak when she chose, that she was no *dummkopf*. She rolled her shoulder at Elisabeth, who was still picking manure off the sole of her boot.

In the darkness of the loft, when Elisabeth's incessant chatter about Hannie and Hugh and this strange cottage and the red-haired children and the maze of stone walls and the endless seaside finally ceased, Gisela had a chance to think in peace. She combed over their journey from Cologne, which began in rubble, in brick-and-mortar dust, doll parts and bent tricycles, dented pots and pans, blasted wires, twisted rebar, shreds of cloth from smocks and aprons. No one confirmed to them one way or the other what happened to their mother, only that she could not care for them, though Gisela knew better, knew what she'd seen with her own eyes. They were told to be grateful they escaped with their lives, grateful to have shelter, grateful that the war was over at last.

From hospital, they were sent to a bleak children's home in Meisenheim, and from there, they were carted off to the Rheinbach, where their father's brother lived, far from the Balkans where his left arm rotted away in a ditch. Little help he was. His fields, like his neighbors', lay fallow, the fear of triggering unexploded mines more paralyzing than hunger. He spent his days and nights rubbing the gnarled stub of his arm, bemoaning all he'd lost.

She and Elisabeth were forced to sleep in a tiny bed with their cousin Herbert, who groped and diddled between Gisela's legs like he was feeling for berries to pluck. She'd squeezed her knees tightly, threw elbows at his temple, hissed at him like a snake, and prayed for morning. By day, he would leer at Gisela, licking the offending digits. After only two weeks, the uncle loaded the girls into a gasping truck and dropped them, and Herbert as well, at yet another orphanage. *Tut mir leid*—his apology hollow and resigned. Gisela was not sorry. She was grateful to be out of the boy's bed.

At the orphanage, rumors of moving German children to Ireland swirled like schooled herring. They would be returned to their families once wounds had healed, once mines were cleared. Gisela heard that some older boys had been taken only a week before. They'd jumped at the chance, eager to escape cold houses with roofs blown off, naked and stripped fields, empty larders and cupboards, sorrow and anger that bled from the adults' open wounds. "There, we will have food not bubbles in our bellies" went the rumors. "We will be clean. At least there is that."

The uncle didn't hesitate to sign her and Elisabeth over to the Irish Red Cross, who would spirit them away to Ireland. Herbert refused to leave, preferring the joyless orphanage. "You'll see," he said, fear chiseled so deep in his eyes it made Gisela cringe. "They'll cook you like we cooked the Jews."

She made a fist and hooked it smack into Herbert's jaw. When he ran off crying, Gisela dusted her hands, done with Herbert.

She and Elisabeth traveled by train to England, by mail boat from Liverpool over relentless chop. A good half of the children had thrown up into the churning sea, onto the splintered deck, onto their own feet. When they'd lost sight of land, Gisela had collapsed into Elisabeth's lap, clutching a stuffed rabbit she'd taken from the orphanage, her face against an empty, gurgling belly. Elisabeth rested her hand on Gisela's hair, and the stroke of it felt like their mother's, as if her ghost sailed with them.

Elisabeth snuggled against her now in their Irish loft, her whimpered breath, her very person, a reminder to Gisela that they would never escape war, that it would always follow them. Gisela's eyes grew heavy in the thick darkness. She gripped Elisabeth's arm. The old women on the street had spat at Mutti, called her "*Rabenmutter*" when she left the girls at the bakery for hours, when they wore tattered clothes. Was Mutti a ghost? Gisela did not know for certain. But she knew that if she closed her eyes, she would dream the same dream. *Mutti will tell me and Elisabeth to put on our good dresses. The dresses are stiff and itchy, but Mutti says people must know that she cared for us. "Even in the end," she will mumble over and over. Mutti is hollow, the bones in her cheeks and jaw sharp as an ax. Her dress hangs from her shoulders, her lumps and curves gone to hunger, her eyes dark and empty. I will dream of sitting on the couch in my good dress, dream of Mutti whispering to me that I must look after Elisabeth, as if I am capable of mothering! She will put a long finger to her lip, one that once played piano so sweetly, hush me, and then I will hear that deafening clank of the bolt turning when Mutti locks us in. If I dream, maybe Mutti returns with bread and a smile. Then I will know I'm dreaming. In real life, Mutti never comes back.*

A man's snoring honked up through the floorboards, snapping Gisela from her shallow dream state. For a panicked moment, she forgot where she was. A night bird hooted, and she remembered. *This is Ireland.*

In the collection of seven cottages, only two other families had children at home. The O'Kanes, closest to the road, had three boys, and the Beattys, the one girl. "Young families don't want to live in the clachan anymore," Hannie said, explaining with careful English and pantomime. Gisela tried to follow, put the gestures together with the lilting words. She wanted to learn, but she wanted to sleep too. She thought of the barracks in Wicklow and the young nurse who taught them with sweet, sad songs, her hands white and smooth. The drowsy sound of the girl's voice had lulled Gisela, transporting her along gentle currents in the melodies to distant fields where small free birds flew. Hannie's hands were rough from husks and the hoe, with tiny cuts in the callouses, her voice pitched and busy. Gisela knew there would be no time to rest or sing with Hannie.

"They up and leave soon as they're grown. Even our boys, gone to Dublin now." She picked up a picture in a rustic frame of two squinting boys in black pants and loose vests. "Seems only those Dalys want to stay here and tend the fields and make babies. How the world is changing."

Bright and early on the first full day in their new home, the Beatty girl, Fiadh, arrived with her mother Jean. Fiadh had square shoulders and brown hair and long freckled arms like her mother. She kept her head down and her hands clasped behind her back, though Gisela caught her sly glances while her mother and Hannie greeted one another.

"And here are our little Germans," Hannie said, flinging the door open so they could step outside. "Fiadh. This is Gisela and Elisabeth. They don't know much English. It'll be up to you to teach them."

Like a hare, Fiadh sprang to life. She grabbed Gisela's hand then Elisabeth's, swinging them to and fro. "You'll be my friends now. We'll have fun and make trouble. Those O'Kane boys won't have seen this coming, that's for sure." She snatched Elisabeth and turned her so they were back-to-back, arms locked. Elisabeth squirmed and twisted to get away. "Hold still! Mam, who's taller, me or Elisabeth?"

Her mother picked up a stick, leveled it on Fiadh's head. "You are, by an apple, I'd say."

Fiadh dropped Elisabeth's arms. "How about Gisela?"

The girl grabbed her like a ragdoll, jostling her into position. Gisela felt Fiadh's shoulder blades match to hers, the bump of the girl's ass against her own.

"This one's closer to you, a plum maybe. But you're a bit chubbier than the two of them," Jean said, poking Fiadh's stomach with the stick.

Gisela stood in awe of the unlikely playfulness between Fiadh and her mother, as if they were friends. And this Fiadh could make her mother laugh! Gisela could hardly remember the last time she saw her own mother even smile.

Fiadh put her hands on her hips. "Mam!" she said, her voice good natured and bright.

"Give them time with Hannie's cooking, and you'll be Irish triplets!" Jean said, and the three of them laughed and laughed.

Gisela tried to understand what was so funny, something about fruit and making fat children. *Hänsel und Gretel, bellies empty, nibbling away at the witch's cottage, fattening themselves to be eaten, blaming the wind.*

That night, Gisela lay awake, thinking of the mother and father below them, what they might be plotting. She rubbed her full belly. Loose shutters clattered in a west wind. "Do you think they're fattening us up to eat us?"

"Don't be silly," Elisabeth whispered. "We are lucky to be here. You worry too much."

Gisela balled up, squeezing her eyes and the brown rabbit tightly. *Der Wind, Der Wind, Das Himmlische Kind.*

The following morning, Gisela and Elisabeth were hardly down from the loft when Fiadh appeared in the doorway with a list of chores and ideas for games and adventures. "Soon enough, those O'Kane boys will be off their boat and just wait until they get a load of you lot."

That afternoon, the sun high in a cloudless sky, the O'Kane boys came up the path like a single, dozen-limbed lobster—boy chests armor-hard, thin carapace, flushed faces, bones bare and pokey. Denis, the oldest, then Jeremiah, called "Jem" for short, and the youngest, Conor. Denis was light haired with a spitting lisp and crossed hazel eyes, looks that reminded Gisela of the boys in Cologne who played at being soldiers, who jutted out their arms and hands in allegiance to *der Führer*. Jem and Conor were his opposite—dark hair, blistering blue eyes, uncommon white teeth. Fiadh had been fighting Conor her whole life, she told the girls. "Denis is the ugly one, Jem is the clever one, and Conor's a rogue—he'll get you cigs if you want. Bit of a temper too." She touched her hair when she spoke his name.

Gisela raised her eyebrows and eyeballed Conor.

"What?" Fiadh said, incredulous. "You think I like him or something? Well, you're wrong. I hate his guts. I hate his stinking, mean guts." She smoothed her hair with both palms and wetted her lips as they approached. "Mark my words, though," she added, grinning mischievously. "I do plan to marry him and make his life miserable."

The boys squared up and blocked the road like brawlers. Fiadh stepped out, hands on her hips, legs spread into an A-frame. Conor did the same.

"I now pronounce you man and wife," Denis jeered. "Kiss your bride, there, Con!"

"Shut your trap or I'll shut it for you," Conor said. "That what you call muscle, Fee? Your girls are scrawny."

The air between the two kids crackled. Gisela's eyes popped when Fiadh blew Conor a kiss.

"Give me a fag," she said.

Conor smirked at his brothers. "Kiss me for reals, and maybe I will."

"We're leaving," Fiadh proclaimed, stepping back and squeezing herself between Gisela and Elisabeth. "No guff from you today, Conor O'Kane."

Jem stepped forward. "Ah, don't leave. Fee, who are these girls anyway. They talk?"

"They belong to Hannie and Hugh. German orphans. Hannie got them at auction by Dublin. They'll be giving them back, though who's to say when. For now, they're mine. Like sisters to me."

What did it mean, Gisela wondered, to belong to Fiadh? To belong to Hannie and Hugh? She'd heard of slaves before, this American thing. Had America won everything? Did everyone have slaves now? Is that what they were? Fiadh grabbed their hands protectively, the way their mother had when she'd pulled them through the streets, past soldiers and shopkeepers, to their grandmother's house before the body wagon took her away. "Stick to me like glue," she'd say. At some point that Gisela could not pin down, Mutti had lost her insistence, had surrendered to fate and war, given them up for dead while they still took breaths. Could Fiadh keep them safe?

"You got your very own Germans?" Jem stepped past Conor. The boys softened, moved toward the girls like Fiadh had come to possess a bundle of firecrackers and punks to light them.

"Ah, sure you're nice now that I've got something you want," Fiadh said.

Gisela stepped back from the advance.

"No," Jem said. "We're not trying to hurt ya." He addressed Fiadh, though his eyes remained on Gisela and Elisabeth. "They come from the war?"

"Aye. Their mum—" She slashed at her throat with the tips of her fingers.

Gisela pressed her tongue into her cheek. The last she saw of Mutti, she was running toward their building after the collapse, her mouth gaped open. Gisela could not hear any sounds she made, though the memory of her own screams echoed in her head. It had happened so fast, the truck that barreled into Mutti, then the strange angle of her neck and hips, the red stains on her yellow dress, the way she wore only one shoe. Gisela forced her lips together and breathed through her nose hotly. She cleared her throat as if it were still clogged with dust.

Elisabeth shook her hand free of Fiadh's, clamped her tiny waist, and thrust her head forward. "*Unsere Mutter ist nicht tot! Nein.* She is not dead!"

Gisela bit her lip, threaded her hand through the crook of Elisabeth's arm. She had tried to tell Elisabeth—*Sie ist tot. Sie ist tot*—but her sister refused to listen. Elisabeth, clinging to this false hope. Now was not the time to try to convince her again. Which would be better? Safer? That they had a mother to return to or that there was nothing left for them in Germany? Best to be quiet, to keep their business secret. "*Sag nichts*," Gisela whispered in Elisabeth's ear.

"Hissing donkey, that one." Denis spat and laughed, a manic sound that went with his bright red face. "I wouldn't want no sister like that. Besides, Fee, how you figure them for sisters? Hell, you're not even cousins. Hannie and Hugh ain't nothing to old Batty Jean."

"I'll call them whatever I like, and you, Denis O'Kane, had better not use that name again. Not like we haven't all seen your own mam running down the lane shaking the rolling pin at your da. You're lucky she's fatter than him, or she'd give him a licking good. Like she ought to be giving you lot, by the by."

"Let's not fight. Come on. We're going to look for periwinkles," Jem said.

Conor thrust out his hand to Fiadh. "Truce?"

"Truce." She spat wetly on her own palm, then clasped it to his, squeezing so tight a drop of saliva dribbled to the ground.

From up the road, a rotund woman hooted, her arms waving above a curly cloud of hair.

"Speak of the devil," Fiadh said. "If it isn't Theresa O'Kane come to fetch her babies."

Conor threw his head back. "Sheesh, Mam!"

"I heard about these girls, Fiadh. I want a photograph." She held up a brown camera that dangled from her neck by a leather strap. "Not often we have visitors." Gisela moved closer to Elisabeth. The woman had the same eyes as her boys, blue patches like shallows in dark waters.

"Have you ever gotten a photograph from that thing?" Jem asked. "You say you're taking pictures, but we never see a single likeness."

"Do as I say," Theresa said, "or I'll whip you. I mean it, now. Go on." She gestured to the wall. Gisela followed Fiadh, who trudged dutifully. Denis jumped on the wall and crouched in a pose. Jem and Conor stood on either side of Fiadh, who crossed her arms. Gisela sat on the wall, her legs dangling, arms stiff. Elisabeth shrugged and did the same.

"Hold still now," Theresa said.

Gisela marveled at the wild black hair, the busy fussing with the contraption. She leaned forward slightly to squint at Fiadh, whose head was cocked toward Conor. Elisabeth grabbed her hand as the camera popped.

"Lord knows what we got there." Theresa blew on her fingertips, stared into the lens as if the photograph was assembling in the camera's guts. She walked away, talking to herself.

"That's done, I guess," Jem said. "C'mon. Let's go."

The girls astride followed Denis down the clover path through the field that led to the water's edge. Jem and Conor brought up the rear. Gisela felt their eyes on her back, flicked her head around periodically to check on them. Fiadh tilted to Elisabeth. "You like Jem? Gisela can have Denis." She covered her mouth and giggled.

Gisela squinted at Denis, seared a dagger into his thick skull. *Yellow hair, like Hitler boys with their spidery armbands. Like Herbert.* She felt a thick pinch on her ass and twisted around. Fiadh gasped at the same time, her face flushing red.

"Conor O'Kane!" Fiadh yelled, stopping the procession.

"What happened?" Elisabeth whispered.

Gisela shook her head.

Conor held his hands out at his sides, threw his head back in wild laughter. "Fee! Your arse is the better handful than the German's, that's for sure!"

Fiadh marched at Conor until they were face-to-face. His bemused look said he enjoyed riling Fiadh up. Gisela expected fists to fly, but instead Conor grabbed Fiadh by the waist, spun her around to the path again, and swatted her on the behind. Gisela's mouth fell open. Beside her, Elisabeth gasped. But Fiadh lowered her chin and pursed her lips. Her eyes drifted from side to side and a tiny smile lifted her lips. Over her shoulder, she said, "The only arse here is you, Conor O'Kane."

Jem punched Conor's shoulder, and Conor rubbed it as if it hurt, but the grin on his face said otherwise. Denis, well up the path and oblivious to the commotion, yelled back, "Ya comin' or what?"

"That boy knows just how to get under my skin!" Fiadh said, wiping at her mouth like she'd bit into overripe fruit. She waved at Denis. "Yeah, yeah!"

They proceeded like the altercation never happened, Conor and Jem behind the girls. Gisela, still smarting from where Conor had grabbed her, stole a glance over her shoulder. Denis reminded her of the brainless Hitler boys, but maybe it was this brother, the one with the dark gleam, who was Little Red Cap's wolf, the real threat in this green place. She would have to keep her eyes wide and her ears perked.

CHAPTER FOUR

1946

And so began a summer of cuckoo birds and lobster pots, shearing sheep and cutting turf. While Hannie kept house, sweeping the soft floor, turning sheep's wool into sweaters and flax into dresses, the girls skipped rocks and rowed the nutshell punt along the shallows, looking for hake and mackerel to scoop up in their nets. They walked paths and fields barefoot, impervious to pokes from bramble and briar and prickly yellow furze. They learned English by singing songs about gypsies and rovers, little birds and mermaids, by skipping rope to rhymes. In the barn, Hugh pointed to the pail, the teat, the milk, calf, hay, sheep, lamb. Words and words and words. Gisela ate them like chips. She didn't want to speak German anymore, the language of shouting and commands, the language of war. She couldn't imagine going back. Not ever.

Most days the girls played together with the O'Kane boys when they weren't busy with chores in the fields and on the docks. In those three months, they'd come to a gentle accord, ribbing more playful than hurtful, though there was still hair pulling and rock throwing. Even Conor settled down, abating Gisela's suspicions.

Twilight to moonrise, the six of them danced along stone walls until the washtub called. And in the attic next to Elisabeth, who no longer whispered her every thought, on a pallet with a wool mattress covered in ticking and quilted blankets, in this green place where there were no land mines in the fields, no bothersome cousins in her bed, Gisela slept dreamlessly.

ꩧ

Gisela and Elisabeth sat on a tree stump nestled against the thick stone wall of the cottage. They had spent the morning weeding Hannie's swede garden and picking potato bugs off green leaves. Fiadh stomped up to them in a pitch.

"We're leaving. Off to America. Off to America the Beautiful. America. Ha." She spat on the ground.

"What do you mean?" Gisela stood and looked around as if a boat that would carry her friend away was waiting in the bay. Fiadh was as much Ireland as the thatched roofs, the dots of sheep on the green hill, the sun-specked sea in the distance.

"You're not leaving! You can't," Elisabeth cried.

Fiadh shook her head no but said yes, as if she were trying to hold two opposing truths—she would leave Ireland and she would never leave Ireland. "Summer and we sail west, never to return. You and our boys will have to go on without me," she said, her voice dripping with melodrama.

"How can you go?" Gisela couldn't find words for the rest of her feelings, that Fiadh was both the open door to adventure and the closed gate that made Gisela feel safe. She was the sea and the harbor. Would she and Elisabeth have a home here without Fiadh? It seemed impossible. And to America, of all places.

Hannie appeared in the doorway, wiping her hands on the thick linen smock she wore for housework. "Slow yourself. What's all this?"

"She's right behind me. Let herself tell you."

As if on cue, Jean rounded the corner of the house, out of breath. "Figured you'd run here with the news."

"So, it's true?" Hannie asked. She touched Jean's arm. "You've received word."

"You knew?" Fiadh shouted. "Did everyone know but me? I'll kick and scream the whole way. I will. I don't want to go. Once we go, we'll never come back. I know it."

"Stop this," Jean chided. "Of course we'll return. Of course. Thomas went to fetch Hugh. He can tell you all more."

Over black tea and biscuits at Hugh and Hannie's table, Thomas, Fiadh's father, confirmed. Their papers had come through. His oldest brother, John, who had been in the state of Maine for decades, had died in an accident, crushed by a curbstone that had fallen on his chest. "I wish I'd have gone to see him somehow, had seen his life. But there's leaving work behind, the journey, the cost, then war, of course—so much more that separated us besides the Atlantic." Along with occasional money, the brother had sent photographs and postcards of craggy coastlines, pine-spiked inlets and red-striped lighthouses, fishing boats in tranquil harbors, promises of jobs and opportunity if only Thomas would come to America. He said there was a shipyard nearby where Thomas could find work. It was a fine time to come, the brother said. Jobs and more jobs. Houses and farms. Not so much backbreaking in the toil. Opportunity. "He died without a wife or family. His debts are clear. What's left, he's left to me. A house, a car. Money for the passage and a cushion for when we arrive."

They would leave at the end of August.

Gisela was surprised to see tears fill Hugh Flanagan's eyes. "Don't know how we'll get by but seems your mind's made up. I'd say this calls for a pint. How's about we walk up the road a spell. Leave crying to the girls." He slapped his hands on his thighs.

With the men gone to the pub, Hannie, at the stove with the kettle, sighed. "Truly, I never thought it would come about."

"Will you go to America too?" Elisabeth asked.

Jean, standing to help clear the table, chimed in. "You and Hugh should. Your boys in Dublin never come this way." She handed Hannie the chipped plates. "And you won't have these little ones forever. At some point they'll want them back in Germany, and what then? Putter around here until heaven calls?"

Gisela's head snapped. Back to Germany. Of course. Fresh air now, then back to ruin and prying fingers and empty bellies. Nowhere was safe.

"I sprung from this holy ground like a wych elm, and I'll go right back into it. There's no going anywhere for me," Hannie said. She flicked a dish rag at the three girls. "Get yourselves air together while you can. Go."

Fiadh took Elisabeth by the hand, dragged her out the door. Gisela held back for a moment, watched as Hannie and Jean, their fingers laced like they would play Ring-a-Ring-o'-Roses, rested their foreheads together. "Aye. Aye," one said to the other.

The Beattys packed satchels with what little they would take, let their friends and neighbors come for the rest. Hannie protested that this was foolish, that when they inevitably hated America and returned to Ireland, no one would give them back what was theirs. Fiadh, still fervently against the plan, teased Elisabeth and Gisela that she would stuff them in a crate and pack them off to America as well. "I'll miss you both! How can I go on without the two of you? Ack! It's all so terrible, to be forced to leave," she moaned. "We must do something big, something so impressive that we'll always remember it."

The sun set, and they gathered, the three girls along with the O'Kane boys, to walk the ferny maze of pasture paths to the stone ledge above a tidal inlet. Week after week, the girls had performed rituals for the last time. This might be the last time we take out the punt. This might be the last time we steal Jem's bicycle. This might be the last time we pick blackberries, until it was the last time and the last day loomed. In two days, the Beattys would leave for Cobh, then on to America.

Denis spat that he wouldn't miss Fiadh at all. "And your little Germans won't have big, bad Fiadh to protect them anymore."

Gisela noted the threat in his voice.

Jem knocked Denis upside the head with his open palm. "Don't listen to him. Talking shite is all. He'll miss you plenty, Fee."

Denis wrinkled his face, jiggled his head until his eyes wobbled. "Yeah, I'm only giving you a hard time. Con's the one to miss you."

Conor shoved Denis, who was still rubbing the spot on his head where Jem had slapped him. "Real pity you never worked up courage to row the punt to Carbery," Conor taunted. He threw a series of rocks into the soft waves, each time harder than the last, jerking his shoulder like he was trying to hit the island itself. In the distance, a kilometer offshore, Carbery Island was a picnic spot for boaters and a lolling spot for harbor seals. "Just as well, I'm thinking. Girls are too soft. Me and the boys, we've rowed out there dozens of times, haven't we boys?"

Fiadh pulled a sprig of toadflax from between two rocks and tossed it at Conor's face. "That's it!" she said. "We'll take a picnic to Carbery tomorrow."

"Hannie and Jean will never let you," Jem said.

"Who said we were asking? No one asked me if I wanted to go to America the Beautiful. No, this is the perfect idea. I could kiss you, Conor O'Kane."

"Why don't you then?"

Fiadh's neck blushed like sunrise. She grabbed his cheeks between her hands. "You wish!" she said, dancing away from him, playful as a faery.

Hannie put together a picnic with apple pies and meat pies, wedges of cheese and berries. The girls played innocent as Fiadh instructed, sticking to the lie that they would hug the shoreline, knowing the real plan was to row out into the bay, have their picnic on the island.

The day was brisk, but the channel was emerald and calm. Gisela and Elisabeth wore marled wool sweaters over their dresses, though Fiadh went without. All three took turns on the oars, one to helm, one to rest. Fiadh jumped from the punt, first onto the island, and whooped with success. "Look at us, girls. Look at us shine!" They pulled the boat onto the sand, clasped hands, spun in circles, collapsed onto their backs, a pile of giggles gazing up into sun-streaked clouds. Gisela wondered if they might live there, the three of them, safe from a world outside of their own making.

They climbed white-stained rocks, collected periwinkles of gold and blue in their pockets, watched fluffed robins flit from tree to tree. They called out to seals and sea otters, spied for dolphins. They vowed to write letters, Fiadh promising she would start when they had an address. And maybe they would hate America and return, or maybe Gisela and Elisabeth would want to go to America someday, she offered.

"Oh, America! No thank you," said Elisabeth. "That would be awful."

Fiadh's face drooped.

"She means because of war. Their soldiers and their tanks and guns," Gisela offered, though she could see from Fiadh's long face that she wasn't helping matters.

Elisabeth went to Fiadh, full of apology. "I'm sure the bombs are gone. They all exploded in Germany!"

Fiadh tightened and shrugged. "I suppose you're right. They did win the war, after all," she said, her voice matter-of-fact and snippy. She turned to the west, raised her palm to the sun to consider the sky and distant shore. "I'm sorry," she said, backing down. "I didn't mean that."

Gisela admired the stiffness of her back, the way her hair caught the breeze off the Atlantic. She seemed carved from the stone she stood on.

Fiadh's head whipped around. "It's out there, you know. America. Waiting to claim my soul, 'tis. Right there." She pointed. "If you squint, you can see it."

Gisela followed Fiadh's gaze. She knew all too well what it looked like to lose a war. What might it look like to win? She nudged Elisabeth, and the two of them went to Fiadh's side. There, the three girls stood a moment, locked arm in arm, Dunmanus Bay before them, the home shore beyond.

"We should get back," Fiadh said, finally. "What a shame we've run out of time."

Would it have been better in some way if the wind had done them in, overturned their boat, sent the trio into the chopping waves? Or malice? Denis O'Kane, that sneaky spider, slipping into the cove with a hand drill to poke a hole in the punt? What it was, though, was silliness, bellies full of sunshine and pie. Yes, the wind had picked up along with the heave, making the rowing that much harder. But when Fiadh scooted over to make way for Gisela, whose turn it was at the oars, she noticed old man O'Kane's boat *The Theresa*, Conor at starboard, pulling in a line. Fiadh stood, waved both arms, yelled, "Ho, there!" and danced a bit of a jig to tell him that they'd made it to Carbery Island just fine, thank you very much. Elisabeth stood, too, always so eager to play along. The punt rocked and the girls laughed, but when Gisela dropped the oars for that moment, stood and twisted to see what the fuss was about, her foot caught on the handle of the picnic basket set against the clinker. She stumbled sideways, banged her hip on the gunwale, and cartwheeled into the white-tipped waves.

Seawater filled her eardrums, her skull and lungs. She gulped sea, doused her eyeballs in it. The sleeves of her wool sweater flopped as she batted against the finned waves circling her. Seals and dolphins and minkes, basking sharks and selkies and pirates and oysters. She could hear the click and yawp of all their voices. She clamored for something to grip. Some part of her rose above the water, struggled to survive, called to Elisabeth like she had called to their mother. The other part gave in, said sad prayers to Mutti and Vati. *Jetzt bin ich auch tot.*

A seahorse galloped toward her, and Gisela imagined lassoing it and riding it to shore. When it neared, it called her name, and Gisela gripped the flowing mane of seaweed on its neck, pulled herself onto its back, pushing it under the waves. It bucked her off, and she mounted again, tightening her knees into its flanks. She took two full breaths, thankful for the seahorse. It was only then that Gisela understood that her rescuer was not mythical but human. Her fingers wound into Fiadh's hair, pulling back on the strands like reins.

She fell away, back into the dark water, only to feel arms pull her up and toss her onto the deck of a boat. And then the seahorse was next to her, Fiadh, soaked as a mop, blue and gasping as if a fishhook were still in her lip. The lobsterman bent over the bow rail to reel in one more catch. Elisabeth. Dry and white as bleached bone.

It took no time for *The Theresa* to reach the pier. The O'Kanes helped the girls off the boat, settled them side by side as a crowd gathered. Elisabeth wept between Jem and Denis, who could only stand by and dumbly watch. Gisela folded to the ground cross-legged, expelled from soaked lungs every prayer she'd prayed, expelled thoughts of sinking to the bottom of the sea, of being dragged into an underwater lair where no one grew old. Beside her, Fiadh, hands on her knees, coughed and belched as Conor pounded his fist against her back, his head bent at the same angle as hers. "You're all right. You're all right," he repeated, his tone calling her out like she was mugging for pity. But as Jean and Thomas, Hannie and Hugh sprinted down the dock, Fiadh crumpled next to Gisela like her body had left her clothes.

Jean wailed and pushed Conor aside. Thomas cradled Fiadh in his arms. "My heart! My heart!" he cried, shouting for someone to go to town for the doctor.

Gisela could still feel Fiadh's shoulders on her palms, though Thomas was halfway up the hill already, his daughter's limp body in his arms. A single strand of Fiadh's hair coiled around her fingers. She stiffened when Hugh tried to lift her, clasping her hands oddly as if she were squashing a bug between them. What had she done?

Somewhere out in the bay, the punt flipped and sank into the darkening sea.

CHAPTER FIVE

1960: Mid-Coast Maine

Faye had not been upstairs in the farmhouse since she and William first started going together and he'd given her an awkward tour, leading her up the main staircase, along the banister that looked over the narrow front entryway. It was the house he and his sisters were raised in, those same Boston sisters who had eschewed the lilies. He'd come late in life for his parents, his mother's pleasant surprise. He'd lived there alone since his mother's cancer diagnosis and rapid decline to death, followed months later when his father, Thomas's friend, pined away until his heart gave out in his sleep.

Now, Faye stood alone in front of the mirror in William's bedroom, the bedroom they would share. She drew her hands down the laced bodice, along her breasts. She pressed her ribs to the bones of her hips that disappeared beneath a swell of satin swirling above her ankles. The dress was exactly as Faye had hoped it would be, exactly how she had described it to Jean, who had insisted on sewing it herself. Simple, feminine, tasteful. Faye's brown hair was pinned back in a gentle roll. A veiled crown of flowers sat on the dressing table next to her, a gift from Aldo. This was her day, and she felt beautiful. The past—hers and William's—could be locked away now where it belonged. She startled when a figure appeared in the reflection.

"You look grand," Jean said wistfully, cocking her head then shaking it, as if she'd surprised herself. "Fiadh. I can almost imagine . . ."

Faye flinched, dared to look around. Her mother hadn't used that name in ages. In the moment, it felt purposeful, pointed. Almost accusatory.

You could hear a pin drop, Faye thought.

Did Jean remember that afternoon long ago in her sewing room, unfolding yards of fabric, the way she held it up to Faye's face and frowned her disappointment? "Not your color," she said, as if that were Faye's fault. "But it will have to do. Slip out of your jumper now, child," she'd said, gripping her own collar and pantomiming pulling up. "Put this on, and we'll see where we are." She handed Faye an old muslin dress pattern off the chair. Faye slipped it over her underthings while Jean fussed at the sewing table.

Faye remembered looking at her reflection, warped in the mirror, an imposter swimming in a shroud, scrawny arms dangling by her side, hands disappeared by the too-long sleeves. When Jean turned, her lips were pursed around a rake of glinting straight pins. Her mouth gaped open, and the pins fell to the floor, tinkling as if they were made of glass.

Not today, Faye thought. *I will not give in to a ghost on my wedding day.* She pressed her chin up, faced her mother. "It fits me perfectly."

"You're ready then? Your father's waiting in the kitchen."

"About," Faye replied. "Thank you. For the beautiful dress." She made a motion toward Jean, thinking this version of a mother might show her tenderness.

Jean's head bobbed. "I'm off to greet guests then." And with that, she was gone.

Faye returned to her reflection, set the wreath of flowers onto the crown of her head. She closed her eyes to rid the room of the shadow that had followed her mother in. When she opened them again, she saw only herself, William's bride.

She descended the stairs into the kitchen where her father waited, his back to her as he watched guests arrive from the window over the sink.

"Papa."

Thomas turned, and his face was instantly aglow. "Oh, look at you. You are a vision, my Faye. A vision."

Faye spun around, the drape of her skirt a step behind like a nipping puppy.

"Your mother knows how to make a dress, and you know how to wear one," Thomas said.

The clock in the dining room tolled the hour. "Before we go out, there's something I want to tell you," Faye said. She took Thomas's hand in hers. "I want you to know how much I love you and how grateful I am for my life here in America."

Thomas adjusted his tie, lowered his voice. "You mustn't talk that way."

"No one is here, Papa."

"Still."

Faye slumped slightly, let out a breath. She swore to herself she wouldn't bring it up, but coming down the stairs, she'd felt that ghost behind her. No one had ever cared what Thomas and Jean Beatty called their daughter. No one gave any of them a second thought. She cursed Jean for surfacing the past as if that was a common discussion when, in fact, they never spoke of it. Not ever. What had burned so bright in her memory for so long had diminished over the years. And if her thoughts turned to darkness, well, it was better to not think about the past at all.

"I don't need to tell him, do I?" Faye asked.

"Faye, please! Someone will hear. Think of your mother."

Faye allowed a speck of fear to seep out. "Would he hate me if he found out? I couldn't bear it. Not after everything."

Thomas twitched, held her by the shoulders. "You are meant to be Mrs. William Sullivan. You two are a perfect match. Everything is in front of you."

"You're right. Of course you're right," Faye said, trying to convince herself. She unwound a single strand of hair from her fingers, watched it flutter to the floor. "But, Papa," she said, her voice barely above a whisper. "My life isn't . . . stolen, is it?"

"Faye! Enough with this now." He kissed her forehead, adjusted a hairpin to straighten her crown. "Let's go get you married."

The red barn had been mucked out and swept clean, and friends of Jean's from the parish in town made food for the reception, which would be held in the barn as well. Aldo baked the wedding cake, vanilla with buttercream, and decorated it with edible flowers.

As Faye and her father stepped onto the farmhouse porch, a final guest entered the barn. Thomas looked at his watch. "Seven past the hour. Fashionably late." He signaled Maybellene Clay, the parish organist, who sat at a piano in the back of a forest green step-side pickup truck. She nodded and, with dramatic flourish, raised her hands and brought fingers down to the keys. The bridal march rose on a grassy breeze. "Shall we?" Thomas asked, offering his arm.

Behind her veil, Faye blushed under the happy gaze of some thirty guests who murmured with delight when she appeared in the doorway. William, in a new black suit with a tidy pocket square, stood flushed and teary at the makeshift altar next to the justice of the peace, who was as thin and sharp as a dart. At the front of the aisle, Jean stood with her arms by her side, her face stricken, eyes bugged with alarm. Faye chose to ignore her mother. Instead, she turned to her father, who kissed each of her cheeks, then presented her to William. Faye handed her bouquet to her one friend, a girl named Trudy Twigg whose parents owned the local grocery store. With eyes only for William, she failed to see Jean grip Thomas, whisper into his ear, failed to see her father's smile fade, his face pale.

Upon pronouncement of husband and wife, William lifted the veil and dipped Faye in his arms, planting a Hollywood kiss on her lips. She let her head fall back so she could linger in that starry moment of her world made right. Guests erupted in laughter and whoops. William pulled her back up and into his arms. The fullness of him against her, the smell of his soap, the shine in his copper hair. In his embrace, she felt safe and complete, fully herself, bursting with joy.

They were engulfed by well-wishers, kissers and huggers and handshakers, many of them family friends of William's parents who'd lived in the area for decades. Faye couldn't stop smiling. Over her left shoulder, William's voice. "Faye, there's someone I'd like you to meet." As she turned, Thomas and Jean appeared on the other side of her.

Thick hair, black as licorice, glacial blue eyes, bushy brows, full lips so deep they were almost purple. In this country place, he seemed gritty and slick. And familiar somehow. Faye felt Thomas tighten next to her. "This is my bride, Faye, and her parents, Thomas and Jean Beatty. Faye, this is Conor O'Kane."

Faye's stomach lurched. That name, the face older but . . . yes. And he seemed equally stunned, staring at them, his face registering a myriad of emotion until a final one washed over him, some wave of recognition. He burst into laughter, forced and hectic.

"Fiadh? You say you're Fiadh?" His Irish accent was thick and rolling, not the green of hills Faye remembered, but the black of troubled water.

William tapped his head with his palm. "Yes, I forget you were called Fiadh. I've only ever known you as Faye. You know each other?"

The day was bright with autumn sunshine, with pig-tailed girls spinning circles, the smell of fried chicken and peeled corn, tomatoes salted in stone bowls. So why did it feel to Faye like war was breaking out? Her mouth fell open. She could not form a single word.

Thomas stepped in front of her, his hand outstretched. "Conor O'Kane. Indeed, the glass of your father. Jean spotted you earlier and said it was like looking at a ghost. I told her it couldn't be, but here you are. And yes, of course, this is Fiadh." He spoke with the authority of a priest declaring the word of the Lord.

"So, you do know each other!"

"We knew Conor when he was a boy, William. Practically in nappies."

The man took Thomas's hand, shook it, but his pained eyes glued on Faye. "I hardly recognize you lot. Certainly not . . . well . . . Though of course I know *your* face." His brow crinkled, his mouth flinched wryly.

"Yes," Faye said weakly. She remembered him, the cigarette out the corner of his boy mouth, those eyes, the way he strutted down the meadow path. Her legs wobbled with the unease of having been on rough seas, shock coursing through her veins so thoroughly it could have been thrill. She searched Jean's face, which had turned wistful.

"Sorry to party crash, but when the fellas said Kevin Sullivan's son was to marry Thomas Beatty's girl, I couldn't believe my ears. Had to see for myself if it was the same old Beattys and my Fiadh after all this time. And here *you* are. Imagine my surprise."

"*Your* Fiadh? A fine surprise then," said William, his voice testy. He put his arm around Faye's waist. "Though she is *my* wife now."

"Oh, we're surprised all right," Jean said, her head shaking with disbelief. "I can't get over how much you look like your father. Like going back in time, that face. How is this possible?"

Faye felt the urge to clamp Jean's mouth shut.

"You know, Dad was part of a network up here, down as far as Rhode Island," William said. "Helped immigrants get settled, including your brother, Thomas. Conor showed up, what? Five years back? Stayed with us for a day or two but ended up in Boston, is that right?"

"More comfortable in the city," O'Kane said. He palmed William's shoulder, then shook his head like a dog caught in a downpour. "Boy, I can't get over this. The Beattys here left and not a word from them again."

"That's our business," Thomas said, his voice clanging like a dropped lid.

Faye was certain she would be sick.

"Left behind a lot of broken hearts. Mine included. What a pistol, that Fiadh! Secretly thought I'd marry her someday. Don't know that I thought I could turn her head one more time the way I used to . . . Still. Like I said, I had to come." Conor's eyes swept over Faye, inspecting every eyelash, every curve. "And now my friend William has captured himself this fine Irish lass. And my poor heart in tatters again." He pressed on each word like a chicken pecking feed. "To think. After that accident."

"Accident?" William asked.

Guests inched closer, eager to extend their wishes to the happy couple and get the party started. "Darling," Faye said, finding her tongue for an endearment she'd never used before. William grinned, clearly amused by it. "We can catch up with Conor later. Right now, we need to attend to our guests. Papa, you and Mama keep Conor company now, won't you?"

"Mama and Papa," Conor said, hinting both mockery and menace. "She's grown into quite the woman, this Fiadh. Congratulations to you both. And to the happy couple. Yes, let's find a table and a drink. Quite the story to tell." O'Kane threw his arm over Thomas's shoulder and swung him toward the table in the corner and a punch bowl spiked with whiskey.

Though Faye tried to keep her attention on William and their guests, she watched as Conor cast aside the ladle and dipped a cup into the bowl. As if some sorcery elevated him a foot above the ground, he was all she could see.

"To the beautiful couple!" he shouted, raising the cup. "Sláinte!" He tipped his eyes into her like a scalpel and drank.

William whispered into Faye's ear. "Bit of a problem, that one. My father wasn't fond of him. I can tell Thomas isn't much of a fan either. Was he a hooligan?"

Shards of memory, sharp as the point of a bayonet, pierced her. Children playing, harmless moonlit shenanigans, the cold water of the bay, a colder body. Hooligan? More of a wiseass then, though the edge he sported now was jagged and hardened. She shuddered, gritted her teeth, pursed out a smile. “Not that I recall,” she said, a smile plastered to her face. It was all she could do to keep her knees from buckling.

CHAPTER SIX

1946: West Cork, Ireland

Still wrapped in blankets from the O'Kanes' boat, Gisela and Elisabeth waited with Hannie and Hugh in the Beattys' cottage. They could hear whispering behind the curtain. At last, Jean and Thomas and the doctor emerged from the room at the back. "She's breathing, thank the good Lord," Jean said. "What on earth happened out there?"

Gisela felt scrutinized, understood the question but couldn't put the whole story together in English. Elisabeth piped up. "The picnic basket. Waves hit the boat. We . . ." She stood, gestured losing their balance. "Gisela fell, and Fiadh dove in. Fiadh saved Gisela."

Jean smiled. "Of course she did. A good swimmer, that one. Always with the knack for it. She could go to the Olympic games. Maybe for America."

"You won't still go? She can't travel," Hannie said.

Jean shrugged.

"A delay," Thomas said. "Until she's out of danger."

Gisela, her stomach full of the roiling Irish sea, moaned and let out a belching cough.

"Let's have a listen to this one," the doctor said. He bent to Gisela, stethoscope in his ears, bell to her chest. He put a finger on his lips to tell her to be quiet. "Big breath," he said, "like this." He demonstrated. "And out." Gisela stared intently, following his instructions. "Again . . .

again." He pulled the scope from his ears and wrapped it around his neck. "No pneumonia, unless I've missed it. If fever spikes, you send for me. Wee girls were lucky today. What, it was last year the Coughlin boy was pulling in traps and"—the doctor snapped his fingers—"just like that, and we never see hide nor hair of him again."

Hannie rose. "We'll leave you now. I must get these girls home and put some broth in them. We'll be back."

"We meant for you to have that punt, Hannie," Thomas said. "You and Hugh. It wasn't much, but it was a fine one. Of course, I'll take our girls over a boat any day." He mussed Gisela's hair in the way her father had.

"Still. What a pity!" Jean said.

"I'm sorry I let it go," Elisabeth said.

"Oh, child! I meant to cast no blame! A bunch of wood is all, not worth a single life, not a one, don't you worry," Thomas said. "We have what matters."

Gisela dropped the blanket and threw her arms around the man's waist, pushed her face against his muddied shirt. For one moment, she was a small child and her Vati was alive and there was no war, no Hitler, no bombs, no Ireland. Only a father's heart beating in her ear. How she longed for it!

Jean put her arms out and surveyed the room as if some great snake were taking the very soul from her husband. "What's this about now?"

Bewildered, Thomas tapped Gisela awkwardly. "There, now. It's fine. We're fine, you hear? We're fine. America can wait if it must."

Before dusk, and already Gisela was on the pallet in the attic, Hannie's quilt wrapped around her, the other blanket folded on the bench by the door. Her body still rode the waves when her eyes drifted closed, like it was seawater and not blood that flowed through her veins. Elisabeth was down the ladder with Hannie. Birds were singing the last songs of the day when the door banged open. Gisela sat up when she heard Jean's voice.

"She's dead. My child is dead."

Keening fogged the room as if the space below Gisela filled with white ghosts. She climbed out of bed, perched herself on the top ladder rung to peer down.

"What? No!" Hannie set a stove pot on the table and opened her arms. Jean went to her, allowed herself to be engulfed.

"The doctor told us to watch her. And we did! He said this could happen." Jean wailed to the rafters. Gisela pulled her feet into the shadow. "What will I do? What will I do? I can't leave her here, Hannie. But I can't stay. This place has taken every one of my children. It will take me next, and I'm about for it."

"I know. You simply can't. No, it isn't fair," Hannie said, patting Jean's arm.

"This is it, I tell you. I cannot bury another child. I told Thomas. We're leaving tomorrow. You'll see to her burial, won't you? You'll do that for me."

"You're being . . ."

"Batty? Am I batty for not wanting to put another child in the ground?"

Gisela had asked Hannie about the nickname the O'Kane boys taunted Fiadh with, and Hannie said that following the deaths of twin sons—one from influenza, the other from a mule kick to the head—only weeks apart, Jean had laid up for months, leaving Thomas to care for Fiadh, who was only a toddler. "'Poor Batty Jean!' they said, like her name was in a drinking song! Then one day, she rose up, got dressed. 'We'll speak no more of it,' she said and never did, though I suppose the name still has a certain ring to it."

"Jean," Hannie said. "Where's Thomas?"

"He's with her. Your Hugh has gone for the priest."

Elisabeth looked up, tapped her finger on her lips to tell Gisela not to speak. She backed slowly to the open door and ran out without Hannie or Jean noticing.

Jean marched around the room. "Curse God. Curse him! Theresa O'Kane and those beautiful boys of hers. You and your sons, and now these German girls are yours too! God gives and gives to everyone and takes and takes from me. God leaves me with nothing!"

"Let's not do that," Hannie said, as if God was in the room taking notes. "You have Thomas. You have me and Hugh. The wee girls need us, especially now. Stay. You must."

"I wish one of those girls had died instead of mine," Jean said.

"You don't mean that."

"I do. I really do. If God wanted a child so bad, take one that no one else wants. Take one who doesn't have a mother who loves her. Don't take mine. It is not too late! Switch them out! I dare you, God. Switch them out!" She raised her fist as if she were throwing lightning to heaven.

Those words that nourished Gisela came together now, what the women were saying about her and her sister. They were castaways. Orphans. Below her, the room turned into the sea. Jean was right. It should have been her. She was to blame. Clumsy fool.

"Friend," Hannie said. "Listen to me. Listen. Stay. Take one of these shamrock girls into your house. They both need a mother." Her voice dropped but, from the shadows, Gisela could still hear every word. "Take Elisabeth. She's easier. She goes along."

"I'll never have peace here. Let me leave!" Jean wailed. "Fiadh. Fiadh!"

Suddenly, the prospect of Fiadh in America didn't seem so bad to Gisela. What had been the fuss? In America, Fiadh would be alive. In America, Fiadh could write letters, maybe someday return. Or maybe someday Gisela and Elisabeth would have gone to visit. Forget the ship. They could have flown in an airplane and visited this New England that Jean and Thomas waxed on about. Gisela closed her eyes and pictured Fiadh alive, living a different life after all. "You are in America," she said out loud. She repeated it. An incantation. "Fiadh is in America." She opened her eyes.

Hannie was staring up at her, a peculiar look on her face. "What did you say?" Hannie hissed, her voice calm but alarmed, a sound meant to let the sleeping rest. "Get back in bed. Cover up. And where is Elisabeth? Where is your sister?"

Jean folded over in her chair, a puppet collapsed, strings limp. A withering look from Hannie again. "See what you've done?"

The twilling light of early evening drizzled in through dirty windows. From the darkening loft, Gisela kept her ears perked. She could not see Hannie or Jean anymore, could not know from their expressions whether what Hannie said next was sinister or generous, but she could hear them clearly in the small house. It was not simply an idea. It was a proposal.

"Or take Elisabeth to America. These girls have no one to miss them. They'll be separated eventually. No one would have them both. You asked God to switch them. I say we do it ourselves."

Gisela gasped, retreated from the opening. The voices lowered to a whisper. Gisela put her ear to the floorboards. Jean's voice pitched and dropped on words like *betrayal* and *grief* and *chance* and *love*. "It's too late," Jean said clearly. "We're leaving tomorrow, and that's that."

"I'll take you home," Hannie said. "We'll talk to Thomas. He'll see it my way."

Gisela crawled into bed. Where was Elisabeth? Had she been taken already? And where would that leave her? Without Fiadh, without Elisabeth, she would have nothing. She slipped into shallow sleep and soon was out to sea in the punt, rowing and rowing, going nowhere, a motorboat full of Nazi boys and cousin Herbert in hot pursuit. War planes buzzed overhead, dropped bodies in bloodstained yellow dresses into the green sea around her. She woke with a start when Elisabeth slid onto the pallet next to her. It was a nightmare. They were still in

Ireland. For now. She rolled over onto her back, stared with Elisabeth into the dark beams.

"The priest came for Fiadh," Elisabeth said. "I saw her through the window. Fiadh is dead. It is so sad. So awful! They'll send us back to the nuns for sure."

"Why would they send us away?"

"Fiadh is dead because of us. They won't want us anymore."

So, they would be sent back. And then what? They'd gotten lucky the nuns had let them stay together. Maybe their luck had run out. Gisela was done leaving everything up to chance. She remembered Herbert, his dirty fingers, his sickening words. She remembered Mutti's bloodstained dress. They had nothing left in Germany, and now Ireland was ruined too.

"I'm so tired," Elisabeth said, burrowing into Gisela. "What a terrible day. But let's not fret. You must think of Mutti waiting for us. You must keep that hope alive."

Elisabeth and her silly fantasy about Mutti! How it galled. She was not coming back. Their life was forfeit. The sea boiled in her throat. Gisela turned away.

"What? Are you angry?" Elisabeth asked. "I'm sorry I wasn't the one to jump in and save you. Is that it?"

It was Elisabeth who always insisted they stay together, even though it meant that they got stuck with Herbert or had to stay longer with the nuns. Gisela turned to face her sister. Though they were close enough to taste each other's breath, Gisela imagined a lifting away, the yank of a paratrooper when the chute opens. "We can't swim."

She remembered a bridge over the Rhine, walking with their father, holding his hand. She had spied a mewling kitten clinging to a drifting branch in the current. Gisela begged him to save it. *"Das Kätzchen, Vati!"* He said if he were to jump in, he and the cat would both drown. *We are in that swollen river now, sister. We must grab hold of what we can.* "We can't swim," Gisela repeated. "You couldn't save me. If you'd fallen overboard, I couldn't have saved you either. We'd both be dead." She felt her knees digging into the seahorse's ribs, felt Fiadh's sea-silked hair tangle through her fingers. She touched her own head. It felt the same.

"I should have tried," Elisabeth said, her voice thick with sleep.

"No," Gisela said. "Listen to me. You did the right thing. You saved yourself."

"Yes, well, we are alive. But poor Fiadh . . . *Wir müssen mutig sein.* Be brave," Elisabeth murmured as she drifted off.

Gisela snuck down the ladder, her ragged stuffed rabbit under her arm. On the tamped grass path to the Beattys' cottage, she watched her brown shoes move beneath her, carrying her as if she were not in control. Her heart pounded. She went to the side of the cottage where a low light flickered. She could see the bed through the window. Fiadh's body lay on top of the covers. There was a blueness to her, part sea, part sky, and a greenness too. Hardly a girl at all anymore. Gisela wondered if vines might come up from the floor, entwine her friend until she turned into loamy dirt, into Ireland itself. She bowed her head, tapped her forehead with her fingers. *Be brave.* She moved to the door and opened it. Jean sat stone-faced at the table, Thomas standing over her, both in traveling clothes. Their eyes were sunken. Hugh and Hannie sat on a bench, hands in their laps. The priest—bent and paunchy, his slapped red cheeks flamed with boil scars—stood next to Thomas.

Gisela did not skip a beat. She went to Jean, bent to her knees, the gritty floor pocking her flesh. She placed her cheek on Jean's lap, sanded her skin against the rough of her dress. She was not fine like that woman in cornflower blue, but she smelt like Mutti, like fire and worry. She felt Jean's hand on her head.

Though Hannie's voice sounded an alarm—"Child! Child!"—Gisela focused only on Jean and on Thomas next to her.

The shoes that carried her, the knees that held her up, her war-torn heart. She would make her own luck now. She would save herself and perhaps Elisabeth at the same time. She croaked in a mix of German and English all that was in her head, spewing every thought and excuse and reason that it should be her they take, not Elisabeth, who was too bossy and too mouthy, who would never tolerate being separated, would never behave. She, Gisela, would do whatever they asked. She would never tell a soul. "*Nicht zurück nach Deutschland. Bitte.*"

Thomas placed gentle hands on Gisela's shoulders. "What is she on about?"

"Take me to America," Gisela said, in plain English. "I will be Fiadh in America."

CHAPTER SEVEN

1960: Mid-Coast Maine

William, his arm around Faye's waist, whispered into her ear. "You're trembling."

Faye scanned the crowd. Near the back of the barn, one of the women from church looked to be talking Jean's ear off. Faye caught her mother's eye, but Jean looked away. No sign of Thomas or Conor O'Kane. "I'm a little overwhelmed. Maybe we can sit awhile?"

William took over, his chin rising as he waved to Clayton Clay to start the music. "My bride and I are going to sit and smooch. Dance! Enjoy yourselves!" William raised Faye's hand in victory. The barn lights flickered on, and guests buzzed into new life as Clayton and Maybellene played "Will Ye Go, Lassie, Go?"

William led Faye to a table set for them. There, she let him pull her to him, tuck her under his arm. She rested her head on his shoulder, her hand on his chest. His heart seemed to beat in time with the music while hers raced with her thoughts. What words had Conor used? *Left behind.* It was true. He had been left, not by her but by an Irish girl he might have loved. He could not possibly blame her for that. Except she was the one who fell into the sea then crossed it with a dead girl's name. An old pit of guilt sprouted in her belly, the memory of staring into the rafters of an Irish cottage. She sat up sharply, sputtered as if the last of the sea she'd swallowed was finally surfacing. Conor might know what became of Elisabeth!

William tilted her face to him. "Faye. What is it?"

She shook her head, jostling loose images of herself as a child, of departing with Thomas and Jean, one dark glance over her shoulder. She considered the children dancing in front of the Clays, creatures of impulse and daring. What could they know of betrayal or regret? What could they know of consequences? She'd had to grow up before she could truly consider the aftermath of her leave-taking, to ask herself what might have happened if she'd stayed behind with Elisabeth, to face whatever fate awaited them together. And what if Thomas and Jean had taken Elisabeth instead? She pictured the little girl she was, a child who saved herself, who made her own luck. Surely, her sister would have done the same.

"I'm happy, William. Happy and lucky to be here with you," she said, draping her arm over his shoulder.

Faye watched for O'Kane to sidle up to William, to whisper and point and accuse. But when he reappeared, he spent his time at a table near the entrance to the barn, Jean on one side, leaning into him, Thomas on the other, his gaze always on Faye when she looked their way. During the bride dance, Thomas took his turn with Faye and told her O'Kane had laughed him off when Thomas had asked point-blank about his intentions. "He said we all got secrets to keep, don't we, Mr. Beatty. *Mr. Beatty,*" Thomas mocked. "The way he said it, like I wasn't myself either."

"You mean an imposter. Like me. I'm certainly not my husband's perfect Irish bride."

"That's not what I meant. Don't talk like that. Anyway, he said it was not his business."

"And you believed him?"

Thomas made a show of twirling Faye when he saw eyes on them. "What choice do we have? He told Jean he doesn't come this way much. He hardly knows William. It was Kevin who helped him get a start. T'was but chance and rumor that brought him here today. Nothing more."

"It wasn't chance. It was Fiadh. He came for her." Her father grimaced, and Faye regretted the jab, though it was the truth. She pulled away so she could see his eyes, check him for an honest answer. "Did he say anything about Elisabeth?"

Thomas looked puzzled. "Who?"

Faye's breath quickened. She had not spoken that name to Thomas nor to Jean. Not to anyone in all the years she had lived in America. This was the lie that she lived as Faye Beatty, daughter of Thomas and Jean, sister to no one. As far as she knew, there had been no word from Ireland. Conor turning up begged the question, though Faye was not at all certain she wanted the answer. "Papa. Elisabeth."

Recognition smoothed the lines around his eyes. "No, dear. No. He didn't offer, and I . . . I didn't think to ask. And Faye . . ." He shook his head. "Don't . . ."

He didn't need to say more. Faye knew. It was one thing, keeping the fact that she was German from William. Surely, a man like him wouldn't care. She had only been a child, after all. But if they had been honest with William from the start, would he have allowed himself to fall for her? Or would she be in the flower shop making bouquets for a different Mrs. William Sullivan? And the rest of it! How they'd stolen away from Ireland like thieves in the night, how the three of them had embraced deception for their own selfish reasons. Thomas passed Faye off as his Irish daughter. Had they tricked William into marrying her? That betrayal, Faye knew William could never forgive. The ring was on her finger. It was too late for confession.

"Come now," he said, pulling her close. "Look at your man there. Your new life begins today. Nothing will stop that."

William had removed his jacket and tie and stood with several friends who took turns slapping his shoulder, their heads thrown back, beer bottles clinking with cheer. He slipped his hands into his pockets, that easy way of his, and winked at her. She didn't deserve him, yet there he was. She blew him a kiss, and he thumped his right hand over his heart and fell into his buddy's waiting arms. She couldn't imagine loving a man more. This other thought she could let slip back into the recesses of memory.

As long as Conor O'Kane kept his mouth shut.

When the last of the guests left the farm, William scooped Faye up and carried her over the threshold into his kitchen, their kitchen now. She'd seen such things in films—Rock Hudson carrying Liz Taylor, Desi carrying Lucy—and had fantasized about how romantic it would be. Her thoughts fled from darkness and worry, and despite herself, she laughed and buried her face in his neck.

Faye didn't know how to be a homemaker or a wife. Her mother kept the house at the cove spotless, couldn't stand mess, but it was not a sprawling farmhouse. Faye didn't know which rooms she was expected to keep clean, how William lived, and what he would want from her. When she'd asked, Jean brushed her off. "It will be obvious. Fill those rooms with children. The rest will take care of itself." She could cook a little, sew a little, skills she'd learned in home economics classes. What she was good at was selecting flowers and making them look pretty in a vase. She dabbled in watercolors, created forgettable images. That was it. When her feet touched the kitchen floor, her life with William, her life as Faye Sullivan, began. She would do anything to protect it. She could figure it all out—how to be the perfect mother, the perfect housekeeper, the perfect lover. She would make herself irreplaceable.

A light was lit over the sink. Everything was spotless. "My mother's been here," Faye said. Vases full of flowers from the tables in the barn were on the counter now. The room smelled of roses. That's when she saw that the floor was strewn with rose petals too. "Oh, no!" She put her hand to her mouth. "What's happened here?"

William put his hands on her hips, pulled her to him, his head tilted sheepishly. "That might have been my doing, wife."

Faye circled her arms around him. "Husband," she said, like she was playing house.

"It was a perfect day, don't you think?" he asked. "And what a surprise, O'Kane showing up. Your parents must have been pleased to see someone from home. Even him."

Faye did not want to talk about Conor O'Kane or even think about him. She wanted to erase him from the day and her memory. "Mm," she said. "Really, I hardly remember him."

"Well, I wasn't surprised he disappeared. I don't want to speak too ill of a family friend, but like I said, bit of a troublemaker, that one. And what was that accident he mentioned?"

She glanced at the rose petals on the floor, let her eyes drift back to his. "Let's not talk about him right now. Don't we have something better to do?" She hardly knew what to expect next, aside from what her friend Trudy had told her when Faye had begged for details—what went where, what hurt, and what felt good.

"Mrs. Sullivan!" William teased. He led her up the stairs along the fluttering path.

The bed was made with two pillows, *W* and *F* embroidered on the pillowcases by a family friend. More petals were sprinkled on the bedspread, and Faye was certain her face flushed the same rose color.

"Your mom asked to put your things away how you'd like it," William said. He showed her which drawers were hers, which were his.

"My mother was in here?"

"Don't worry. I did the rest after she was gone. Jean doesn't seem the romantic type."

Faye did not want to think of her parents that way, in a bed together, doing the things one must do to make the babies they'd made.

She shook the image away and sat on the bed to remove her shoes. "My feet are so tired!"

William bent before her and undid the straps on her low heels, held each foot in his hands, caressing firmly. How could his touching her feet cause whooshing everywhere, thrumming in private places that drove her mad? She wanted to put her fingers in his hair, pull and push. "William, I—"

"Don't worry," he said. "There's no rush."

"It's not that. It's, well, I don't really know what to do next."

"Come," he said. "Let me help you with the buttons."

She stood, turned her back to him. William's fingertips and knuckles grazed the length of her spine as he moved down. A shiver coursed through her, and she held her breath. With the last button released, Faye slipped the shoulders down and stepped out of the dress, carefully laying it over the arm of the chair in the corner. She stood exposed in her foundations and stockings.

William took a step back, and for a moment, Faye thought he might be disappointed. Instead, he let out a whistle on a sigh. "You are a beauty."

She smoothed her hands down her body, the stiff boning and rough fabric, and realized she'd forgotten something important. She looked around the room and spotted the little valise in the corner. She couldn't do this in front of him, not yet. "I need to change. Into something else."

In the bathroom across the hall, Faye stared at her gold rings, the perfect little diamonds. Her hands were small and soft, childlike, which to her made the ring set look like something from a gumball machine. She had assumed she would live at home with Thomas and Jean, never marry, never allow anyone close enough to see her flaws. All her fine thoughts about taking the money she skimmed from the flower shop and embarking on some grand journey of reconciliation—that was the wishful thinking of a child squirreling away for a toy from a catalog. The truth was that she had taken dollars back out here and there, for lipstick, perfume, for matinees on her own. Truth was there were not that many bad men who came into the flower shop who deserved to be swindled out of their hard-earned money. Truth was she had not amassed a small fortune in her coffee can. She had seventeen dollars left, an amount she'd put in her pocketbook when she packed up her room. She thought of Conor O'Kane, the way he had looked at her, in her white dress, her hair pinned up and curled under the floral crown . . .

No, no, no. He would not take anything from her. She would not allow it.

She pulled her slip over her head, removed her hose, slid both over a towel rack. She unhooked the stiff bra, pulled down the girdle, which held her young belly in place, and cast both aside. She stood on her tiptoes on the cool pink-and-black tile to consider her breasts in the small mirror. She unwrapped the package she'd placed at the bottom of the valise. The palest blue, the softest nylon, simple and elegant. She'd seen the chemise through a shop window and had bought it for herself. It slid over her body and fell into place like scales on a mermaid.

When she returned to the bedroom, William was under the covers, propped on his elbow to watch her walk in. His shirt was off, his bare shoulder as naked as any man she'd ever seen. The lamp was lit next to his side of the bed. The covers were turned down on what would be hers, from here on out, for all the days of their marriage.

"Oh," he said, awe pouring out of him. She slid into the sheets, warm from the heat of him, laced with his smell. His hand wrapped around hers. She curled to him, put their clasped hands to her lips, sighed warm breath into them. Love slipped over her like a nightgown.

CHAPTER EIGHT

1960: Mid-Coast Maine

The leaves were down, and they'd already had snow when Faye, home from the grocery, noticed a strange car in the driveway. She set the packages on the counter. She'd planned a romantic dinner for William with music and candles to celebrate Kennedy's victory. Was he home early? "William?"

Unlike her husband's reedy voice, this one from the other room rumbled like thunder.

"In here."

She walked into the living room. Conor O'Kane was on the couch, his arm extended across the back, legs crossed like this was his place.

Her *Life* magazine was open on the table in front of him to the spread that Faye had so admired about the young senator from Massachusetts that all the women went on about. His glamorous wife, like Faye, was more than a decade younger than her dashing husband and, unlike Faye, was quite pregnant that November.

She'd read the *Life* article while William watched the news, peppering him with facts as she read them.

"You know Jackie was twenty-four when she got married."

"And John Kennedy was a decade older than her."

"And he was in the navy."

"She is going to have that baby any day. What an exciting time for them!"

Faye had hoped she might be pregnant by now. They'd been married for months, had been intimate plenty by Faye's measure, though what was too much or too little was hard to say. She liked it enough, especially the attention William paid her afterward, when he collapsed into her, flushed with exertion, the way he murmured and stroked her hair, as if grateful to her for something essential. He would ask sometimes if she was okay, and she was, though her body felt a wanting. Wanting what, though, Faye didn't know. Maybe if they made a baby, that feeling would go away. But her cycle had come three times since the wedding, and with each one, a rising panic. William had done his part. Clearly, the failure was hers.

Faye had gone to bed the night before, hopeful Kennedy would defeat Nixon, that this elegant family would go to the White House. She had hoped for it as if it would say something about her own prospects for happiness. At twenty-three, it was Faye's first time voting. She and William had gone to the ballots together. "For the Irishman, of course," William had said, when a neighbor asked how they'd voted.

But as she stood now in her own living room, all hope and happiness drained from her at the sight of Conor O'Kane.

She knew from her father that O'Kane had come to the cove house a few times, that for some odd reason, Jean welcomed him, made him tea and buttered his bread, even smoked cigarettes with him, which bothered Thomas to no end. "She stops short of mending the holes in his socks," her father had quipped. "Though to my knowledge, he hasn't asked." When Faye about fainted with worry the first time he mentioned it, Thomas reassured her that Conor seemed wholly uninterested in Faye or William. "They talk about Ireland and the old days, stories upon stories. I don't like to hear . . . I walk away when they start in. He doesn't say much about what he's up to now."

Those words echoed in Faye's head. What is he up to?

"I let myself in. Hope you don't mind." O'Kane leaned forward and closed the magazine. "What a victory for the Irish!"

Faye took notice of the bottle of Jameson on the side table, the glass of whiskey that O'Kane now held up to her before taking a swig. She looked at the clock on the mantel. "William should be home any minute." She tucked her shirt into the waistband of her slacks.

"You look scared . . . Fiadh. You don't need to be frightened of me." He held his hands up as if to show no trick was up his sleeve.

"I prefer Faye."

"I'm sure you do. Now c'mon. Sit down. I won't bite. Let's be friends, like we were when we were kids."

She softened, a memory popping into her head of Conor and his brothers splashing each other on the rocky shores of Dunmanus Bay. Those days seemed fuzzy and waterlogged, like she was looking at them through a damaged lens, the edges dark. She wasn't lying. William would be home any moment. She sat tall on the couch next to Conor, trying to be firm.

"You know who I am and who I am not."

"Do I? Let's see. You're the new bride of my friend, William. You're the daughter of neighbors I knew as a lad. You were my friend. Briefly. But you were my friend."

He was not mocking her, but she could sense his wheels turning.

"Yes, all of that is true. But I need to know something from you, Conor. You must tell me what happened after our ship sailed." He could put it to rest. Put her at ease. "You must tell me what happened to Elisabeth."

"Elisabeth? Now, there's a name I haven't heard in a long time. And you were . . . Gisela. Hard to get it straight. Quite a trick you lot pulled." He snickered, put his palm to his forehead, pushed black hairs along his crown. He could only be a few years older than Faye but seemed weathered somehow. "Lots of confusion. The priest drunk for days . . ." His voice drifted, and he cocked his head as if spies might be in the next room. "The one left behind? That girl blubbered on about how it wasn't what it seemed. Of course, no one listened. Me, I cared only that Fiadh had gone without saying her goodbye. No one cared about a weeping orphan, poor thing. Father Doyle tried to quiet her, you know, 'God's will and all that.' I remember she spat at him."

Faye tried to picture what he described. The only priest she could conjure was from the orphan home in the Irish mountains, the one whose fingers wiggled in her mouth along with the body of Christ between them. She recalled Hannie and Hugh and their kindness. Surely, they'd helped Elisabeth despite her carrying on. "What did Hannie do? Did Elisabeth stay on with them?"

O'Kane's blue eyes shot side to side like comets. "I'm sorry to tell you. But, well . . ." He shook his head.

"What? Say it! What?" She could not bear it. Her heart pounded like she'd run a footrace. To what end had she consigned her own sister? Shame swelled in her like high tide. Headlights shot across the room. William was home. He would not poke his head into the barn first, not with a strange car in the driveway.

"Where is Elisabeth? I demand to know!"

"You demand, do you?" He poured himself another shot and downed it, setting the glass next to the magazine with a thud. Then, with a hand on Faye's leg, he pressed himself to standing. She cringed when he made a pitiful face then tilted his ear to his shoulder as if to imply she was stupid for asking. "What difference does it make to you?"

"How can you say that?" Faye rose in fury.

"You'll give all this up? Oh, I doubt that very much."

He rested his arm on the mantel, picked up the framed wedding picture, then set it back down. "Fiadh was supposed to meet up with me. The night before she sailed. She was me *mot*, you know. My girlfriend. Figured we'd try wearing each other's faces off before she left for America. Then she got fished from the bay, and I figured that was the reason she didn't show. Shocked I was, the next day, that the Beattys were gone. See it now, though. The likes of you is what got her killed off."

"It wasn't my fault!"

O'Kane grabbed Faye's waist with both hands, pulled her so tight she could see the creases in his dark lips, smell whiskey on his taste buds, feel the bulk of him against her pelvis. "Like I said, thought it'd be me marrying Fiadh Beatty." His hands slid down. "There's that arse I remember. What do you say we—"

Faye pushed his hands off her, stepped back. Blood coursed through every vein, swelling her like a tick. She was mortified, embarrassed as if she had done something wrong in that moment, invited his advance. "Don't you touch me!"

The back door shut then, and William's voice ran between her and Conor like a lance. "You're home!" She shoved past O'Kane, who slouched himself into the doorway as if the conversation they were having was nothing at all. "Conor stopped by—"

William's mouth opened slightly, and he squinted like he was laboring to figure out the scene in his own home.

Conor held up the bottle of Jameson. "Let's drink to the Irishman! How about it?"

Faye could do little except go along, though what Conor said consumed her. Did she truly want to know about her sister, even if it would upset her life? And what would William say? How could he trust her if he found out she'd kept such a thing hidden from him? And Thomas, her father! William would never forgive the betrayal. It was all too much.

She put the lamb chops aside for another day, made a quick meat loaf, then drank with the men into the night, to the bottom of the bottle, the whiskey warming the cold spot O'Kane exposed with his insinuation that she cared nothing about her sister. They put records on the player, and William and Conor sang along with the Irish songs they knew, their arms around each other's shoulders like they were in a pub. There had been little music for Faye in America, none in the house, Jean especially preferring a kind of reverential silence in her daily routine. Thomas recited poetry, his Yeats, which certainly had lyricism, though it wasn't the same as music. But William had grown up with parents who listened to the radio and brought records home to play on the console. "Jean is too stern," he'd confided. "A good Irish home should be filled with music. I promise you. We'll fill our house with children and song."

William crouched next to the record player, searching for another album to put on when O'Kane suggested "Danny Boy." "For Fiadh," he said. "To remind her of home."

"Let me find it here," William said.

"Oh, come on! That one we know by heart."

O'Kane started singing, really singing, not slurring or shouting. His voice was crystalline, the key higher than might be expected, given the looks of him. He closed his eyes, but the corner of his lip on the left side drew up on certain notes, like a conductor had it on a string. The effect was almost spectral. *'Tis you must go, and I must bide.* Faye pulled her sleeves down to cover her shivered gooseflesh. He drew out the notes, and William sang along with him to the end of the verse. *"Oh, Danny boy, I love you so."*

"That was lovely," Faye said, clapping politely.

"Oh, but of course there's more, Faye," O'Kane said.

"You sing it yourself," William said. "I'll mess up the words."

Conor sat on the arm of the sofa. This time he kept his eyes open, singing to Faye, singing to that question she still held.

"*But when ye come, and all the flowers are dying. If I am dead—*" He dropped the word like a stone and spoke the next line. *"As dead, I may well be . . ."*

He held her gaze for an eternity, toying with her. Then his voice soared. *"You'll come and find the place where I am lying and kneel and say an Ave there for me."*

Faye bent and buried her face in her hands. She could not bear the thought of Elisabeth in a grave, coldly waiting for her return. It had seemed so obvious. If only one of them was bound for America, it should be her and not Elisabeth. A child's logic, but still. Whatever Elisabeth's fate, it was Faye who'd condemned her sister to it.

"Ah, my singing has broken your bride, Will," O'Kane said. "Best to stop now. To tell you the truth," he added, "it usually ends better than this for me."

William put his arm around Faye. "I have never loved you more."

She paused in the darkness she created by covering her eyes, in the life she created by denying another. She sat up, wiped her cheeks, smiled at her husband.

"There's my girl!" William said. "A testament to our new president! Who wouldn't weep at that one, I ask. And Jesus, Con. That voice of yours! Like a choir boy!"

O'Kane scratched at his face, lifted his brow, a sadness about him. "My mam said that. 'Angel voice, demon heart.'" He shrugged largely, twisted his neck as if wresting away a burden.

Faye spotted an opening. "Yes, it's all so emotional! And I'm a little drunk, I'm afraid. I think I need to call it a night."

"No worries. I can take a hint." Conor slung his black leather coat over his shoulder. "And the night is young!"

"You're welcome to stay here," William said, though Faye detected that the offer was less than heartfelt.

"Oh, let him go," Faye said, hooking his arm. "He's had enough of us."

"Yes," Conor said. "Think I'll try my luck in town. Plus, seems the fox ought to go on into the hen house, if you know what I mean. Your wife is a wee bit sauced."

William's back straightened. "Watch yourself. My wife's none of your business."

O'Kane held up his hands in surrender. "She is not. That's true." He glanced over his shoulder at the door, his face half in darkness. "Grand evening. Really grand." He winked, then disappeared into the November night.

Upstairs, Faye washed her face, put on her nightgown in the bathroom as was her practice. She brushed her hair with her right hand, smoothed with her left, examining her reflection. She and Elisabeth had looked so much alike as children. Years she'd spent remembering her sister only as a girl, never imagining her as a woman. Maybe something inside her feared Elisabeth would never live to comb gray hair, as the poem went. She yanked at her hair, wishing she could brush out the knots in her stomach. Conor O'Kane and Fiadh. Conor O'Kane and that voice of his. She didn't know what he was trying to pull, singing the way he had, talking in riddles, touching her that way. She could have wrung his neck for toying with her, for stirring her up and making her restless. She leaned in closer and wet her lip with her pinkie finger. *Him and his whiskey.*

The lamp was lit when she entered the bedroom, William on his side, his back to her. She turned out the light and slipped in behind him, resting her forehead to his bare shoulder blades.

"Are you awake?" she whispered.

"Mm." He rolled over, concern wrinkling his brow. "Can I ask you something?"

"Yes. Anything. Of course."

"Conor didn't . . . he didn't make a pass at you, did he?"

Her stomach flipped, the feeling of Conor O'Kane's hands sliding down her ass. She did not want the man here in her bed. "No. No! Nothing like that."

"I felt I interrupted something when I walked in. He gets under my skin."

"No, he was reminiscing is all, talking about when we were children."

"Yeah, he did say he had planned to marry you."

Faye shuddered at the thought. Maybe Fiadh had loved Conor, even though they were only children. Maybe if Fiadh hadn't come to her rescue, Faye would have drowned in the bay instead, and Fiadh and Conor would have married. She drew a black curtain over the thought.

"Dear," she said. "That girl is long gone. You have nothing to worry about there."

"Well, I'll kill him if he tries anything."

She put her hand on his chest, and he drew her in with a rush of movement, new and insistent. She said his name, and he covered her mouth with his. He took her hand and put it on him, releasing her mouth, groaning at her touch. Lifting her hips, he pulled her nightgown up to her belly. He slid his palm between her legs, and Faye gasped at her body's wetted response to William's hand cupped over the whole of her like a mouth, fingers like a tongue. She was embarrassed at the thought of it until it became the thing that was happening, William diving there, airless and searching, then back to her lips, the flavor of him now so foreign. When he found his way inside her, the joining flung their eyes open to each other. Some great fever broke, spilled into hidden tributaries beneath her skin. She belonged with William. The wanting, she understood it now.

CHAPTER NINE

1961

Faye pushed herself to standing, mopped sweat off her neck. The flower garden was in full bloom, but it was a fight to keep the weeds out now that her pregnant belly made bending that much harder. She pulled the cloth gloves from her hands. *I give up,* she thought. *Let them grow.* Plus, this bending couldn't be good for the baby. Her doctor had told her to avoid overexertion, and certainly this weeding would count. She'd promised William she wouldn't take any risks with her pregnancy. She'd even given up cabbage and raw apples, though she did sneak a little chocolate here and there. She sat on the steps, spread her legs, and leaned back to give the jutting baby more room. It wouldn't be long now, and as much as she'd marveled in the strangeness of pregnancy and her changing body, she was ready for the baby to arrive. She was about to go in for lemonade when William pulled into the driveway, towing a rickety trailer. Her heart sank at the sight of it.

William, beaming, practically skipped around the front of the truck. "She's a beaut, right? And before you say it, I know we need things for the nursery. But I got a great deal on her."

A wooden rowboat not ten feet long, buxom yet sleek, white paint peeling, varnish chipped. But fine somehow. Faye did not know boats, did not want to. She and William had seen *The Philadelphia Story*, Katherine Hepburn and Cary Grant reminiscing about some boat they had once sailed. They'd called it "yar." A thing beautiful and safe, capable and solid. Fishing boats in the harbor would never be called "yar"—beautiful to some, she supposed, but so unsleek, gulls chasing them like street urchins begging for coins. But she often admired the sailing boats, their red and white wings on blue horizons, how free and American they seemed. It was one thing to admire boats and their purposes. It was another entirely to be in one, at the mercy of a boat.

"Even came with Shaw & Tenney oars," William said, as if that meant anything to either of them. "I'll fix her up, and we can put her in at the cove next summer. I don't think your folks would mind us keeping it there. We can christen her with a bottle of Jameson! We'll have to come up with a name of course, for the boat and the baby soon enough."

Faye couldn't get a word in edgewise, though she was too stunned to speak.

"Not exactly a yacht, but it would be fun to paddle around. We could take a picnic, you and me and the baby. How does that sound?" He ran his hand along the weathered gunwale, knocked on it for good measure.

Faye stared at the needy tender, at her husband and his gleaming eyes. Her legs wobbled as if she'd spent a week at sea. "My," she said. She felt a stab in her hip so sharp she expected someone had cast a stone at her. She reached for the pillar to steady herself. She'd had a purple bruise on her swollen hip, big as a grapefruit, from slamming into the gunwale before spilling into the bay. On the passage across the Atlantic, she found a knot of rope to sleep on, to aggravate the injury, a penance for sinking Fiadh and taking her place in terrible America. In terrible America, it had taken weeks to heal. She had stood with Jean on great granite boulders behind a new house, their dresses flapping like sails in the wind in terrible America, where food was good, doors were solid, where bedding was clean and neighbors smiled, where bruises and memories faded. In terrible America she'd found a home and a man that was beautiful and safe, capable and solid. The terrible America that she and Fiadh and Elisabeth had feared was not so terrible after all. As it turned out, America herself was yar.

William ran to her side, propped her up. "Are you okay? Is it the baby?"

She smiled as kindly as she could muster. "No, no. I'm fine. She's yar. Truly."

"Then what is it?"

All this time in America, living so close to the water. She'd spent hours upon hours walking the beaches, collecting rocks and shells and tiny treasures. She loved to wade into the water, swim a little if the temperature was right. But, in her life, she had been on four boats: a mail boat, a clinker punt, the O'Kanes' boat come to the rescue, and a great ship crossing the Atlantic. Would this be the fifth? A wooden tub made seaworthy by her own husband, who knew little of her seasickness and from what it was truly born?

Her tongue was a cold stone in her mouth. She did not want to deny William but struggled to keep the hesitation out of her voice. Tiptoe, tiptoe. "Do you remember at the wedding, when Conor mentioned an accident? I told you it was a local tragedy, a girl who drowned." She could do it. Right now. She could set the record straight. He would not leave her. She was carrying his child. The baby kicked her then, a reminder of everything she stood to lose. No. She couldn't risk it.

But that boat would not do.

"Sure . . ." William said, confusion in his voice.

"It was the day before we left Ireland. A boating accident actually." Faye flicked at her ear like a watchful pest had lit there. "A family in the village had taken in two sisters. Refugees." She found a way to make the lie a truth. "German girls. The three of us were friends."

"Germans? How did German girls get to Ireland of all places? Were they Jews?"

"Jews? No. The Irish wouldn't accept Jews. In fact, I believe the children had to be Catholic, not even Protestants were allowed. It was a humanitarian program. Meant to be temporary. Shamrock Something. They got them from"—the gray stone, the iron fences, Elisabeth—"a barracks or church, somewhere near Dublin. I don't recall specifics." Truth and fear tugged Faye in opposite directions. "We were playmates, in the fields and on the shore. They didn't know much English." Faye ached for Fiadh then, for the girl who took in these strangers. "We played with the O'Kane boys, sometimes. But then my parents decided to move to America. And these girls and I, we took our little boat out into the bay. But there was an accident, William. A terrible, terrible accident."

"Oh. I see."

"I stood up in the boat. And then the German girls did too. And one of them fell in." Faye rubbed the phantom pain on her hip. "I dove in and tried to save her. And she kept pushing me down, down and under the water, over and over." Faye remembered her hands in Fiadh's hair, her fingers tangling. "A fishing boat came to our rescue and pulled us out of the sea. But . . ." Tears poured down her face. Such a betrayal! To deny Fiadh and Elisabeth this way! "She didn't survive. It was my fault. If I hadn't been so careless . . . standing up in the boat like that." A breeze blew up the path, swirling the clippings and weeds Faye had pulled.

"But you tried to save her. That was brave of you." William put his arm around her shoulder, and she tilted into him. Oh, she was not brave. Not one bit.

"The boat was like this one. It would be a terrible thing for . . . for my parents. To see that boat. They felt guilty because we girls shouldn't have been allowed to take it in the first place." Faye sat up, wiped her eyes. "I'm sorry I didn't tell you sooner. It's such a . . ." She stuttered. "Such a sad, sad story. But truly, she's a fine boat, William, and your heart was in the right place. But no. We mustn't let them see it. Especially not my mother. She is so tender in her way. And please. Never mention the accident. It would be too much for them."

"Whatever happened to the other girl? Back to Germany, I suppose?"

Faye's eyes glazed over. She did not want to imagine Elisabeth anywhere—not dead or alive, not in Ireland or Germany or a grave. Her head ached. "I don't know." That, at least, was the truth.

Faye let William help her inside where he insisted she lie down and rest. She waited until he was out of the house then went to the window to see what he would do. He walked around the little boat, ran his hand along the gunwale. He glanced back at the house as if he might make an argument. Faye retreated from the window. Relief washed over her as he climbed into the truck and towed the boat out of their lives.

CHAPTER TEN

1968

It was a Saturday morning, late in the fall, and the farmhouse was freezing cold. Faye was running late. They had lost power during a storm the night before, lights flickering with each moan of wind working its way around the barnyard, early snow spraying the side of the house like paper spitballs. Thankfully William made it home from work before the worst of it had started, time enough to bring in wood before dinner, to find candles and matches and flashlights. When the blackout came, he'd brought blankets down to the living room to pin up in the doorway to keep heat from escaping and to make a sleeping pallet in front of the fire. Maeve, seven years old, found the whole thing a delight, snuggling between Faye and William on the floor, begging for book after book until both parents were hoarse from storytelling.

Faye called for Maeve, who she'd sent upstairs to change now that power was restored and heat banged through the house. "Let's go! Let's go!"

The phone rang, and Faye threw her head back in frustration. Probably William calling from the hardware store. She hopped to the receiver, pulling on her second boot as she did. She cradled the phone between her jaw and neck. It was her father. The wall clock said they were nearly half an hour later than she'd told him.

"I know. We're late. We lost power last night."

"I have a problem," Thomas said.

"I'm on my way, Papa." She covered the receiver with her hand and yelled into the house for Maeve to hurry up. "What is it?"

"It seems your mother is dead."

Faye felt a club to the chest, touched the wainscot to ground herself. She'd never heard those words from anyone, not in the hospital, the orphanage. Not from her uncle or from the nuns. She was a girl again, her Mutti in the dirty street. "Your mother." Had Jean ever been her mother? Faye could hardly recall a day when she'd felt love from or for her. But Thomas had more than made up for it. She wondered sometimes if it hurt Jean even more than Fiadh's death, that her own husband loved Faye so completely, especially since their relationship was borne from such sorrow. Yet how Jean could pour herself into Conor O'Kane had perplexed Faye. He'd tried to forge a relationship with William, but Faye suspected William continued to be dubious of his motives, especially after finding Conor alone with his wife, that grin of his always taunting. But Jean had been another thing entirely. Thomas had once—only once, given his nature—complained to Faye that O'Kane and Jean seemed to share something unnatural, some huddled secret that always excluded him. He said Conor had confessed to Jean that he'd fallen in with a tough crowd and that Jean worried about him, cared about his safety. Faye could not bring herself to say it then, and it pained her that it was the first thing she thought of now, that Jean loved Conor like a son but could not love her like a daughter, could not love her at all.

When she was pregnant with Maeve, Faye had had doubts about whether she even knew how to love a child. She watched other young mothers cradle and caress their newborns and hoped it would come to her naturally. She'd certainly not learned it from either of her mothers. Her memories of Mutti were clouded by war. If there had been tenderness, the fight for survival had torn it from her. As for Jean, grief occupied the space where love might have grown.

"Did you hear me?" Thomas's voice brought her back. "I said Jean is dead."

Maeve bolted down the stairs and plowed into Faye. The punch of her was solid and alive and made Faye breathe deeply. She was not Mutti. And she was not Jean. Loving her child was easy. Protecting her and keeping her safe was Faye's job. She lifted her daughter onto her hip and gripped her waist. In a flash, Faye remembered when Jean held Maeve for the first time. Her shoulders had eased, the lines in her face had softened even in the harsh hospital light. What was it that she said? "She's beautiful, dear." That was it. Jean had called Faye "dear." Maybe some scrap of love had been there after all, even in its smallest measure. Faye boosted Maeve higher onto her hip.

"Papa! What happened?"

There was not much to it. Thomas woke that morning like every morning since his retirement, without an alarm, when the sun poked through the window, when his eyes opened, when the bathroom called. Next to him, Jean lay cold.

"I tried to wake and warm her, but she was having none of it. I have quite a mess, I'm afraid." Thomas explained that Jean had wet the bed, and he couldn't bring himself to clean it up. "I didn't want to leave her alone. You know she's always been so alone."

"Oh, Papa! Is she still there?"

"Aye," Thomas said, his voice cracking. "She is that."

"Hold on. William is out. I'll drop Maeve at the Delaneys' and be there as soon as I can."

She hung up, put her nose into Maeve's hair, searching for the smell of baby scalp gone since the toddler years. Faye thought of her father sitting alone in the quiet house.

"Sweet girl," Faye cooed, closed her eyes. "I love you so much, you know that?"

Maeve cuddled into Faye like a big bear cub climbing a tree, legs around her body, arms around her neck, her grand heart knowing without asking that this was what her mother needed most. "Don't cry," she said, nuzzling into the crook of Faye's neck.

The funeral mass was held at the church Jean attended regularly, Thomas only on Easter and Christmas, as demanded. Faye and William sat with her father, Maeve fidgeting between them in a navy plaid jumper and white ruffled blouse, knee socks bagging into her Mary Janes. That morning, she asked Faye to help her write two lists, each with its own intent. It was Maeve's way of sorting her feelings, one that Faye and William knew well. One was titled "Grandma" (sweater, strawberry pin cushion, rhubarb pie, rocks, be quiet, tea, Grandpa) and the other "Dresses" (knees, collars, legs, armholes, zippers, boys, girls, monkey bars, lipstick, teeter-totter). Faye could see that Maeve had a wad of paper in her little hand, sweated up from the handling. She was waiting for her chance to slip a list into the casket before they took Jean away. It was the deal. You can give Grandma one last list, but you have to wear a dress to the service. And Maeve had a condition of her own: She wanted to write the list herself and keep the contents secret, like a wish. Faye had allowed it. Why would she not? Maeve knew her letters and was learning to use them to form words. If the list mattered at all, Jean would be able to read it.

With her eyes set on the priest delivering the sermon, Faye reached over to Maeve and gently drew her hand away from where she fussed with her hem. "Not much longer."

When the priest nodded to the family, Faye asked Maeve if she was certain she wanted to go first and alone, and Maeve swore she did. They had all seen Jean's body privately so it wasn't Maeve's first glimpse. "I have a bad feeling about this," William said, as Maeve, hands in her dress pockets, scooted past Thomas and made her way on tiptoe to the casket. She glanced over her shoulder once, then again, and Faye knew she'd made a mistake. It was too much. She stood, as did Thomas and William.

"I can do it!" Maeve shouted. The congregation seemed to cringe collectively.

Faye put her hand on Thomas's shoulder. "I've got her. I'm sorry."

Maeve, merely a foot from her grandmother's cold face, grunted out her frustration and threw the wadded paper into the casket. It hit Jean's icy cheek and bounced onto the dais. The congregation murmured with some mix of sympathy and scorn. Maeve's face burned fury red. Faye knew what it was, that terrible despair, that embarrassment, as if even in death, Jean found a way to reject Faye by rejecting Maeve. She picked up the paper, then, squeezing Maeve's hand, stuck it in next to Jean. "It's okay. Grandma has your list now. She knows you love her."

That word. She cast a glance at Jean's body, her face made to look calm, her skin and visage stone cold. She had not loved Faye and had tolerated Maeve at best. Maybe all the love she had in her died with Fiadh. Faye had thrown herself at Jean as surely as Maeve had thrown the wad of paper. Jean had rejected them both. She joined Maeve in crying hot tears as the two of them returned to the pew.

Inside the doors to the parish center, the family greeted mourners who offered condolences for a woman they hardly knew. Faye had spotted Conor O'Kane at the service, so she wasn't surprised to see him on the line. According to Thomas, the woman hanging off his arm was the new girlfriend, a bombshell who tended bar in Camden where Conor had been living for the last month or more. Too close, as far as Faye was concerned. At least when he was in Boston, news of his comings and goings was sporadic.

As they approached, Faye marveled that the woman appeared older than Conor. It was the one thing Jean ever criticized about him, that he only brought around girls barely out of their teens. Otherwise, he was perfect in her eyes. "It's like I have a son again," she'd said once. The comment had so annoyed William, he had reminded her that she had a son-in-law, a retort completely out of character for him. "You know that's not the same," she'd replied.

As they made their way closer, William whispered, "How old is she, do you think?"

"Maybe close to forty?"

"Yeah, maybe. Hard forty."

O'Kane took a long drag on his cigarette, then snipped the edge with his thumb like he was taking the head off a dandelion. Embers arced to the cement as smoke poured from his mouth and nostrils. He mashed it out with his boot tip, put the butt in his jacket pocket, then made his way inside. "What a blow." His voice cracked with emotion. He shook Thomas's hand.

Thomas nodded coolly. "Yes."

"I have to say, Fiadh, she was like a mother to me," Conor continued, his eyes swollen and red-rimmed.

Faye's heart thudded the way it always did when Conor O'Kane appeared, a snake on a trail. She had encountered him a couple of times at the cove house, jawing with Jean over cigarettes and coffee. Only in those situations did he call her Faye, out of deference, she figured, to Jean. He'd make himself scarce when Faye showed up, though with a slanted eye. It gave Faye the creeps, the way her mother looked at him as if theirs was a clandestine relationship, as if they were lovers. "Mm. The two of you did have something special, all right."

"Don't take it personally. I made her happy." He drew Faye into a lengthy embrace. That menacing scent of him—burning paper, pomade, the leather of his jacket almost feral. It was the smell of an animal that lurked where humans gathered. She recoiled as William stepped up.

"Okay, Con. You've made your point."

"All I'm saying is what Jean meant to me. Isn't that right?" he said to his guest. "Oh, everyone, this is Glenda."

She was a big woman, hair dyed rubber-ball red, as tall as William and heavier, all of it magnified by blue eyeshadow and overwhelming breasts impossible to ignore, even for Maeve, who stared in that way of children.

"Sorry for your loss," Glenda said, her voice husky. "Con has talked nonstop about his friend Jean since I've known him."

"Conor thinks everyone is his friend," Thomas said.

O'Kane, shrugging off the jab, patted Maeve's head. "This wee one had a time of it."

"Are you a good witch or a bad witch?" Maeve asked.

"Maeve!" Faye admonished.

Glenda roared with laughter. "Trust me. I've heard it before."

"Quite the spitfire you got there, Fiadh," O'Kane said. "I've got half a mind to kidnap her to Ireland with me. Fiery Irish lass . . ."

"What's wrong with you?" William asked. "Hardly the occasion for gallows humor."

O'Kane tried to pat Maeve again, but this time she ducked behind Faye. "Settle down. It's a joke. Though it's true you've never been one for humor." He regrouped, slicked up his voice. "So, how about that? Glenda and me, we'll go to Galway soon, then to see her brother in Derry. Been more than a decade for me. You lot must miss it. The homeland and all. Too bad Jean couldn't go back."

The scoff slipped out of Faye's mouth on a blast of breath. She shook her head, rolled her eyes. She'd had it with him. She wished she could shove him into the hole they dug for Jean.

"My wife had no desire to return to Ireland," Thomas said. "Surely in all your ear-bending with her, she'd told you that much. Her home was here. And I will miss her in it."

Maeve squirmed next to Faye, fussing with her skirt and shoes until it was too late for anyone to thwart what she had planned. Her hand balled like it had earlier with the message for her grandmother. She wound up like a major league pitcher and threw her underpants, hitting O'Kane in the nose with white panties scotched with urine and a child's poor wiping habits.

"I don't like him," Maeve wailed, her face red as a washed tomato.

No one does, Faye thought in an instant, though outwardly she was aghast.

"Dear God," Faye said, scooping up Maeve and her underwear. "Okay. William. You have to take her home."

He took Maeve from Faye. "I don't know what on earth got into her."

"Little young for my taste," Conor said, wiping his face with the back of his hand.

"You know," Thomas said, his finger shaking as he pointed. "Jean said you reminded her of our boys. She was right on one count. They, too, were snickering idiots. I'd ask you to steer clear of us now that she's gone."

"Thomas," Conor said, his head cocked.

"Papa," Faye cautioned. *Leave trouble untroubled.*

"I mean it. You're not welcome."

The black hearse from the funeral home approached the front of the church, followed by a car to take the family to the graveside.

Conor stared at Maeve, who glared at him from the safety of her father's arms. "Changed my mind about that kidnapping. I don't like you either," Conor said, taking Glenda's hand. They walked away without a backward glance, though Conor tossed his arm in the air. "See you lot."

As the black car pulled away, Faye and Thomas slouched in the seat. Thomas stifled a laugh as best he could, and Faye covered her face. "Oh, my," she said, turning to look at her father. "Papa. I'm sorry. I should have known better."

"Don't mind that. Not a proper funeral until someone makes a scene. Good for Maeve. Maybe she drove that snake away." Thomas turned to the window. The pool-blue sky shimmered against the dappled gold of autumn. "Jean would have liked it this way."

Faye squeezed his hand. "It is a bluebird day."

"That too, my little Faye. No, it's better this way. Her going first. She would have been too lonely." Blue and gold and gray whisked by the window as he spoke. "I have you, after all."

Faye drew in a breath, held it with her tears.

"Still, I wish I could have buried her there by her rocks. Kept her close."

It was Jean's favorite place from the very beginning—the massive granite rocks along the cove. "That's the future," she would say. "Out there somewhere is Ireland. They've had their breakfast, and their day is half done." She would sway her arms back and forth, closing and opening doors to the past. "If only we could clear this away."

Other times, she would sit on the rocks and jot in a leather journal not much bigger than a hand, small enough to drop into a pocket. As a teenager, Faye had gotten up the nerve to ask about it, and Jean had told her flat out, "It's not your business. A woman is entitled to her story." Faye had been so overcome with curiosity she'd gone in search of it, rummaging through drawers, walking her hand along closet shelves when Jean was out of the house. She'd never found it.

Faye closed her eyes now, lulled by the motion of the heavy black sedan. It was the last place Faye had seen Jean alive. Buoys bobbing in fog soup, seabirds ranting in circles, the laughter of lobstermen drifting from ghost ships somewhere out in the snug cove. Jean had turned when Faye called to her, and a girlish wisp of gray hair fell from her loosely spun bun. She'd brushed it up onto her head, then let her hand rest over her mouth in surprise as if she were expecting anyone but Faye. It was a lasting image for sure, a hunched woman, her motion slowed, caught in a world she was never a part of, alive there but not living.

"That would have been nice, Papa," Faye said, patting his hand.

The winter that followed was dark and deep, storm after storm, a nor'easter that marooned them between drifts of snow and spotty power. Faye worried about Maeve's safety when the marigold-colored bus ferried her off into a sea of white drenched red by brake lights tapping out warnings. The world outside her window was blue and gray, white on white, as if spring would never arrive. Snowed in, she baked and cooked in survival mode, stored casseroles in the deep freeze. It made her feel useful and necessary to keep her family warm and fed, and she hoped it would distract William, at least for a while, from the fact that she had not given him another child, despite their efforts. Faye longed for William, for his body on hers. She thought sure she'd recently had another miscarriage, her second, but it had been so early it was difficult to know. Lately, when she reached for William under their heavy covers, he pulled away, leaving Faye broken and blue.

They tucked Maeve in one night in February, a nor'easter pelting the house with horizontal snow. In the hallway outside Maeve's bedroom, Faye touched William's arm. "Let's go to bed."

William flinched as if her touch was repulsive, rolled along the railing perched above the foyer, and retreated into their bedroom.

Faye followed him. "Enough of this!" she shouted. William pulled her to the bedroom and shut the door. She crossed her arms in a huff. She felt petulant and ugly. "Is it me? You no longer . . . want me?" A horrible thought crossed her mind. *Had William seen Conor O'Kane?* The scene at the funeral had been so horrific maybe Conor had finally exacted his revenge. Is that what her husband was grappling with? Her betrayal? She tried to keep fear out of her voice.

"No, honey, no." Deep sorrow rent across his face. He turned away, stretched his hands out to grip the edge of the dresser before facing her. "I would be a wreck without you. I don't want to . . . upset the order here. We're happy, right? The three of us?"

"You're not making sense."

He sighed. "I know. I keep thinking maybe something is wrong. I'm afraid I've gotten myself sick with worry that if you do get pregnant again, after all this time, something will go wrong. I couldn't bear it. And what would happen to Maeve?"

Faye wiped at her face to remove the web of fear she'd woven. "The doctor said I'm fine. Nothing is wrong."

"I don't know." William pulled at the waves of his hair as if the right answer had burrowed in there.

"Look. I come from—" A flip-book of images fluttered in her mind, a patchwork of her stitched-together life. "I'm a strong woman. Don't push me away."

By spring, Faye knew she was pregnant. When she was confident she was out of the woods, she told William, and they both told Thomas. She had worried about her father's loneliness with Jean gone, but he assured her that he had books to keep him company and pints when he wanted one at the pub near the docks. "Such lucky news, and right when the lilacs are blooming."

Maeve, when it was her turn, ran from the house. William chased her down in the barn, held her in an abandoned goat stall while she cried and cried. Faye arrived close behind.

"I don't want a *baby*. I told Grandma Jean. On the list." Faye had never asked what was on the crumpled paper that wound up in Jean's casket. Maeve held up her fingers. "One: A kitten. Two: Pennies from heaven, like Daddy's song. Three: A baby *doll*. She never listened to me. No one ever listens to me!"

Faye opened the gate, collapsed cross-legged next to Maeve and William, her heart bursting. "I'm sorry, sweetie. We're listening to you now. Tell us anything."

"Will it be a boy or a girl?"

Faye shrugged. She hoped for a boy. For herself, for William, so Maeve would have a brother. She tried to shake off her ambivalence about having a girl. On one hand, it might be nice for Maeve to have another girl in the house. But the thought of sisters sent Faye to a place she didn't want to be or to think about anymore.

"It will be a surprise!" Faye said. "Now, let's talk about that list." The three of them, plus baby on the way, sat on stacked crates among William's growing collection of woodworking projects, toppled bean pots and crocks, antiques, and rusted tools, and they talked about kittens and pennies and dolls and all the ways their family might grow.

Molly was born the day after Thanksgiving, bleating like a lamb, William's red hair curling off her waxy scalp. Though she was smaller than Maeve, labor had been harder and longer. Torn and depleted, Faye could hardly move her head from the pillow when William brought Maeve into the room. She scrambled onto the hospital bed to be close to Faye and the baby who rested against her. "Careful, careful. Mommy's a little sore and tired," Faye said. Maeve touched the baby's swaddling, and a tiny arm escaped, wrinkled fingers clenched to fight.

"I wanna hold her," Maeve said. She stiffened, stuck her arms out. "Can I hold her?"

Faye petitioned William with a raised brow, and he replied with an easy nod. Faye swiveled and placed the baby in Maeve's arms. "Be gentle. She's very tiny."

The baby fussed, and Maeve brought her knees up and curled her arms around the flannel blanket. "I'll be careful," she whispered, cooing until the baby settled again.

From a green metal chair next to the bed, William stroked Faye's hand. "They're pretty cute. She's a natural, that one."

Faye put her arm around Maeve, snuggled her daughters closer. She felt a serenity that bordered on euphoria, though every part of her throbbed. "You're not disappointed? That it's not a boy?"

"What? No!" William said. "Look there. One of you holding one of me. They're perfect. Keep hold of her head there, Maeve. Don't let go."

Maeve pipped her lips, made kissy faces. "Don't worry. I won't let go, Daddy. Not ever. I'll be a good big sister. I promise."

Faye covered her mouth, quieted a sigh, let a water-drenched memory wash over her. Two girls—indigo skirts, billowing peasant tops, blistered hands carrying tin pails—blurred together in a greenwashed field. New life and old ghosts. And second chances.

PART TWO

1976–1995

CHAPTER ELEVEN

1976

Faye held Molly's hand as they passed the ice cream parlor and hair salon on the way to the five-and-dime for a new hair ribbon. She had never seen more red, white, and blue. Maine, like all of America, was crazy for the bicentennial celebration. Every house was festooned with buntings, and flags of every era—thirteen stars, forty-eight, fifty—hung from porch rails and makeshift flagpoles. Planning had been going on for a year or more, so decorations went up before the snow was gone. Aldo at the flower shop where Faye used to work had died two years short of his own centennial, and his granddaughter had taken over—first the shop, then the local Chamber of Commerce. Hers was the first business to go all in on patriotic trinkets and spinners and carnations dipped to match.

As much as Faye loved America, she struggled with the celebration, especially the fireworks. Bursts of mortar, fire raining from the sky. She wanted to thrill in the display the way William and the girls did, but in truth, each explosion shook her to the core, surfacing childhood fear she could hardly name anymore. She'd dared ask William once if the fireworks brought back memories of war, and he'd brushed the question off, said that they signified endurance and victory to him. She wished she had even one fond memory of when she was a little German girl, of Elisabeth and Mutti and Vati, when they weren't dodging bombs, hunting for butter and coffee on the black market, averting their eyes for fear of being questioned. There had been a train ride with Mutti and Elisabeth to the countryside where they ran through fields to the shelters when the sirens blared. Maybe she had smiled over pea soup in some kitchen there, maybe there were games and pranks and laughter. But every memory Faye retained seemed to end in an explosion, with Mutti unfurled in the street. Even blue skies sometimes glistened silver with phantoms of whistling bomber formations circling overhead.

And then there was the matter of that song. Even now, "America the Beautiful" followed her and Molly down the street, piping from crackling speakers hung from phone poles. Faye knew it by heart, of course, had learned it in elementary school. But every time she heard it performed—and so often in July—she was reminded that Fiadh had spat that phrase to the ground. What Fiadh might have made of America, or America of her, Faye could not know. But three decades later, the song still felt more like an accusation than an anthem, reminding Faye that the freedom she celebrated, and her own beautiful life, had been meant for another girl.

Molly struggled to keep on her new sandals—flip-flops with a rattan foot bed and a puffy thong—and her gait alternated between halting and skipping. Faye, her shoulder sore from the yanking, had grown testy with the music and rising heat. "Honey," she said, exasperated. "Try to keep up." The last thing they needed was for Molly to stub a toe. Distracted, Faye didn't see the woman before she ran smack into her.

"I'm so sorry!" Faye said before she recognized her. "Oh!"

"Glenda," the woman said. "Hi, Faye."

Was it possible she'd grown more colorful since Faye had seen her last?

"Glenda! No, of course. Hello. So much happening here." She laughed awkwardly. "Good to see you."

Their lives had been blissfully free of Conor O'Kane for years. After Jean died, he'd gone back to Ireland, resurfacing only for a couple unwelcome visits to Thomas at the house on the cove, each time trying to gloss over the past. William had run into him once a few years back in Boothbay and had been shocked by his appearance, both eyes swollen and black, his arm in a sling. "What you get when you mess with a man's woman. You shoulda seen the other guy," was what William told Faye he'd said. Taking it apart, it wasn't clear whether Conor had been the affronter or the affronted. All he'd said otherwise was that he moved back to Boston and implied connections William wanted no part of. They hadn't seen or heard from him since. And now here was Glenda.

She looked the same, old and ageless at the same time. She'd caught the bicentennial fever, an eagle and flag T-shirt over cutoff jeans, star-shaped sunglasses tucked into the cleft between her boobs. "This the baby? She got big. How old is she now?"

"Six. Going into first grade." Faye looked around. O'Kane must be lurking somewhere.

Glenda followed her gaze. "I don't know where he is. He was supposed to pick me up."

"Conor?"

"Yeah. Actually, I'm surprised to see you here. He said he was heading to your place."

Faye did a quick scan of their plans for the day. Like a typical teenager, Maeve wasn't even up when Faye and Molly left the house. William was having breakfast with Thomas—a regular Saturday outing for them since Jean died—then he was supposed to run errands, which could mean early afternoon before he was home. It was past eleven now. "No one's home so he should be around here somewhere," Faye said with as much cheer as she could muster.

"You're a funny little thing," Glenda said to Molly. Her husky tone was stilted and shouty, as if Molly were hard of hearing or thick in the head. "And those sure are odd-looking sandals. You don't look one bit Chinese." She winked at Faye like they shared a secret.

Faye gripped Molly's hand. "We have to get going. Nice bumping into you."

"I'm in the parade," Molly said, as if that explained her vaguely oriental shoes.

"I'll watch for you. Throw me candy if you see me."

Faye wanted to get away from this woman, this conversation. She wanted to check on Maeve. But Molly pulled her arm, and Glenda stood there, not catching the hint. "Irish step," Faye said, exasperated. "Her class is performing tomorrow. I don't think they'll be giving out candy." It came out wrong, like she was talking to a child.

Glenda looked at Faye like she was the dumb one. "I can get my own candy, you know."

"Right, right," Faye said, eager to end this. "Okay, well then. You take care."

Glenda's face soured as they snuck past her.

Molly, miffed they had to leave in a rush, huffed all the way home, right up to when they pulled into the driveway. A black car with racing stripes was there. William's wagon was not. Faye didn't bother grabbing her bags or holding the door for Molly. She ran to the house, pulled the screen door, cursing that the paint stuck in the humidity.

Conor O'Kane sat at the kitchen table, an open can of beer in his hand. "Finally," he said. "I wondered when you were coming home."

"Why are you here? Where's Maeve?"

"Hello to you too. She came downstairs a while ago. I don't think she was too happy to see me." He wiped his brow with the back of his hand. "It's hot in here. Helped myself to a beer. Don't you have fans? And why are you lot never here when I come by? I always have to let myself in."

Faye scrunched her face, confused. "Have you been in our house before? You can't just walk into someone else's home!"

Molly burst in, jabbering about wanting to go back to town. She stopped in her tracks behind Faye.

"There's the little sweetheart!" O'Kane said. "Come sit with your Uncle Con." He patted the spot next to him. Molly dipped her head, glowered over a pinched brow like she was casting a spell, turning a toad into a smaller toad.

"Go upstairs and find your sister. Go on." Faye nudged Molly, but she bounced back into her hip, drawn like a magnet to steel. She spread her legs, crossed her arms. She wasn't budging.

O'Kane guffawed a lungful of cigarette smoke. "Ah, well, she reminds me of someone I used to know. Will you look at that! Even her little mouth is sealed shut."

"I saw Glenda in town," Faye said, ignoring his comment. "She's waiting for you. You should go."

O'Kane pushed himself up like it was a great burden. "Was hoping to talk to William, and your—well, and Thomas too. I've a sort of investment opportunity."

She wished she could get rid of him for good. When she'd heard about the bar fight, she had secretly hoped it had been debilitating. When he flew to Ireland, she'd been ashamed of herself for thinking about the plane crashing. He brought out the worst in her. More than a thorn in her side or a pebble in her shoe. He was a bullet loaded into a gun, a lit fuse. She did not believe he wouldn't crack eventually, his very presence a reminder that she'd blown the opportunity to come clean with William herself. He was a threat, simple and true.

"Jesus, will you stop staring at me!" O'Kane said. "If I didn't know better, I'd think you might have a thing for me. Little too late to get the ride, don't you think?"

Faye shivered her thoughts away, hardened herself. She didn't want him to get the best of her. "I'll alert William and my father that you have returned to town after a long absence with a money-making scheme I'm certain they shall not want to miss. Now, if you don't mind . . ."

"Well, happy Independence Day to you and to your beautiful family, Fiadh."

She stifled the urge to bare her teeth, to roar like a lion. Instead, she smiled sweetly, watched him retreat until the car was gone from the driveway, out of sight. Only then did she unclench, taking the stairs as quickly as possible. "Maeve!"

The bedroom door flew open. Maeve, in bell-bottom jeans and a blue checkered crop top, fumed.

"Mom! What took you so long? That guy was sitting there when I came down. I was in my nightgown!" she wailed. "I didn't see him and I walked into the kitchen, and he didn't say anything and then I came out and about had a heart attack. He was like, 'Do you remember me? You threw your dirty underpants at my face. I'm your long-lost Uncle Conor.' I mean, Mom! Why would I remember him? God! I wanted to ride into town, but I couldn't, I was so scared. So, I sat up here. Dressed. Waiting for him to leave. Nothing to do. What is wrong with that guy?"

Faye could not land on a proper answer. The worst thing about him was that he acted like something had been taken from him, that he was owed something he'd never received. It was infuriating that he'd stumbled upon this life of hers and had nothing to offer except his silence. She couldn't figure out what it was that he wanted in return. How could Jean have let him into their life? And for how long would Faye have to keep up this charade?

"Mom! God. Snap out of it!" Maeve rolled her eyes, pushed past Faye along the railing.

"He was Grandma's friend. From Ireland. You remember. I'll tell Dad we need locks on the doors," Faye offered, shuddering at the thought of him prowling around their home.

"Great. Fine. That guy gives me the creeps."

"Forget him," Faye said, to herself as much as to Maeve. "Wieners and beans for lunch. And I thought I told you not to wear that shirt. It's inappropriate."

Maeve shrugged, headed down the stairs ahead of Faye. "I like it. And, by the way. Locks don't stop rats, you know," she said over her shoulder. "They squeeze in through cracks."

The next day, Center Street was lined six-deep with spectators spangled in stars and stripes, parents craning for children performing, tourists covered in cotton candy and waving their flags. Faye and William stood with Thomas along a sawhorse barrier while Maeve and her friends perched on a nearby curb, ignoring adults with teenage precision. The grand marshal on the back of an open convertible led the procession, followed by antique cars and fire trucks and Shriners in clown cars, festooned floats for the garden club and the rotary club and Friends of the Lobstermen. Queens and princesses and sea goddesses waved like royalty. Sailors in dress whites escorted the Bath Iron Works float, which elicited big whoops from Thomas and William. Right after the high school marching band passed, Faye spotted the dance studio's homemade banner, girls in green dresses and Mary Janes with ankle socks behind it. She nudged William and pointed. "Here they come!"

Only nine children took step class, and Molly, the smallest, was positioned at the point of the *V*, lead goose with her chin high, red springs bouncing around the white ribbon Faye had found buried in a drawer, and a grin that could bring ships home. Molly's arms were stiff at her sides, feet crossed, toes pointed as piped-in music from a nearby float started playing. The older dancers were in perfect sync, while Molly and the other two littlest girls did a basic jig step.

"Looking good, Pix!" Maeve, standing now, yelled. Molly let herself get distracted for a moment, waved at her family, and they all waved back, charming the crowd even more. Mission accomplished. Her bounces got bigger, her toe-kicks higher. She was having a ball.

A voice drifted across the crowd from the other side of the street, chanting, "Good golly, Miss Molly! Good golly, Miss Molly!"

Conor O'Kane was half in the road, clowning an Irish dance. Faye could tell from the looks of him that he'd already been in the whiskey. When Molly saw him, she stopped in her tracks. Arms that were supposed to be stiff at her sides shot up to her waist, and the girls dancing behind had to stop with Molly in the way. He made an exaggerated gesture, his mouth in a circle, hands up to the sides of his head. Faye gripped William's arm. She read Conor's lips, an "Oh, shit!" followed by guffawing laughter. Glenda backhanded him then pulled him toppling into the crowd, setting off a stumbling chain reaction.

Molly, lost for a moment, stared at Faye and William.

William patted Faye's hand. "You got it, Pixie!" he shouted as the dance teacher got her back in step. They marched by, and Molly kept her eyes only on her family, her steps slightly muted now, but the smile back on her face. Livestock brought up the rear, followed by street sweepers, the final act. The crowd dispersed, and O'Kane loped across the street toward them.

"I stopped by yesterday to see you, Will," Conor said, panting a cloud of stale alcohol.

"So I heard."

"How've you been?"

"Maeve!" Faye shouted. "Will you please go find your sister?"

Glenda fluttered her fingers, and Faye raised her hand dismissively. She had no interest in yet another conversation with Glenda . . . something. Faye didn't even know her last name. Mostly, she wanted to throttle Conor.

"Gladly," Maeve said.

"Why don't I catch up with you all by the bandstand?" William said, squeezing Faye's shoulder. "I want to talk with Conor alone."

A taunting look passed from Conor to Faye, as if they were children again, as if Conor were daring Fiadh, the other Fiadh, to say a dirty word, to lift her skirt, to secretly row a boat out into a bay. *Ooooh, what do you think I'm going to say, Fee? Who's going to stop me, Fee?* Faye had a look for him too. *Don't test me, Conor O'Kane.*

Over blueberry pie and strawberry ice cream, and with the girls out of earshot, William told Faye and Thomas what Conor was cooking up. "Says he's collecting money to send to Ireland, to the IRA. He figured we'd be in a mood for revolution and independence today, me and your dad. Apparently, Glenda's got brothers back home all wrapped up in The Troubles."

Thomas dropped his paper plate on the grass, wiped his mouth with his fingers. "My guess is he's not trying to send money. You hear things, down at Kelly's. Fellas in Boston and New York, connected." Thomas tapped his nose twice. "Been sending ArmaLites for years. Conor is the right fool to think gun running is like cigarette running. Feds are on those guys."

"Guns, William? The IRA? Please, tell me you didn't give him money!" Faye said. "He'd only come back for more."

"Faye. No. I humored him but made it clear that I want nothing to do with his stupid schemes. He'll wind up in jail or dead, mark my words."

Maeve wandered over for seconds. "Claire's dad says the IRA are terrorists." She cut a slice of pie from the tin perched on top of a picnic basket and plopped it on her plate.

"Stay out of it, honey," Faye said.

"Does he now, and what would he know?" William asked. "Here we are, celebrating America's independence from the British. Does Claire's father think our revolution was won with sweet talk and daisies? Perhaps Claire's dad, the Loyalist, would like to go back to living under British rule here as well. Is he here then?" William asked, looking around mockingly. "Flying the Union Jack?"

"Sheesh," Maeve said, eyes rolling. "I was trying to participate? In the conversation?"

"Are you going to continue to argue Irish politics with your high schooler, or can someone get an old man more pie?" Thomas asked, nudging his empty plate with a flick of his finger.

"Sorry I snapped at you, Maeve. Sensitive subject," William said. "I told him to beat it, and him and that goofy woman of his took off. Maybe that's the last of him."

"Your mouth to God's ear," Faye said. "What a blessing that would be. Really, there's not much here for him with Jean—with my mother—gone."

Molly wiped a ring of berry juice off her lips with her wrist. "Are you talking about Fonzie? We saw him."

"Fonzie?" Faye asked.

"That Conor guy," Maeve said. "After Claire and I picked up Molly. He made a crack, some 'little pixie doll thing' and then Claire asked who he was, and he was all gross, like, 'Who's your friend?' What a creep. I mean, who wears a leather jacket in weather like this?" Maeve bit her lip. "I may have mouthed off a little."

Faye's heart sunk with worry. Every encounter felt likely to provoke him. "Oh, no. Maeve. What did you say?"

Maeve shrugged. "I just said, 'Mind your own business, Fonzie.' That's all."

Molly scooted closer and tapped Maeve's thigh. "And then we ran, didn't we?"

"Yeah," Maeve said. "Then we ran. But don't worry, Mom. I had Molly's hand the whole time. I didn't let him touch her."

"I should hope not!" The thought sent a shiver up her spine. And Maeve, with her navel showing again below the tied-up ends of her blouse. She really had no idea what men like Conor O'Kane might read into her choices. "I wish you'd listen to me and cover up more."

Maeve rolled her eyes. "It's fashion, Mom. All the girls do it. Besides, he wasn't looking at me. He was looking at Claire. Everyone looks at Claire."

"Boy's a lost soul at best. Bad penny at worst," Thomas added, his head shaking.

"Hope he stops turning up," William said, adjusting his aluminum chair. "I told him to get on with his own life and leave us out of it. And

I, for one, would like to get on with this day. Can we agree? No more talk of him?"

"I couldn't agree more," Faye said.

Someone tapped the mic at the bandstand, and the topic was dropped. The grass thrummed from the bare feet of scampering children, leaves quaked with their laughter. Pop music filled the park. Relieved, Faye stretched out on the blanket, leaned back on her elbows, crossed her bare legs at her ankles. She let her head drop so the sun could blaze her neck and chest, closed her eyes, and played out the remainder of the day. Later, Maeve would take Molly to the midway for rides and games. There would be more food—corn dogs and lobster rolls, caramel corn and candied apples—until bellies ached. Finally, her whole family would reconvene on the blanket to watch what would seem like two hundred years' worth of fireworks explode overhead. The girls would shriek with delight. Faye—while trying to keep old wounds from aching—would welcome William's embrace and his gentle ribbing over her delicate nature, knowing they would return to a home still standing, their girls safe and sound under a solid roof with only stars overhead. America the Beautiful indeed.

CHAPTER TWELVE

1979

Molly sat on the end of Maeve's bed, knees drawn up but splayed, painting her toenails a gaudy purple while Maeve, her back against the headboard, thumbed through the *Tiger Beat* she'd bought that afternoon. She'd thought about shoving the magazine down the front of her jeans, but shoplifting was pointless without anyone to see you get away with it. It had been funny and conspiratorial to steal with friends, to run to the park afterward and lay out the loot on a picnic table, the risk worth the reward of pulling off a petty heist. But her old friends were gone. And she didn't have new ones who she could hang out with in the same way. She missed basketball. She missed Claire. She'd bought the nail polish but told Molly she'd swiped it. *Talk about pathetic! Lying about stealing to impress your little sister.* She watched Molly slop polish all over her cuticles, pursed her lips, and closed the magazine. "You'd better not get that on my bedspread, or Mom will kill me. Or you."

"I'm trying to be careful. It's hard. Toes are so far away from hands."

Maeve rolled her eyes. She knew Molly was fishing for attention. "Give me that." Molly handed the bottle and brush over with a satisfied grin.

Maeve didn't want to admit how much she needed Molly's company. Here she was, seventeen years old, and her best friend was a third grader who didn't know the first thing about boys or basketball or rumor mills or periods or bras or how snaky and fickle girls can be. She didn't know what it felt like to be an outsider, how saying or doing one stupid thing could change everything. But, then again, it wasn't just one thing that got Maeve into this situation.

"Don't tell Mom and Dad, okay?" Maeve said, Molly's big toe pinched between her fingers. "I'm going to a party tonight. In the woods."

Molly bent forward, blew on the nail. "A birthday party?"

"No, not a birthday party. More like a party to blow off steam," Maeve said.

Molly scrunched up her face. "Huh?"

"Remember that boy Oskar I was telling you about? The exchange student?"

"The German boy. With the tongue. I remember."

Maeve had had a nonspeaking townsperson role in the spring play, and at the cast party after the final curtain, the bottle pointed at her when Oskar spun it. He'd lurched across the circle, and suddenly his tongue was down her throat.

"Yeah, so he and a bunch of other kids are going to a party. He asked if I wanted to go, too, so I said yes." Maeve put the cap back on the nail polish and used the magazine to fan Molly's nails.

Molly flexed her foot to admire her purple toes. "Are you going to kiss him again?"

Maeve did not want to kiss this Oskar again. But she had to admit, there was some satisfaction in it. It had all started freshman year. If only her parents had let her switch from Spanish class to German with Claire and Robin, she wouldn't be in this situation. But no. They'd been firm to the point of ridiculous. Her dad had raised his voice—something he never did—shouting at Maeve that he would not have German spoken in his house, and that was that.

And her mother had almost burst into tears! Then Claire and Robin grew closer, and Maeve was the third wheel. To make matters worse, Robin decided to go out for basketball, and before Maeve knew it, Robin and Claire were both starters, and Maeve was a reliable benchwarmer. No, she didn't want to kiss Oskar. But she did want to shut up that stupid, pimply dullard Kim who peeked over Maeve's shoulder in class one day and saw Maeve had doodled Claire's name in bubble letters. It wasn't framed in a heart or anything. It was nothing. A thing between friends. But loud enough to make sure someone else would hear, Kim said, "Oooh! Maeve has a crush on Claire!" And somehow, somehow, it had stuck. No matter what Maeve did or said, no matter how hard she tried to prove otherwise, she knew that people still snickered about her, and she'd let it get under her skin and it had made her act weird around Claire, which made Claire act weird around her. Then, beginning of junior year, Maeve and Claire were assigned to the same homeroom, and some random boy said, "Look, Claire. There's your girlfriend!" Claire told the kid to go fuck himself, which made Maeve's heart leap until Claire turned to Robin, made a gagging motion, and said, "Gross," which pulverized Maeve's hopeful heart. Weeks later, at tryouts, the varsity roster was filled until Maeve was the only junior left standing. "Looks like one more year of JV for you," the coach said. In front of everyone—Claire, Robin, her teammates, even the hotshot new girl from Canada, Wendy Walker—Maeve told the coach he could stick JV and had walked out of the gymnasium, away from basketball and the only friends she had. If it hadn't been for the theater kids, she wouldn't have any social life at all. And the German boy was a theater kid. Did she want to kiss Oskar? No, she absolutely did not. But she would. To get back at her parents. To prove something to Claire. To clear her name. Sure, she'd kiss him again.

Maeve smacked Molly's foot playfully. "Wouldn't you like to know . . ." she said. "Now get out of here. I have to change and come up with a story for Mom and Dad. And Pix, seriously, you have to promise. You can't tell."

"I know!" Molly said. She crossed her heart with an *X*, locked her lips with an imaginary key, then snatched the nail polish off Maeve's side table.

"Thief!" Maeve cried and threw the magazine at her.

"Ha! Mine!" Molly said, grabbing the magazine off the floor before hightailing from Maeve's room with her loot.

Maeve huddled in a folding chair, her jacket on backward to keep her warmer. She'd settled on jeans and a pink sweater, a pink barrette holding her bangs to the side. Pink, the color for girls who wanted to kiss boys. It was early, but she was already buzzed. She surveyed her new friends next to the campfire, small groups of misfits and weirdos smoking grass and swigging cheap wine, others drinking flat beer from a week-old keg in the back of one of the two cars parked close by. Oskar sat across the fire, chatting in German to the girl whose family hosted him. He glanced at Maeve, then past her, and shot up so fast he about dropped his beer.

"Oh, man!" he said, waving furiously. Maeve, confused, looked over her shoulder. Voices on the path, giggles and laughter in the orange light. Becky Glover, the senior center on the basketball team appeared first, followed by Claire and Robin, then the broad-shouldered Nordic twins—sophomores no one could tell apart, who were also on the varsity team—then Wendy Walker, that point guard who'd transferred from Canada.

Maeve sat a little taller.

She had spoken to Wendy Walker exactly once, and it was the day Maeve quit the team. She was sitting on the sidewalk outside the back door of the gym, waiting for her ride home, and out came Wendy, basketball under her arm.

She kicked Maeve's foot. "Rad decision in there," she'd said.

"Huh?"

"Telling off Coach. I mean, you're a good player. The team's deep, is all. But that guy's a douchebag, and sorry, but he doesn't like you."

"Yeah, he's never been a fan. He doesn't like my shot. He says I don't know how to protect the ball. He's a jerk. I could make a list of things he's said to other girls. So, I don't know if it's just me."

"Yeah, I think it's you. And me, but let's be honest. He can't be mean to me. I'm going to be his star for the next two years." She'd smiled when she said it, but she wasn't joking. And Maeve knew she wasn't wrong.

"Modest much?" Maeve asked and immediately regretted it.

"It is what it is. Anyway. Glad you stood up to him." She let the ball drop to the pavement and dribbled it, making two scissor steps. "See you around."

That girl was so cool.

Maeve finished the beer in her cup and dropped it onto a bed of pine needles. When she stood, she realized her coat was still on backward. She fumbled dumbly until it was on straight.

Oskar ran around the fire. "I invited them!" he said to Maeve, as if he'd pulled off some huge social feat.

There were whispers, awkward hellos, warring parties making nice. Claire stood close enough to Maeve that to say nothing would be awkward. "Hey, congratulations," Maeve said, touching the barrette. Her body bobbed with discomfort. "Good season. Great season. Really."

"Yeah, thanks. You were in the play, right? I heard it was good. Sorry I missed it."

Robin joined them with a beer that had a remarkably full head of foam. "Don't think the nerds knew they needed to pump the keg," she said, tipping the foam across her lip. "Hey, Maeve. What's shakin'?"

Maeve bubbled like she was drunk on champagne. Had it all been in her head? Was she the one who'd snubbed them? The conversation turned funny and dark. They filled her in on the coach walking into the girls' locker room when he knew they would be undressed, catching several girls "tits out," as Robin put it. Becky Glover had gone to the principal, and the principal had gone to the superintendent.

"Doubt he'll coach next year," Claire said. "You should try out. Wendy really thinks he had it in for you. She said you knew he was a perv all along."

Maeve tried to sound casual. "Maybe." Wendy Walker talked about her? To the team?

A log split, and the bonfire crackled with molten sap. Across the fire, Wendy Walker stood holding a red cup, blond twins on either side of her like Norse goddesses protecting their liege. All three wore letter jackets, the keys to the kingdom. Wendy cocked her head and locked on Maeve.

Heat rose in Maeve's cheeks. *What I wouldn't give . . .*

She didn't know what that thought was, what she had to give, what she would want in return. But looking at Wendy made her want. She wanted to be in the world the way Wendy was—assured, head up, carefree. She stayed in the game, holding Wendy's gaze. Holding, holding. Sparks flew like kite tails trailing into the black woods. There was a quick eruption of gleeful laughter, and the intensity of two girls staring into each other's eyes broke. The mood surged and shifted into high gear. Maeve unclipped the barrette, stuck it in her pocket, let her hair hang heavy and loose. Around her, bodies swayed as if on a cusp, trying to speed up and slow down the beat, searching for the never-ending. Maeve swayed too.

She crept into the kitchen, way past curfew, dragging the stink of campfire and beer and mud in behind her. Her own sneaking cracked her up. Nothing had been fun or funny for months. Suddenly, everything was. She hadn't intended to drink so much, but it all caught up with her now. The panes rattled when she shut the door too loudly. She snickered, covering her mouth. She just had to get up the stairs without waking her parents.

"Maeve." A voice in the dark. The light flickered on.

Maeve giggled, forced a serious frown. "Father."

He pulled a wooden chair across the pine floor. "Sit."

Maeve leaned against the closed door, rested her head back. "I'll stand." She let her eyes drift closed, let the room spin. She took a wobbled step forward.

"You're drunk."

Maeve sighed. She straddled the chair and rested her head on her arms across the back. "I know, Dad. I'm sorry." Even her apology was funny. She let out a guffaw.

"Keep your voice down. You'll wake the whole house."

As if on cue, Molly bounded down the back stairs in her nightgown, red hair pointed every which way. She plopped onto William's lap and plugged her nose. "What's that smell?"

Maeve noticed then that her pants were torn and caked with mud. The party had drawn cops to the woods, and she'd spent the last two hours huddled in a ditch with Wendy and the twins, hiding until the coast was clear. She was covered in bug bites, and her neck was kinked. She'd never been happier.

"Go back to bed, Pixie," William said.

"Pixie, Pixie, Pixie," Maeve said. Maeve tapped the words out purposefully, moving her fingers along an invisible keyboard. "Did you rat on me?"

Molly tossed her arm around her father's shoulders, casually, a simple affection. "I told you I could keep a secret."

"I was worried, Maeve. You're so late. I forced it out of her. Molly said you went to a birthday party in the woods. Is that true?"

"What the heck, Pix!" Maeve railed. "You promised!"

Molly leaned toward Maeve. With her hand to the side of her mouth, she whispered, "I didn't tell him about the German boy you kissed . . ."

"What's this? What German boy?"

"You did that on purpose! You're such a brown-noser, Pix," Maeve said. She spat the *P* sound. "I'm never trusting you with a secret again!"

Her mother appeared at the foot of the stairs, velour robe over her nightgown. "Oh, God. Okay. Molly, you heard your dad. Back to bed." She clapped her hands, and Molly slid off her father's lap like a pancake off a spatula.

Maeve knew she was in deep trouble but couldn't stop giggling. Wendy had stifled her laughter earlier with a finger pressed to Maeve's lip. She bit the spot, tasted bug spray and beer. All worth it.

"You know what?" Her mother circled her finger in the air. "Everyone. Go to bed. William, you better walk behind that one so she doesn't fall and break her neck. We're really disappointed, Maeve. You know better."

Upstairs, Maeve collapsed into bed. She didn't like that her mother was disappointed, and her father had said there would be punishment in the morning. Plus she'd probably get a talking-to about that business with Oskar, but Maeve didn't care. Nope, Maeve couldn't care less. She'd led the girls through the woods, down a path to a ditch where they wouldn't be found. She was the one who made sure the cops were gone. She was the one who'd spotted Wendy's keys on the ground. And the way Wendy had looked at her when they found their way back to the parked car . . .

A persistent knock made Maeve open her sleepy eyes. The bedroom door creaked, and a moment later, Molly stood next to her bed.

"What do you want, snitch?"

"Sorry I told. It slipped out."

Even though she got caught by her parents, Maeve still felt like she'd gotten away with something. And it felt way better than shoplifting ever did. "It doesn't matter. I don't care."

"You're not mad?"

In that hazy light, Maeve saw Molly for what she was—her little sister busy with child's play, her little sister, too little to understand Maeve at all. In a way she hadn't in ages, Maeve felt full grown. She wouldn't need Molly to be her best friend anymore.

She steeled her voice, tried to sound like their mother. "I'm not mad. Go to bed, Pix."

CHAPTER THIRTEEN

1979

On the roof outside her bedroom window, Maeve braced her feet against the shingles, tucked a flashlight into her armpit. Spring peepers chirped in the distance. She listened for the sound of a purring motor, the low rumble of a car moving slowly. She could hear the television from the living room below—*All in the Family*, *Mannix*, *Gunsmoke*. It didn't matter what they were watching. Wendy Walker had asked her at school that day if she could sneak out to go to a party with her and the Nordic twins. "Absolutely," Maeve said, no hesitation, though she still felt the sting of her parents' disappointment, not to mention she had a week left on her grounding. But this was worth it. It had to be.

It was eight on the dot, and for a moment, Maeve feared she'd fallen for a sick joke. But then, headlights flickered, went dark, flickered again. She slid her switch on and off, on and off, on and off. *I'll be there.* She shimmied down the tree trunk, stashed the flashlight under a bush, and ran toward the car waiting darkly in the road.

The paneled station wagon idled beneath the pine trees. Wendy was behind the wheel, overpowered by the size of the beast, the sink of the seat. Her hands at ten and two, she hunkered down, turned to Maeve, and grinned, accentuating a slight overbite. "Let's go, let's go, let's go!"

Maeve glanced at the farmhouse and hopped in. Wendy hit the gas, and the house was out of sight before Maeve turned to say hello to the girls in the back seat. It was empty. "No twins?"

Wendy eased up on the accelerator, relaxed her hands on the wheel. She cranked her window down, glided her hand along the current. "Would you be mad if we skipped the party?"

The back road was curvy and narrow. The headlights skipped along tree trunks and branches, briefly green in the spray of light. The center line was faded, and Wendy used the whole road. Maeve rolled down her window too. She didn't want Wendy Walker to know what was happening inside her body, though surely, she could hear Maeve's heart beating, could hear her chaotic thoughts bursting like popcorn.

"Yeah, I could skip the party."

"Cool. I have an idea. Do you trust me?"

Please, don't let this be a trick. "Yeah."

"What time do you have to be home?"

Maeve did not want to think of her dad waiting up again, of her mom coming down the stairs, the way she wore worry on her face like foundation every time she looked at Maeve. She wanted to be like the other girls—go to parties, cruise the drag, kiss boys. Whatever it was. She was finally fitting in. Wouldn't they want that for her?

What could she say to impress Wendy Walker, to let Wendy Walker know this was no big deal? "Before sunup?"

This time they caught each other's eyes and grinned.

A gust billowed Wendy's hair. "Cool." She smoothed it down with a laughing gasp.

Maeve looked ahead, shimmered like the northern lights.

On the empty beach, a fat waxing moon rising behind Seguin Light, Wendy spread a scratchy wool blanket next to a burned-out log.

She pulled two bottles of wine from a paper bag. "Apricot Splash or Plum Hollow?"

Maeve was glad to be sitting. Her legs were mush. "The good stuff first—Plum Hollow."

Wendy twisted the metal top, sniffed it snootily. "A fine choice." She took a swig, swirled it around, swallowed, and handed the bottle to Maeve.

Maeve put the bottle to her mouth, pressed the ridges of glass that had been on Wendy's into her lip too. She didn't want to do anything; she only wanted to think about why she was thinking about it at all. The wine slid over her tongue and down her throat, burning and sweet and warm. The second time they shared the bottle, Maeve let her tongue glance the rim.

"Sorry if this is weird," Wendy said. "I wasn't in the mood to be around everyone tonight."

"Is something wrong?"

"No, I just—" She looked at Maeve, shook her head and shrugged.

"I get it. It's nice to hang out with a friend sometimes." Maeve tried to keep the conversation light. But Wendy's mouth, the wetness on her lips, sparked other thoughts that flickered like fireflies. *Concentrate, Maeve.* "Do you miss your friends in Canada? What was it? Quebec, or something? My parents went on their honeymoon there."

"Ottawa. And no, I don't miss it. My dad teaches college. That's why we came here."

"Mine works at BIW."

They talked like that, back and forth, about their families and school, rumors about the basketball coach. When the first bottle was gone, Wendy grabbed the second.

It was the best night of Maeve's life. She didn't care if her butt was cold, if she was getting damp in the sea air. She didn't care if she froze to death.

"Are you cold? Scoot closer," Wendy said, as if she could read her mind.

There it was again. That electricity. Maeve didn't know if she could stand it much longer, the feeling of Wendy's shoulder next to hers, their bent thighs pressed against each other.

"Can I ask you a question? It's kind of personal."

"Um, sure," Maeve said. She wrapped her arms around her knees.

"You really are cold," Wendy said. "Maybe we should go."

"What did you want to ask me?"

Wendy moved away from Maeve, twisted to sit cross-legged so they faced each other. "I heard this rumor, about you and Claire."

Maeve's heart sank. She looked around, certain someone would pop out from behind a dune or stump, point at her, make fun of her for what they could see and for what they couldn't know. She stood, brushed off her pants. "Yeah, I knew it. You're like them. I didn't do anything, okay? Nothing. One time, I wrote her name on a piece of paper. That's all. Then everyone turned it into something it wasn't. I mean, I like boys. Like everyone else. I like . . . Oskar. The exchange student? But my parents wouldn't approve, so I keep it a secret."

Wendy was on her feet now too. She tried to interrupt Maeve's rant but couldn't get a word besides "no" in edgewise.

"Maeve!"

"What?" Maeve's arms were crossed, her hip jutted. She could see that Wendy was upset, almost to tears. "What?" she asked, more gently this time.

Wendy sucked in the wet sea air and huffed out breath after breath. "I thought . . . I thought maybe you . . ." Her teeth scraped her lips. "That maybe you . . . were like me. I mean, I like you."

Maeve didn't know what she was supposed to do. Cry. Laugh. Run. It dawned on her. If she did or said the wrong thing, it would all be over. She would be over. "I like you too." It was enough. She hadn't said or done anything that couldn't be explained if she misunderstood the situation.

"No. I like-like you." Wendy's posture sank, and her face softened into a grimace like she was ready to take a punch.

Maeve looked up, tried to make sense of the whole universe. A trillion stars, pinpricks in tar paper. "There's a star up there for every crazy thought I'm having right now." There was no turning back now. "To tell you the truth, I'm scared to death you're joking me and that I'm going to say something and all of this is going to be a giant fake out. I would die."

Wendy took a step forward, put her hand inside Maeve's jacket, resting it on her waist. Maeve's own hands were paralyzed by her side. Wendy moved closer until their bodies were practically touching. A moment closer, and Wendy's hand brushed Maeve's face. They tilted toward each other awkwardly until their lips touched, plum wine on apricot, kissing each other in little waves and then more fully, with a current as deep as the sea.

At first it was exciting to have a secret. Maeve was inflated, floating. They had to be careful, not letting on to anyone that they were . . . what? Maeve wasn't sure. It was like that thing with the tree falling in the forest. Could they be going together if no one knew? And they didn't go on dates. They didn't hold hands in the foyer or by their lockers. Wendy's prom date was the captain of the boys' basketball team, though she assured Maeve they were just friends.

"Does he . . . know?" Maeve asked. They sat on a picnic table, eating lunch outside, spring in full bloom, a safe distance between them. Maeve marveled at other girls touching each other playfully. That she and Wendy wanted to touch each other made it necessary to avoid each other completely. Instead, they shared a Coke from the machine, the can sitting between them.

"No one knows," Wendy said. "No one can know."

"I wish we were going to prom together," Maeve said, though she couldn't imagine it, not really. A boy and girl could go together as "just friends," so why couldn't two girls do the same? "Or that I was going so I could see you get crowned prom queen!" She shoved into Wendy playfully, and Wendy shoved back.

"Yeah, right," Wendy said. "As if." The bell rang, signaling the end of lunch. "Hey. I have an idea. Could you come over this afternoon? My mom is picking me up, but I could drive you home after."

Wendy's mother was a formal woman, elegant to Maeve, the way her shirt tucked neatly into a fitted skirt, pantyhose matched to her skin tone, silver-blond hair pressed into a tidy bun. She was on the board of the historical society, a member of the garden club. "Ladies who lunch," Wendy said. The dusky scent of her filled the car.

"Maybe I know your mother?" Mrs. Walker asked on the short drive to their house. Maeve tried to picture her mother chatting over tea, musing about preservation, but it was impossible. Faye Sullivan was not a joiner.

"I don't think so, but she might like the garden club. She loves flowers. She worked at Ransoms—or what used to be Ransoms—when she was a girl," Maeve offered.

"She grew up here?" Mrs. Walker said to Maeve's reflection in the rearview.

"Mostly, yes. She and my grandparents came from Ireland when she was little."

"I see."

Maeve wasn't sure what Mrs. Walker saw, but whatever it was had shut down the conversation. Wendy said her mom was like the heirloom roses in their garden—showy and groomed and prickly. It made Maeve smile, as she stared at the back of Mrs. Walker's stiff hair, to think how much her own mother would not like the woman's fussy ways. Maeve's mom didn't wear makeup, except occasionally lipstick. She did not paint her nails, though she kept them clean and filed. Her hair was thick and straight, brown like Maeve's, but instead of hints of red, hers was streaked with random silver strands that glinted like tinsel. She cut her hair herself, evenly across the bottom, and pinned each side behind her ears. She wore pants most days and a shirt that buttoned or a sweater that did not. She was not much for chatter and would often hush her or Molly if they went on about most any subject. "Enough talking," she would say. But she was also playful and funny. She was the first to take out board games or a deck of cards and, as far as Maeve could remember, had never turned down an invitation to take a magic carpet ride on the rug in the foyer, a flight of fancy Molly made up after hearing the story of Aladdin.

In Maeve's literature class, her teacher lectured about a character's interiority, the life and thoughts lived on the inside that are not meant for the light of day. "A good character will have a rich interior life that either seeps out from the cracked and broken places or explodes under pressure." Maeve could not imagine her mother's interior life. If Mrs. Walker was a prize-winning rose, grown for show, then Maeve's mom was a wildflower cropped up in a field or a violet that could bloom in the cracks of a sidewalk. She never talked about her childhood other than coming to America on the ship with Maeve's grandparents, how she had been a quiet girl who kept to herself, and how she only bloomed after she met Maeve's dad. Maeve had to admit that it sounded romantic but also a little sad, too, like her mom was nothing at all without her dad. He had tons of stories about growing up with his big sisters and a father who was a big talker and a big drinker. But her mom's childhood stories were flat as paper dolls. Even when Maeve's grandfather told stories about Faye, they were lacey, delicate, and filled with holes, like her inner life was dandelion fluff.

Wendy stole a look over her shoulder. Maeve smiled, shuddering to think what her mom would do if she could read Maeve's mind. What a mess! Maeve felt like two different people—one was some version of herself who made her parents proud, who learned from her mistakes, who didn't lie or sneak around, and the other was this Maeve, the one riding in the back seat of some fancy car who wanted nothing more than to jump the bones of a girl smiling at her from the front seat.

Wendy lived in a centuries-old clapboard-sided house near the river, chosen by her mother for its history and by her father for the fact that it was close, but not too close, to the college where he taught political science.

"Leave your bag here," Wendy said, once inside the door. "Shoes too. She doesn't like clutter." The house was light and formal with curving furniture tightly upholstered, still-life paintings of fruit and flowers, maritime images of ships at sea. A shining banister swirled up the staircase like the inside of a conch shell.

"Your house is really nice," Maeve offered as they climbed.

"It's a museum. C'mon."

Her mother's voice followed them up the stairs. "Doors."

"Doors?" Maeve asked.

"Yeah, uh, no slamming doors, so close it super quietly."

Wendy's room was wallpapered with blue stripes, but everything else was white—the sheer curtains, the bed and dresser, the thick pile carpet, the lumpy quilt. Posters of men papered the walls—Larry Bird, Bill Walton, John Havlicek, Kareem Abdul-Jabar. A shelf of gold trophies, two rows deep, all basketball. Next to the trophies, an eight-by-ten glossy photo of a women's basketball team. Maeve picked it up. "What's this?"

"Only the 1976 US Women's Basketball team. I saw them in Montreal, at the Olympics." She came up behind Maeve, rested her chin on one shoulder, her hand on the other. "See there? Pat Head and Ann Meyers? They're my favorites, but I like the guards too. They all give me hope that I'll be able to play in college."

Maeve set the photo back on the dresser and turned into Wendy, wrapping her arms around her waist. She had learned in the weeks since their first kiss where to put her hands. She had also learned more about kissing, about closing her eyes and letting herself drift like she was doing now. Wendy pulled away. "Um," she said, looking over her shoulder. "I'm going to open the door for a second, and let's laugh and talk a little so she doesn't start to wonder." She opened the door silently. Maeve realized that despite its age, this house didn't creak like hers. Wendy laughed at nothing, repeated what she'd said before about the basketball players, made some noise about going to the bathroom and left the room.

Maeve checked out the trophies idly until she felt eyes on her. Mrs. Walker was in the doorway. "Oh, hi again," Maeve said. "I was looking at Wendy's trophies."

"You play basketball?" Mrs. Walker asked in a way that suggested she knew the answer.

"I used to. I wasn't good enough for the team. I'm more into theater now," Maeve offered, trying to sound interesting.

Mrs. Walker looked around the room.

"Wendy's in the bathroom."

Mrs. Walker smiled tightly and whisked herself away.

Wendy came back and closed the door gently. She told Maeve to sit on the end of the bed, then she opened the closet, pulled out a hanger with a blue dress. "Since you're not going to prom, I wanted to show you this. My mother wore it in college. I couldn't imagine putting on some frilly thing, and she let me have it altered. What do you think?"

It was the most elegant dress Maeve had ever seen—midnight blue satin, liquid straight, with wide straps and a curved neckline, and a matching bow at the empire waist. She touched the fabric. "It's so beautiful! I wish I could see you wearing it."

Wendy glanced at the door, a mischievous look on her face. "Should I try it on quick?"

Girls got undressed around each other all the time in the locker room. How was this any different? And yet it was. She had never been in a locker room with Wendy, had never seen her bare skin. They had touched each other under shirts, under the cover of darkness. But here they were, in a bedroom, in Wendy's bedroom. Maeve bit her lip, nodded.

Wendy took the dress off the hanger and laid it on the bed next to Maeve. She shimmied out of her jeans, pulled her T-shirt over her head until she wore only tiny striped bikini underwear and a white cross-your-heart bra with a pink bow. It was like putting a face to a name, seeing the skin she had touched. Maeve felt the urge to meet Wendy there, to shrug off her clothes and stand naked. Wendy's stomach was hard and flat, her waist gently sloped. "I have to take my bra off or it'll show. The dress has it built in." She turned her back. "Will you unhook it?"

Maeve hesitated, not certain she even knew how to unhook a bra, which was stupid. Of course she knew. She wore a bra. She reached up, freed one hook and then the other. Wendy turned slowly, brushed her hair out of her eyes.

"Wen," Maeve said. Maeve wanted to tell Wendy that she loved her, that she loved everything about her, loved her teeth and her eyes, loved how good she was at math and biology, how dumb it was that she only knew basketball stars and not movie stars. She wanted to tell her she loved her even though she was kind of a bad driver, that her taste in music could be better. "I mean . . . You're so pretty."

The bedroom door swung open. "Wendy!"

Wendy snatched the dress off the bed and covered her naked breasts. "Mom! Stop it! I was showing Maeve my prom dress, and I didn't know if the boys were home. Do you mind?"

Mrs. Walker swept into the room and stood between Wendy and Maeve, shielding her daughter. "Put it on. I'll zip it up."

Maeve was pinned in place, unable to move, let alone stand. She knew her face was ablaze, as if they'd been caught between the sheets. Girls do this all the time, she told herself. *This is fine, this is fine.* But that cinched look on Mrs. Walker's face, like she stepped in something filthy that Maeve had drug in.

When Mrs. Walker nudged Wendy toward the wall mirror, Maeve stood. "You look really good. That color is pretty." She tried to keep the comment flat and unflattering.

"It was mine, you know," Mrs. Walker said, admiring her daughter's reflection. "I was a freshman in college when I got engaged to Wendy's father. Not much older than you girls. I wore this dress. Who knows? Maybe Brett Overton is the one."

"Mom, I told you," Wendy said, aggravated. "Brett Overton is not the one. Now will you unzip me? Please."

"I should go," Maeve said, gesturing to the door.

"Yes, why don't you wait downstairs for Wendy to get dressed. She'll meet you outside."

Maeve could not get out of the room and down the stairs fast enough. She wished she could evaporate. Outside, Wendy's brothers played basketball in the driveway, the hoop shaking and clanging on the misses. She sat on the narrow step, her body quivering. She could hear an argument in the house but not the words. The boys pushed on each other, threw elbows, shoved, called each other names. Maeve had half a mind to join their game if only to have the pleasure of laying one of them out on the pavement.

Wendy emerged from the house, the car keys in her hand. "I have to be back here in twenty minutes, so we'd better haul ass."

Wendy drove too fast through town, too fast out of town. "Slow down," Maeve said. "You're going to get us killed."

"I don't care," Wendy said, her voice petulant and seething.

"Well, I do. I'm sorry if I did something wrong. I tried to be cool."

Wendy sighed, laughed a little. "You know you were not very cool, right?"

Maeve shrugged. She knew. "I couldn't help it."

"I'm grounded until prom. And it's going to be strict."

"Because of me?"

"Officially, because I violated the door rule. It's so stupid. My brothers and I aren't allowed to be behind closed doors with anyone except for family. No exceptions. She said I should have gone into the bathroom or their bedroom to change. But yeah, it's because of you. She'd probably be thrilled if I closed the door with Brett."

Maeve let out all her breath. She did not want to imagine Wendy with Brett Overton.

"Look," Wendy said. "It's not you. She doesn't like me. She doesn't like that I'm not girly like her. She doesn't like sports. She doesn't like that I play basketball. I heard her and my dad fighting once, and she was yelling that it was like she had three boys. She thinks girls should be girls and boys should be boys. She even slapped Caleb when he called me a lesbo. She thinks someone is going to turn me into one. None of them know I already am."

"You're already what?" Maeve asked.

Wendy swerved off the road onto the gravel. A black car zipped around them, honking. She blinked at Maeve incredulously. "A lesbian, Maeve. I'm a lesbian. You're a lesbian. We're lesbians." She shook her head. "Is this some kind of revelation?"

Maeve's parents had their own chairs in the living room, like Edith and Archie Bunker. Normally, after dinner, they would occupy their spots in front of the television, and Maeve would retreat to her room to do homework or listen to records. But it was Wednesday, and Wednesday night was family night. On family night, there was no bickering between her and Molly, everyone lingered at the table, even Maeve's grandfather, who came for meat loaf and mashed potatoes, then stayed for hot chocolate and an episode of *Eight Is Enough*.

Her father leaned back in his chair, set his crumpled napkin on the table. "Oh, you won't believe who I saw today. Conor O'Kane."

Maeve only half paid attention, her thoughts still on Wendy, what she'd said in the car. She startled at her mother's response. A fist on the table that rattled the dishes.

"Ugh! What now?" She tapped three fingers into her forehead, a tell, like a squirrel hiding a nut for later.

"Says he's trying to clean up his act. Guess he did some time down in Massachusetts. Counterfeit gun licenses. Something about grenades."

"Guns? Who has guns?" Molly asked.

"Papa, take Molly out to the living room and set up the television, would you?" Faye said. "We'll clean up and make the popcorn. Maeve, grab the plates."

In the kitchen, William continued. Maeve washed and her father dried, while her mother wrapped up leftovers. "Yeah, he said he and Glenda got married, but she walked out on him when he went to jail. He said he wants to win her back, though from the looks of him, he hadn't made much improvement. He was pretty sauced. He wanted to know if I'd put in a good word for him at BIW. I told him I didn't think I could. He wasn't very pleased with me."

"I don't like this," Faye said.

Then Maeve remembered. "Um, do you think he still drives that black muscle car?"

Her father put the dishcloth over his shoulder. "Yes. Why?"

Maybe she was wrong. But she could picture the red streak on the side of the car that had sped past her and Wendy earlier. "I think I saw that car this afternoon. Close to here. Wendy—" She faltered. Even saying her name made Maeve blush.

"What's wrong? Did you talk to him? Did he say something?" her mother asked.

"No. Nothing like that. Wendy wanted to show me her prom dress after school—" Maeve's eyes fluttered. *God! Spit it out!* "She drove me home, and a car kind of sped past us, annoyed and honking, you know? I guess maybe Wendy was driving too slowly?" She shook her head. "Anyway, maybe it was that car?" She stuck her sweating hands back in the dishwater.

"William," her mother said.

"I'll deal with it. Don't worry."

Maeve sat on the floor, her back against the couch, a bowl of popcorn between her legs. Clearly, the conversation about that stupid guy still bugged her mom, based on the way her arms were crossed. Not Maeve's problem. She had bigger ones.

It was family night, and Maeve wondered what would happen if she was what Wendy said she was. While Molly giggled with their grandfather about the family on television, Maeve ate her popcorn absentmindedly. The week before, Wendy had sucked salt off Maeve's finger at the drive-in burger stand, tongue to fingerprint, fingerprint to lip. She tapped her salt-puckered lips, remembering the sensation. What would happen to family night, what would happen to her family—this one or the one she dreamed she'd have with some mystery man who would come along and love her the way her parents loved each other, who would carve their initials into a tree trunk and frame it with a heart? What would happen to her?

When the show was over, her grandfather went home, and Molly was sent to bed. Maeve wanted to stay up to watch *Charlie's Angels* but thought better of it, certain her parents would see the way her eyes followed Sabrina rather than Jill. She felt like her insides were on her outside, her interior life exposed. "I'm heading up too," she said.

She thought about sneaking into the kitchen to call Wendy, but Wendy's voice was already in her ear, telling her she wasn't normal, wasn't . . . straight. This couldn't be true. Wendy made Maeve feel special, pretty and smart and funny. Her head spun while she got ready for bed. Maybe that was the plan, to confuse Maeve, corrupt her. No, that couldn't be right. She brushed her teeth, staring into her own eyes as her mouth foamed. Where was the part inside her that had gotten mixed up? Could she brush it away, pluck it out, scrub until this thing was not a part of her anymore? She put her toothbrush in the cup, ran her hands over her chest, down her stomach. Go lower, she thought. That's where the problem is.

Monday morning, Wendy met Maeve by her locker. She fumed about her mother, the silent treatment she'd been given over the weekend. She slammed the locker shut. "I'm so sick of her."

They walked together, Maeve's books clutched to her chest. She felt newly self-conscious, all eyes on her and Wendy, sizing them up, a scarlet *L* pinned to her shirt. She'd lain in bed the night before, unable to sleep, fretting over which was worse—her parents or the kids at school finding out about her. Profound disappointment or relentless scorn? Exhausting questions, wrapped in midnight blue satin, tied with an empire bow.

"You look wiped out," Wendy said.

Maeve had noticed the dark circles under her eyes that morning but didn't have the energy to try to conceal them. "Couldn't sleep."

The earth sciences teacher slowed down as he approached them. "Girls," he said, eyes flicking up and down, back and forth.

Maeve groaned. "What was that about?"

"Pervs everywhere."

The pressure felt like a sack of flour on her chest. She steered Wendy into an open doorway, peeked inside. Empty. "Listen. I think we should cool it. Your mom and everything. And I don't want to tick off my parents."

"It's almost summer break," Wendy said, her head tilted. "And then mayhem, right?"

Maeve scratched at a patch of dry skin on her forearm. "Mayhem." That was the plan for summer—have as much fun as humanly possible before senior year of high school. "I don't think we should be seen together right now. I have my friends. You have yours . . ."

"Lots of the same people . . ."

"No, I mean. You know, prom and all. Let's lay low." Maeve tried to ease her way back into the flow of hall traffic.

Wendy's mouth fell open slightly, and she tipped her head forward. "Are you breaking—"

"Wendy!" Maeve interrupted, shaking her head. She lowered her voice, talked through her teeth. "Call me when you're done being grounded or something." She jump-skipped to get past a throng of freshmen, shoved a scrawny boy for good measure. She felt safer already.

CHAPTER FOURTEEN

1979

It had been two weeks since Maeve sat on Wendy's bed, her bra on the floor at her feet, nine days since they'd spoken. Three days since Wendy walked past Maeve in the hall and hadn't even looked at her; two days since Maeve saw Brett leaning into Wendy at her locker, not looking like they were "just friends." The day before, the theater kids came up with an alternative to prom, a dress-up party, misfit style. The theme was simple—dress as your favorite character from a book or play. What the hell. She would go.

Maeve sat on the living room floor, leafed through an old photo album searching for a particular picture to complete her outfit, to remind her exactly who she was. Each page was a part of her family story, starting from the beginning. She had looked at this album often, memorized the photos so that the photos themselves had become memory.

In one, her pregnant mother, sideways to show off her belly in a tented dress. The pine tree next to the house is so small! Her parents on the same day—someone must have purchased a roll of film for this particular occasion—standing next to a silver car they no longer owned, her father in dark pants, mud boots, a solid flannel shirt from the looks of the black-and-white picture. Another, this one with her grandparents. Maeve inspected it more closely. Her mother's careful smile, her grandmother's mouth thin and tight, like she's holding a watermelon seed between her teeth. Maeve could almost remember her but not quite. She smelled a little like dirt, Maeve thought, though it might have been her cigarettes.

Then she found it. A picture taken from a distance, probably from the back porch of the house, probably taken by her mother. In it, Maeve and her father stand side by side, both in jeans and plaid shirts with the sleeves rolled up. Maeve removed it from the plastic sleeve. There was no writing on the back, though the date was machine printed along the zigzagged edges of the photo. APR 69. Maeve's hair is so short she could be mistaken for a boy. They are in the garden, and her father is leaning on a shovel. He is hardly a half inch tall in the photo, Maeve even smaller, but still, it is clear that she is happy. They had fixed a fence post together, and he was proud of her. She remembered him singing, his voice cracking. "Please, don't take my sunshine away."

She thumbed through the copy of *To Kill a Mockingbird* her father had given her on her thirteenth birthday. When she found the page she was looking for, she marked it with the photo, then stuck the book in her back pocket.

Her parents were sitting on the porch swing at dusk drinking bottled beer when Maeve came out the front door. As annoying as they were, she couldn't help but smile. Her dad still put his arm around her mom; she still tapped his chest when he said something silly. They were perfect together. Somehow, even that made Maeve sad. Could she ever be happy like they were, considering how messed up she was on the inside?

"There she is!" her father said. "Glad you decided to go."

Maeve had been sulking, it was true. She buried herself in her favorite books, moped herself to tears listening to records. She'd snapped so often that even Molly steered clear. But she had to keep trying. The more she let on, the more her parents pried. She told them she was embarrassed she didn't get invited to prom. She had to fake everything.

"Aren't you supposed to be in a costume?" her father asked.

"I am," Maeve said. She was wearing denim overalls with a star embroidered on the back pocket, flat red sneakers, and a honey-colored checkered blouse.

A brown four-door sedan turned into the driveway.

"And?" her mother asked.

Maeve turned and pointed to the paperback in her pocket.

"Ha! Scout Finch!" William said. "My ray of sunshine in pants."

Maeve flourished her hands, happy and sad that her dad remembered it like she did. It felt like a thousand years since she'd been his little girl. He'd said Maeve was a tomboy, like Scout, told her the importance of being principled, though Maeve hadn't really known what he meant by that. "Be honest. Stick up for what's right." She was a tomboy. A girl who liked sports. A girl who didn't like dresses. That was all. She could have said that to Wendy. Her stomach knotted again. How had she let this all happen? She never wanted to be a disappointment to her parents, especially not her father. She choked back tears, faked a cough for distraction.

"Home by midnight, sunbeam."

"Dad, it's prom night. One a.m."

"You're not going to prom, remember? Twelve thirty."

She remembered. "Fine. But don't wait up."

"Maeve," her mother said, caution in her voice. "Please, be careful."

She'd been weird since that Conor O'Kane guy came around even though William said it was a chance meeting.

"Don't get into strange cars," she'd said to Molly. "Even if someone says they know you. You don't go. Never ever. That goes for you, too, Maeve."

Now, Maeve looked at the car full of theater kids but saw only strangers there. A lump lodged in her throat. The horn honked, whoops and laughter erupted. Maeve looked over her shoulder at her parents on the swing, how they glowed in the fading sunlight. They could not see her, not what she really was. She felt invisible. She wished she *was* invisible.

"Maeve? Honey?" Her dad stood.

Maeve squeezed her eyes closed, gritted her teeth, pasted on a smile. "You know," she said, "I'm not sure how late I want to stay out, after all. If I promise, seriously, I promise, I will not even sip a beer, can I please take your car?"

Maeve had her license, but she wasn't one of those kids who drove their parents' car around town. "I don't know . . ." her mother said.

"Dad, seriously." She pointed again to the novel in her pocket. "Ray of sunshine, remember?" She twirled her fingertips into her dimples.

"Eleven," her father said, pulling the keys from his pocket. "Don't let me down."

Maeve breathed out, caught the keys her father tossed. "Wouldn't dream of it."

She followed the brown car through town to make sure she knew where the party was but circled back to the high school. She parked in a spot where she could see couples arriving, girls with corsages and curly up-dos, boys in suits with jackets too big and pants too short, their hair slicked unnaturally.

As the last few couples trickled in, Brett Overton's white pickup squealed into the parking lot. Maeve wanted to see Wendy dressed up, see her arm looped through Brett's, queen to his king. Then maybe she could let this all go. She had a clear view.

The passenger door flung open before the truck even came to a complete stop. Wendy hopped out, her feet bare, shoes in hand. She stuck her head back into the cab. She was clearly enraged, though Maeve couldn't hear what she was yelling. Brett stormed around to where Wendy stood, gripped her arm. Wendy tried to yank it away, but Brett squeezed tighter.

Maeve sat up, heart pounding. Her mouth went dry. She reached for the door handle, hesitated. If she jumped out now and made a scene . . . was that what Wendy would want her to do? Wendy was inches shorter than Brett, and he loomed over her, his mouth chomping down at her. She adjusted the back of her dress like it had gotten caught in her underwear. She wiped her eyes with both hands. Brett motioned toward the doors to the gym. Maeve rolled down the window a crack, hoping to hear. Wendy sat back in the truck, pulled her feet up. Maeve thought of the day they shot hoops at the court behind the junior high, how Wendy insisted they switch shoes. Same size, though the fancy shoes Wendy strapped on now looked too small for real feet, dainty as glass slippers. When Wendy stood again, her stance was more fitting for a basketball court than a dance floor. Brett put his hands together like he was praying, and Wendy held up a finger of warning. Maeve felt a pang of guilt, watching as if it were a performance. But it seemed to be over.

She wanted to follow them through the double doors like a shadow. A gleeful voice shouted. Brett and Wendy turned. One of Brett's teammates loped up, dragging a girl in a poufy dress behind him. Brett threw his arm over Wendy's shoulder, his hand landing above her breast. She flung it off, and Maeve could hear her then.

"I said keep your hands off me!"

Maeve rolled the window down a little more.

"You know what? I'm done. I'm going in. You can do what you want." Brett and his buddy laughed, the other girl shrugged.

Maeve read Wendy's lips. *Take me home.*

"I'll take you home after prom, or you can walk. I don't care." Then: *You're a bitch.*

Wendy took one step back. She swung wide, a forehand shot. Her palm connected with the side of Brett's head. "You fucker."

He twisted his mouth like he was counting teeth. *Fuck you.*

They left Wendy in the cement courtyard. Maeve looked around. No more kids, no more headlights. She got out of the car, walked smoothly to Wendy, who had taken off the shoes again.

"Wen," she said, the name floating off her tongue like a butterfly. "What are you doing here?"

Mascara ringed Wendy's eyelids, and the clasp of her pearl necklace was skewed to the side. She was missing an earring. Maeve brushed a strand of hair from Wendy's cheek. She was beautiful. In that moment, Maeve wasn't afraid anymore. She was with Wendy, and Wendy was safe. They both were. "Are you okay?"

In a flash, Wendy's arms flew around Maeve's neck, her hot breath puffing into Maeve's ear. She wrapped her arms around Wendy's waist. She could smell her Ivory soap, sticky hair spray, the gentle funk of the vintage dress. They pulled away from each other.

Maeve's head bobbed. She couldn't stop it. *Yes, yes. Do this. Yes. It'll be fine.* "Let's get out of here."

They stopped at a store, and Wendy suggested maybe they find someone to buy beer for them. "Watch for someone to come out and ask. Guys will do that. The creepier the better." Maeve couldn't keep her eyes off Wendy. The dark blue of the dress popped against her white skin. Her hair up in ridiculous curls. She looked like the Hollywood version of herself. "Ask that guy," Wendy said, pointing. "He's already got a six pack."

But Maeve shook her head. She wanted to stay clear. She could at least keep one promise to her dad and not drink. "Nah, I'll just get Cokes and chips and be right out. Wait here, okay?"

Wendy laughed and put her bare feet up on the dash. "Where would I go?"

On the ride out to the beach, Wendy told Maeve she'd let Brett kiss her, and he said she was a prick tease for not doing more. She'd had to push him off several times.

Maeve did not want to think of Brett kissing Wendy, of his hands on her. "He didn't hurt you, though, right?"

Wendy shook her head. "No, but, man, I can't keep doing this. I don't want that. Not ever. Pull over," Wendy said, pointing to a dirt lane. "No one will be out here this time of night."

Maeve shut off the engine, and the world went quiet. When she shifted toward Wendy, the paperback in her back pocket fell free and landed barely under the seat.

Wendy picked it up. "Reading?"

Maeve leaned across her to open the glove box. She shut the book inside.

Maeve did not see the car come up behind them. It was possible the lights were dimmed. It was possible she was wrapped up in Wendy, buried beneath her. By the time she heard rapping on the fogged window, it was too late to make the situation less clear. She righted herself, though there was no fixing the straps on her overalls that had been undone. She buttoned her shirt while Wendy pulled her dress down over her hips. Maeve expected to see a cop or, worse, her dad. Instead, the door opened, and Conor O'Kane peered into the back seat. His mouth fell open as his stony eyes moved from Maeve to Wendy and back again. He seemed to pick up something he'd dropped then stepped away from the car.

Maeve twisted to secure the toggles of her overalls. *This can't be happening.*

"I think that's the guy from the store, the one carrying beer out," Wendy said.

Maeve heard the flick of a lighter, smelled tobacco burning. "Wait here."

O'Kane was leaning against the hood of his car, which had Maeve's pinned into the lane.

"Hello there, Maeve. Fancy bumping into you. You remember me, right?"

"I know who you are."

"I saw Will's car in town and thought, now that's funny," Conor said. He sucked on the cigarette, blew smoke in her direction. A memory of her grandmother swirled in the scent of it. "Strange seeing it parked on this road on a Saturday night. I figured I'd check it out." He stared at her, squinting as if he was trying to solve a riddle.

"Did you follow me?"

"What if I did? Seems you got up to something, I'd say."

The moon was full and as bright as an interrogation light. There was no story she could invent. He saw what he saw.

"Are you going to tell?"

"Tell?" His laugh was outsized and fake. "You think I'm some kind of narc? Ask your mother. She knows I can keep a secret."

"What's that supposed to mean?"

Conor stepped forward, put a hand on her shoulder. She flinched, tried to shrug it off.

"Your strap is twisted," he said, hooking a finger into her overalls. He detached the metal toggle, unwound the strap like he was twirling a lock of hair, his eyes never moving from hers. "So, girls, huh?" He gestured toward the car. Wendy was staring from the back window.

He was the villain of every story—the wolf in sheep's clothing, the needle on the spinning wheel. His accent was as thick as her grandfather's, who said more than once that Conor O'Kane was full of shite. Up close, he was an abyss. What made it worse was that he smelled good. Not like cologne or soap or a firepit or oil or car exhaust. He didn't smell like leather or denim or cotton. It was not some herb or flower or fruit or piece of wood or fish in a net. Something earthy oozed from him—mushrooms or moss in a cave. Maeve wished she could smell like that, push up earth just by breathing. If Conor O'Kane could transform into a bear or wolf, she would not be surprised. She stared off to the right, repulsed but something else too. She was afraid to even look at him.

"I bet you've never even given a man a go. You never know . . . the right one might fix you up." He hooked the toggle around the metal button, grabbed the other strap, and yanked up hard. The seam of her pants dug into her crotch. Maeve let out a yelp.

"You and your girlfriend there best get home. Wouldn't want William and Fiadh to worry. Where do they think you are, anyway?"

"It's none of your business what I do." Maeve thought of conversations she'd heard over the years, her parents' distrust of this Conor O'Kane, how they'd both wanted to be rid of him, how her mother pounded the table at the mention of his name. She would be doing them a favor. She could end it for them all. "You know, Mom and Dad don't even like you. Nobody does. And they sure don't trust you. They know you're a liar. Even my grandfather doesn't like you. He said he wished you'd go away. You don't have proof of anything."

Maeve saw a flinch. Good, she thought. Maybe her jab landed. His white smoke circled her, and she remembered being a child scared by him but thrilled too. She could feel it again, the danger of him manifesting as desire. She throbbed where the seam had cut in.

"Don't be so sure. You have no idea what I know." He pulled a flat woolen flask from inside his jacket, unscrewed the lid, and took a long pull. He wiped his mouth with the back of his hand then held the flask out.

She scoffed. "Drop dead."

His head tilted. He filled his cheeks with air then blew the boozy breath into her face. "Maybe I do have proof. Maybe I could sink your whole perfect family."

"You don't. And it's your word against mine. Now, if you don't mind . . ."

He wagged his finger at her. "Have it your way."

Behind the wheel of the car, Maeve shook. "Oh, I hate him!"

Wendy climbed from the back seat into the front. "He's still there."

Maeve looked in the rearview mirror. A flash of high beams blinded her, then retreated. The black car spun and peeled in a circle, pebbles plinking against the fender like hailstones.

Maeve checked the time. She was past curfew. "My dad is going to kill me."

Wendy laughed oddly, put her hand to her mouth. "Oh, no," she whispered. Maeve pointed at a rip in that precious dress as if that were the problem. "That? That's from before. No, I was thinking. If I was voted prom queen, my parents would definitely find out I wasn't there. I didn't think of that. I was so mad. And fucking Brett. It's almost funny how embarrassed he would be." She laughed wryly. "Guess we're in for it now."

Maeve turned the key in the ignition, and the engine sputtered to a purr. "Do you want me to take you back? To the school?"

Wendy shrugged. "It's too late. Doesn't matter."

Maeve drove in silence, relishing the feeling of Wendy's hand on her thigh. She imagined telling her parents about Wendy, about herself, imagined finding the words to make them understand. She thought of Wendy's mother and how cruel she had been. No way her parents would be like that. But then again, they were there on that porch swing, that perfect couple, golden and true, the American dream. Could they reject her? What would rejection even look like? The truth was Maeve had no idea what they would do. What Wendy said looped in her head like a skipping record. *We're in for it now. We're in for it now. We're in for it now.*

CHAPTER FIFTEEN

1979

Every light was on when Maeve pulled up to the house. When her mother opened the back door, Maeve braced herself for another scolding, for the grounding that would come at the end.

"Where have you been? Jesus, you had me worried sick. Your dad took my car. He's out looking for you right now!"

"Mom, I'm only an hour late."

"Wendy Walker's mother called me."

One thousand thoughts fired in Maeve's brain, a hail of arrows. She swore words at herself she'd never dare say out loud, certainly not in front of her mother. *Be cool, be cool, be cool.* "What did she want?"

"You don't know? There was an accident. Apparently, Wendy's prom date hit a tree. He's in the hospital. Him and another boy."

At Wendy's request, Maeve had dropped her off at the corner in case her parents were waiting up. What if Brett had been waiting at her house? Had he forced her into the truck? Was she with him? Was she hurt?

"There was a girl with them, but it wasn't Wendy. They can't find her!" Her voice was shrill. "She was frantic, calling all Wendy's friends.

Dad even tried to find you at that party. He called from a pay phone and said the car wasn't there."

Maeve tried to think of what to say, but it was like she was turned to stone.

"Maeve. Maeve! For God's sake! Snap out of it. Get in the house!" Her mother followed her in, let the screen door slam. "Have you been drinking?"

"No!" Maeve said, answering a question she knew she could be honest about. "You can smell my breath, I swear."

Lights shone in the driveway. Her mother exhaled hotly. "There's your father. We can straighten this out now."

"When did Mrs. Walker call? I mean, like, what time was the accident?"

"Over an hour ago! We've been frantic!"

An hour. Wendy had been with Maeve an hour before. She couldn't have been in the wreck. She wanted to run to the phone and call Wendy. But there was no way. The hammer would come down now that her father was home. The door opened.

Maeve shuddered.

It was Conor O'Kane.

In the kitchen light, the creases under his eyes were deeper, the strange darkness of his lips more purple, his hairline blacker, his eyes bluer. Here was the wolf Maeve feared.

Her mother's head lolled. "Now's not a good time, Conor."

"I saw the lights on," he said, as if that was an open invitation to any house.

"William's not here," she said, then added a second thought, ". . . but he should be back any minute."

"I'm not here for him. Or for you, Fiadh." His eyes flicked to Maeve then back.

He was the only person Maeve ever heard refer to her mother by her given name, one that was not even on her driver's license. And the way he said it, biting down on that *F*, as if the name itself was a curse. Maeve's shallow breaths heaved. She could not let Conor O'Kane say what he saw.

"What do you want then?" her mother asked.

He uncorked the flask he held in his hand, emptied the contents into his gaping mouth, then tossed it in the direction of the table like it was a paper airplane. It hit the floor with a hollow clang. He rummaged his right hand around in his jacket like he was sorting a junk drawer then turned his attention to Maeve. "I think you dropped this. Earlier."

Maeve patted her empty back pocket. It was the photograph from the paperback. It must have slipped out of the car when he opened the door. Blood rushed to her head.

Her mother snatched the photo from Conor's fingers, considered it, a look of confusion on her face. "Why do you have this?"

"I saw Maeve tonight. This fell out of the car."

"What do you mean you saw her?"

"Well, Maeve and her little girlfriend . . ." he began.

Her mother's head jerked like a predator had snapped a twig. "What?"

That leer. *My, what a big mouth you have!* "He was at the Quick Stop," Maeve blurted. "I was there. Before the party."

Conor crossed his arms, an amused look spreading over his face. "I told you I had proof, remember? But, by all means, dig your hole. I have all night."

She had to think fast, get rid of him before he said more, before her father came home. "He said he would buy beer for me, and I told him no. Then . . ." She remembered the way he'd pulled up on her overalls. He knew what he was doing. "He touched me weird." She was shaking. She would not let him say what was only hers to tell. "I don't want him here. Mom. Make him leave."

She turned, squeezed her eyes shut to wish him away, then bolted to the stairs as shouts erupted behind her. Accusations. Her mother and O'Kane, gnashing at each other.

". . . Frenching some girl!"

". . . kill you if you touched her, so help me God!"

". . . a liar, just like you!"

"Liar!"

"Fiadh!"

"Liar!"

Molly was staring over the railing in front of Maeve's door. "Go to your room!" Maeve shouted, taking steps two at a time. Molly retreated as the wolf clamored up the stairs. Maeve flung her door open. Her mother's hollering shook the whole house. Conor O'Kane was steps away from gobbling her whole.

"Trust me," he said. "You want to see this!"

Molly, weighing in at sixty pounds, got between Maeve and this wolf.

"Leave her alone!" Molly yelled. She kicked him in the shin, and he swatted at her. Molly ducked and pushed him in the belly. A fierce little thing, their father called her. O'Kane took two steps backward, almost with a laugh. But it was the extra step, a heavy stumble into the railing, the crackling of wood. O'Kane busted through, grasping at air, disappearing into the hollow. Then, the pumpkin thud of a heavy skull.

Her mother was caught halfway up the stairs like she'd stepped in cement.

Molly took a step toward the broken railing like a siren called to her, her hands out as if they were smeared with blood. Shock ran through Maeve like she'd been struck by lightning. She yanked Molly back, wrapped her arms around her. Everything from there was a blur—her mother bounding into the entryway, her sickening yawp. Then her shocked father appeared in the doorway. Maeve pulled Molly closer, pinned her sobbing sister against her body.

"William! The girls!" Her mother was on the floor. Maeve caught her eyes as she looked up. Her face was a galaxy of emotion.

And then their father was with them, and Maeve could breathe again. He was Atticus and she was Scout, and he would make everything okay. He backed the girls into Maeve's bedroom, sat them down, and told them not to come out, no matter what.

CHAPTER SIXTEEN

1979

Faye stared at the broken railing as the door to Maeve's bedroom closed. That moment, stuck in a loop: Molly, defiant in a worn flannel nightgown, a hand-me-down from Maeve. Her foot kicking out, the villain swiping at her children, the shove—so righteous and powerful coming from something so small. *Atta girl!* Then, surreal horror. A failed railing, a flailing man.

Like a ship captain's wife in a widow's walk, Faye had lit every lamp in the house when William left in search of their daughter. She'd wound herself up, fearing something terrible had happened to Maeve while also replaying that woman's accusations. "Your daughter is unnaturally attracted to mine. I'm worried she might have absconded with her." Faye had been too shocked to respond, much less defend Maeve from this ridiculous accusation. *Unnaturally attracted!* Still. She'd kept that part from William, only telling him there'd been an accident, that a friend of Maeve's was missing, and that the girl's mother was worried.

That all fell away now. Conor O'Kane was sprawled on the fringed rug in the narrow vestibule, one leg twisted strangely at the hip. The air around him seemed charged, life and death in conversation about what was there for the taking. Blood oozed over his tobacco-stained teeth, and Faye had the strangest memory of him as a boy when those teeth were fine and white, the way he left his shirt unbuttoned after they dipped in the bay, the way he spread his legs when he talked to Fiadh. His hand juddered and twitched. His eyes pleaded with her as he breathed in ragged gasps soggy with blood. She did not think he could move his head.

One word sniveled out of him, suffering and clipped. "Help." His hand flopped near hers, a fish on land.

Faye picked at her lip. They had been children together, briefly, long ago, far away. But she did not owe him anything. She could not save him. She would not try.

She backed away, out of his reach. She did not want to feel his touch.

"*Du hättest . . . Du hättest . . .*" Faye said. It was the language she'd spoken as a child, but it would not come back to her. "You should not have come here."

His eyebrows flicked, and he grunted. "Fiadh."

Faye could not see the images that flashed before Conor O'Kane's eyes then—the green paths, the mossy shore, stones in a churchyard, pebbles that rattled in crashing waves, Fiadh's blush when he'd dared to touch her cheek. She could not see Conor's mother, Theresa, waiting at a white gate. She could not feel his anger and resentment fall away, ribbons of a heavy robe untied, a burdensome yoke lifted.

His furtive eyes closed, his breathing stopped. A bloody bubble popped into drool.

Faye sunk back on her feet, the knots on the fringed rug digging into her knees. She screamed at the world of her making that had brought them to this place.

William rushed down the stairs. He stopped in his tracks as he took in the scene—splintered wood, stunned wife, dead man. In the pause, Faye imagined rolling Conor's body up in the rug, wrapping it with rope, weighting it with stones. She could almost picture it, her and William rowing out in the darkness in the yar little boat she'd made him haul away, how they would hurl Conor overboard into the deep green sea, that same sea where her own story ended and began, let the currents ferry him to wherever he would rest.

William eased toward her, breaking the spell. "Give me your hand." Faye took it, let him pull her to standing. "Now, step over. Yes, like that." She was in his arms. Safe again. The tears came, fear and sorrow falling from her onto William. "There now. No, don't look at him anymore. Look at me."

Faye lifted her eyes. "Are the girls okay?"

"Tell me what happened. Quick now."

Faye wanted to shroud O'Kane, but William said they shouldn't touch anything. She told William the story that Maeve told her. "He had the photograph. He must have come to apologize. But Maeve was scared and ran from him."

"He tripped then, on a loose rug. On his way to the bathroom."

"No! William. Molly pushed—"

He pointed his finger, cut her off. "No, you listen. He tripped on the rug. Honey, he tripped on the rug. He was drunk, he had to use the bathroom, he tripped on the rug. The girls didn't see him. They didn't see anything. No one did. Do you understand? You go up there, and you make them understand and then we are done with this. Done with Conor O'Kane." His face was hard, his eyes wide and certain.

While William was on the phone with the sheriff, Faye climbed the stairs, armed with the story. She bumped up the runner in the hallway, made a lump a person could trip over. She opened the door and found Maeve and Molly huddled on the bed, Maeve's bedspread wrapped around them. It gave Faye a start, these sisters next to each other, so unsure of what would happen next. A flicker of memory, arriving in the barracks in Ireland, trembling on a cot with Elisabeth. She crouched in front of Maeve and Molly, put her hands on their legs. She could control this for them. She could make certain they wouldn't be hurt by this one terrible, troubled night.

"This has nothing to do with you, not with either one of you, you understand? Not a single thing. This was an accident had by one man and one man alone. He was a bad man. He was drunk. He tripped on that runner," Faye said, pointing to the open doorway. "That's what happened. If anyone asks, you didn't see it. No one saw it. Conor O'Kane was heading to the bathroom. You heard a noise. That's it."

Maeve sat up, wrapped the bedspread back around Molly. "But Mom, earlier tonight . . ."

Faye had caught Maeve's eyes before and tried to tell her then that her secret was safe. No one had to know. Faye would say it one time, then it would be forgotten. She lowered her voice. "Was Wendy Walker with you when you saw him?"

Maeve nodded.

"And did you see anyone else tonight other than her?"

Maeve shook her head.

"Listen to me. There was no earlier tonight. You did not go to the party. Nothing at all happened. Nothing. You make that clear to that girl and don't speak about any of it again. Not to anyone." Despite herself, she thought of the phone call, of what Conor said he saw. That was dead now too. "And that includes Daddy. It would break his heart, you understand that, right?"

Maeve nodded.

"Get your pajamas on. Quickly. And brush your teeth."

She turned her attention to Molly. Her little face was ashen. "Pix." Molly sat up, and Faye zipped her lip with an invisible pull. "Not a word. It's very important. Not a single word. Never, ever speak of it. Mama and Daddy will take care of everything. That man fell. That's all. He fell. You understand?"

Molly's eyes were wide, glassed. She nodded, the barest gesture. Her mouth opened and closed twice, like a fish out of water.

"You do it, honey," Faye said. "Zip that lip."

Molly lifted her hand slowly, drew her pinched fingers across her mouth.

Faye touched her cheek. "That's a good girl."

Maeve whispered, "Is he . . . ?"

Faye squeezed between the girls. She wished her arms were wings, that she could fold her daughters beneath them. "Yes," she said. "He's gone. He can't hurt us anymore."

The sheriff arrived with the ambulance, lights blazing in the night. Maeve stuck to the script when the police asked questions. Molly, obedient, didn't say a word, didn't shake her head yes or no. "She slept through the whole thing," Faye said.

William answered their questions with earnest ease.

"Honestly," he said, "I don't know what brought him here tonight. We've known him a long time. The families were connected back in Ireland years ago."

The sheriff took perfunctory notes. No one seemed much interested in the details of the common story. An ex-con, a known drunk and pain-in-the-ass dead at the bottom of a flight of stairs. No sign of foul play, no bloody knuckles or torn clothes, no weapons. Only distraught parents and children in nightgowns, cheeks tight with dried tears.

Conor O'Kane went out on a stretcher, black boots poking out from under a white sheet, his hands empty. Faye and William, Maeve and Molly, watched from the open front door until the police car and the ambulance pulled away, sirens silent, emergency lights dark, and all was quiet.

William rolled up the stained rug to carry out to the trash. Only then did Molly speak. "My magic carpet."

"We'll get another one, honey. I promise," Faye said, though she could see the defeat in Molly's eyes. She loved to play the game, especially with her big sister or with Faye if Maeve wouldn't give her the time. Molly would sit on the rug, whatever playmate straddled behind her. With an old vase for the lamp to rub between her palms, she'd say something like, "My carpet is a hot air balloon!" or "My carpet is a bird!" and then whisk them away to magical places, weaving stories of colorful beasts, of planets and stars, seas like the bluest diamonds, impossible mountain peaks—flights of imagination and wonder. If only we could fly to a place where Conor O'Kane had never darkened the doorway, Faye thought.

"No," Molly said, resigned. Her eyes drifted to the splintered railing, darting as if a murder of crows circled above. She flinched, then furled into herself. "It's ruined."

Faye and William lay in bed, grave still. "Is this the same day, or is it tomorrow?" Faye whispered. If not before, she knew she was old now.

"It's tomorrow."

She sighed. "Okay, good."

"They'll come for his car."

"We'll need to call Papa in the morning. Or maybe go over. That'd be better."

"Suppose Glenda'd be next of kin if they really did get married."

Faye thought of the three brothers. They had seemed inseparable, but of course, that was false. Distance or death separated everyone eventually. She did not want to think on him anymore. And yet. "I wonder if he ever told Jean what happened between him and his family."

"I can only imagine."

"It must have been bad. He and his brothers were close. From what I recall." She sighed again, heavy and effortful. Floorboards creaked in the hallway, and her first thought was of Conor O'Kane's ghost out there, come to haunt her family. "Did you hear that?"

"I didn't hear anything," William said, his voice sleepier.

She listened, but there were no more sounds. "I guess it was nothing."

William touched her hand in his way. "Try to sleep."

Faye dreamed about Fiadh crashing through waves, seawater splintering like wood around her. Neither she nor William heard the floorboards creak again under the weight of tiny feet outside their door. They did not know that their child tiptoed down the stairs, splayed herself out like a chalk outline by the front door, and flew away in her imagination on a magic carpet, looking for the place where dead people go so she could give back the inky impression that Conor O'Kane left behind on her shoving hands. They did not know that her little fingers crawled along the bare floor and found a portal to the past, missed by lazy authorities, behind a blocky table leg, there, in the empty vestibule, in the windowed moonlight.

CHAPTER SEVENTEEN

1979

It was the Wednesday before Halloween, and the days were noticeably shorter. William had turned new spindles and repaired the man-size gap in the stair railing, glossy paint the only sign that Conor O'Kane had been there at all. Thomas was over early for family night and the promise of apple pandowdy.

Maeve and Molly dutifully sat with their grandfather at the kitchen table, sipping hot cider while he regaled them with stories of death and Samhain and shape-shifters, how the veil thins between the living and the dead, how this is the time to watch out for evil faeries who steal children and unsettled ghosts looking to even the score. "Light little fires to keep them away."

"Papa," Faye admonished. Molly had been having nightmares, though she was not one to cry out in her sleep. Instead, she would come into Faye and William's room, tears streaming down her face, and stand next to the bed—for how long, Faye didn't know—touch one of them on the shoulder or slip a hand between the mattress and their sleeping body to wake them.

It had been a long, difficult summer. That girl Wendy's prom date had died from his injuries. Faye and William had gone with an insistent Maeve to a memorial in the packed gymnasium. The sickly floral odor barely masked the standing stink of sweating teenagers. "Lilies and carnations," Faye whispered to William. He stuck out his tongue to feign a quick gag, the two of them still in agreement after all the years since the flower shop. Faye had watched Maeve scan the crowd, assumed she was looking for Wendy, even though Faye had heard that the family left even before the school year ended, citing the girl's grief as the reason they couldn't stay. Conor O'Kane's death the same night was hardly a footnote compared to a star athlete dying young. Faye had tried not to feel relief.

Thomas flipped his wrist at Faye. "You know your grandmother Jean thought that pile of boulders behind the cove house was a thin place. That's why she stood there so often—commune with the dead, talk to Fiadh and the boys."

"What do you mean, talk to them?" Maeve asked. "Mom's right here." William, too, home from work, gave Faye a puzzled glance.

Faye could only roll her eyes, dismissing her poor father, who himself seemed to dwell in some in-between more often these days. The wind howled, and doors rattled like spirits knocking for entry. "Stop now," Faye said, harsher than she intended. "You're scaring the girls."

Thomas startled, let out a laugh. He put his hands on either side of his face and made a show of rattling it back and forth. "You're right, my little Faye. Of course."

"No, tell us more," Molly pleaded. "About ghosts."

"I don't think that's a good idea," Faye said. She dug through the utensil drawer for peelers. "Here," she said, laying them next to a bowl of bright-red apples. "Are you three going to peel or just sit there?"

Thomas picked an apple from the bowl and handed it and a peeler to Maeve. "Now, Maeve," he said. "How old are you? You must be about ready for a husband."

"I'm in high school, Grandpa. Besides, I don't want a husband."

Thomas poked at her. "Every girl wants a husband! Humor an old man. Peel that apple but don't break the skin. When the ribbon drops, it will reveal the first initial of your beloved."

"I want to marry you, Grandpa," Molly said, grabbing her own peeler and apple.

"See?" Thomas said, his hand on the top of Molly's head. "Even your sister wants a husband. Even if he is a crusty old man."

Faye tried to appear distracted but listened intently. Maeve had been in a mood for months. Even William had noticed and mentioned it to Faye, who dismissed his concern. "Senioritis," she told him. He'd wondered aloud if Faye thought it had to do with "the accident," which was how they referred to Conor O'Kane's death when they mentioned it at all. There had never been a discussion about that girl Wendy, but Faye was glad she was gone. A problem that solved itself.

"Fine," Maeve said with a huff.

The girls went to work on their apples, Maeve carefully keeping the peel intact. Molly hacked almond-shaped shards onto the table.

"My mother swore by it," Thomas said. "Cunning, she was. She made witch bottles to hide in hearthstones. Ward off evil. She was long dead, my mam—bless her soul—by the time our boys died so close to each other. I thought we needed a witch bottle, but your grandmother wouldn't allow one in our house. Too superstitious." He sucked at his teeth. "Maybe if she'd listened to me, Fiadh would be here, and things wouldn't have gone the way they did."

"I swear," Faye said, a warning in her voice. Shame rose in her, unwelcome as always. She did not want to scold her father, not in front of William and the girls. But she couldn't let Thomas slip into the past like that, and after all this time. She hadn't told him about Conor's last word, how he, too, had invoked Fiadh. It made her feel small, the way she resented Fiadh's staying power so long after her death. She felt her cheeks flush as her shame doubled. "I'm right here. What's gotten into you?"

The girls' eyes widened, and their heads dipped.

"Don't mind an old blabbermouth like me," Thomas replied, rapping his head with his knuckles. He gave Faye a weak smile. "The attic's empty."

Molly inspected her slashes of peel. "What does that mean?"

Thomas looked at the pile and laughed. "Means you have to wait until you're better with the peeler!"

Maeve's crimson peel slipped to the floor.

"Oh, look," Thomas said. "What's your letter?"

Molly squatted next to the elaborate coil, traced the ragged peel. "Could be an M." She tilted her head. "Or W."

Faye caught Maeve's eye in a sideways glance. "Oh, please," she scoffed.

Maeve bent over in her chair. "That's not a letter. It's a broken heart, Grandpa," she said, her voice small and blue.

Thomas tapped his lip thoughtfully, considered the peelings, considered Maeve. "Cursive," he said. He told her the peels don't lie, that hers would be a winding path with twists and turns to find true love.

After dinner, Faye cleaned up the apple peels from the table and floor, went about washing the last of the dishes. William had taken her father back to the cove. Thomas didn't like to drive past dark anymore, part of whatever it was that was going on with him, this desire to be home more than anywhere else. Molly had asked to stay over at the cove house again, to sleep in Faye's old bedroom there, but Faye couldn't risk it, not with her father being in such a mood, the way he slipped up and slid back. She had waited with him at the front door while William warmed up the car. "She won't use these stairs," Faye said. "Molly. She doesn't think I notice, but I do. She only goes up and down the back ones."

He stared up at the new railing. "You'll all forget soon enough," Thomas said.

"I hope so." The girls well out of earshot, Faye sat on the step, remembered the body that had broken there months before. "I used to sit on our stairs at home and eavesdrop on you and Jean in the living room."

"Overhear anything good?"

Faye pulled her knees up. "Nothing really. I think I was trying to figure out a way in with her, figure out what she said to you or what you said to her that might help me. I never could unlock her. I've been mad for years that she treated Conor O'Kane like family, but I never got that from her."

Thomas sat next to her, surprisingly nimble, put his hand on her knee. "If it makes you feel any better, she was nicer to him than she was to me, most of the time. The two of us, you and me, we reminded her of something she wanted to forget. Conor O'Kane reminded her of something she wanted to remember. He was tricky that way, sinister how he wheedled his way in. Doesn't surprise me, him falling to his death." He twisted his mouth and made a clicking sound. "Tough to stay upright on cloven hooves."

"Papa!" Faye said, smiling despite herself. "You're sure you don't want to stay?"

But he said no, he only wanted her man to take him home.

Faye dried the last dish, felt the mist of Thomas's thinning veil around her. She took the dirty washcloths and dishtowels down to the laundry in the basement. She did not want O'Kane's ghost to skulk and stomp the dust of her home, disturbing thoughts she guarded. She would need to smudge him from this house, forget he was ever here. She spotted a leftover box of sparklers on the shelf next to the powdered detergent. Just the ticket.

Maeve and Molly huddled in the living room watching a rerun of *Family Affair*, the Uncle Bill in that show a spitting image of her William. Molly curled next to Maeve, head on her sister's lap. "Look what I found in the basement. Why don't we light them off and scare those ghosts away." She put on her brightest smile, thought her brightest thoughts, forgetting that light reveals shadows.

"Sparklers!" Molly screamed, jumping out of Maeve's embrace.

"Come on. You too," Faye said to Maeve, who pulled herself up off the couch.

"Oh," Molly said, more seriously. "I need gloves."

"Honey, you—" Faye stopped herself. Let Molly wear her gloves if it made her feel better. "Hurry up and get them."

In the driveway, Faye lit Maeve's sparkler, and Maeve lit Molly's. October frost coated the pumpkins and the field behind the house. Snow couldn't be far behind. Tonight, though, wool sweaters kept them warm, and sparklers made it like summer with stars hanging so low they seemed to fly from the ends of their metal wands. Dancing shadows rose from the darkness.

"Let's make wishes," Faye said.

"Write your husband's name, Maeve!" Molly said, her voice mocking.

Maeve's brow furrowed in the flashing light, and she spun around like leaves on a dust devil, circles and circles, drawing cyclones up from the ground like she was spell-casting, no name at all as far as Faye could tell.

Molly leaped, feet twisted, eyes closed, muttering words Faye could not make out.

Faye saw it then, the milky veil. *Everything will be better now,* she thought as she blazed names—Thomas and William and Maeve and Molly—into the stars. She added *Fiadh* and *Jean*. She wrote *Mutti* and *Vati* because she had forgotten their given names. She thought of the boy marching on the wall by the sea, a wild thing like in the children's book. *Go away!* she thought and wrote *Conor*. When she wrote *Gisela*, her old name, a flurry of leaves lifted around her. She spun, relieved and unfazed, torching the night with the last of her sparkler.

Elisabeth, she wrote as her sparkler flickered out.

Molly's scream tolled crisp as a bell. Faye grabbed her outstretched hand, pulled off a singed glove, and held the child's palm close. A red streak blazed her little lifeline. "What happened?"

Molly sputtered. "It hurts!"

"Well, duh," Maeve said. "Why did you grab it like that?"

"Maeve, leave her alone! I know it hurts, honey," Faye said and put her lips to the burn. Pangs, sudden and sharp, wrenched Faye's heart. She'd released them, all the unsettled ghosts. "Let's go put ointment on this. You'll be okay now." She rushed Molly inside as darkness fell and the veil thickened.

CHAPTER EIGHTEEN

1987

White paint peeled away from the clapboards of the cove house in cheesy strips, and a green shutter dangled from the window frame like a rock climber. Faye used her foot to shove aside a twine-tied stack of newspapers moldering on the step. It had been one of those days—ferrying Maeve's five-year-old, Dylan, to preschool, grocery shopping for family night in the pouring rain, picking up Molly at the high school when her ride fell through. And Faye had been trying to get her father on the phone for hours, but he hadn't picked up. She opened the unlocked door. "Papa?" The house was quiet. "Hello?" she hollered up the stairs.

Faye knew the locals snickered at the old Irishman, his silver hair akimbo, the way he wore a battered wool coat in all but the warmest weather. She checked the hook. The coat wasn't there. He spent most of his days on the docks now, watching boats and feeding gulls chunks of bologna out of paper cones he crafted from *The Irish Times*.

Thomas and his love affair with *The Irish Times*.

He stuffed the newspaper into shoes to keep their shape, laid it in the flower garden to tamp down weeds, stuck it under rugs to prevent slipping. He used it where others used rags—to clean windows and mirrors, to change hot lightbulbs. Jean had never stood for Thomas's newspaper hoarding and had insisted he throw out any that started to accumulate. Faye was surprised he hadn't papered the walls with it after she died.

In the living room, *The Irish Times* was stacked like cairns, sedimentary memorials to news of bombings and riots that increasingly captured headlines in America too. Thomas's subscription came by mail more than a week late, but he was still in the practice of reading each issue cover to cover. Even Molly had noticed that he'd been strange about his papers recently, cutting open stacks and leaving them strewn everywhere. Faye piled the few in the way, then went to the kitchen. It was a mess, even for her father.

Dishes sat dirty next to a clogged sink, mail cluttered the table. It couldn't have been more than a week since one of them had stopped by, but the place was a disaster. Even the couch cushions were askew. Had Molly been there that weekend? Surely she would have straightened up or at least mentioned if the kitchen had been this bad. Faye made a mental note to ask. A red checkered cookbook was splayed face down on the linoleum floor. On a spindly chair pushed way back from the table sat a single envelope, yellowed and stained. Faye picked it up. It was addressed to Jean, postmarked Ireland 1947. She turned it over. There were no other markings, no return address.

Faye's pulse quickened. She had never known of any mail to come from Ireland. She lifted the crisp flap and puffed out the envelope. It was empty. She shook the pages of the cookbook before placing it back on the shelf, rifled through the papers on the table—utility bills, grocery store circulars, newsletters from BIW. Nothing stuck out that looked almost forty years old, no letters or certificates. Envelope in hand, she climbed the stairs, calling for her father. There was no answer. She checked every room. Nothing.

His coat. Of course. She could guess where Thomas was. She tucked the envelope into her purse and went to find him.

She crossed the main road, walked up the little hill. At the top, she climbed the familiar weathered stairs and pushed open the thick door of her father's favorite pub. The air was skunked with spilt beer and wet planked wood, rubber and gasoline and fish in a fryer.

"Hey, Faye. You just missed him," the bartender Lonnie said.

Faye scanned the long bar. "When did he leave?"

"Maybe five, ten minutes ago. He was loud-talking his faery tales again. I was about to call you, but then he left on his own."

Faye huffed out a frustrated breath. "Maybe stop serving him if he gets like that."

Lonnie raised his eyebrows, thick as woolly bears, and rolled his bloodshot eyes. "A man can drink himself dumb if he wants. That's not my business."

She went back down the hill, scanned the rickety boat dock. She didn't see him at first but then spotted familiar boots sticking out, toes up, from behind a column of lobster traps. Faye ran the length of the dock. Her father was there, flat on his back, arms crossed over his chest like a corpse, eyes open and calm.

"Papa, what are you doing? Are you okay? Here, let me help you up." She bent, tried to pull him to sitting, but he let out a gasp of pain.

"*Macushla!*"

Faye looked around, frantic for help. "You can't sit up?"

When he lifted his head, Faye could see there was blood on the dock. He attempted to sing. "Your sweet voice is calling me, softly again and again. Do you know this song?" he asked. "Fiadh! *Macushla!* My heart. It aches."

She took off her coat, balled it up to pillow her father's head, then ran to the pub as fast as her feet could carry her to call for help.

Faye had gone over and over that day, and she was doing it again, all these months later, while the doctor went on about end-of-life. She didn't want to hear it anymore. If only she'd checked the docks first instead of stopping by the house and pub. William admonished her when she got like this. "You're being silly, kicking yourself. It's good that you found him when you did. Give yourself some credit."

Thomas had suffered six broken ribs, a laceration and contusion on the back of his head, and a concussion severe enough he had been kept in a darkened room for a week. In the hospital, he developed pneumonia, which turned to double pneumonia and a thrush infection from antibiotics. Over weeks and weeks of decline through the winter—in and out of the hospital, to the rest home for rehab and back to the hospital—Faye sat at his bedside, pushed the wheelchair, fetched the nurse, refreshed bedsheets. Thomas begged to go home. He lost weight, became dehydrated. They pumped him with fluids, but the doctors said it wasn't enough. His organs were failing.

She held her father's hand, cold and bruised, while the doctor whispered his doctor-speak, as if Thomas was dead already. *How on earth is it April? How many nights has he spent in this hospital? Staring at these walls? Papa.*

"Don't let me die here!" Thomas pleaded, squeezing Faye's hand with what little strength he had. "Please, Fiadh. Take me home."

Fiadh, again. Always Fiadh.

"He should stay here," the doctor said, "where we can monitor his pain."

Faye didn't want her father to die. He had been hers for so long. But she would do this. For him. She could be whomever he needed her to be. "I'll take you home, Papa. Don't worry."

Faye sighed, checked her watch, though she knew the ambulance still hadn't left the hospital with Thomas. She surveyed the living room of the cove house again. It was good. Her father would be happy to be home.

Molly had been so angry when they told her that her grandfather wasn't going to get better. She'd yelled about the stupid doctors and the stupid hospital and yelled at Faye and William for going along with the whole stupid plan. Maybe Molly was right to be angry. It seemed impossible that Thomas should die.

Faye had to coerce Molly into helping her clean the cove house, though she'd been belligerent the entire time. They neatened the mess Thomas left in the kitchen, straightened cushions and slipcovers and ran the vacuum, tossed out molded cheese and cold cuts from the deli drawer in the refrigerator, Faye all the while on quiet lookout for what might have been in that envelope from Ireland.

Before her grandfather had taken the fall, Molly had spent most Fridays with him, sleeping over in the room that used to be Faye's, waking up there on Saturdays to make pancakes and bacon that she and her grandfather shared. Sixteen now, Molly didn't make friends easily, didn't play sports or an instrument. Besides Thomas, she only had one friend, a girl Jonie who shared Molly's penchant for dark eyeliner and cut-off gloves and layers of lace and cheap jewelry, who talked incessantly, ping-ponging between dragons and Madonna and a stepmother she hated. Mostly, Molly liked to read, and it was a thing she shared with Thomas, a love of poetry and mythology, words on a page. Faye had hoped Thomas might talk sense into Molly, encourage his granddaughter to ditch her trashy thrift-store style, make friends, maybe even get her driver's license.

Now, as she waited for his arrival, Faye recalled Thomas chuckling at the suggestion that he'd have sway over Molly. "Her and that Jonie. The sullen sisters," Faye had lamented. "I've tried, but it's like we don't speak the same language. I bought her a sweater I thought she'd like—black, of course—and you know what she did? She took the scissors and cut the neck out of it! It's all frayed now!"

"'What could have made her peaceful with a mind simple as fire?'" he'd responded in his lofty poetry voice.

Simple as fire, indeed.

Faye took his wool coat from the hook by the door and wrapped herself in it. What would this house be without her father? She still had time. Outside, she traced her finger down the door frame, stood the coat collar up, pulled on her hat and mittens, then set off to walk her father's favorite path to the docks.

She was certain it was the coat the gulls recognized as they circled, their bird voices shouting for the old Irishman to toss a bit of fish or a slice of bread or popcorn from the pub. Faye went to the spot where her father had fallen, sat on the splintered bench. She took off her mittens, held out her hands to prove to the birds they were empty. She set the mittens beside her, stuck her hands into the coat pockets in case Thomas had left some stale treat behind.

She withdrew a sheet of oniony paper, swollen with ink and creased from decades of folding and unfolding. Her eyes darted to every corner of the page before she could focus.

> My friend, my friend, it is me, Hannie. I have burned your letter. You must not correspond. Grass covers ground that should not be disturbed. What we did cannot be undone. Nothing here for you but the risk of Fr. and his outstretched hand and loose tongue. He is a man first and would so save himself if it were Big Seamus to start with the questions or worse, the Sisters. I looked about and found nothing to soothe you. I went to Theresa, tho the two of us have little to speak over, her being so full of herself. I drank her weak tea and fluffed her feathers so she would show me photographs from that Camera of hers. Boys and Cows is all except the one here included from Summer and the six of them, strange as it is, the way they stand there out of time, though maybe that is but the light upon them. I stashed it when her back was turned. It is dagger and salve, I fear. I think of you fondly and wish for God to carry you in the palm of His Righteous Hand. We sinners meet in the Churchyard soon enough.

Frantic, Faye turned out all the coat pockets, even felt along the hem and seams as if he might have sewn the photograph into a hiding place. Only crumbs and cracker bits. Her parents had never even owned a camera, which seemed so strange to her now, the way she brought out her own Kodak for special occasions. The letter said "the six of them." Faye's math only went one way. Three O'Kane boys. And three girls—herself, Fiadh, and Elisabeth.

Elisabeth.

She wheeled around like one of the gulls, practically screamed at the notion that somewhere in the cove house, the image lived on. She'd been on the lookout for something from Ireland, but it had never occurred to her that what was missing might be a photograph. After Conor O'Kane died, she'd had dreams of her lost sister, dreams that bled into daytime thoughts as if a ghost were trapped on the wrong side of the veil. She'd even bought a little diary like the one Jean had, thinking she would secretly write it all down, reconcile that she had a sister and that she, Faye, had left that sister for Fate to do its business. She'd hid the diary in the back of a kitchen drawer, though it didn't matter who found it. The diary sat blank. To commit the truth to paper felt impossible. Yet here was part of it, obscured by time and Hannie's cryptic words.

If only she could see the photograph, hold it in her hand. She closed her eyes. *My Dear Elisabeth,* she would write. *Forgive me. Just now I've seen a photograph of us together as children. Forgive me . . .* She could get no further. This letter from Hannie did not mention Elisabeth at all. Had Jean written to Hannie, begging to come back with the sorry imposter who'd drowned Fiadh? Had Elisabeth been sent away? *If I am dead, as dead I may well be.* Conor said those words to her. What had it meant? And how could it matter now? It had been forty years. But the photograph. She had to see it. She hurried to the cove house in time to watch the ambulance back up to the door.

Faye walked alongside the gurney as the medics brought Thomas into the house. "Here she is!" Thomas said. "My little Faye, my good faery, my beautiful girl." They transferred him to the hospital bed by the big stone fireplace positioned so that Thomas would be able to see out the window. Faye hung Thomas's coat on its hook but put the letter in her own pocket. She stopped herself from tapping her foot impatiently as the medics finished settling Thomas. She thanked them, ushering them out the door like unwanted guests, then turned her attention to Thomas. The sight of him there—his favorite quilt tucked around him, his silver hair spilled onto the propped pillow like a furry halo—took her breath away. For all the questions she had about the letter, what was in front of her was quite real.

She pulled a chair up next to the bed, dabbed a cool washcloth onto his forehead.

"Papa," she said, holding out the letter. "I found this in your coat pocket."

Thomas groaned, flicked his brittle wrist, turned away from her like a stubborn child. "I don't want to see that."

Faye scooted closer, pulled his shoulder gently toward her. "Papa, where is the picture? The one from the letter?"

"She would be your age. She would be you." He squeezed his eyes shut. "But you are you, Faye, aren't you? Where have you been? I haven't seen you since you were ten years old. I've been so worried."

"I'm fifty years old, Papa. I've been here the whole time," Faye said. "The letter, Papa. It says there's a photograph."

Suddenly lucid, eyes wide, Thomas glared at Faye. "That letter, it fell from the cookbook, which itself jumped from the shelf. I looked everywhere." He threw up his hands weakly, a washed-up magician disappearing a long-toothed rabbit. "She didn't let me even have a look at it, not the letter or whatever picture it held. I looked everywhere! Oh! To see her face!"

Faye tried to calm him. "Jean? You want to see Mama again?"

Thomas gaped at Faye, his neck tensed. "Fiadh. Fiadh! God, if I don't miss that child still. How could she keep it from me? My own wife!"

Faye could almost remember the day the photograph was taken, the boys' mother with a camera, the way Fiadh grinned and the boys put their hands in their pockets to look tough. Who among those children was dead now, besides Fiadh and Conor, besides the girl she once was? Seeing her father's pain was too much to bear. There had always been reasons to keep the door closed. Besides, who was she to criticize Jean for keeping the letter a secret? Look at the pain it caused her father even now. If anything, this confirmed Faye's own decisions to keep the past hidden. She looked at Hannie's letter again. *What we did cannot be undone.* It was far too late.

"Go to sleep now," she said to Thomas, gently lowering him onto the pillow.

He did not sleep well that night, in and out of quiet and rest, moans of what sounded like pain, though it was impossible to pinpoint. Faye tried to sleep on the couch but woke in the chair next to his bed when Thomas cast a line of ache into the room pinked with sunrise.

"Fiadh," he said, smiling as if he had reunited with a bold, brash child with strong arms who could stand up to boys, who could row the little punt, who did not live to smoke a cigarette or kiss a boy or sail to America. He said it over and over, wistfully, pleading, scales on his eyes.

"I'm right here, Papa," she said. "I'm right here."

"Rose of all Roses!" he said. "Rose of all the world."

"Yes, Papa." Faye pulled a book of poetry from the shelf, scanned the pages for the poem he was remembering, the one about dim tides hurled upon wharves of sorrow, a sweet far bell, the same white stars. "I have it, Papa," she said, her hand on his. She read to him in distilled light, waiting with him for the angels.

"Fiadh. *Macushla*," he said, his voice small.

When he fell back to sleep, Faye called William. "Come this morning. Bring everyone."

࿋

Faye pushed the breezy curtain aside at the sound of cars in the drive. The reflection on the windshield of William's truck—trees beginning to bud, patches of blue in a gray sky—made it hard to see inside. She raised her hand, fingers spread, like she was putting it to prison glass. Maeve's red sedan pulled in behind William, who was out of the truck now. Maeve's husband, Sam, took Dylan from the back seat, and the four of them walked toward the house. The front door opened quietly, reverently even. Dylan's head was on Sam's shoulder. Faye hugged Maeve, touched Sam's arm, pecked her grandson's cheek. "He had a rough night. He's resting now, kind of in and out."

"Ahhh," Thomas said weakly. "What have we here?" His eyes were open, still lit.

"You have visitors," Faye said.

Maeve and her little family went to Thomas's bedside. William hung back with Faye.

"No Molly?" she asked.

William shook his head. "I tried. She slept at Jonie's last night. She said she didn't want to come. I didn't want to force her."

"She understands, though, right? You made her understand?" Faye asked. "It'll be worse for her if he dies and she doesn't come. We can't stop this. I wish she wouldn't be so—" Faye stopped herself. She knew her criticism wasn't helpful, but Molly's anger at everything was exhausting. William told Faye to stop trying to change Molly. "Let her be," he said. "She'll come around." Faye had tried every trick. Anger only fueled more anger. Offer sympathy, and Molly screamed to stop feeling sorry for her. And making light of her mood enraged her even more. Whatever it was, it was certainly not funny. Nothing was funny.

"Yes, she knows," William replied. "I told her to be home by noon. We can try again."

Faye glanced at her watch, as if it would show the sand spilling out of what was left of her father's life. *Don't wait too long.*

Maeve's little boy stood next to Thomas's hospital bed, hands stiff by his side. Maeve was only a little older than him when Jean died, and now, here she was, married with a child of her own and another on the way, though she wasn't even showing yet. Faye took a step closer when Thomas put his hand on the boy's head.

"Be a good lad," he said, managing a wink at Maeve, who bent to talk to her grandfather quietly. Sam, still a practicing Catholic, bowed his head.

Faye watched as if she were hovering over the scene. Maeve wiped her eyes, made room for William when he put a hand on Sam's shoulder. He was so kind to the boy—the man—though, privately, he confessed he found Sam dull.

"You know," William said, not quietly like Maeve, but in full Irish voice, "You're probably the best friend I've ever had. Thomas, do you hear me? Thank you for trusting me with your daughter. Thank you—" His voice cracked as he bowed his head. "For everything."

Thomas's eyes fluttered. He struggled to speak. "You're a good one," he croaked, patting William's hand.

William nodded, blinking back tears. Thomas closed his eyes again.

Sam hoisted Dylan onto his hip. Maeve came and stood next to Faye. "I'm so sorry, Mom. This is awful."

Faye glanced at Maeve's belly. "How are you feeling?"

"Don't worry about me. I'm fine."

Faye swallowed. "Did you make any headway with Molly?"

"I called her last night. She told me to lay off. She's really mad. I guess at Grandpa for dying?"

Faye knew Molly was hurting almost as much as she was. "Dad said she should be home by now. I hate to ask, but could you maybe sit with Grandpa a little more and then go check . . . ?"

"Yeah, Mom, sure," Maeve said. "I'll drop Sam and Dylan off then go out there."

Faye hugged Maeve, marveling as always at how she had feared Maeve's life would be so difficult. But it had come together so neatly. She had a part-time job at a law firm. She was a good wife and mother. When William had a mild heart attack, Maeve had been right there to pitch in while he recovered. And Faye knew she tried to be a good sister, although Molly made it hard on everyone. Faye hoped it wouldn't get worse.

CHAPTER NINETEEN

1987

Molly pulled Jonie from the sidewalk to the curb. She looked left before jaywalking to the thrift store across the street. It was a Saturday, nearly spring now, though it might take until June for Maine to truly give up on winter. At least the tinsel bells and decorations were gone from the lampposts, months after Christmas, replaced by egg and bunny banners that would likely be up until flag season.

"Today's the day," Molly said. She hadn't told Jonie about her grandfather, how her mom acted like Molly didn't understand what dying meant. She knew about dying. She could tell them all a thing or two about it if they ever thought to ask.

"Seriously? You have the rest of the money?"

Molly had obsessed over a leather jacket in the window of the thrift store, "visiting" it as if it were a prisoner serving out a sentence. The more times she found reason to pass that window, the more it had become an object of desire. She'd liked the way she could see her own reflection against it, how she could superimpose her life onto another one. She imagined putting it on, wearing the pain that looking at it caused.

The new window display hadn't changed since the day Molly put the coat on layaway. Pink dresses, pink shoes, pink handbags. A pink sweater with a green alligator. *Pretty in Pink*. It made Molly want to gag. She stared at it one more time before heading in.

Jonie stifled a guffaw. "I still think that's hilarious. You're, like, the opposite of Molly Ringwald, even though you both have red hair."

Molly jerked. She wanted to punch Jonie but charged into the store instead, stomping her second-hand combat boots on the soft floor. She pulled a five-dollar bill and six quarters out of her pocket along with the layaway ticket and slammed it on the counter. The tiny clerk wore John Lennon glasses and went braless, wheat-colored hair cascading down a tie-dyed T-shirt with the neckband cut out. Her head bobbled like it was on a spring. "And hello to you too."

Molly moved her hand off the money, chewed off a chipped black hangnail, and spat it on the ground. "Final payment," she said.

Molly had drained her meager allowance savings and filched in tiny increments from her father, who kept small bills and coins in his pants pockets hanging in the closet. It didn't make sense to steal dimes and nickels. Stealing it all would get noticed. But stealing only quarters might not. And quarters added up. Molly offered to go into the grocery store for her mom then conveniently forgot the receipt but gave back only most of the change. She stole a ten out of Maeve's purse, which was pretty daring, considering Maeve was so uptight. She remembered when Maeve used to brag about shoplifting. Now she acted like she was perfect. And their mother was constantly telling Maeve what a good mom she was and praising her for every little thing. There was only one right way to be in their world—cheerful and carefree and clean. Molly never felt clean. She washed her hands obsessively, but they always felt grimy. She painted her fingernails black to match the rest of her.

It served them right. If they cared about money, they'd pay more attention. If they cared about her—well, there were so many things they would do differently if they actually cared about her.

And besides. Everything was chaos. There had been a time, years ago, when everyone stared at her, when they asked how she was but didn't want to hear the answer, when she got sweets without asking, when Maeve was nice to her, took her to the diner for fries and shakes, and let her sleep with her in her bed. Then Maeve got knocked up and married Sam, and all the attention turned to her. Maeve even moved Sam into her actual bedroom, right next to Molly's! Then came the baby, Dylan, who was cute, fine. But the crying in the middle of the night, footsteps, loud whispers. How many times had Molly muffled her ears? They all pretended it didn't wake the whole house, but of course it did. Everything revolved around Maeve and Maeve's kid and Maeve's this and Maeve's that. It was like Maeve forgot she even had a little sister. This had gone on for over a year until Maeve and Sam found a tiny apartment in town and moved out. Even then, her parents doted on Dylan, tried to force him on Molly. The baby sat on her dad's lap. When Molly tried to do that, he said she was too big, even though she was only twelve at the time.

And then there were the nightmares. Everyone called them "bad dreams" as if the ghost were Casper and not a devil in black leather who sailed backward over the railing, who floated in the open stairwell, who put his finger to his lips and shushed her like her mom and dad did. *It's not real. It was only a dream. Dry your tears. Go back to sleep.*

And then, boom. Everyone forgot. The rail got fixed, the rug got replaced, Maeve got married, and Dylan was born. It was like nothing happened. But something did happen.

Now, the only person who paid her any attention was dying. Her grandfather told her stories, read to her from his Irish books, played Go Fish and Crazy Eights with her. He made her tuna fish sandwiches with extra mayonnaise on soft white bread that stuck to the roof of her mouth when she took a bite. Her grandfather taught her to stuff barbecue potato chips into sandwiches for the crunch. They listened to Eddie Albert and Bert Humperdinck and Tom Jones together on the little phonograph in his house, though

Jonie would die if she knew Molly actually liked that music. What she liked most was her grandfather. He'd even let her practice driving long before her parents had given him permission. She felt in charge and trusted when she got behind the wheel and he leaned back against the headrest. But she didn't want a license anymore.

Once, she'd gotten her period at the cove house and bled through the sheets onto the mattress. She'd scrubbed but couldn't get it out, and she couldn't exactly throw out a mattress like a bloodstained rug. Her grandfather had found her crying on the floor, and when she told him what happened, he flipped over the mattress. "Problem solved," he said. Her grandfather was the only person who didn't make a big deal out of everything. But he never told her to stop crying either, never told her to save her tears, as if some greater tragedy would befall her someday and she'd need them all then.

Yoko Ono brought the black jacket out on a hanger and gave Molly the layaway ticket. "Here you go. Paid in full." Molly put her nose to the tough leather. Asphalt and oil and a patch of dead grass. No magic carpet, this. No. This was a getaway car.

She dropped her own jacket on the floor and kicked it under the rack. She felt the heft of leather square on her shoulders, hugged it around her body, and stuffed the layaway slip into the pocket. Outside the store, she stared at her black reflection in the pink window display. The collar was stiff at her ears, the sleeves long beyond her wrists and fingertips. She swam in it. One tough cookie. "I love it."

She and Jonie made one more stop.

The guy at the pharmacy held up the bottle. "You know this is permanent, right?"

"Nothing's permanent," Molly said. "Ring it up."

Jonie giggled next to her. "Your parents are going to flip out."

"Let them." She put the bottle in her backpack. "No one's home at my house. We'll do it there."

ꩮ

In the bathroom of the farmhouse, Jonie dyed Molly's hair coal black. Molly considered her features while she smoked her eyes—green like her dad's—and penciled in her faint eyebrows. Her lipstick was dark and slick as an eggplant and filled out lips that were thin and inconsequential, entirely not kissable. Her skin was ghostly white next to the black hair. A gray shadow of dye smudged her hairline. She licked her fingers and tried to rub it off. Her hair was dry and frizzy, a black cloud where before it was a penny in the sunshine.

Jonie rested her head on Molly's shoulder and stared at her in the mirror. "Absolutely wild. Wild, wild, wild. I wish I had a camera."

Molly wrinkled her nose, scrunched her hair in her hands.

"I wish I could stay and watch," Jonie said. "I mean they're going to freak, but I told evil stepmother I'd be back for lunch."

"Go," Molly said. She touched her bottom lip, drew it down. "I'll call you tomorrow or see you Monday if I'm not grounded for eternity." She put the leather coat on and walked Jonie out to the ancient station wagon in the driveway.

Jonie hugged Molly tight. "It looks amazing."

Molly raised a punk fist in victory as Jonie drove off.

Back in the house, she stared at her face in the mirror while she scrubbed her hands. She loathed Molly Ringwald, hated when she was teased about their similarities. That Molly was so perfect—pink, desired, pampered, fresh, and creamy. This Molly looked on the outside how she felt on the inside. A killer freak. She dried her hands, then spread her fingers against her cheeks, skewing her features. No one wanted to know what went on inside the head of a killer freak. No one wanted to love a killer freak. Now they wouldn't have to fake it anymore. When she heard the front door unlatch, she braced. *Showtime.* She stepped into the hallway, looked over the railing like she'd done a hundred times, and there was Maeve. Jeans, purple sweater, some sort of ugly clogs. She looked up, and Molly reveled in her shock.

"Oh, shit. Pix! What did you do?" Maeve took the stairs toward her heavily.

Molly headed down, met Maeve on the landing.

"God. That looks awful!" Maeve said. She reached out to touch Molly's hair, but Molly ducked her hand. "What were you thinking? And where did you get that . . . that . . . jacket?" She closed her eyes, shook her head in exaggerated disgust. "What is the matter with you? What would it cost you to just . . . go along? Does everything have to be a fight?" She threw up her hands. "You're a lost cause, you know that?"

She knew she was lost. Couldn't Maeve see that? "Look who's the brown-noser now? What would it cost *you* to stop being such a suck-up? I wanna go see Grandpa," Molly said. The pit in her stomach felt like tar, black as death.

Maeve blinked and blinked. She threw up her hands. "Fine. Let's go. It's your funeral."

Maeve sighed, and Molly could tell that she regretted her word choice. Molly pressed her tongue into her cheek as she opened the front door. She wasn't about to let her sister off the hook. "No, Maeve. I think it's Grandpa's."

She and Maeve rode in silence to the cove, Molly imagining the talking-to her father would give her about respect and family, how her bad attitude and brazen disregard for others would not be tolerated. He would remind her that they had expectations, that her defiance would not do her any favors. She was ready for him. When they arrived at Thomas's house, Maeve switched off the ignition. "I have to warn them," she said and rushed inside. Before Molly even reached the porch, her father was outside.

He yanked her arm, not brutally, but not gently either, and pulled her to the side of the house. "Jesus Mary Almighty, Pix," her father hissed. "What did you do?"

"I like it," Molly said, her voice barely a mew.

"Oh, you do not. It looks terrible. It's like a bird's nest in hell." He pulled up her fried coils of curl, stinging her scalp. "And what's with that?" He slapped at her new leather jacket. "Looks like—" He shook his head. "Take that off before your mother sees it. Did you even think . . . ? Honey . . ." William pulled her into him, wrapping her up so tight she could hear his heartbeat.

"What are we going to do with you, huh?" he whispered.

Molly wanted to scream, to hit and kick, to make every bad thing stop happening. She wanted to be a raven or a grizzly or a shark, something deadly and fearsome. But nothing she did ever seemed to change anything. Why wouldn't they all just quit loving her? Did they understand that she was broken? She cried and cried in her father's arms, wished she was small enough still that he could pick her up, small enough to fit in his pocket.

Her father leaned over her, smoothed her hair in his big hands. "We have to go in now so you can see Grandpa. Let's take that coat off, though," he said, easing it off her. "You wait here while I put it in the truck."

Molly nodded.

Before they stepped through the door, he squeezed her hand. "Be nice."

Molly tiptoed in, her head low. Even without the jacket, she was dressed for a funeral, all black right down to the fingerless gloves and heavy liner smudged around her eyes. Her mother's arms were crossed, hands on her shoulders like a shawl. Molly ignored the exhausted look she gave her. She could pay hell later.

Thomas stirred at the sight of his granddaughter, and his mouth went into a big circle. "Oh!" he said, his brow twitching.

Molly thought she saw a little smile. She tightened her lips, touched her hair, and leaned in. She didn't want anyone else to hear her talk to her grandfather or for them to hear what he said to her. "The Morrigan. Shape-shifter. Up for a battle, I see," Thomas said, resting his hand on her head, piercing her armor.

Molly broke open, sobbed onto the ugly quilt. *Some warrior.*

"There, there, faithful one. Fight your fight if you must. Dance for me? One last time?"

Molly did what he asked, tears falling, chest heaving with sobs. The Irish steps felt odd in her heavy boots, and she knew she probably looked ridiculous, like some prancing imp. She didn't care. Thomas managed to clap twice. His smile was all that mattered. She leaned in, kissed his smooth cheek.

"Go and love, my Molly. Go and love."

"Bye, Grandpa," she said and ran from the house.

She did not see her mother crumple a section of the *Irish Times* and fold Thomas's creped hand around it one last time or the way his blue veins pulsed like rivers. Molly was already halfway home when loss bore down on Faye, and the sky seemed to open up and the flap of great wings and the delirious laughter of gulls filtered in through a cracked window at the cove house.

Only her mother saw Thomas's eyes widen. Only she heard a note of wonder sound from his throat.

"My birds!"

The paper fell from his hand.

Her father dropped Molly home without even turning off the engine. "I have to get back to your mother. You're sure you'll be okay here? I can take you to Maeve's . . ." Molly told him she would be fine, that she would take a shower and see if she could get out some of the hair dye. They weren't wrong. It did look like shit. She got out of the truck, put the leather coat back on.

"I don't understand why you'd want that," her father said, through the open window. "It's not you."

"It is me, Daddy," Molly said. She couldn't make her insides better, so she was making her outside worse. That's what none of them understood. This is what she felt like on the inside. This was her skin.

Molly sat on her bed, stared at the layaway slip with her weekly payments, a log of tiny thefts she'd pulled off to secure the black jacket. She dug an old cigar box out from under her bed, put the ticket on top of other artifacts she'd collected or stolen. She went back down the stairs and arranged herself like a broken man, the weight of his life finally material and hers to bear. She imagined the roof lifting off, a sky full of stars above it, and, beyond the stars, her grandfather feeding white doves in a perfect heaven.

CHAPTER TWENTY

1987

Early in December, Maeve woke to another contraction, the tiny feet inside her pushing her spine, her uterus wringing itself out, her husband snoring gently next to her in their double bed. She had drifted off since the last one, but they were getting stronger and closer together. "Babe," she said, shaking his arm.

Sam bolted upright, practically flew out of the bed. "Now?"

She nodded, pushed herself up to sitting so she could get dressed. He would follow the plan: call her parents to meet them at the hospital and take care of Dylan until this baby was born. Everything would be fine. Maeve knew she was a good mother. That had come naturally to her once she recovered from the shock of pregnancy itself.

The first time she'd had sex with a boy was in the back of a Toyota pickup during the summer before her senior year. She'd hated it, his slobbering kisses, the slippery penetration. What got her through was how mad she was—at herself and her parents, yes, but mostly at Wendy for leaving without saying goodbye. The first chance Maeve got, she'd called Wendy's house. The line had been disconnected. That's what she'd thought about—disconnection—as she stared blankly at the underside of a camper shell, this boy and his icky condom moving in and out of her.

She had a real boyfriend after that, a theater kid named Tal Martin. He had a beautiful singing voice and spotless skin and played Ali Hakim in the senior production of *Oklahoma!* He was fun to be around, read all the books she read, liked going to movies, and didn't complain at all when she brought Molly along on their dates. He smelled like aftershave, which didn't make much sense because he hardly had any facial hair. Maeve thought she might have sex with him, too, imagined a smooth body under tight shirts and bell-bottoms. They held hands and kissed for months. One time, she made the move in the front seat of his car, rubbing her hand along the zipper of his jeans. But he'd pushed it away without a word. In the end, that had been fine with Maeve. He talked to her about his plans to move to the West Coast, to pursue an acting career in California. He was wistful and gentle, and eventually they were only friends. After graduation, he left, and she never heard a word about him again. It would take her years more to understand what she was to Tal and what he was to her.

Sam was different.

He was quiet and dutiful. When he'd asked Maeve to coffee, everything about him seemed long—his lashes, his fingers, his doe-eyed gaze. His parents were stern, he told her, and expected him to marry and have children and take over the business—an office supply store—so they could retire. He paid for everything on their dates, and his studio apartment was above a bakery, so it always smelled like bread.

She liked the attention he gave her, the way he demanded so little. She liked his company, the way he held a book with both hands when he read. On Friday nights, once they were a couple, he'd make lasagna or spaghetti and set the table in his front window with a lace tablecloth and lit candles.

The first time he kissed her, he asked for her permission.

The night he proposed, the night she said yes, was likely the night she got pregnant with Dylan. She had to admit that she'd been less than careful with birth control, often forgetting to take the pills, then doubling up or skipping days altogether. She had been stunned by the pregnancy test, somehow in disbelief that their perfunctory, sporadic sex life had produced anything at all. Still, there was something about Sam. He was nice, and she felt safe with him.

Her parents had been happy about the engagement, if a little muted. Sam's bland, centuries-old European nothingness couldn't compare to her family's immigrant Irishness, and she'd figured they were disappointed that she'd carry on neither the family name nor the Irish bloodline. She knew her dad wasn't all that impressed with Sam's bookishness either. And although her mother defended him—Grandpa was bookish, after all—Maeve knew it was different. Her grandfather, in his prime, had been skilled with tools, always ready to lend a hand or a solution, quick with quotes from his favorite poem, with anecdotes from his reading, whether it was a book or an article from *The Irish Times*. Sam, on the other hand, absorbed and absorbed but rarely discussed what he was reading beyond a line or two. When she held out her finger with the delicate engagement ring, her mom stared at her as if she was trying to see what it was that Maeve was hiding.

"You're awfully quiet, Mom," Maeve had said.

Her mother snapped out of her trance with a forced smile. "Oh, I'm sorry! No, I'm just getting excited thinking about all the things to be done. Flowers! Cake!"

"And Pix," Maeve said. "Maybe you'll be my maid of honor?"

Molly had shrugged her off, tilting her head while she shook it. "Yeah, I don't think so, but congrats."

Maeve and Sam decided it would be better to drop the bomb about the pregnancy to their parents separately since Sam's were devout Catholics and might have something to say that he didn't want Maeve to hear. But it was Molly who was the cruelest.

"Well, I would rather be alone than marry a corpse like Sam," she said. "I hope your baby is more interesting than its dad."

Maeve had wanted to slap her but thought better of it. Forget Molly and her petty jealousy. She and Sam married at the courthouse and moved to the farmhouse until they could find a place of their own, suitable for their family.

Maeve had breastfed Dylan, though no one had expected her to, not even her mother, who told Maeve she could afford formula. But it felt like a miracle, the way her breasts filled up with milk, how the baby took to it, his whole mouth open, milk seeping out the corners of his lips, full over her nipple. When he was done and she put him to her shoulder, his head tucked into her neck while she rubbed his back. Then out the burp would come, satisfying them both. The rest of it—the diapers, the long nights, the milestones—Maeve didn't mind at all. At the end of every day, she felt accomplished, a natural at something. She had done it. She'd made herself into a woman who could be a wife and mother, who could have a family. It was bittersweet when she allowed herself to recall how afraid she'd once been that she'd never have any of this, that she'd never find the kind of happiness that her parents had. But here she was, ready to bring another baby into the world. With her husband. With Sam.

With Dylan secured in the back seat, Maeve gritted her teeth. "Babe, you have to . . ." She paused to let the latest contraction subside. She rounded her mouth to keep her breathing in check. "Slow. Down. The last thing we need is to hit a deer and end up having a baby by the side of the road."

Sam took the corner tight then put his hand over hers. "Not far now. Hold on."

Maeve focused on the road, how it was lined with pine tree sentinels marking the way. She was twenty-six years old, about to have her second child. She stared at her husband in the lull between contractions—his earnest face, sleepy eyes like dark commas, square bony shoulders, tidy haircut. A thin scar from a childhood bicycle accident creased his right cheek when he smiled. It was dented with anticipation. "Are you excited to meet the baby?"

"I can't believe it." He flashed her a giddy smile.

She was grateful for him, for the way he made sense to her, made sense of her. "I don't deserve you."

It was minutes before midnight, and snow was in the forecast. Maeve grimaced, said a little prayer of thanks that they weren't driving in a storm. She swore she could hear the baby crying inside her, could hear her voice. *Her voice,* she thought. A girl. She dug her nails into the back of her neck, trying not to bear down. Sam pulled her arm toward him. "Hang on."

౿

In the hospital parking lot, Faye and William swept up Dylan before Maeve was out of the car. Wet snowflakes as big as dimes fluttered on a cold white wind, confetti shot from a snow cannon. Sam ran around the front of the car and opened the door for Maeve, holding out his hand to keep her from slipping. As she stepped out, her water broke, running down the legs of her sweatpants, soaking the snow. "Oh, God. Okay," Maeve said. "Here we go."

"Call with news!" her mother said.

"Love you, sunbeam," her father said, Dylan perched on his hip.

Sam splinted Maeve with his body as he guided her to the red cross of the neon emergency sign.

౿

"You're in luck," said the receptionist, an apple-faced woman with steel-colored hair. "Slow night in maternity. You'll have the place to yourself. At least for a while. Shift is changing, so you'll even get a fresh nurse."

"Swell," Maeve said dryly, immediately regretting her tone. "I'm sorry . . ."

The woman brought a wheelchair around and guided her in. "No worries, honey. You're probably scared. All first-time moms are."

Maeve pointed to the chart the woman held. "Not my first time."

Sam brushed white flakes from his hair. "Can I push her?" he asked.

"And you are?"

"The husband. Husband and father."

Maeve could hear the pride in his voice.

"I see. But no. House rules."

Sam put his hand on Maeve's shoulder, and she put hers on his. "I'll be right here," he said. "I'm not going anywhere."

Maeve was in a hospital johnny, and the doctor had already checked her cervix when the shift changed and a new nurse walked in. Jockish sway, tumbled hair, that bit of overbite as she reviewed the chart. Sweat rose on Maeve's scalp. She wished she'd put on lip gloss or curled her hair. Something. Anything. When the nurse looked up, her face shot through with recognition. "Maeve?"

Wendy and Brett had been the talk of the school in the weeks after prom and Wendy's disappearance. The group-sorrow of the star athlete's shocking death eclipsed the fact that some ex-con, suspected gunrunner, IRA sympathizer had died in a freak accident at a Maine farmhouse. And in all those years, Maeve hadn't spoken a word to Wendy, hadn't seen her since she dropped her off barefooted in a ripped prom dress a block away from home.

So much had changed. And yet, here she was. Wendy Walker in the flesh. Blood rushed to Maeve's head. She thought she might pass out.

"Hey, Wendy," Maeve said, her voice breathy from labor. "Long time, no see." *I can't believe I said that. How stupid can I be?*

Wendy hung the chart at the end of the bed. "Jeez, yeah. Wow."

Shared memories chattered around them like hens at the fence rail. The pause was ironically pregnant.

Maeve mopped her sweating brow, smoothed her johnny. "Not my finest moment."

"What are you talking about? You—you look great."

Wendy glanced at the open door. "Boy, you're really far along. Um, I guess this is a little weird. Are you okay with me being your nurse? Since we . . ." Those memories. "Since we know each other? I can switch with Pam."

Maeve had spent years trying not to think about Wendy, about their days and weeks together. So much had changed. Pain came from all sides, crushing every part of her. "It's fine. You've seen me now. I must look terrible."

Wendy took the stethoscope from her neck and readied it to listen to Maeve's heart, to listen to the baby. "Seriously, you look beautiful. You're about to be a mom! First time?"

Maeve shook her head. "I have a little boy. He's five."

Wendy moved closer, swooning Maeve with honeyed breaths. "Oh," she said, her voice so noncommittal Maeve could read nothing into it.

Wendy made notes on the chart. "When was your last contraction?"

"Like three minutes ago?" Maeve winced. *It's been what? Seven years? Eight?*

"What's your little boy's name?"

"Dylan." The 8-track was in Wendy's parents' car. *My heart a sunken ship.*

Wendy paused, looked up from the chart.

That smile, the way her teeth buckled her bottom lip.

"Bob?" Melancholy in her voice.

Maeve nodded. Dylan Thomas Reed. Maeve figured it was no one's business that she'd named her son after Bob Dylan and her own grandfather.

"Hm," Wendy said and sighed, pivoting to the end of the hospital bed. "Okay. Looking good, Maeve," she said, making herself professional again. "Can you put your knees up and kind of let them fall apart? I need to check your cervix. Is that okay?"

Maeve couldn't stop the wild thoughts. *Wendy Walker is looking at my crotch. What if something gross is going on down there? Well, of course something gross is going on.* They had fantasized about running away together. Kansas, maybe. California. Mayhem. She groaned as her body turned molten.

Wendy calmly pulled the sheet over Maeve's knees and went to her side. "Maeve, you're almost there. Dilated to nine. We need to get you to ten, and then you push. Let's work together on this breathing." She put Maeve's hand in hers, told her to squeeze if she needed to and not to worry, no one had broken her hand yet.

Maeve stared into Wendy's brown eyes, locked with them, mimicked the breathing Wendy showed her. Hoo, hoo, hoo. Ha, ha, ha. *God, the pain.* "It really hurts, Wen."

"I know. I know it does. That's it. That's it. You're almost there. And rest, rest." Wendy's voice all around her.

Wendy's hand on her forehead. Like a basketball. Maeve drifted, thinking about the way Wendy handled the ball like it was on a string, dribbling between legs that chopped like shears. Hoo, hoo, hoo. "You were really good," Maeve eked out. Ha, ha, ha. "Basketball."

Wendy laughing, throaty and full. Wendy's hand on her arm, moving down her body. Wendy's scrubs, taut over athletic thighs and butt. Maeve couldn't keep track of the sounds and movement, the rushing in her own body. She was swollen and ugly. She panted like a thirsty dog. She had felt so powerful when she gave birth to Dylan. She'd been home when the contractions began that time. Her mom had held her waist, walked her around the farmyard while Maeve begged to go to the hospital. Her dad had pulled a slab of bacon—Maeve's favorite—from the refrigerator as they walked out the back door. "I'll fry up a little for us," he'd said. Maeve had given him a weak smile, knowing bacon was a treat he wasn't supposed to have anymore, since his heart attack.

At the hospital, when she was wheeled away from her parents, she'd felt real panic for the first time in years. Maybe this was all a mistake. Maybe she was pretending to be some *thing*, some *one*, that she was never meant to be. And she'd briefly let in the possibility of a different life. But a terrible loneliness threatened to consume her, and she swore she'd never think about that again.

And now, of all times, Wendy Walker was the only person in the room with her. Wendy Walker, back from whatever exile she'd endured. Pain shot through Maeve, a lustered aura slicked her field of vision—white and pink and blue, opalescent. "Wendy."

The doctor swept in. Wendy leaned closer to Maeve. "You ready? C'mon." She extended her hand, palm down, and Maeve put hers on top. They made a huddle of two. "Baby on three."

Maeve burst into tears when their hands parted. "What if I shit myself?"

Wendy winked. "All the good ones do."

"Quick look here, Maeve." The doctor lifted the sheet, stared between Maeve's legs. A gloved hand touched her thigh. "Perfect. Perfect." He appeared above the sheet. "Okay, Maeve. Next contraction, and you're going to push."

"Bear down when it comes, Maeve," Wendy said. "It's a wave. Work with it. Your body knows. Your body will carry you. You can do it." And she took Maeve's hand, squeezed as the contraction began.

The pain was everywhere, pushing out of her, flooding her, rays like bursting stars behind her eyes. It seemed endless. And then nirvana, where pain bursts open, scalding water on raw skin. Maeve roared and roared, felt almighty as her daughter entered the world. The baby's cries made the room laugh, and Maeve let out a sob.

"They're cleaning her up quick. They'll bring her to you in a jiffy," Wendy said. "You were amazing, Maeve. Really."

Maeve reeled and reeled.

The neonatal nurse gave the swaddled baby to Wendy, who placed her in Maeve's waiting arms. "She's a beauty!"

Her pink face was rosy with color, a thick swash of dark hair, eyes closed, full red lips. Maeve unwrapped her carefully. Her little chest rose and lowered with each breath. She counted fingers and toes, took stock of her perfect body. She looked up at Wendy. "Could you get my husband?"

Wendy lowered her head, smiled, her lips a knowing pout. Beautiful, yes. Maeve remembered. It was an expression she had loved once.

"You bet. I'll have him meet you in recovery. Who's the proud father?"

Maeve stroked the baby's cheek, shaking her head at this moment, deeply profound, deeply weird. "His name is Sam Reed."

Maeve watched as Sam approached almost reverently, though nurses scurried around without a care, talking at full voice. He radiated pride, his hands clasped in delight. "Can you believe it?" Maeve asked. She certainly could not. In the background, Wendy smiled and not awkwardly at all, even though Maeve felt a rush of guilt, remembering the first time she kissed Wendy at the beach, the sand sucking at their feet.

Wendy touched Sam's arm. "Maeve and I went to high school together," she said. "She was quite the basketball player."

Sam leaned in, kissed Maeve's forehead, his hand warming her cheek. Her eyes tipped closed like a doll. "Ooooh," Sam cooed to the baby. "Maybe you'll play basketball one day."

"I'll leave you all to get acquainted," Wendy said.

Maeve wanted to put up her hand, to say something. Stay? Go? But words jumbled with memory and the awesome present. She stared at the baby—her perfect nose, thick hair, eyelashes already long, cheeks red and welted from the journey. But she was here and hers, and Maeve was in a different reality, as shiny and smooth as the inside of a shell.

"Let's name her Opal."

When she looked up, she saw only Sam. Wendy was gone.

Opal's pediatrician and Maeve's OB-GYN both had offices at the hospital clinic, and because Opal had chronic ear infections and Maeve had pelvic floor issues, they were there constantly in the months after she was born. But there'd been no sign of Wendy since she'd brought Sam in from the waiting room.

Maeve told herself she wasn't looking for Wendy, only looking *out* for her. She didn't want to be rude, after all. She thought she should thank her somehow. Flowers seemed weird and aggressive. A card maybe? But she didn't know where to begin, other than to call the hospital, which she didn't want to do, or check the phone book (which she'd done but had found nothing).

In the parking garage at the clinic for Opal's monthly visit, Maeve and the baby were both clammy from early summer heat. Sweat drizzled between Maeve's spine and sundress, into thick cotton underwear she wore in case of inadvertent piddle. Opal wore only a diaper and onesie. A car pulled into the empty spot next to Maeve. Until that moment, seeing Wendy Walker emerge from her sedan in powder blue scrubs, Maeve suffered the indignities of motherhood without much complaint. She used her thumb and middle finger to brush her damp hair away from her forehead. Could she not catch a break? Once even? What she wouldn't give for a new dress, for a bra that actually flattered her, for empty arms and air conditioning.

"Hey," Maeve said, giving a weird wave she immediately wished she could take back.

Wendy jogged around the car to Maeve. "Oh, wow! There you are. I wondered if I'd ever see you around here." She jiggled Opal's toes and made a face until she gurgled. "How are you?"

"Good," Maeve said, trying to think cold thoughts. "Opal's had ear infections. And I keep peeing myself, incontinence, you know." She clamped her mouth shut, shook her head. "Sorry."

"We should get together some time," Wendy said. She pulled a little notebook out of her bag. "What's your number?"

Maeve flashed to Wendy playing basketball. "Lucky seven," Maeve said.

Wendy gave her a quizzical look.

"That was your number. In high school. Number seven," Maeve said. "Stupid. Sorry. My phone number, I know. I was just . . ."

Wendy laughed, and Maeve peed a little.

"C'mon. I'll walk you in." Wendy grabbed the diaper bag off Maeve's shoulder, and they walked into the clinic together like it was the most natural thing, the two of them side by side.

Their conversations, usually over coffee in the hospital cafeteria before or after a doctor's appointment, were reserved at first, catching up on details as if they'd been casual friends. Wendy had finished high school back in Canada. Her father took a sabbatical so they could move. "After that night, Mom didn't want to stick around." She'd gotten her degree in Ottawa, then moved to Freeport for the job in Brunswick. She told Maeve she'd thought about getting in touch. "But it had been so long. So much had happened." Maeve understood. She told Wendy about meeting Sam, that he was a "good guy" and a great dad, that Dylan loved him, that her parents seemed to like him fine. Wendy gave her an odd look but didn't ask the question Maeve wanted to answer. *I'm straight.*

It wasn't until their third coffee date that they talked about Brett Overton, what happened to him, how Wendy walked into the house, shoes in hand, her mother's precious dress ruined. "She was—I don't know—livid, I guess. I honestly thought she would hit me. She asked where I'd been, and I told her with Brett. Obviously, I didn't know about the accident so she knew I was lying. She pulled the phone cord out of the wall, it was ringing so much. She packed the whole family up the next day, and we stayed in a hotel in Portland. It was nuts. She watched me every second. She told me she'd called your house. I always wondered if you'd tried to call me."

Maeve had gotten used to the idea that Wendy Walker, everything about her, had been some kind of dream. She'd pushed it down, aside, away, anywhere so she wouldn't have to look right at it. There was before, and there was after. And now there was this. Maeve didn't know what it was. She added more sugar to her coffee, sipped while Opal slept in the infant seat next to her. "Something else happened that night. At my house." And she told Wendy about Conor O'Kane, how he'd come to the house. She told Wendy about his accusations—"Frenching"—as if it hadn't been so much more. She looked around the cafeteria for eavesdroppers. "You can't tell anyone." And then Maeve gave up the secret her family kept. She'd never told anyone because to talk about it would mean she'd have to talk about Wendy, and she'd never, ever wanted to do that. Until now. Until it was Wendy herself sitting right there. Even Sam had no idea a man had died at her parents' house. The whole thing had been swept up in the rug that her father had thrown out.

Wendy's hand was on her mouth the whole time. "Holy shit. How's your little sister? She must have been fucking traumatized."

"Molly? She's fine. It wasn't *her* fault. She just gave him a shove. *I* felt terrible! It was because of me that he was there." Maeve hesitated then added, "Because of us. But it's in the past. I don't even think about it. I'm sure Molly doesn't either."

"That's wild. I mean, I was severely depressed my whole senior year. I felt guilty about Brett. Guilty that my family had to move. Pissed at myself and my parents and, like, everyone around me. I even considered a degree in psychology to sort myself out. It took me forever. I still think about it. So, you and your sister don't even talk about it? Ever?"

"God no! You don't know my family. We don't talk about anything."

Maeve kept her friendship with Wendy Walker from her mother for months. It wasn't her business and, besides, Maeve told herself, mentioning Wendy's name would resurface everything that happened that terrible night. No one wanted to talk about that. But Sam mentioned Wendy over dinner one Sunday, and her mother practically bit her fork in half. "Wendy? The same Wendy from high school?"

Maeve had kept eating, trying to be cool about it. "I told you a girl from high school worked at the hospital," she said, casually. "That's who it is. We've been hanging out sometimes. It's no big deal."

"You didn't tell me who it was," her mother replied.

Sam seemed confused. "You don't like her, Faye?"

Maeve could tell her mother was trying to regain her composure. "It's not that. I never met her."

Maeve leaped to the rescue. "Wendy was a really good basketball player. I was jealous of her and probably talked about her. That's all."

Her father cut into his pot roast, his head down. "That's the girl whose boyfriend died in that car accident." He hesitated, exchanged a look with her mother, who passed it on to Maeve like a game of telephone. Maeve didn't think she'd ever been more grateful that Molly had skipped the family dinner that week.

"Boyfriend?" Sam said.

Maeve kicked him under the table.

Sam had encouraged Maeve's friendship with Wendy, said she needed to get out of the house more. He had bowling buddies and went fishing and camping with a rep from a paper company he'd known for years. Maeve kept to herself, complained about the bowling wives, most of whom were older than her. She knew moms from Dylan's school but didn't like them or their preference for gossip. So, when Wendy started coming around, when Maeve went shopping or to movies with her, Sam said Maeve seemed happier than she had in ages. But when he asked why she never brought guys around or talked about dating, Maeve let on that Wendy liked women. He'd wrinkled his nose, citing his Catholic upbringing and his discomfort with that "lifestyle."

"She's not, like, into you, is she?" he'd asked.

Maeve had balked, told him to look around. "I have a husband and two kids. I don't think I'm exactly her type." He'd laughed in a way that stung, like the idea that she could be attractive to someone like Wendy was ridiculous.

But she was not about to have a conversation about who Wendy preferred now.

"Forget it," she said. "Who wants dessert?"

Maeve made a point to have one of the kids with her when she met Wendy for coffee or lunch or at the park. But sometimes they talked on the phone while Sam was at work and the baby napped. She knew what days Wendy had off and would call. Sometimes Wendy would be home. Other times she had to leave a message. Maeve knew Wendy had a girlfriend, Carla, in Freeport, that they'd been dating for less than a year, that she worked for L.L.Bean as a guide. She'd shrugged off that twinge of jealousy by talking about Dylan and Opal, how they were growing, the cute things they did and said. She talked about the house on the cove, what a gift it had been for her and Sam to be able to move in after her grandfather died, how she and Sam had really made it their own, and how much they liked living close to the water. Wendy confided that she was estranged from her parents, that she'd come out to them freshman year of college, and that they couldn't accept "her choices," as she put it. "But Carla's mom is cool, and so is her sister, so they're kind of like family in some ways."

They met at the park the following spring. It had been months since they'd seen each other, and Wendy talked about having brunch with Carla's mom for Easter.

Something about the way she said it boiled Maeve's blood. "Do you think you two will have kids together, then? Like get inseminated or something?"

She was pushing Opal in the kiddie swing, trying to be nonchalant.

Wendy took a step back. "Why are you being cruel?"

"How is that cruel? You like kids, don't you? Why else would you be an OB-GYN nurse if you didn't?" The next words shot out of her. She felt ugly saying them. But wasn't Wendy rubbing it in? Her relationship with this Carla? "I mean, besides the obvious."

"Oh, you are not implying that I went into obstetrics and gynecology because I'm a lesbian, right, Maeve? That's not what you're saying. Because that would not only be cruel but homophobic and kind of sick. And we're friends, so that's not what you're saying, right?"

Maeve grabbed the swing to stop it and pulled Opal out. The baby reached for Wendy, but she stepped back. "I'm sorry," Maeve said. "Really. I don't know why I said that. It's—" If she admitted what it was, what would that make her? She was losing her mind. "I'm jealous of your relationship with Carla, okay? Is that what you want to hear? And before you get all weird about it, I can be jealous of the time you spend with her because we're friends, and I don't want to share you . . ." She rolled her eyes. "God, that is *not* what I'm trying to say. I love Sam, okay?"

Wendy let out a knowing laugh. "Okay, Maeve. You've got yourself tied up in knots again. Just like high school. And let me add, since we're being, you know, *straight* with each other . . ." She stepped forward and put her arms out to Opal, who fell into them eagerly. "I love kids. I care about women's health. Carla and I—we're good, but we're not great. She's not the love of my life or anything. And I'm a little jealous of you. I'd like what you have—a home, a family, someone who loves me for me, even a little girl of my own someday." She rubbed noses with Opal, who threw her head back in a giggle. "Maybe you don't get lonely, Maeve. But I do."

Maeve could not begin to tell Wendy about her loneliness, how murky it was, this feeling that she was wading in her own life, staying in the shallows because something scary lurked in the deep end. She'd thought having a second child would round her out and quiet the nagging part that resented being a paper salesman's dull wife, a part-time office worker, a woman expected to raise perfect children and keep a house running. Opal had made it a little better—how could she not?—but Wendy resurfacing made the other part so much worse. So, yes, she did get lonely. She just couldn't tell Wendy that without falling into the deep end.

"I'm sorry, Wen. Truly. Can you forgive me? For being a jerk."

Wendy squeezed Maeve's hand, her brow knit and sincere. "Always, Maeve. Always."

They walked hand in hand to Maeve's car as if the child Wendy held was theirs.

CHAPTER TWENTY-ONE

1990: Mid-Coast Maine

Molly, first through the tavern door, scraped her boots on the bristle rug, pulled off her stocking hat, and shook pellets of snow onto the wood floor. She pulled up on her bleached blond hair to respike the curls. Her dorm mate, a long-legged girl from Bangor named Shelby, shoved in behind her along with a small group they'd gathered on their bar crawl. The Salty Siren was the fourth stop. A flaking wood sign above the bar in the shape of a mermaid read, **Est. 1972 Sailors and Whores Welcome.**

One of the joiners, a guy named Chris, whistled. "Wow. This is the definition of dive bar. You guys sure about this? It's kind of seedy."

Most of the light in the bar came from green lamps over six pool tables and neon beer signs. The back wall was lined with racks of pool cues and pinball machines and arcade games and bearded bikers and flannel shirts. Empty shot glasses accumulated at the end of the long busy bar, next to jars of pickles and brined eggs. A movie-theater popcorn machine in the corner dumped out a fresh batch into the glass bin.

Molly grinned. Stop number four. It was perfect.

"I can't believe we've never been here," Shelby said. "I honestly thought we'd been to every bar in town. And don't be such a baby, Chris. It's cool."

Molly's skin prickled to life. *Something wicked this way comes.*

Her advisor had grabbed her after class earlier that day. She'd been avoiding him, ignoring his summonses. She knew what he wanted. Academic probation. Again. She had barely eked out a C-average in her first semester, an A- in literature balancing out a D+ in economics. She'd promised her parents over Christmas break that she'd knuckle down, that it was jitters of being away for the first time. But in truth, she couldn't put her finger on what her problem was. When she was home, she couldn't wait to get back to college, away from the farmhouse and her parents and Maeve and her perfect little life at the cove. She and Sam had painted every room, pulled down the kitchen wallpaper with the floral ribbons, replaced the linoleum. Worst of all, they painted the shutters blue. The green was gone. It was like they'd erased her grandfather completely. But when she was at school, in the dorm room she shared with Shelby, in the bathroom down the hall that she shared with every girl on her floor, in classrooms she shared with clusters of strangers she didn't care about, she was pathetically homesick. She missed her mom and her dad and the couch and television and the way she could do nothing, hours and hours of nothing. She missed the porch swing and her dad's cluttered barn. She missed the honeyed smell of fields in the fall, an oven with cookies baking, fresh sheets on a bed that someone else made for her. She missed those things like a poet, her yearning existing only on paper. In real life, her entire world itched. In real life, she was always looking for an escape hatch into some other place entirely.

"This is awesome," she said, already buzzed from earlier stops. "It's like something out of a Stephen King novel. And I think I'm up. You guys see if you can find a table, and I'll get a couple of pitchers."

Most people at the bar were men, most of them too old and too crusty to be college kids. At first glance, two women in short denim skirts and tank tops—clothes that didn't make any sense in the dead of a Maine winter—looked her age but, up close, Molly could see that they were much older. She wondered if they'd changed into those getups in the bathroom. She made a yuck face, mostly for herself, and squeezed in beside a burly guy with a long broad nose and antlers of hair that made him look like a moose.

"You want a shot?" he asked, pushing one of two amber-colored glasses her way.

Molly gave him a skeptical look. He seemed harmless. "Sure."

They tapped rims, took the shots. Molly's teeth floated, and she shook her head.

"Dan," he said.

"Thanks, Dan. Molly."

He nodded and turned his back. Definitely harmless, Molly thought. Now where is that bartender? A heavy-set woman wearing a howling wolf sweatshirt dumped a bucket of ice into a bin then put her hand on the bar in front of Molly. "What can I get you, sweetie?"

Molly played cool in her most adult way, channeled someone who didn't give a shit. "Two pitchers of Bud," she said, smiling at Dan, who was looking her way again.

The bartender stared for an extra beat. "Yeah, I'm gonna need to see some ID."

Molly sighed, rolled her eyes at Dan like she was too old for this nonsense, and rummaged through her purse for her wallet. She'd had the birth date on her driver's license altered to make her legal to drink, even though she was only twenty. The guy hadn't done a great job, but it worked fine in dimly lit bars and careless liquor stores. And since she refused to drive once she passed the test, she'd never have to show it to a cop. "Here you go."

The lady looked at the card, then back at Molly, then at the card again. She ran her fingertip over it, feeling, Molly suspected, for scratch marks. "This is you? Molly Sullivan?"

Molly nodded.

The bartender looked down at the identification again, ran her tongue visibly over her teeth, bit at her lips and nodded. She stared at Molly. "You don't remember me?" she asked.

Molly racked her brain. She was sure she'd never been in this bar. She and Shelby had gotten tossed out of a bar in September after they got fall-down drunk pounding well drinks on ladies' night. But that bartender was a man. This woman looked to be in her sixties at least, her hair, streaky with different colored dyes and grown-out roots, up in a messy wad of flyaways. Her skin was smoky and wizened with creases. Molly did not know her. *Something wicked . . .*

"Your mom is Fiadh, right? And your dad is Will?"

Molly nodded. The ice around her thinned. *Fiadh . . .* "Faye," she said. "My mom is Faye."

The woman's eyebrows flicked. "You remember the name Conor O'Kane?"

Molly's eyes widened. Her stomach churned like a whirlpool. Dan's shot plus others rose in an urp. Molly swallowed. Didn't this woman know that was a name no one said out loud? Didn't she know that person hardly existed at all? That person was a figment. "What?"

"I remember you from when you were little. You had red hair then."

"For Chrissake, Glenda, give the girl her pitchers!" Dan said. "And while you're at it, pour us a couple more shots."

Glenda laughed, loud and hard.

Molly grew small. Good witch or bad witch? *Sardonic.* She'd learned that word in lit class. Her bones rattled in her eardrums. In fact, the whole bar seemed to shimmer as if none of it were real at all, as if she were imagining the whole thing. Glenda set two pitchers in front of Molly with a thud that sloshed the foam. She grabbed a bottle of Jameson and put three shot glasses out.

"Whoa, there," Dan said. "No one asked for top shelf."

"On me," Glenda said, filling the glasses. "We're drinking to my dead husband. He might not have been the best man, but he was a good man. And he was *my* man."

Glenda and Dan lifted their glasses. Molly stood paralyzed. This man, Conor O'Kane, loomed over her entire life. To her, he must have been eight feet tall, rangy and muscled like a werewolf. He took every step she took, laid out in front of her, long and distorted like a late afternoon shadow. Good? *He was a bad man.* That's what her mother told her. A bad man and a drunk. She could see his hands clawing the air even now. He had sideburns. Dark lips. That's all she could remember about his face.

"Come on, big girl, big college girl," Glenda mocked.

Dutifully, Molly lifted the glass. Her palms were sweaty. She wished she had her gloves.

"To Conor O'Kane," Glenda said. "The love of my life. May he rest in peace. Sláinte."

"To Conor," Dan said, clueless.

"To Conor," Molly whispered.

Glenda filled the glasses again. And again. And again. Molly gagged on the last shot.

"That ought to about do it," Glenda said. "Banjaxed proper now. Here's your fake ID, Molly Sullivan. You can tell those parents of yours that I said hello and tell them it would have been nice if they'd come to the service or sent flowers or even picked up the goddamned telephone when I called. All he ever wanted was a family to care about him, you know. I hope you lot pay for how you treated him. So, yeah, you tell them I said hello. You'll do that for me, won't you, Molly Sullivan? Tell them Glenda said hello?" She pinned Molly's wrist to the bar, stared her down accusingly before releasing her again. "Oh, and nice jacket, by the way."

Stunned, Molly touched her cuff and backed away, bumping into a skinny guy playing pool, who gave her a shove. As she stumbled out the door, she heard Glenda laughing, Dan's moose voice saying something about pitchers of beer. And another voice, this one dark and filled with dirt. *I see you. I see you.* Outside, under a blistering cold sky, she emptied her stomach into the dirt-stained snow.

CHAPTER TWENTY-TWO

1992: Mid-Coast Maine

Maeve pulled the duvet up to her chin, scooted farther under. She'd left the office at noon, stopped at the grocery store like she always did on Fridays. Dylan and Opal had after-school activities, then her parents were picking them both up for pizza night. Sam would close the store then go to bowling league. No one would be home for hours. Fridays were predictable.

The crisp sheets felt good against her warm skin. She rolled over, let her hand glide down the sloping line from her waist to hip. She longed to drift toward sleep, to float in that heady place where wonder was possible. The candle on her bedside smoked and flickered. Bergamot and cedar and tangerine swirled around her like a finger in a cocktail glass.

Wendy, next to her, let out a gentle sigh and rested her hand on the curve of Maeve's neck. "I should go," she said.

The candle was a gift from Wendy. Wendy, on fire. When they weren't together, Maeve sniffed the unlit candle to trigger what she felt at that very moment. To remind her that it wasn't all a dream.

"No! No one will be here for at least two hours. Don't go. Close your eyes."

Wendy looped her leg over Maeve. "A few more minutes but then, seriously. I have to get out of here. Unless, of course, you're ready to tell them."

This was Maeve's favorite time, the moments after sex when she pretended this was her life and this was the way she lived it, with Wendy and the kids and somehow with Sam too. It was fleeting, an unburst bubble. *Why can't it be this way? Who says this wouldn't work?* But how could it? Sam would be heartbroken. The kids would be disgusted. And her parents. Maeve couldn't imagine how let down they would be. They held her up like a model wife and mother, especially to Molly, who continued to struggle to find her footing. Yet here was Wendy Walker, in her bed, the same one she shared with Sam. She wiggled out from under Wendy, swung her legs so her feet touched the floor. "You know I can't."

"It's getting ridiculous. Strike that. It *is* ridiculous."

Maeve and Wendy had been sneaking around for over a year. If Maeve were to say this to Sam, he might assume it was Wendy who had seduced Maeve, Wendy who had tricked his wife into a relationship. But that wasn't the case.

It was Maeve who put her hand on Wendy's thigh when they went out together. Wendy gently removed it.

They'd hugged once in a simple greeting, no eyes on them, and Maeve had lingered at Wendy's neck, taking in her scent. Wendy registered shock, and Maeve relished even that. "Stop it," Wendy hissed. "You're being a jerk."

Maeve told Sam she was going to a movie with a friend and instead had stopped by Wendy's apartment unannounced with a bottle of cheap wine in a paper bag for old times' sake. When Wendy opened the door, Maeve was surprised to see the lights dimmed, a different candle burning in a jar on the kitchen counter. Another woman—straw hair, dull eyes, man hands by Maeve's account—sat on the couch weaving a macramé plant hanger out of white rope, a glass of wine in front of her on the coffee table. Carla was long gone, but Wendy hadn't said anything about someone new. Wendy had put her arm casually on the woman's shoulder, a signal to Maeve that she wasn't welcome. Maeve made a lame excuse, thanked Wendy for a favor Wendy hadn't done, and left the bottle of wine on the counter. She drove to the theater, sat in the back row of a movie in progress, and sobbed her way through murders and car chases on the screen.

Wendy had called her at work the next day. "What was that about?"

Maeve ducked down at her desk so the other clerks in the office wouldn't hear. "I could ask you the same thing."

"We need to talk. Can you come over after work?" Wendy asked.

"Will your girlfriend be there?"

"Maeve. Just come over."

At the apartment, Maeve batted at the plant in the new macramé holder when Wendy told her to back off. "I hope you and Man Hands will be very happy together."

"You don't get it," Wendy told her. "I walk this line at work where everyone knows I'm gay, but we don't talk about it. I'm excluded from every conversation with other women when they talk about boyfriends and husbands. They're talking about letting gay people be out in the military but in real life? In hospitals and law offices and classrooms? It's harder than you know because you have the cover of this." Wendy snatched Maeve's hand roughly and held up the ring. "And for your information, 'Man Hands' has a name and it's Laurel, and Laurel's partner parked her car in a shed and stuck a hose from the tailpipe through the window and took her own life. I'm one of the few people who listens to her. So, don't pretend life is hard for you."

Maeve pressed on her stomach. The scolding hurt, but it was the image of the woman's death that struck her. She didn't want to picture that kind of sadness for anyone. "I'm sorry. I didn't know."

"You come over here and . . . I don't know what you want. But you have to stop fucking around like this. This isn't a game for me. This is real life." Wendy turned Maeve's hand over. She caressed Maeve's palm with her fingertip, and Maeve had felt the shock everywhere else.

"Don't start something with me that you don't want to finish," Wendy said. "Don't pull me into your life unless you want me in it forever. It's always been you for me."

They laughed about it later, a scene made for Hollywood, the way they devoured each other, a frenzy of mouth and tongue, hands and fingers. Maeve told Wendy it was like being in another dimension. "Like I was surfing strands of my own DNA."

Now, she heard frustration in Wendy's voice again like she'd heard every time over the last year that Wendy called her out. She had a fair point. Maeve was stalling. She rested her elbows on her knees, buried her face in her hands.

A sound came from downstairs. A voice?

"Did you hear that?" Maeve checked the clock. It was early still. She wiggled into the jeans bunched on the floor and yanked on a top, not bothering with a bra. She tiptoed to the door and cracked it, her finger to her lips. Wendy rolled her eyes as she grabbed her scrubs.

The sound of a cabinet closing, the refrigerator door sucking open.

Maeve pushed the door closed. "Someone's here. Hurry! Make the bed." She blew out the candle, twisted her head left and right, trying to find an excuse for Wendy to be in her bedroom. "Fuck." She smoothed her hair in the mirror over the dresser, licked her fingertips to wipe smeared mascara away. "Wen." She pointed to Wendy's bra on the floor.

Wendy balled it up and shoved it into her pocket. "Now what?"

"Shh," Maeve said, gesturing wildly. "Follow me."

They tiptoed out of the bedroom, then down the hall to Dylan's room. Maeve flung the door open and the smell of boy—potato chips, sweaty socks, and must—wafted out. Maeve made a gagging face to Wendy then said loudly, "I don't know if paint will do it. I think maybe we should empty it out and wallpaper it."

She motioned for Wendy to follow then marched down the stairs. "But if I wallpaper that room, Opal will want hers done. Sam will want to paint but, I don't know . . ." When Maeve turned the corner, Sam walked through the kitchen door, a glass of milk in one hand

and a half-eaten sandwich in the other. He choked down the bite in his mouth.

"There you are! Didn't you hear me calling?"

"We were upstairs in Dylan's room. It needs to be painted or something."

Sam's eyes tracked from his wife to Wendy. "All right." He took another bite of sandwich.

"Wendy has a better eye than I do."

"Hey, Wen," Sam said, overly casual. "Why didn't you ask your mom's opinion? Seeing how it's still her house. No offense, but Wendy doesn't strike me as the interior decorator type."

He'd been snottier about Wendy lately, and this dig seemed especially harsh. Maeve let it slide, resisting the urge to argue. "What are you doing here?"

He held out his right hand. The middle finger was swollen, and the fingernail looked like it would turn. "I slammed my finger in a filing cabinet. I'm not bowling tonight. I thought maybe we could go out instead. It's been a while."

"I have to go," Wendy said, waving awkwardly. "We can talk more about the . . ." She waved her thumb in the direction of the upstairs bedrooms, and Maeve felt heat rising in her neck.

"The paint?" Sam offered.

"Yeah, the paint."

"Okay, bye. Thanks!" Maeve said, waving stupidly as Wendy walked out the door.

Sam took another bite from his sandwich, chewed a couple of times. "That was awkward," he said, his mouth still full.

"She didn't want to help. I basically begged her."

Sam turned his back, returned to the kitchen while Maeve stood paralyzed. Though Wendy was gone, Maeve could smell her still, on her skin and in her hair. She cupped her hand around her mouth and exhaled, certain Wendy was there too. She wished she could twitch her nose, magic herself out of this situation. What was she doing?

When she'd used the word "experimenting," Wendy had lost it. "Experimenting? You're not dabbling in pastels. If this is an experiment, well, you've safely reached a conclusion. It's a success, Maeve. Trust me."

She heard water running in the kitchen sink, the clank of silverware. She closed her eyes, felt the room vibrate. Her lips tingled as her mouth dried up. She stared at the stone fireplace, the couch by the window. She remembered her grandfather dying right there, remembered the day that she and Sam moved in with Dylan, Opal on the way. She had a life. And it was this one. It wasn't too late. He hadn't walked in on them, hadn't seen something he couldn't unsee. She could talk her way out of this bind. She could quit this thing with Wendy.

She breathed in, took a single step. "Babe?" She could see the suspicion in his eyes. Hurt. It was the last thing she wanted. There had to be a way. She could do this. "I was thinking. I'm ready to try for another baby."

"Really." It was not excitement in his voice. It was disbelief. He set his plate on the counter, pulled Maeve to him. Her body, still tingling from Wendy's touch, felt foreign in his arms. She willed herself not to recoil. She loved her husband. That wasn't the problem. He kissed her the way only he ever had, his palm cradling the back of her head. She didn't know who taught him to kiss like that. It was the most unexpected thing about him, the way that palm in that spot had always turned her on. She gripped his waist, tried to will herself into a different way of loving, the one that should feel natural to her. He was the father of her children. He was her husband. *You keep telling yourself that.* Wendy's voice.

He pulled away gently. "I know you're not in love with me anymore. I know something's going on between you and Wendy."

Her ears rang, the façade cascading like shattered glass around her. "That's crazy. What are you talking about? She stopped by to help with the paint colors, that's all."

"Don't insult me. That candle. You never light it, but it burns down anyway. It burns when I'm not here. I figured something was up, then it dawned on me when it was happening."

Maeve looked at her husband's injured finger. "Did you do that on purpose? To have an excuse to come home?"

"Not really. No. But maybe subconsciously. I wanted to be wrong. But then her car was here. I was kind of hoping it was some man. That would have made more sense to me, I guess. I didn't take you for—but then again, this thing with Wendy. Anyway, I sat outside awhile, thinking maybe she'd come out. Then I came in and sat down. I didn't hear anything. But I could smell that candle."

That look on his face. Bitterness and pain. She could deny it, make promises and vows. Her mind raced. He could take the kids away. Take her to court. Sue for custody. Would cheating with another woman make it even worse? He would run to her parents, tell them what she'd done, out her. She had no defense. She was what he said she was. She'd done what he feared, and these were the consequences. Maeve held her hand over her mouth, ran to the bathroom, and threw up.

Maeve splashed her face, swished and spat and drank. She looked at her own reflection as if it was a stranger there. She was a wife. She was a mother. A daughter and a sister. She was her father's ray of sunshine. She was a stranger to all of them. A stranger to herself. She had done everything that was expected of her. She remembered that awful night, the way her mother had looked at her when she'd asked about Wendy. Maeve swore when the ambulance drove off with Conor O'Kane's body that she'd never put her family in this kind of jeopardy again. She'd drawn him to their house. That's what got him killed. But they'd survived it, hadn't they? As long as Maeve toed the line, nothing bad would happen again. She stared herself down. Strands of wet hair clung to her pale cheeks. *But you crossed the line, didn't you? And now what?*

Sam sat stiffly on the couch next to the fireplace, his right hand resting in his left. Maeve sat next to him. "Let me look at that."

He held his hand out to her.

"Can you move it?"

His finger flicked back and forth.

"It's not broken. Damaged but not broken."

He took his hand back. "This isn't a metaphor."

Maeve mirrored his posture, his demeanor, the placement of his hands, the tightness of his face, the direction of his gaze, as if it might help her figure out what to do next. Ten years together. Around them, furniture they'd chosen, pictures of their kids on the mantel, books they'd added to the shelves along with the ones left behind by her grandparents, a bin of toys in the corner.

She could not imagine what might come next. She waited.

When Sam finally moved, he went up the stairs in a steady stride. Maeve assumed he was packing a bag. She waited.

He returned with the candle in his hand, walked through the kitchen and out the back door. Maeve watched from the kitchen window as he stood on the big rocks by the cove and hurled the candle underhand like a bowling ball. It arced high then disappeared from sight. When Sam turned to the house, Maeve went to the same spot in the living room. The screen door slammed, and Sam sat back down.

"Fucking thing," he said. "I hoped it would sink, but it bobbed right to the surface again." He paused, then added, "And yeah, that probably *is* a metaphor."

They sat together silently, into the darkness, until her mother called to let Maeve know she would be dropping off Dylan and Opal soon. "We're all bushed," she told Maeve with a happy laughter in her voice that broke Maeve's heart that much more.

So much would change now.

That June, Maeve and her father drove up to Rockland for an estate sale, early enough in the morning that Maeve hoped her quiet wouldn't be perceived as something wrong. She'd offered to go with him, using the excuse that she was lonely with Sam and the kids gone to Virginia to see his parents, who had retired there after he took over the store. It had been a hard two months, and Maeve welcomed summer, a break from the school schedule, the reprieve of Sam taking the kids. Pretending was exhausting. Maeve sipped coffee from her thermos. The tire wheels hummed as they took the exit ramp. "A couple of miles down this road," Maeve said. The FM station played soft rock. "Can I ask you a question?"

"Shoot," William said.

Sam slept on the couch that first night, told the kids he wasn't feeling well and didn't want to get Maeve sick. Ten years of marriage, and the thing the two of them couldn't do anymore or ever again was lie down next to each other and fall asleep. The intimacy of that, trusting the person next to you, feeling safe in the quiet of slowed breathing. That was lost. Maeve had searched herself for regret, for remorse, but found only sadness. She wanted to sleep for days. She wanted to sleep forever.

"Have you and Mom ever had a fight so bad you didn't sleep together because of it?"

William switched the radio off. "Oh, no, honey! What happened?"

"No, I was just thinking about . . . seriously. Have you ever grabbed the blanket and pillow and slept on the couch? I can't remember that happening when I was little. I know you must fight sometimes, but it always seems like everything is perfect between you two."

Her father scrunched up his face. "I can't think of a time I was angry enough that I didn't want to put it to rest before I fell asleep. You know the saying, never go to bed angry. I've been mad with her a few times over the years, I suppose, but nothing I couldn't get over."

"She's never done anything—or maybe you did something, and she told you to sleep on the couch?"

William shook his head, kept his eyes on the road. "No, though, truth be told, I'm a bit of a pushover, as you may have noticed. You didn't know your grandma all that well, but she was a hard woman.

Nothing like your grandpa. I think your mom had a pretty lonely childhood. You know she's not great with conflict, bottles stuff up. And I tend to let things slide. I was raised in a noisy house with opinionated women—like you and Molly," he added with a laugh. "My dad always told me, 'Go along to get along.' Guess that's how I keep from sleeping on the couch."

Maeve unfolded the map again, checked the road signs for the turn. She pointed. "There. Baxter Lane."

"So, what's going on?"

Maeve promised Sam she would tell her parents while he was gone. When he returned, they'd tell the kids together. The plan was to make summer the best it could be under the circumstances. Then, in the fall, unless something changed, which neither of them believed it would, they would separate. Sam had made her promise she wouldn't see Wendy during that time, wouldn't risk embarrassing him that way again, or worse, having one of the kids catch them together.

They had tried to lie in bed together, and it had been too much for both of them. When Maeve heard Sam's muffled sobs, she'd rolled over onto her side, tried to comfort him. He'd flinched, out of what she read as disgust. That was when he grabbed his pillow a second time and slept on the couch again. Dylan was eleven and old enough to know something was up—Maeve had noticed him averting his eyes, ducking out when conversations went ice cold—but savvy enough to keep his head down and not ask questions. Sam spent more nights out, used bowling for an excuse, though Maeve suspected he was sitting in his office at work until the last possible moment, slipping in late with murmurs of "accounting" and "inventory." The solution was to make a demarcation line down the middle of the bed with pillows. They slept with their backs to each other. A temporary solution to a permanent problem.

Maeve's other problem was Wendy.

It was one thing that the marriage had failed. The reason it failed was an entirely different problem. She missed Wendy desperately, but there was something exciting buried underneath all this uncertainty and confrontation and disclosure. When Maeve called Wendy after that first confrontation with Sam, she'd been sympathetic but encouraging too. Maeve heard relief in her voice. She'd felt it too. They talked about really being together, out in public, out with their friends and family. Out, finally. But there were hurdles to clear first.

"Must be up there," she said. "Looks like a crowd."

William parked behind a white utility truck. "Okay, kid. Out with it."

Maeve took a deep breath, shifted to face him. She had planned to deal with it on the way home, not now, not when they'd have time to talk and talk and talk. She tightened. "Sam's leaving at the end of summer. It's over."

William wrinkled his nose. "Maeve! No! What happened?"

Maeve covered her face. She remembered doing that as a kid, thinking if she couldn't see her dad, he couldn't see her. His hand pulled her wrist down, exposing her. She clucked her tongue. "Oh, Daddy. I'm no ray of sunshine, that's for sure."

And she told her father, who she revered above all others, about having feelings for someone else and that someone else was a classmate from high school and that they'd reconnected and that one thing led to another.

"How long?"

"More than a year."

William puffed, straightened his ball cap. "Jesus, Maeve. How did Sam find out?"

She didn't say anything, just stared him down.

"Oh, no. Poor guy. Well, I know Sam well enough to know he didn't throw any punches. Not exactly his style. How bad was it, with the other guy?"

A van pulled up behind them, and lookie-loos parked up the street. "We'd better go in," Maeve said. "We can talk later."

"Maeve. Come on. It's me. What happened with the other guy? You're not still seeing him, I hope. No way you and Sam can make this work if you're running around with—Jeez, at least it's not your boss! Who is it? Do I know him?"

Maeve's skin prickled, and she rubbed her arms like she'd caught a chill. She was not trying to be dramatic, but she couldn't make herself speak. Once it was out, they could never go back. "It's Wendy, Dad."

"What about Wendy? Sam's not with Wendy! No way. C'mon. He's no match for her."

"No. Dad. It's Wendy. Wendy's the other guy. Just not, you know, a guy."

William shifted his attention forward, so Maeve did too. "We better get in that line. Don't want to miss out on something good." His voice was low and even.

Maeve's heart sank. She didn't know what she'd expected to happen, though she'd run through every scenario. He couldn't leave her here. He wouldn't. It wasn't like him to shout, especially not with so many people around. "Dad. Say something."

He stared. "Does Mom know?"

The question was a simple one, but the answer was far more complicated. Maeve thought about that night, years ago, her mother's expression. And then when she and Wendy rekindled their friendship, the way her mother had said she didn't like her, didn't trust her. "No. She doesn't know. I'll tell her when we get home. Daddy, if Wendy didn't matter to me, I wouldn't have bothered telling you. I know this is hard. She . . ." Maeve choked on the words, thrilled at the thought of saying them out loud. Pride bloomed like a sprout caught in a time-lapse. "I love her. I want to be with her. I want you to understand."

Color rose in William's cheeks, flushing his hairline. Flustered, he reached for the door handle. "We gotta get in there."

Maeve followed him up the walk like a chastised child. At the top step of the brick house, he paused. Maeve halted, braced herself. "A lot's going to change," her father said. "But not the way I feel about you. Not ever. You understand? Now let's go hunt treasures."

After they unloaded the estate sale haul into the barn—a primitive apple cart, a box of depression glass, an oak secretary desk—Maeve begged off. "You mind if I go find Mom? May as well do this now since never isn't an option anymore."

The conversation on the way back had been mostly a diversion, though her father had asked about Wendy's job, whether it was stable. "You think she'll be around after the summer?"

"I hope so," Maeve had replied. "Would that be okay with you?"

"Not gonna say it won't take some getting used to—the idea and all. But I would never turn you away, so I would never turn her away. Easy as that."

Maeve left her father to sort his antiques and thoughts. Her mother would be anything but easy, never one for airing dirty laundry, not metaphorically or literally. Buttercups creeped along the lattice under the back steps. Glass clanked in the kitchen. Her body told her to run.

Faye sat at the kitchen table, twisted in her chair, bent over a scrap of paper taped to a cutting board. A child's watercolor tray in front of her, she dipped a red brush into the muddy water. "Let me guess," Maeve said, surprising her mother. "A seascape. For a woman who's not fond of boats, you sure do like painting them."

"Prettier from the shore to me."

"A ship in the harbor is safe, but that is not where ships are meant to sail," Maeve said, reciting words from a poster that hung in Opal's kindergarten classroom.

"So, I hear. Lucky me. I'm not a ship."

"You want to take a break, sit on the porch with me for a second?" Maeve asked, pushing away from the safety of the dock.

They sat facing each other on the porch in her parents' wicker chairs, the table between them a growing chasm. Faye went white, stiffened like a stoic. "You didn't tell him about before, about back in high school?" she asked. "I never did, you know. I kept your secret."

Maeve couldn't understand why her mother focused on that detail above all the others as if she deserved a medal for keeping a secret Maeve never asked her to keep in the first place.

"No. I figured—look." She didn't want to think about that night, about the way Conor O'Kane had peered into the car, the words he'd said to her, or about the guilt she'd felt watching a dead man's boots go out the door. "That's the past. I want to focus on these next couple of months. I have to think about Dylan and Opal. And Sam. I never meant to hurt him."

"Poor Sam! So, your father . . . he was fine with . . . with Wendy and all?"

"I wouldn't say fine, but he said that there was nothing I could tell him that would make him stop loving me."

Faye's eyebrows twitched and flicked like she was having a complete and separate conversation in her head. "That's always seemed so strange to me, when people say things like that. Of course, you could say something—or do something—that could change everything. Even dogs run away when they're treated badly. Love is full of conditions."

"I think he meant I didn't need to keep anything about myself secret from him."

"Well," her mother said, a million miles away.

"Are we going to be okay, Mom? You and me?"

Her mother refocused, returned to their conversation. "Like you said, you've got a lot to deal with, the kids, Sam. With Wendy, I suppose. Your job. You'll have to call Molly. She'll be disappointed. You know she looks up to you."

There was that word Maeve feared. Disappointed. She nearly doubled over. "Does she, Mom? Look up to me? I'm not so sure about that." It occurred to her then. "Wait. Do *you* have conditions for loving me? Which is worse: That my marriage fell apart or that I was in bed with Wendy? Is it worse that I'm a cheater or that I'm a lesbian? You made it pretty clear a long time ago that I was an embarrassment to you. I'm sorry I'm not the daughter you thought I was." If that hurt her mother, Maeve didn't care. She was done pretending. She sat up straight, wished Wendy was there to hear her say the word, to own her feelings after all these years.

"Maeve! That's not true. I have loved you every single day of your life. I will always love you. You are not an embarrassment. Not at all."

She could not read her mother's face, flushed now, her expression far away again like she was trying to remember the verses of a poem or the thing she'd forgotten from a long list. Finally, "I don't understand why you would choose such a difficult path, is all."

"Mom. I didn't *choose*. I want what you and Dad have—a happy life, children, the whole thing. As much as I have that with Sam, I hid this part of myself, even *from* myself. I thought I could keep faking it. Then Sam found out, and it spilled all over the place into this mess."

Her mother shook her head like she'd been swarmed by bees. "I can't believe your father threw up his hands and accepted this."

"Why are you so shocked by that? You don't give him enough credit."

"But you lied to us. I would have thought . . ."

Maeve bit her tongue, remembering that it was her mother who told her to keep the part about Wendy a secret. *It would break his heart, she'd said.* There was no use trying to fix blame. This was simply the way it unfolded. "If I lied, I did it because I thought I had to. I was afraid you guys would hate me if you knew. I tried to be what I thought *you* wanted me to be, Mom. The worst part is that I lied to myself. If I'd been honest from the start . . . who knows?"

"Well, you wouldn't have Dylan and Opal," her mother snapped.

"That's true," Maeve said, dismissing her mother's accusatory tone. "And as hard as that is to think about, I'm also glad I don't have to keep pretending to be something I'm not."

"We all do our best to not hurt people. I did my best to protect you, to protect this whole family, to keep you all safe. That's all I've ever done. But no one is perfect."

"I never said I was perfect, Mom."

"And neither did I, Maeve. Neither did I." Her mother leaned forward, arms extended, both hands open. Maeve accepted the gesture. "Honey, I'm sorry if I made you feel like you weren't enough for me. Jean, my mother, held me—" Faye's voice faltered, and Maeve tightened her grip. "She held me apart from her. I would never want to do that to you or Molly. I swear."

Her father came around the side of the house, his white shirt sleeves rolled to the elbow, jeans and boots tired from wear and overuse. Still, the sun hit him in a way that for the briefest moment caught Maeve by surprise.

Tears welled in her mother's eyes. She must have seen it, too, that halo. She let out a rough laugh and slapped her own knees, putting an end to the conversation. "You're braver than I ever was, I'll give you that," she said before turning her attention to William, who lifted his shoulders, surrendering to the moment.

"Quite the bombshell, huh?" he said.

This can't be it, Maeve thought. No screaming, no cursing. She wasn't disowned or told to stay away from the house, the family. "So," she said. "What's next?"

"I don't know about the two of you," her father said. "But I sure could use a beer. Anyone else?"

CHAPTER TWENTY-THREE

1992: Washington, DC

The cabbie left Molly's suitcase on the curb in front of a house with faded peace flags blowing on the porch, concrete pagodas in the yard, happy Buddhas plopped among ferns. Molly sucked the last breath of cinnamon out of a spent piece of gum then spat it into the gutter. She hoped the girl Brenda was home, hoped that she wouldn't have to stay in some cheap hotel or the Y. The place gave off hippie vibes, and the word "ashram" popped into Molly's head. She briefly considered the possibility that it was some kind of religious cult or sex cult. It would be just her luck. If Brenda let her stay, this would be the fifth place she'd lived since she'd dropped out two years before.

She'd spent her last weekend at college getting drunk with that guy Chris, having sex in the top bunk of a double while his roommate slept below them. Shelby was pissed at her for bailing, but after—no. She hated even thinking about it. She'd called home and asked her dad to come get her. So, the first place was back home. The dreaded farmhouse.

She spent over a year living there, babysitting for Maeve when she absolutely had to, working at the same florist where her mother had worked. She dip-dyed white carnations in orange for homecoming, red for Valentine's Day, green for Saint Paddy's. She made corsages and boutonnieres and wristlets and bouquets for confirmations and weddings. She stuck it out through all the seasons—black fly, monster mosquito, tourist, brief autumn, deepening snow, through nor'easter season, stick and mud. She made deliveries when she was forced to, though she hated driving. Then her old friend Jonie walked into the shop.

Her hair was long and straight, pulled back in a plaid cloth headband. The white collar of the polo shirt under her Colby College sweatshirt was tastefully upturned. Molly endured her going on about how peachy everything was for her, how much she utterly adored college. "Dean's list every semester!" Jonie had barely gotten to the question mark about Molly and college when she stopped herself. "Tell me that is *not* the same leather coat!" she chortled, pointing to the jacket draped over the swivel chair behind the counter. "You were *obsessed* with that thing!"

That afternoon, Molly saw a flyer in the grocery store. Nancy's Nannies. A nanny service that paired girls from Maine with families in Washington, DC, run by the wife of an environmental lobbyist. Molly called the number, jumped through all the hoops, and cleared all the screenings. She chopped the last of the bleach blond off the ends of her natural red hair. She bought a floral dress and sensible shoes for the full-body photograph she had to send in with her applications. She did it all without telling anyone until she was placed. Maeve had been the worst, of course. "You don't even like kids!" she'd said, and Molly had replied with the only reasonable response. "No, Maeve. I don't like *your* kids." Her parents—ever hopeful—had driven her all the way to Boston to take the train.

House number two: A ten-year-old boy who hardly needed a nanny, and his sister, a seven-year-old, who definitely needed a psychiatrist. Molly had tried but, when the girl escaped the house for the third time, Molly was referred back to the agency like a poorly trained stray.

House number three: A lucky break. Fancy place in Chevy Chase, two attorney parents, doting grandparents who lived nearby, swimming pool, one adorable little boy who needed a European nanny, according to his mother, so he could learn French before he started preschool. Molly had the gig for seven weeks between the time Inga returned to Denmark and Vivienne arrived from Paris. Good while it lasted.

House number four: Molly interviewed with Sideny ("Not Sidney," she'd said politely. "Sideny.") and Charlie Grant together. They looked like models—her, Ralph Lauren, him, Banana Republic. She was a political consultant. He was an economist bureaucrat. They'd held hands. Their entire house, inside and out, was painted some shade of mint green. All the wood was dark. Their two boys were adopted. They had a beloved golden retriever called Walter. They were lovely and perfect, and Molly couldn't believe her luck. They made Molly want to be lovely and perfect too. Sideny traveled constantly for work, was on the inside track with an Arkansas governor planning a presidential run. But then there was Charlie. Charlie snuck into her bedroom when the boys were sleeping and his wife was out of town. The day Maeve called to tell Molly that Wendy was more than a friend, that Maeve and Sam were splitting up, that Maeve hoped Molly would be okay with all of it, that she'd told their mom and dad and "Molly, they were so cool about everything" was the same day Charlie told Molly that he had chlamydia and that Molly needed to go to the doctor, that he'd arranged for an appointment with a trusted friend, that she'd need to stay quiet about it all, of course, but that "this thing" between them couldn't go on, that he'd need her to submit her resignation, but that he'd pay her "a severance" of course, but that Sideny couldn't know, that she must never know, that "it could negatively affect her career, you see," and then ripped up the first check he wrote to double the amount if she would please go to the doctor, get the pills, and be gone by the end of the week.

Molly was on a stiff course of penicillin when she pulled the rope that rang a gong somewhere inside house number five. Brenda, a "retired" nanny who Molly had met months before at one of Nancy's mixers, opened the door. "Hey," Molly said. "I need a place to crash."

In the backyard, the soggy heat curling her hair like rollers, Molly broke down. She told Brenda it was all a show—the Grants and their perfect marriage—how Saint Charlie would walk in at the end of the day, drop to his knees like he'd been rescued from a hostage situation so the boys could run into his arms. She told her how it all started with Charlie talking dirty into the baby monitor, how he'd forced her to give him head under their Christmas tree when Sideny was upstairs in the bath, about everything else that happened on the days when Sideny was out of the house. Molly told her about the check in her purse but not about the diamond bracelet she'd stolen from Sideny's jewelry box or about how she'd cut Charlie's designer neckties in half. She didn't tell her about the STD. She didn't confess her feelings, muddled as they were.

"First things first," Brenda said. "You have a bank account, right? You need to turn that paper into money pronto. My dad was a gambler—high stakes poker—and his rule was, 'Never trust an IOU. Not worth the paper it's printed on.' That's all a check is."

They walked to the bank, Molly fuming about Charlie all the way there and all the way back to the house, egged on by Brenda's rage. It felt good to talk, though it was hard to get a word in edgewise with Brenda. "Jesus, what is wrong with this town? First Gary Hart, then Clarence Thomas. I'll vote for Clinton, but man, I do not trust that guy. Men are so gross. You're like Anita Hill. This is harassment."

In the common room, Brenda pulled down double-hung windows. "Open at night, closed in the day. That's the worst thing about this house. No AC. Let's go outside."

Molly followed her through the kitchen lined with open shelves and mismatched plates and glasses. Brenda pulled a bottle of pink wine from the refrigerator.

"It's ten in the morning."

"Who cares! You deserve to get drunk after dealing with that pig." She grabbed two jelly jars with her fingers, then pushed the screen door open with her hip.

Outside, Brenda went on and on about the Anita Hill hearings and how some group of congressmen—"Biden, Specter, Kennedy, and the rest"—looked like they were getting off on the spectacle of this young Black woman having to sit there while they questioned her integrity.

Molly had hardly paid any attention to the hearings and couldn't keep up with Brenda's rant. "Yeah," she said, offering the only detail she knew. "I heard about that thing with the pube on the Coke can."

Wendy scoffed. "Yeah, what was it that old fart said? 'Are you a scorned woman, Miss Hill?' Like I said, men are gross."

Molly had not wanted this thing with Charlie, not at the beginning at least. But she liked the attention, the risk of playing with fire. She'd daydreamed that their clean life was her own, that she could walk away from every mistake she'd made into a new life. How had she tricked herself into thinking Charlie was a good guy? That morning, he'd stood on the porch, holding a coffee cup, making sure she got into the taxi like it was carrying his bad rubbish away. Scorned? Maybe. Used and stupid? Definitely.

Molly's head was dizzy with wine and fury. "I am no Anita Hill."

"You're acting like only the most virtuous women can rightly claim abuse. Charlie had power over you. Simple as that. I don't care how many people you've slept with. He had no right to do that. Honestly," Brenda said. "Let's call the agency. Right now. Tell Nancy what he did."

"God no! That would be mortifying. And Sideny would eat me alive. She went to Wellesley. Like Hilary Clinton. She's always talking about that. I think that's how she got on the campaign. Plus, I mean, the money. He bought my silence, right? That's how it works." *At least I'm getting paid to keep my mouth shut this time. At least there's that.*

"But aren't you worried about the next girl? Charlie's a predator." Brenda emptied the last of the wine into Molly's cup. "Drink."

Molly wiped her mouth with her fingers. Her lips felt thick and numb. "She'll be smarter than I was."

"You're plenty smart. He abused his power," Brenda said. "How old are you even?"

"I'm twenty-two." Molly fingered the bracelet she'd put in her pocket, each perfect stone. It must be worth thousands, chump change for the Grants. Knowing how careless Sideny was with her jewelry, it would probably be months before she even realized it was missing. She wanted to wipe her brain clear of all the memories of the past year. And back. And back.

"That prick! You really should report him."

"No. Mouth closed, case closed. I'm done. The new nanny's on her own. Glad I cashed that check." Molly sighed. She fell against the musty pillow on the weathered teak chair. "I wish I could be someone else."

Two weeks later, Brenda took off on an extended trip to South America. "This place is great," Brenda said, turning over her key to Molly. "Just be yourself."

Molly didn't warn Brenda that she didn't know who that girl might be. She hung her leather coat up in the closet, signed the hippie co-op agreement, and took over her room.

On the swing in the gazebo behind the house in the middle of a sweltering and soggy day, Molly watched Yarrow, one of her new housemates, quietly pull weeds from the skimpy lawn and put them in a tin pail. Tedious, Molly thought. And pointless. They would grow back. Why bother? Let them be green while they could. As if she could read her thoughts, Yarrow sat back on her feet, wiped her brow with her dirt-speckled arm. She smiled at Molly. "It's meditative," she said. "Feeling for the roots, asking the soil to give them up."

Molly smiled back. "Cool."

"You should try it. It's great for tension. It helps me with patience."

Molly suspected that Yarrow was not her real name. Like the others in the house, Yarrow seemed to dwell on the fringes. Molly knew she worked in some crystal shop in Silver Spring. She did not know where she had lived before or how old she was. There was a guy named Larry who called the house looking for her, but she always shook her head "no," and whoever had answered—Molly rarely picked up the phone and Yarrow never did, probably because of Larry—would kindly tell him that Yarrow was not ready. Larry had apparently lived in the house for a while and then in Yarrow's room. They'd had a falling out involving a bird and a cat, though Molly wasn't certain which one might have been Yarrow's pet. Either way, the housemates decided Larry should leave. And he had done it, gone and left his heart behind with this woman who probably kept it in a velvet pouch in her drawer.

Molly crisscrossed her legs, stuck her hand into a bag of Doritos that she could only eat outside since junk food was frowned upon in the house. "I'm pretty relaxed."

Yarrow tilted her head. "May I have one of those?"

Molly held out the bag in question, and Yarrow crouched next to her, took one chip from the bag, and put the whole thing in her mouth. Molly could see she was sucking the flavor off it, softening it with her saliva.

"God that's good. Can I have another?"

Molly held the bag out, and this time Yarrow took her single chip and nibbled small bites, crackling it with her teeth, the crunch echoing out of her slightly open mouth. When she was done with that one, Molly held the bag out again. It was like feeding a chipmunk.

Yarrow shook her head. "Two's good. So, you don't have a job anymore?"

With Brenda gone, Molly was a clean slate. She didn't have to tell anyone anything. "I was a nanny, but I quit."

"Hm. My friend Maxx owns the new organic bakery by the Metro station. She needs help. I can put in a good word for you. If you want."

Molly turned the bag sideways and dumped the rest of the chips into her mouth, alternately crunching and sucking. One slipped down her tube top into her cleavage. She fished it out and ate it. "Do you think I'll fit in?"

Yarrow got back on her knees and continued her weeding project. "I think you'll be fine. We can go tomorrow."

Molly faked the part of a health nut for her job at the bakery. She didn't feel like a liar. Everyone wore some sort of costume, some disguise, designed to signal where they belonged. Punks in Georgetown conformed to black-lipped, fishnet anarchy, dirtbag headbangers thrift shopped for flannel shirts. Was the uniform of the monied—pencil skirts and blazers, hair back in a tight bun, feet squeezed into shoes shaped to fit a knife blade—any different? At least she was comfortable, and her uniform didn't strike fear or envy or pity.

She wore her hair longer now and piled it on top of her head for work, bandana tied in front, strawberry bangs to the edges of her eyelashes. Yarrow gifted her two pairs of loose linen overalls with gaping pockets that dangled to her knees. Somehow it all looked okay with the black leather jacket and boots she'd worn for years.

She walked to work, often before sunup. The bakery itself was airy and clean. It had a free library of books, stools along the window, mismatched coffee and teacups, Fiesta ware dishes and jelly jar glasses. The food was wholesome, a little bland. It was a spot for commuters and a retiree walking group during the week. On weekends they were inundated with corporate earth mothers from Bethesda or Chevy Chase—pretenders who made their kids eat healthy but probably stashed Oreos on the high shelves. Molly saw a little of Sideny in all of them.

Yarrow's friend Maxx was expanding to another location and rarely came around, which was fine by Molly. Most days she worked with three other people—a baker, a cook, and another counter person named Camille, who, like Molly, wasn't a dyed-in-the-wool granola type. She was twenty-seven, though her round face and glowing skin made her look younger. She came from a big family that gathered weekly, and she often brought in leftover pasta gooey with cheese and meat to share with Molly. Before the bakery job, she'd worked as a cocktail waitress where she said the pay was better, but the hours and the customers way worse. The bakery gave her an excuse to stop wearing a bra during the day, though, when they went out together some nights, she favored a push-up and low-cut shirts. It was her philosophy that Molly was actively trying to embrace—you can be two things at once. "You are not what you eat for breakfast or what you do for a living or what you wear to a club."

Around Camille, she did what Brenda had suggested before she left—soul-search, let go of expectations. When Camille brought in a flyer for a punk show on U Street, said they should tart it up and go, Molly agreed. The place stunk of spilled beer and White-boy rage. The lead singer from a band called SKAlarship, his spiked hair dyed neon yellow, screamed incomprehensible lyrics with a fake British accent and threw himself into the crowd. When the drunk crowd surfed him back to the stage, it was clear the screaming was from the broken arm he'd suffered in the dive. Molly tugged at Camille, and they fell out into the street, gasping for fresh air in the sweltering heat. "That was fucking awful," Molly said. "I can absolutely cross punk rocker and punk rock groupie off my career list."

She felt like Goldilocks. That place was too hot, the Hill bars too cold. They found their favorite hangout in midtown at a bar called The Wren on the second floor of a brownstone with a decent little kitchen and a takeout window below. The bar was long and narrow with a measly row of high tops and otherwise open space. The ceiling fans were propellers, and there was a vague flying theme, leather flight hoods and goggles here and there, framed newspaper articles and pictures of Amelia Earhart nailed to the walls, avian wallpaper behind the deco bar.

Molly liked it there, liked sitting at the bar, talking smart, imagining herself as a person with her shit together. In midtown, she could be fun Molly, nice Molly. She wore dresses in a favorite color like periwinkle blue or persimmon, or the perfect shade of olive green to set off her eyes. The first time she'd kissed anyone since Charlie was at The Wren.

He was very sweet, blond and balding, too short for her. They made out over drinks, and she gave him her number, though he didn't ask for it. When he called (he really was sweet), it was to say he was Jewish and that his mother wouldn't approve of her, so even though he liked her and she was pretty, it was pointless to date. She hung up and shrugged, told Yarrow the story.

"What were you drinking?" Yarrow asked.

Molly couldn't remember. "Maybe 7 and 7?"

Yarrow nodded knowingly, handed Molly a slice of peach. "You should try gin," she said and left the room.

The night Molly met Leo, The Wren swarmed with G-men. She and Camille staked out a spot at the bar. Molly was about to order her usual and thought about Yarrow's weird comment. The bartender was almost a friend since they were almost regulars. "I'll have a gin gimlet," she said.

"Who are you? My grandmother?" Camille asked. "I'll have a rum and Coke."

The drinks came, and Molly sipped hers. It tasted like a kamikaze but without the threat of blackout. Maybe Yarrow was onto something.

"Don't look now, but there's a live one behind you," Camille said, sipping her drink through a thin cocktail straw.

Molly checked him out in the mirror behind the bar. The guy was tall and thin, his nose long and pointed. His skin was clear and flawless, whisker free. He put his arm up to get the bartender's attention.

Camille leaned in. "You know what they say about a guy's wingspan . . ."

Molly elbowed her and looked in the mirror again.

"What do you gotta do to get a drink in here?" he said to no one in particular.

Molly spun on her barstool. "Let me help you." She lifted her eyes and chin, put her arm out on the bar. The bartender came straight to her. "Whatcha need, Molly?"

"Two more and whatever this guy's having. He can pay for ours."

"Got it. What'll you have, pal?"

"Sheez, that was fast. Guinness for me. Hope that's not top shelf," he said. "Leo." He put his hand out to her, but it wasn't like he was offering to shake, more like he was asking her to take a spin around the ballroom. He had a look to him that reminded Molly of yesterday, like he'd stepped out of a time machine, bewildered. He had dark hair, cut close but not military close. Hint of a dimple. Strong jaw. And blue, blue eyes.

Molly rested her hand in his, dramatically, delicately. "Molly."

As the night drew on, The Wren grew louder, and Molly found herself leaning into this Leo, putting her mouth next to his ear then slouching back to laugh, to see his reaction, to wait for his mouth next to her ear, her neck. His smell, a hint of some expensive cologne applied hours before, a spiced deodorant, breath and body warm with brown beer and the blue day.

Another round courtesy of Leo's friend, Henry. They'd formed a circle—her sitting next to Leo, Camille, Henry, two more of Leo's friends, and a couple of random women. She knew she wasn't being cool, but she could not take her eyes off him.

"So, what do you do?" Leo shouted.

She wished she worked in an office. "I work in a bakery."

"You're a banker?"

She crinkled her forehead, and then realized what had happened. "No," she shouted. "A bakery. An organic bakery."

He nodded. "You're a chef?"

She shook her head. "No. I'm not a chef. I just . . . you know . . . work there." She forced herself not to roll her eyes at how dumb she sounded. "What about you?"

"Clerk."

"At like . . ." She almost said a store, but that wasn't right. Then it dawned on her. ". . . the Supreme Court?"

He laughed. "You're adorable," he shouted. "No, I wish. District."

The theme song for *Hawaii Five-O* came on, and Camille threw her arms up in the air and whooped. Molly finished off her drink and grabbed Leo's hand. "Wanna be in my canoe?"

"What?"

"My outrigger. My canoe. Behind me. Get in my canoe!" She sat on the sticky floor, pulled up her knees. "You guys get in behind Leo!" she shouted to Camille and Henry. Leo wrapped himself behind her, his thighs encircling her hips, his body bracing her spine and tailbone. It seemed to Molly he was as close to her as he could possibly be.

He rested his chin on her shoulder. "It's like a magic carpet. Did you ever do that, when you were a kid?"

The bartenders squirted water into the air like sea spray. Molly turned her head, kissed Leo's cheek. He wrapped his arms around her waist, and she rubbed his hands with hers. *My carpet is a canoe,* she thought, *and we're going on an adventure together in this deep blue sea. Porpoises leap all around us, and the ocean glistens with scales of sunfish and rays of sunlight. We eat pineapples and drink from coconuts and cool each other with palm fronds on a fine golden beach soft as powdered sugar.* Her boat rocked now, side to side. Molly took up her make-believe oar and rowed, Leo's laughter in her ear.

She woke on time, thankfully, in her own bed, thankfully, alone, though Leo was still on her mind. Camille had hopped the Metro back to Silver Spring, but Leo insisted Molly hail one of the cabs waiting at the curb. Then he picked her up and set her on the hood. She wrapped her legs around his butt and made out with him until the cabbie laid on his horn and said it was time to go. "I could come with you," Leo had offered. She shook her head. "I gotta work in the morning, and I don't . . ." She almost said she didn't sleep with a guy on the first date. But that wasn't true. Sex on the first date, even the first night, was fine. What she didn't like was the second date, conversations over dinner, the getting-to-know-you phase. She liked intimacy of the body, not the heart. As for the affair with Charlie, that had been one long one-night stand. He didn't care a thing about her, and she'd been dumb enough to let her guard down and entertain her own fantasies. When he dismissed her so summarily, he had confirmed that she was not worth getting to know. She was good for one thing while that good thing lasted. But, even as drunk as she was, and as tempted, in that moment she didn't want to treat Leo casually. It was only after the cabbie drove away and she turned to look back that she realized he hadn't asked for her number.

She was in the bakery in plenty of time before the pre-church rush. Gavin was in back; Ruthie brought out trays and filled the pastry case. What Molly wanted was something to put into her stomach that would soak up the hangover and the fatigue. Where was Camille with a pan of lasagna when she needed her? Her day off. She made herself a latte with the good milk—not the soy or almond the hippies demanded. The muffins and croissants were too proper and fussy. She needed pizza. She needed a burger.

"What kind of music this morning, boss?" Gavin asked. He called everyone "boss."

Molly thought of the outrigger. "Island vibes," she said, her hand a dolphin surfing imaginary waves.

"Steel Pulse it is."

Three hours later, her hangover caffeinated into a manageable throb, the bell on the door chimed, and Molly came out of the back, wiping her hands on the apron tied around her waist. A young woman with a baby in a sling was ordering from Ruthie at the counter. The person behind her leaned to look. He held two paper Popeye's bags—contraband in an organic bakery.

Molly pushed the half-door divider and swiped a bag from him like it was dope. She called over her shoulder, "Ruthie! I'm taking a quick break! You," she said to Leo, "Follow me."

They walked up the street, out of sight of the bakery.

"How did you find me?"

"I mean, it wasn't hard. You told me where you worked. Thought you might need a fix."

Molly squeezed her eyes shut tight. "I did? I guess I did."

"Hey, if I'm out of line, say the word."

She sat on a park bench in the shade of a magnolia tree, patted the spot next to her. She opened the bag, and a delicious waft of steam rose. Fresh. Her stomach grumbled. "You come bearing gifts. I'm hungover. How could I be mad?"

"I get the whole vegetarian scene," Leo said, gesturing to the bakery. "But the way you talked last night made me think you might be down for something else."

"Well, I don't know what I said to deserve this, but please, tell me there's a spork in here," she said, rifling around in the bag until she came up with the utensil wrapped in flimsy plastic. "Yes!" Molly held the foam cup in her left hand, sporked beans and rice into her hungry mouth with her right. "Biscuit chaser," she said, tilting her head back slightly to keep the food in before biting into the biscuit. She put her hand to her mouth, chewed quickly, trying not to talk with it full. "God, this is so good. Thank you!" She swallowed hard, her body bouncing to the rhythm of her chewing, trying to hurry the process along. She wiped her oily fingers on her pant leg. "I can't believe you're here . . ."

"Leo. Leo Doria."

"I didn't forget your name!"

Awkwardness caught up with them, strangers bonding over fast food. They both tried to speak at once, to fill the quiet.

"You go," Leo said.

Molly laughed, suddenly self-conscious. She'd rushed into work that morning and worried that, at a minimum, her pits stunk. "You must have been first in line at Popeye's. Where do you even live?"

"Adams Morgan. I share an apartment with Henry. From last night?"

"Of course."

"So, me, Henry, and another guy. Not a great place, definitely too cramped. But it's fine. Close enough to work, the Metro. Great food. And you, you live here?"

"Yeah, Takoma Park. Hippie house."

Leo nodded. "And the bakery? How long have you been there?"

"Why are you here, Leo? Don't get me wrong. I'm happy for the red beans and rice. I mean." She fluttered her eyes. "We drank a lot last night. Made out a lot. But why are you here?"

Leo's left leg shook, and he let out an exaggerated breath, like a kid blowing out a candle. "Well, I hope maybe you're glad to see me and not just the bag of hangover food I brought. Look, maybe you think I'm some kind of weirdo. But I couldn't stop thinking about you after you left. And then I realized I didn't get your number. I should have chased down the taxi. I woke up thinking about you—well, you and my headache. And I wanted to see you and I wanted Popeye's and . . . two and two . . . here I am."

Molly tapped her teeth together. This Leo made her nervous, jittery, like he might be able to kick down that heavy door she'd closed after Charlie. No one ever went out of their way for her, did something for her that didn't serve themselves first. Was he just another guy who didn't take no for an answer? But there hadn't been a question really. He brought food. She sat on a bench and ate it with him. "Sorry," she said. "I got up in my head for a minute there. No, that's really nice. I had a good time last night." She cringed, hearing that needy sound in her voice, that dippy flirting. "And I woke up thinking about you and *lasagna*, so you are really, really close to perfect right now."

He reached for her biscuit. She slapped his hand before he could pull it away.

"Killer instincts."

Her heart skipped. "You have no idea."

In the daylight, the glow of youth and ease on him was almost unbearable. His skin was absolute butter. Molly was dying to kiss him. She popped the bite he tried to steal into her mouth. "Sadly, I must return to the vegetable mines."

"What time are you done? That's me," he said, pointing to a motorcycle parked at the curb. "I could come back. We could go for a ride or something if you want. I brought another helmet, just in case."

"Pretty confident, aren't you?"

He cocked his head, touched her hand. "Nothing wrong with a little hope."

They locked eyes, both playing the game now. Heat rose in her cheeks, thinking about Leo leaning into her on the hood of the cab. Okay, a little hope, then.

"Clean up this mess, yeah," she said, pushing the paper bag toward him. "I cannot be seen with poison. My granola universe can't handle it. And three. I'm done at three."

Leo was outside at three sharp. He reached for the bandana to help Molly get the helmet on. "You mind?" he asked, his hand hovering.

"Go ahead."

He undid the knot, and she shook her hair free, knowing the moment was charged. She'd refreshed her lip gloss already, the only makeup she kept in the bag she took to work. "Sorry I'm not in motorcycle gear," she said, adjusting the helmet. "Well, the boots maybe."

Leo tightened the straps for her, snapped her in. "You're fine. It's not a hog. It's easier to get around in the city. Plus, it's fun. We can ride through the park."

He put his own helmet on and mounted the motorcycle. "Not quite the magic carpet from last night . . ."

"Oh, it'll do." She got on the motorcycle behind him, the seat slightly raised so she could see over his shoulder, put her feet up on the pedals, her arms around his waist.

"You ready?"

Molly had never been on a horse or a dirt bike, even. She loved the feeling of shooting forward, ahead of the moment, only a second behind the future. She let her body join to Leo's, riding the languid motion of sun-dappled curves through Rock Creek Park, the humidity low for a summer afternoon. She loosened her grip and leaned back, the asphalt wave rising up to greet her, the green of the park cool on her face.

CHAPTER TWENTY-FOUR

1992: Washington, DC

Camille steered her lemonade-colored sedan through the DC traffic. She and Molly were picking up Leo and Henry at Dupont Circle, heading out of town early in hopes of beating traffic on the way to Rehoboth Beach. The hotel rooms were cheap, and the place would probably be scuzzy, but none of them cared. It was on Leo's tab, and it was a chance to escape the city, to frolic in waves, to cut loose.

"This is going nowhere. Seriously. I can't believe he's still hanging out with me. I should break it off with him." Molly couldn't help but second-guess herself. There had to be a catch. She'd tried for weeks to keep her feelings about Leo in check, but every time they were together, she let herself imagine something more with him. But as soon as they were apart, her fear crept back in. How could she be worthy of someone like him? He didn't know the first thing about her.

"You're crazy," Camille said. "And why does it have to go somewhere? Can't you have fun?"

"Oh, I'm having fun. Pointless fun. He graduated from Tulane. Studied abroad. He talks like we're going to travel the world together, how he wants to show me New Orleans, how he wants to live there someday. I'm a college dropout from the boondocks. I'm sketchy.

He's a law student at Yale. Classic summer fling. Better to dump or be dumped? That's the question."

"I think you're selling yourself short. And you're hardly sketchy."

Molly put her head in her hands. She was trying to play it cool, but she really liked Leo. And the more she wanted something real with him, the more certain she was that she could never have it. She was leaving herself unguarded, and it felt terrible. "God, I'm a mess."

"You really are. But look there." Camille pointed over the steering wheel. Leo and Henry were on the corner. They'd changed into swim trunks but kept their suit jackets, shirts, and ties on. Henry was shorter, stocky, wavy brown hair. Hilarious and perfect for Camille, who was a cutup too. "Molly, Leo is a stud. Look at him. He looks like a Greek god. You can have nice things, you know. And that man is *nice*. Don't self-destruct."

Molly smiled. Half Italian, half Irish. He was too good to be true, and soon enough, one way or another, she'd lose him. It was only a matter of when. And how. "Oh, fine!" she hollered as Camille beat her hands on the steering wheel. "One more weekend, stud!"

Molly called him the night after they returned from the beach, told him over the phone that she thought he was great, really, but that they should call it. "You'll be leaving DC at the end of summer, back to Yale." They'd gotten their picture taken together on the beach, and Molly held the little plastic viewfinder up to her eye while she talked. They were kind of beautiful together.

"That's weeks away. And, even then, it's not that far. You could take the train."

Their photo booth strip was stuck into her dresser mirror. In the pictures, in her reflection, she looked happy. Why couldn't she let herself be happy? "We're on different paths, different wavelengths." It sounded unconvincing, even to her ear.

Leo laughed. "You've been dipping into the organics. I see you with your wavelengths, Sullivan. You're not getting rid of me that easily. Listen. Did you have fun at the beach?"

Endless fun. Sand in all the places. "Of course."

"Did you have fun skinny-dipping in the Dumbarton pool?"

They'd gone out to dinner in Georgetown one muggy night, drank too much wine. One of the many upsides of dating Leo, Molly realized early on, was that he had money, came from money, and never hesitated to drop money to have more fun. "I have an idea," he'd said. "Trust me?" His question hit hard. Had she ever trusted anybody? Someone from the Italian embassy had told him about it, the one place you could get past the guards and onto the closed grounds behind Dumbarton Oaks. She put her trust in him, and they stripped out of their clothes, slipped into the dimly lit pool, lightning bugs setting the lawn aglow. They floated, made out buck naked, screwed in the loggia. They'd walked off the grounds right past the guard. Leo had that way about him, like he belonged everywhere he went.

"Yes."

"So, why break up? Everything is going great. No pressure from me, no pressure from you. Is there someone else you'd rather be with?"

She looked into the viewfinder again. "It's not that," she admitted.

"Then what? You want me to fight for you, is that it? You *want* pressure, Molly? I'll give you pressure. I'll fight for you. I'd kill for you. Is that what you want to hear?"

He had no idea what he was saying, who he was talking to. She wouldn't wish that burden on anyone. She didn't want anyone else to die because of her. "No," she said. "I'd rather be the one to take the bullet."

"All right," Leo said. Molly could hear the exasperation in his voice. "This conversation has gotten way too serious. I'm sorry if I'm freaking you out. I'll back off if that's what you want. But don't push me away."

Molly laid back on the bed, listened to Leo breathe into the receiver. *Tell him the truth and let him decide for himself.* The problem was that the truth had gotten too complicated, even for Molly. And it was more than that "first thing" that he didn't know about her. It was every other thing since. Guilt had taken root inside her. When she was little, she'd imagined extracting it with a scooper or syringe. Then she tried to assuage it, but it became unwieldy and vicious. Now it felt systemic, elemental. She was mean and careless and self-destructive.

Leo had been such a surprise, so unexpected. He laughed at her caustic humor, he liked how she dressed, whether she wore girly skirts or combat boots. If he cared that she didn't have a college degree or even a great job, he didn't let on. She told herself that trying to be the right kind of girl for Leo was exhausting, but maybe the truth was that she wasn't trying that hard and that he liked her anyway, maybe loved her even. And if he loved her, really loved her, she could tell him anything, and he would listen. Maybe worrying was exhausting her.

"The truth is I'm freaking myself out. I'm sorry," Molly said, grimacing as she allowed Leo to get that much closer. "Forget I said anything?"

Leo laughed, sounding relieved. "You really are a tough nut, Sullivan. You know that? See you Friday?"

They had dinner at an Ethiopian restaurant in Adams Morgan a week before Labor Day, a week before Leo would leave for Connecticut. He said pressure, and he'd been applying it. He'd given her his new phone number already, his new address, made her promises about weekends and holidays, how they would figure it out. Molly wore a white dress with yellow embroidered daisies, a dress she wouldn't have been caught dead in when she was a teenager. It was a little too cute and country club, but it was practical for a muggy DC night, and most importantly, she knew Leo liked it. At the last minute, she'd put on the stolen bracelet she stowed in her underwear drawer, admired how it fit loosely, expensively on her wrist, more diamonds than necessary. It would match her fake earrings, make her that much shinier for their night out.

They fed each other spongy flatbread dipped in spicy dishes, sipped sweet honey wine. He put her fingers in his mouth, and she giggled. He held up her palm. "That scar's kind of badass. Knife fight?"

"It's from a sparkler," she said. "I grabbed it after it burned out." She didn't know what had made her do it. Some impulse to brand herself, to cause pain on top of pain. "I didn't know how much it would hurt." She ran her finger over it, felt the tingle of touch, the flutter of opening her heart to him. *Ask me more.*

"Wow, and speaking of sparkler! Where'd that come from? That would set a guy back."

Molly shifted, immediately regretted wearing the bracelet. She brushed off both conversations. "This? Fake. Are you kidding?" She felt like a kid playing dress-up, the real fake.

"More wine, please!" she said, bending the conversation away from her.

After dinner, they made their way through the bustling dining room to the exit. Lacquered fingernails parted the beaded curtain. Leo stepped Molly back to make way for the incoming party, their laughter already too much for the small space. The woman, turned to someone behind her, was unmistakable. Stiletto heels the same temptation red as the fingernails, tasteful dark suit impeccably tailored, blond hair up in that high ponytail. In those heels, she was as tall as Leo. Molly's mouth went dry as the party of four backed her and Leo even farther from the exit.

"Excuse me," Leo said politely, tapping the woman to get by.

Molly wanted to duck between their legs, scurry off like the pickpocket she was.

Sideny Grant glanced at them, dismissively at first, but then stared at Molly blankly like she was searching a card file for the name that went with this face. "Ha," she said. "Molly? What are you doing here?" The tone was exactly right. What *was* Molly doing here?

Sideny elbowed Charlie, who stopped guffawing long enough to see what it was that his wife wanted. His mouth flew open, and he made an involuntary sound like a crow's caw.

When Charlie booted Molly from the house, Sideny had been on the campaign trail. He'd put Molly in a taxi headed for the train station, with a ticket to Maine in her purse and her tail between her legs. As far as Charlie Grant was concerned, he'd bought Molly Sullivan out of his hair and his city.

"Hi," Molly said. Her voice was pipsqueaky. She raised her hand in a small wave to match, cleared her throat.

It took barely a second for Molly to realize that Sideny and Charlie had registered the bracelet. She jerked her hand behind Leo.

"Charlie," Sideny said, her voice sing-songy and accusatory. "I thought you said Molly had to go back to Maine, some family emergency . . . I thought you went back to Maine," Sideny repeated. Her eyes scanned Molly's face, then Leo's, scanned the darkness between them for another glance at Molly's wrist.

"Nice to see you," Molly said merrily, as if her stomach weren't in knots. She tugged Leo's arm. "We have to go. Enjoy dinner." She pulled Leo past the other couple, through the beads, down the steep stairs, and to the street.

"Molly! Hang on," Leo said, laughing, unaware of Molly's mortification. "Let me catch my breath! That woman is so familiar. Who was that anyway?"

Sideny was on all the television news programs, talking about the Clinton/Gore ticket. Molly had told Leo she'd been a nanny and had given it up, that she couldn't stand the dripping entitlement or the way the parents treated nannies like commodities they could buy and trade. She'd let him believe that the hardest part of leaving the profession was leaving the kids behind, though in truth, Maeve had been right. Molly didn't like them much.

"Sideny and Charlie Grant. I nannied for them." Molly tried to quash the images that flashed from her memory of other things she'd done for Charlie or allowed him to do to her. And the bracelet. She had no idea what it was worth, though the way Leo had whistled when he thought it was real confirmed it was a lot. She looked over her shoulder at the door, sure that one of them would crash through at any moment, chase her, demand it back, have her arrested. "She works on the Clinton campaign. You've probably seen her on television."

"She said you went back to Maine? I thought you hadn't been home since last year."

Molly hated lying to Leo, but this was what she'd been afraid of—getting too close, baring her rotten soul. "Honestly, I lied to get out of the job. Their kids were a nightmare and the pay was terrible and I got the offer at the bakery—all of the above, you know? I probably should have given more notice but . . . yeah."

The bracelet felt like a vise. She wished she could unclasp it and drop it in her purse, but she'd called enough attention to herself already. She wanted to recede, like the tide or a shadow. "Anyway, can we go now? Back to your place?"

In Leo's apartment, Molly took off her clothes, tucked away the bracelet, and laid on her stomach on top of his down comforter. She was glad to be out of the entire getup. She wanted to forget all about Charlie Grant and her past and to just . . . be.

"You should leave that bracelet on. It's sexy."

She shook her head. No more Charlie. She'd pawn it and be done with him. "Play naked for me," she said.

He sat in a slip-covered recliner, wearing only his boxers, his guitar next to him on a stand against an exposed brick wall. "I'm not sure I know that one."

"Play something. Anything . . ." *Take me anywhere.*

"That one, I know." He grabbed the guitar, strummed an F chord followed by a B-flat.

His guitar skills were above amateurish, and his singing above average, barely on both accounts. But the sweetness of having someone sing to her and play guitar, the smell of him in the room . . . *Don't fall in love. Don't fall in love.*

"Something . . ." He moved toward her, crooning lyrics she knew by heart, where they were going, the uncertainty, the mystery. She cocooned herself in the comforter.

"Are you wooing me?" she asked.

He set the guitar down and unfurled her from the blanket. "And how."

Leo's room had gone dark except for a beam from the streetlight that streaked across their tangled feet at the end of the bed. She stroked his stomach while he dozed, the gentle strip of hair that ran up to his navel, the animal grooves of his abdomen. Even though it scared her, she let the dream in. He would go back to Yale, and they would keep seeing each other, as often as possible because they couldn't stand to be apart, and he could come to Maine and she would show him the railing and tell him that crazy story, and he would tell her that none of that mattered to him, that she was good. "Go and love. Go and love." Her grandfather's final words. How strange that they came to her now. She closed her eyes, put her scarred palm to Leo's cheek. *Tread softly because you tread on my dreams.* "I love you." She said it so quietly it felt like the words were still rattling around in her mouth.

"Hmm?" he mumbled dreamily, half asleep. He pulled her hand down, cupped it with his against his chest. "And I love . . . your hands." He turned into her, nuzzled, and fell asleep.

She didn't blame Leo. It was a dumb moment to say something so important. She'd been caught off guard. But it was clear to her too. Whatever this was, it was not love, would never be love. At least not for Leo. All Leo loved about her was her damaged hands. *Walk away now.* Love and go.

Molly slipped out of bed, stepped into her underwear, pulled on the dress Leo had draped over the chair next to his guitar. She watched as honey wine lulled Leo into deeper sleep, watched him spread and curl like a nocturnal plant. She didn't need to embarrass him or try to break his heart to make him see she was no good. She didn't need to make a scene, wouldn't guilt him into professing love because he felt sorry for her. She didn't need his excuses, didn't need him to pretend. What he loved about her was what she did for him in the darkness. She wasn't about to stick around to see how ugly an end could be. Instead, she left the room, the apartment, the building, Leo.

She told her housemates she didn't want messages, didn't want to know if he called. "If he comes to the door, tell him I left town." Camille had only hooked up with Henry a couple of times, so his departure a week before hadn't been the same thing. Still. Molly didn't want to endure Camille's questions until after Leo was gone, and it seemed likely he would come by the bakery. She called in sick, feeling sick enough. One night, she heard a motorcycle revving by the house, the noise disappearing around the block. When it came by again, revved and went quiet, she knew he was there. She went to the window. He stood next to the motorcycle, arms folded, looking up. She turned out her lamp. In the darkness, they watched each other for minutes. It didn't feel to Molly like they were fighting for each other. It was a standoff. Who was tougher. He didn't know her at all. She was the tougher one. Finally, Leo reached into his back pocket and walked toward the house until Molly couldn't see him anymore. She waited. When the doorbell rang, she almost gave in and ran down. But then she saw him walk back to his motorcycle. She imagined flinging open the window, yelling something that would change the fact that he didn't love her. But he didn't look up. He jump-started the bike and took off. The revving faded, and Leo was gone.

There was a soft knock at the door and Yarrow's voice. "Molly?"

Molly opened the door.

"This was on the mat. I think you might want it."

Molly took a cassette tape from Yarrow's open hands. *Swimming Eyes 1992.*

꩜

Molly listened to the songs over and over, pouring over the lyrics but also reminding herself that it wouldn't do her any good to read something into it. The mixtape was a gesture, a booby prize. That was all.

She tried to make Camille understand. "We had a perfect night together. Why ruin it with a bunch of goodbyes? I've known the whole time. Leo wanted to be the good guy and pretended this thing mattered to him, but it was a summer fling. Nothing more."

"Was that all it was for you?" Camille asked.

Molly deflected. "He probably has some preppy girlfriend back at his cushy Ivy League school. The last thing I need is to try to get in touch and have him completely blow me off."

Camille slid a tray of muffins into the case. "Suit yourself. But I would have tried to hang on to him if I were you."

She didn't want to admit that when the phone rang at the house, she jumped to answer it. Yarrow's man Larry had been persistent, and she'd given in, allowed him to come over in person to apologize to everyone in the house for laughing when his black cat, Dante, had slipped out and killed an oriole in the yard. "It was easier for me to make the bird's death something small and inconsequential than to confront my own mistake." Molly had looked around the room, searching for eyes she could catch that would second her own skepticism. But everyone listened in earnest, until Yarrow told Larry that laughing at someone else's pain wasn't cool but that he'd redeemed himself, which made everyone relax, apology accepted.

The house got an answering machine, and at the end of her shifts, Molly checked it first thing when she got home. It was never Leo.

"You should call him," Yarrow said one night. They were sitting at the kitchen table, eating tabbouleh salad and whole wheat bread Molly had brought home from the bakery. She'd lost her desire for junk food, craved sours to suit her mood. "He might be your soulmate."

"Is Larry your soulmate?"

Yarrow smiled. "No. But that doesn't mean Leo isn't yours."

It wasn't like she hadn't thought about it. She missed everything about him. "I don't know what I would even say. We're beyond small talk."

"You could thank him for the poem."

Molly furrowed her brow. "Poem?"

"The mixtape?" Yarrow said, tilting her head. "The song titles? It's like a poem, don't you think? That's the beauty of the mixtape as a form of expression. You get the songs and lyrics. But then you get the arrangement. And that tells a story. Leo left you a love poem." She took Molly's empty bowl to the sink. "I like you, Molly. But you're not very perceptive."

It was a rare confluence—sunny day, Saturday, and Halloween. Shops and vendors set up booths and tables, and kids in costumes ran screaming through the closed streets lined with pumpkins and cornstalks and bales of hay. Normally, Molly didn't work Saturdays, but it was an all-hands event with ghost-shaped vegan cookies, vats of hot apple cider, and pumpkin-spiced everything else. She still had hours to go in her shift, but she was already exhausted.

Her back was turned to the table, but she recognized his voice. Unmistakable. She balled up her hands for courage, cursed that she was wearing stained overalls, as if that were the problem. Yarrow was right. She wasn't very perceptive. She'd finally taken a test. What was wrong with her that she couldn't figure this out? Twice, she'd called the phone number that Leo had given her, but she couldn't bear the thought of him telling her to get rid of the pregnancy. Whatever she decided, she would do it on her own. But she was running out of time. And this? This was the last thing she needed. She caught her reflection in the bakery window, could see him behind her now. She gritted her teeth, conjured a hard smile, and turned.

"Hi, Charlie."

Charlie checked over his shoulder like a witch was tapping it, which made Molly look too. She scanned the crowd for Sideny, who would be easy to pick out among the dowdier people. But it was almost election day. No chance she'd be strolling around Takoma Park. Then Molly spotted the boys across the street. They were dressed as burglars in matching costumes, holding hands with a sturdy girl who looked a little older than Molly. She approached with the boys, who seemed entirely uninterested in Molly.

"That the new nanny? Doesn't look like your type. Unless of course your type is young and vulnerable. Then, yeah, she's your type."

"Maybe my type is conniving little thief," Charlie hissed. "She saw the bracelet. She'd been looking for it everywhere. I had to buy a new one exactly like it and hide it so she could find it. You're welcome. She was planning to call the agency. Or the cops."

"Stick it." Molly wiped her hands on her apron, took off the scarf over her curls, and let them drop to her shoulders. "You're hardly the one to hand out morality lessons."

Charlie fumbled his bag of apples, and they rolled into the gutter next to the curb. The boys ran to grab them, and the girl with them stood back. "I think they've got it," Molly said. "I'm Molly. I was their nanny before."

"Boys," Charlie said, setting the reassembled bag onto the table between them. "You remember Molly."

The boys didn't react.

"Guess you didn't leave much of an impression," Charlie said. "This is Helen."

The girl's face turned crimson. Up close, it was clear she was quite young. Young and frantic. She was petrified. That asshole. Molly felt physically sick, thinking about what might be happening to the girl. She swallowed hard, tried to keep her legs from buckling. The boys stared off at the cotton candy machine, no longer paying attention to the adults.

Molly walked around the table and put both hands on Charlie's chest. "How's this for an impression?" she said, and shoved him hard. She pictured him sailing through the air. Instead, Charlie stumbled into Helen.

Molly looked at her hands like they weren't her own.

She could have told Sideny right away. She could have refused Charlie's advances. She could have quit and gone back to Maine, and she'd considered it. But the thought of that house, that ghost. No. She swelled with regret. She should have hidden a warning for the next girl in the basement. She shouldn't have accepted Charlie's hush money. Keeping quiet had never done her any good. She spiraled around thoughts of protecting herself, protecting other people. She'd even thought she was protecting Maeve when she pushed Conor O'Kane. And look where that got her.

She pointed at Charlie. "Leave her alone. Or I swear . . ." She said it evenly, like a killer.

She retreated coolly into the bakery, through the swinging gate, into the kitchen, to the staff bathroom. She closed the door, pressed against it, and hung her head. The checkered floor tiles shifted in a slick of tears. She boiled at the unruliness of her life. It came at her, blunt and thudding, tomatoes thrown at a bad actor. *What a colossal fuckup I am.*

She grimaced into the scratched mirror, wished she had ever bothered to ask Maeve what it was like to have a baby, what it was like to be someone's mother. What had it been like to be her mother? That busted-up girl staring back at her was clueless and dumb and irresponsible. "What do you even have?" she asked. "You don't have anything."

But she did have something. If only she could figure out how to fight for it.

CHAPTER TWENTY-FIVE

1993: Mid-Coast Maine

Faye took Molly's sheets from the dryer, held them to her nose, breathed them in like fresh air. Cotton as whipped as the color white, as scorched as sunlight on the bluest day. She remembered being a girl, pulling sheets off the line from the house by the cove, Maeve's house now, Maeve's chaotic household now. Back then, the sheets might have been out for days, through rain and mist, dry enough to bring in when the sun got around to doing its job. Back then, Faye would shroud her whole body in her bedsheets, suck in the taste of sea and grass and brine through her open mouth, her tongue licking the threads. She would imagine herself mummified, the sheet a layer of protection between her dead body and what would readily consume it—fire, maggots, shrapnel, tire rubber, tank tread—though it was these morbid thoughts that she longed to escape the most. The time that Thomas found her like that, cocooned head to toe on a bare mattress, was the only time he or Jean ever laid an angry hand on her. He'd dumped her out like a potato from a bag. When she recovered her footing, he swatted her firmly. "Never do that again," he'd said, then pulled her to him, enfolding her a surely as the cotton sheet had done. That may have been the day Faye knew for certain that Thomas loved her.

She flattened the top sheet against her body, folded and smoothed, right over left, until it was a neat package to be delivered to the upstairs bedroom, the yellow one, Molly's. She folded the bottom sheet next, making a clever tuck of the elastic corner that she'd learned from Jean. Perhaps she had learned from Jean how to tuck away worry too.

When the girls were little and helped with the laundry, she had tried to teach them to fold their sheets instead of impatiently wadding them around their forearms like they were winding an electric cord. She never told them about wrapping herself in sheets. It was not that she didn't want to imagine them doing the same, wondering what it would be like to be dead. It was more that she didn't want them to know that's what she had been like as a girl. She hoped her girls would be happy, that their lives would be uncomplicated, clean and dry, carried on a gentle breeze. Maybe she had hoped that the worst thing that would ever happen to them was that they'd be bad at doing chores.

"You two are hopeless," she would say, snatching the sheets back to fold them properly. "You'll make terrible wives."

"Oh, no. Not that," Maeve replied, flipping her hand to her forehead. "Whatever shall we do with ourselves, dear sister?"

Faye remembered the laughter, when Molly collapsed on the floor, a curtain on a stage gone dark. "We are doomed!"

Faye breathed in the sheets once more before they cooled and the scent was gone. She shouldn't have said that, the thing about them making terrible wives. In her head now, it sounded like a curse. She pulled the string to turn off the overhead light and carried the sheets and a few towels up the stairs.

The door was open, so Faye went in without knocking. She set the towels on the dresser and paused to stare out the window, holding the sheets to her chest. Her mind wandered as her eyes followed the line of the barn to the silver maple. William's son would be in his mid-forties if he had lived. And where would Faye be now if he had? She was fifty-seven, and it was true what people said. She looked young for her age. She celebrated Fiadh's birthday, after all, not her own. Maybe she was really fifty-six, or fifty-five even. Could she have been a stepmother if Sterling had lived? When she was pregnant with Maeve, she'd secretly wondered whether William would save her or the baby she carried if something went wrong during childbirth. She kept her question to herself, though she imagined telling William to choose the baby over her, secretly hoping he would choose her anyway. What kind of woman was she, to have such a terrible thought! And then there were pregnancies she wasn't able to carry to term. She'd feared it was punishment for her selfishness. Her life, her family, might have been so different if she'd chosen different paths. But it had not gone a different way. Only this one. The maple was beginning to leaf out. New life, like Molly, ready to burst. There must be a phrase for when a woman is near birth, like a leaf bud waiting for spring.

Faye pulled the fitted sheet over Molly's bare mattress. Maybe clean sheets would help. That morning, Molly had been so uncomfortable, the baby kicking at her relentlessly. She had no sense of modesty, that girl, pulling up her shirt, leaning into the sofa cushions to rub her exposed belly with nut cream Wendy had given her. "I didn't sleep at all," she complained. "Please baby, please baby, please baby!"

"It's bad?" Faye asked.

Molly rolled her head, stretching her neck and jaw. "She's right there. If I could—" She paused and her teeth clenched—"stick my fingers in, I could touch her and take care of her and make whatever is bothering her better." She held her belly with both hands like a medicine ball, shushing the baby.

Faye had carefully twisted a lock of Molly's hair around her finger before letting it spring back. Oh, if only a mother's touch could solve all a child's problems! "If it's any consolation at all, you look good. You're almost there." She hesitated but brought up the sore subject anyway. Molly had been clear. She would do this on her own. The father was out of the picture. "We can still call Leo . . ."

Molly yanked her shirt down. "Will you please—I'm begging you, Mom. You and Maeve and Daddy. Wendy! All of you. Please, drop it."

"I'm sorry. I am. It's just—"

"No, it's not just anything! God, I can't believe I'm here." Molly had stuck it out as long as possible in DC, but those people she'd been living with—"the hippies," Molly called them—had told her she couldn't live there with a baby because a baby couldn't follow the quiet hour rules, of all things. And finding a new place that she could afford when she was seven months pregnant had proved impossible. Her petulance, while understandable, was hard to take.

"We're not so bad . . ."

"I don't know what I'm doing, Mom. I'm not you. Maeve was right. I don't even like kids. I hardly like anyone."

"Oh, Pix. That's the hormones talking. You're being too hard on yourself."

"Am I? What if I'm terrible at it? That's why you all want me to call Leo. You think I'll fail at this."

She fell into Faye's arms then, her little girl, suddenly so at odds with the world. Was it sudden? Molly had been fighting for so long. Maybe motherhood would be the thing that would correct Molly's course, though it was true that Faye had her doubts. "You'll be happy to have her," Faye said, rubbing Molly's shoulders. "Like I was happy to have you girls. We both were."

Molly cinched herself in. "I'm going to find Dad."

Faye smoothed the flat sheet, then whipped the quilt into place. From the window, she could make out Molly's splayed legs now, stretched into the sun that flooded through the white-and-black barn. Only William could keep her from blowing her top these days. He had stripped the crib that Maeve used for both Dylan and Opal, giving it a fresh coat of white paint for the little girl Molly would have any day. He'd walked her through every detail of his process, lulling her like a hypnotist. Since his heart attack he'd honed that gift, her husband. The gift of keeping his cool. It seemed nothing could rattle him anymore.

"She doesn't want advice," he said, when she'd come home bearing news that she was not going back to college after all. Instead, she was having a baby. "Not from you and definitely not from Maeve. Her little wheels are spinning up there."

The revelations had happened right on top of each other—boom, boom, boom—the thing with Maeve and Wendy, then Molly calling to say she was done with being a nanny, that she found another job and was staying in DC. Faye had doubted both of her daughters. But Maeve had proven her wrong—so wrong. She had been steady through the breakup with Sam, both of them so patient with Dylan and Opal. And the transition of Wendy into their lives had been . . . well, it had been fine. More than fine. Faye was charmed by Wendy, her ease, her air of assumption that she could be herself and that everyone could come around at their own pace. She was as fresh as those clean sheets. Now, if only Molly could surprise her too.

Faye sat for a moment, pressed Molly's pillow to her face. She couldn't hear a single sound except the gentle buzzing in her own ears. Soon enough there would be baby noises and baby smells again in the house. Oh. And laughter! God how she missed Molly's laugh! She never wanted to admit to herself that maybe she and William had let Molly down, that maybe they shouldn't have been so quick to dismiss her sullenness. It was so long ago, when her laughter faded.

She straightened a bobby pin that had come loose behind her ear, fighting the urge to flop down and swaddle herself in the freshly laundered bedding. "Pshhh," she said, flipping her hand. No time for nonsense. No time to dwell in the past. Molly needed her.

CHAPTER TWENTY-SIX

1993: Mid-Coast Maine

Molly woke from shallow sleep to the sound of Nola Wren mewling. She stumbled to get to the baby before her tortuous crying began. When Molly got any sleep at all, it was in the only thing that kept her cool, a white poplin nightgown smocked with ribbon that she bought when she was with Leo, thinking it was romantic and sweet and virginal. She hushed the baby, writhing now as Molly changed her soaked diaper. Moonlight doused the yellow room in blue, and Molly felt dunked in it. She looked down. What had she stepped in? What was on her feet? At first, she thought she'd bled through her nightgown. But it was her own milk, summoned by the baby's cries, cascading onto her bare feet. "No, no, no," she whispered, hurrying to finish the diapering, to get to the rocking chair to feed the baby before what milk she had went to waste.

She held her boob like a sandwich and tickled the baby's lip with her nipple. "Pastrami on rye," she tempted. "BLT . . ." But the baby squirmed and wailed, snapping at the nipple like a turtle. Her breasts would never be sexy again. She felt like a dairy cow, a wet nurse, reduced to what her body could produce to sustain another person, which, it turned out, was not enough.

She propped the baby with a pillow, trying to balance her weight and get that nipple into the mouth. Finally, Nola Wren accepted it, reluctantly sipping and whimpering. Molly's shoulders burned, but she couldn't risk adjusting herself and jarring the baby free. She put her head back, closed her eyes. She was stretched thin, tenterhooked.

Wendy had come over to the house with Maeve the day Molly brought Nola Wren home. Everyone was together, including Dylan, Opal, and even Sam, each of them taking turns holding the baby, counting tiny toes, nibbling tiny fingers. Molly collapsed into a chair next to Wendy and mentioned she'd had a lactation consultant in the hospital.

"Plenty of new moms have trouble breastfeeding," Wendy said. "It's not your fault."

"Tell that to my sister. She managed it with both kids. If I can't do this—I mean, it's literally what boobs are for—what good am I?" She knew she sounded hysterical—God, that word—but she felt that way. "Plus, I'm bleeding to death."

Wendy went right out and got Molly heavy-duty pads and put them in the upstairs bathroom. While Molly practically wept at the gesture, it also left her feeling shut out and wanting, witness to the kind of life she herself would never have.

Maeve had told Molly breastfeeding was the easiest thing and cheap too. No formula to mix, no bottles to clean. "Trust me," she said. "It's a breeze." But where was Maeve now? Where was Maeve when she needed her? Sleeping with Wendy Walker at the cove house while Molly was here, alone, trying not to wake up her mom and dad (the last thing she needed was advice from them), trying not to disturb the ghost that haunted this place. No one else noticed or, if they did, they didn't mention it. But the white paint on the section of railing in front of Maeve's door had a different quality. It lacked richness of years and layered coats and had a blue tint, skim versus whole milk. When Molly ran her scarred hand along it, she felt the texture change, felt it grab at her then let go, the way Glenda had grabbed her wrist at the bar.

Her head snapped forward, and she jerked awake when the baby unlatched and slipped down her relaxed arm. "I've got you. I've got you," she whispered.

Molly could not pinpoint when it started. The lowts, she told herself, opposite of heights. It simply washed over her, liquid despair. She would sit down to nurse, turn on the music, drink a glass of cool water the way Wendy had instructed, and hold Nola Wren to her breast. The moment the baby latched on, Molly was swallowed. If she had been on top of a tall building, she would have jumped. *Do it,* the voice told her, though she had nowhere to jump to, no height around her, only her child at her breast, the lowts choking her like quicksand. And Nola Wren would suck away, extract all life from her, until it was over and Molly could hold the baby, rub her back, and catch her own breath.

When the baby rejected her, Molly assumed her milk tasted like her body felt—sad, bitter, and regretful. Ashamed.

Nola Wren was nine weeks old the day Molly stepped out of the house while the baby slept. She walked along the boundary of the property along a decrepit fence rail. Asters and Queen Anne's Lace bloomed wild in the field behind the barn. Honeybees with pollen-dipped legs moved heavily at her feet. How long would it take to die if she were to lie down here, to sink into the soil and wait for weeds to sprout through the knobs of her spine, storm her gated ribs, eat through her broken heart? She willed her feet to keep moving. The baby would wake soon and need to be fed.

Back in the house, Molly could hear crying upstairs. She wiped the yellow field from her shoes and climbed the stairs to the howling baby and her beet-red face. She unbuttoned her shirt, picked up Nola Wren, and cradled her gently, shushing, shushing. She'd left a half glass of water on the table next to the rocker. She took a drink as she sat down and sighed so deeply she wasn't sure she wanted to take another breath. Her mouth hung open as the baby tugged on her nipple, on her spirit, on what rooted her to her own life. She could almost see it, slender as steam, wisping out of her mouth into thin air around her.

"I can't do this," she said to no one. She released Nola Wren gently. Her nipple, cork-like and scarlet, throbbed in the open air. She put the baby on her shoulder and stood. She became aware that she was bare-breasted, standing in the room she'd occupied when she was a child, before . . . She could imagine that little girl staring at her, baffled by the person she was seeing now. *Go downstairs, wait for Mom.* That was the plan. She needed a break, that was all. She was overwhelmed. She would go for a drive, to the beach, to the lake. Anywhere. Get her head straight. At the top of the stairs, she hesitated, held in place by shackling hands coming up from the floor. Over and over, O'Kane went through the rails. She closed her eyes. When she opened them, something worse happened, something horrible.

She pictured it like she intended to go through with it, her sweet girl sailing over, tiny arms backstroking, eyes in that dream place of wonder, asking, "How could you?"

Molly's feet unstuck, and she ducked back into her room, Nola Wren safely on her shoulder. "I'm so sorry," she said, over and over, tears drenching the soft spot on the top of her child's head that throbbed with heart and blood and real life. She had fought, and she had lost.

Over the next month, Molly declared herself done with breastfeeding. She pumped enough to relieve the engorgement but bought baby bottles and fed Nola Wren formula instead. She would not subject her daughter to whatever poison was bottled up inside her. She let her parents feed Nola Wren, liberating herself, distancing herself. She took Nola Wren to Maeve's house, watched how sweet Dylan and Opal were with her, how Wendy and Maeve doted on her. Molly was in awe at the way her sister deftly moved between mothering an adolescent girl and a pubescent boy and a newborn baby that wasn't her own. "I really admire you," she told Maeve. "I mean it. I wish I had what you have." What she couldn't bring herself to tell Maeve was that she missed her. She missed everything about being a little girl and being Maeve's little sister. Maeve hugged her the way she once had, enveloping her from behind. "You have no idea how much that means to me."

She told Maeve and Wendy she was invited to spend Labor Day weekend in Portland with an old college friend. Just until Monday. Would they, could they, watch the baby?

"Go. Go!" they said.

When the bus arrived in Portland, Molly thought about getting off, spending the weekend there, making a friend, then going home. But she'd bought the ticket to go through, knowing she would. In Boston, she switched to a westbound bus, afraid that if she continued toward New York that she might get off in New Haven. She needed time and distance and nothingness. The bus hummed beneath her, racing through a tunnel of trees like water in a garden hose.

A boy in his early teens boarded the bus in Syracuse and took the seat next to her. He wore a John Deere hat over hair so short Molly couldn't see the color of it. Pink and pimpled, he grinned widely at her as the bus pulled out of the station.

"Ridin' the dog," he said wisely, an old soul.

"I'm sorry?"

"You know, riding the dog. The Greyhound. I'm heading back to Rochester. Go back and forth all the time, riding the dog. How about you?"

"Oh, right," Molly said. "The dog. Yeah, west I guess. I'm not sure."

"An adventure, then," the boy said. "I've got an extra bologna sandwich if you're hungry. My grandma makes me a whole bag every time I come.

She don't think my dad feeds me right even though I tell her I'm naturally skinny, is all."

Molly hadn't eaten since she bought an ice cream bar at a stop back in Massachusetts. Bologna sounded good. "Sure," she said. "Thanks."

The boy handed her the sandwich and a bag of barbecue potato chips. "They're good smashed right between the bread. Mixes with the mustard and mayonnaise. That's the way I like it. My mom likes it that way, too, but she can't really eat right no more on account of the stroke. I visit her with my grandparents in the nursing home. My name's Brandon, by the way. We don't got to be friends or anything but good to know who you're sitting with."

"I'm sorry," Molly said, and the boy shrugged. She crushed her chips on top of the bologna, squished the whole thing back together. "My grandpa did that, too, with his potato chips. Molly," she said, before taking a bite.

"Anyway," Brandon said. "Nice to be riding the dog with you. Usually it's me and a bunch of losers."

"How do you know I'm not a loser?"

"You been on the dog as often as I have, you can spot a loser easy."

She wanted to ask Brandon what he saw in her but thought better of it. The boy didn't need her bullshit.

When she finished her sandwich, she balled up the plastic wrap and stuck it in the seat crack. Brandon was turned around now, chatting up someone she couldn't see over the head rest. She pulled out her aging Walkman, put her headphones on, and pressed play. Leo's mixtape. She'd almost left it behind in her old cigar box. But she'd grabbed it at the last minute, in case she actually went through with her plan.

At the cove house, she had held Nola Wren close, searing an impression of the baby into her before handing her off to Maeve. *This is me fighting for you, I swear.*

"Have fun," Wendy said, hugging Molly in her hugger way, as if everyone welcomed intimacy. *See me and stop me from doing this,* Molly wanted to yell, returning Wendy's hug uncharacteristically. When

Wendy pulled away, she took a gift bag off the table and handed it to Molly. "I know it's been hard, and I don't want to overstep. But it might help to write about your feelings. Even a single word or phrase can be empowering. Give it a try while you're away."

Molly opened the floral notebook, flipped to the first page, blank as her mind. She didn't know what she was chasing or running from. Didn't know how or why she'd done what she'd done except for what she told herself. *You are saving a life.* She was not a poet, not religious, not a deep thinker or even a caring person, for that matter. *I am . . . , I am . . .* She wrote down how she filled in the blank. *Riding the Dog.*

CHAPTER TWENTY-SEVEN

1995: Mid-Coast Maine

Faye kept two pieces of lined paper taped on the wall next to the telephone. The first was a long list of typed numbers that included the fire station, the police, Sam's business phone number, the number for the cove house, which hadn't changed since her father lived there. She had Maeve's number at the law office, Wendy's number at the OB-GYN office where she worked now, the numbers for Dylan's junior high school and Opal's elementary school. In blue ink off to the side, William had handwritten the number of his estate-sale buddy Noel Delaney who owned an antiques shop in town. He'd also jotted down the number for the pizza place that would deliver.

It took all of them to care for Nola Wren. Faye and William babysat on the days Maeve and Wendy's work overlapped. Dylan and Opal came through in a pinch too. Even Sam helped when he was with his kids. The pediatrician's number was there above the family doctor.

The other piece of paper was a reminder:

COLLECT CALL
"Pixie" = All Okay
"Molly" = Please pick up

Faye, her hand on the receiver, was about to call Noel to find out whether William had left the antique store yet. She looked at the numbers. It was her life there, everyone she loved and cared about. Except Molly. Maeve had a number she could call to get a message to Molly if it was a real emergency. And Faye had had it, too, for a while. But seeing it made her want to call, made her want to force Molly to explain herself. *How could you walk away from your own child?* Other questions burned at her, resurfacing wounds she thought were healed. *How could you give her away like she was a thing and not a person? How does any mother walk away from her child? What makes a mother give up? What kind of mother turns her back on a child?* And even deeper questions that Faye could hardly allow herself to consider. *Did I do this to you? Is this my fault? Am I looking for absolution for my own sins? Comfort for my own pain?*

The last time Faye called the number, she'd asked Molly the same questions of why and how. Molly had given the stock answer. "I told you. I thought I might harm her, Mom." But that time, Faye had persisted until Molly said something that made it crystal clear. "I had a vision that I threw Nola Wren over the railing and that she died on the floor. What would you have done if you were me? If you thought leaving would save her life, wouldn't you go too?" Faye handed the phone to William, too stunned to say another word.

While William sat at the kitchen table, the phone cradled in the crook of his neck, Faye had eavesdropped on the rest of the conversation from the front hall. He was full of warmth and understanding, acknowledging to his missing daughter how hard it must have been to leave her own flesh and blood, how he understood that she didn't know why she'd done such a thing, that yes, yes, he knew she'd been so afraid, that yes, he'd heard how hard it can be on a woman, childbirth, especially if she was already dealing with loss—"that Leo sounds like a nice young man"—and no, no, he wasn't trying to tell her what to do, only that he loved her and wanted her to know they were taking good care of Nola Wren, and that, "Molly, Pix, darling," that everyone missed her, everyone wanted her to be safe out there, and they all wanted her to come home as soon as she was able. "Molly, you're so young," he'd said, unwittingly knocking Faye to the ground. "Oh, honey! Don't cry. It's okay. I know you weren't trying to hurt anyone. No one blames you. No, Mom doesn't blame you, honey. I promise. We know you were only doing what you thought was right at the time. Fear and heartbreak are powerful, powerful emotions. You did what you thought you had to do to keep the two of you safe. Yes, I know. Even if that meant leaving without her. No, honey. It's never too late to come back. But do it as soon as you can. As soon as you can. We all love you. We do. Okay, honey. Goodbye for now."

A memory had erupted, buried so well and deep Faye could not recall ever having thought on it at all, a memory so old and new that she was not sure it was real. It was her own mother, her real Mutti, in a room so distant Faye had to close her eyes to see any details. There was a red chair, velvet, and her mother in a yellow dress, her eyes sunken and hollow and colorless. Faye could feel her mother's hand, gentle on her cheek. She could smell her unwashed skin, see the stains and wear on the once-lovely dress. "I have to go," she'd said, though Faye couldn't be sure because, in this memory, her mother spoke English, a language she hadn't known. The memory must be distorted, she reasoned. And yet. Her mother walked out the door. Faye waited for it. The click of the lock. She'd thought it was their mother who'd locked them in, left them for dead. But William's words to Molly: *You did what you thought you had to do to keep the two of you safe.* She remembered. It was Elisabeth who got up from the couch and bolted the door, Elisabeth who said they must stay put and wait for Mutti to return, even as bombs exploded around them. Faye felt it like a slap on her face. *Wake up! Your mother did not abandon you. She did not lock you and your sister in, she did not leave you to die alone. She simply went out—probably in search of food—like she had many times before. She left you to keep you safe. And you left Elisabeth. And now Molly left Nola Wren.*

How desperately Faye had wished in that moment that she had one complete memory of her German childhood that did not include war. But even the softest fragments had faded with the yellow of

Mutti's dress and the velvet of a once-fine chair. Mutti and Vati must have known love. They brought two girls into the world as a monster was gaining power, after all. They must have had hope that love would endure.

William had found Faye cross-legged on the floor in the very same spot where she'd watched Conor O'Kane die, crying tears for herself and her daughters as she had done that night, hoping silence would keep them safe. "You heard all that?" he asked, crouching next to her.

Faye nodded, unable to even speak. And, like he had that night years before, William pulled her to standing and took her in his arms. "It's like she's fighting a war, our Molly," he said. "We have to hope eventually it will end, and she can forgive herself."

Faye spent every moment since trying to minimize casualties. That's why she had rewritten her list of phone numbers that she stared at now, left off Molly's emergency contact. In return, Molly—or rather "Pixie"—called every couple of weeks to let them know she was fine.

And the baby, Faye thought now, how she had grown among them all, a wild daisy! She learned to walk, to use a spoon, to say one word then two then to speak her toddled sentences. Her home was at the cove house with Maeve and Wendy, Nola Wren—fair skin, hair black and curly, with Molly's eyes only blue as flame.

At the sound of the nasally honk of the pickup horn, Faye startled, set the receiver down again. She and William had talked about taking a drive up to Camden or maybe into Boothbay. Maeve and Wendy had Nola Wren for the weekend, and Sam was camping with Dylan and Opal. But from the back porch, Faye could see that William had made other plans.

After he retired, he built himself a wood shop out in the barn, where he tinkered with his own designs for stools and did some restorations with Noel. His knuckles ached with arthritis, but Faye knew how much he loved finding treasures under layers of paint and rotted veneers. Noel sold the better pieces at his antique shop, but over the last few years the rest had stacked up, William's imagination outstripped by the limits of time and the aches in his back. His simple painted milking stools were hits at the farmer's market that buzzed with tourists in the summer and early fall. William had sold out for the season two weeks earlier.

"I know what you're thinking," he said when Faye came out onto the back porch. "We can unload this in no time, then take our drive. I couldn't resist. Noel and I went out to that estate sale I told you about, and would you look at that? Matching Morris chairs, and they're not in that bad of shape. I'll strip them and see if I can get Sandy to make me a couple of cushions. We could keep them or give them to Maeve and Sam—er, Maeve and Wendy. But maybe Sam would like them too. Right?"

"William Sullivan," Faye said. "Have you not looked in your barn? You could open your own antique store. Forget Noel all together."

"I guess I best not tell you about the box of glass and figurines in there. Told you keeping that stack of newspaper in the truck would come in handy. *Irish Times* to the rescue! I'll get them unwrapped so you can take a look, see if there's anything you want before I let Noel have a crack at it." He was like her father in that way. His devotion to *The Irish Times*. How many conversations had he started over the years with, "I saw in the *Times* . . ."

At almost seventy, his hair had thinned some, had gone to white, though the waves were still there. He had the belly of a man who drank beer, laugh lines of a man who enjoyed his friends, ruddy neck and forearms of a man who spent time outdoors.

The house phone rang across the yard. William jumped. "I'll get it. Hang on." He'd stopped adding, "Could be Molly," though Faye knew it was his thought. He was quickest to defend her, likeliest to bring her up, the one who said he prayed every night for her safe return. They weren't big believers in God, yet William told Faye he said this one prayer. "Just in case."

When William didn't come out, she followed him into the house. He was sitting at the kitchen table, hands on his lap.

Her first thought went to Nola Wren. An accident. "William, what is it? What happened?"

"It was Molly. She says she's coming home, Faye. Our girl is coming home."

CHAPTER TWENTY-EIGHT

1995: Boston, Massachusetts

As the train left Providence, Molly pulled a worn notebook from her backpack, the floral cover bent and tattered now, the pages warped with two years of ink and tears. One last stop, and she would be home. She had been all over the country, passed time in moments and months, hurt herself and healed herself in a thousand ways. She had never meant to stay gone so long.

It had been difficult at first to write anything, thinking it would need to be profound in case someone found her body somewhere and that the notebook would eventually get back to Nola Wren. She had starts and stops—dear baby, dear daughter, dear Nola Wren, dear Mom and Dad, dear Maeve, dear Leo, dear Leo, dear Leo. The looking back killed her. And looking forward was too grim. So, the notebook became a day-to-day account of what had mattered to her when anything mattered at all. It was all there now as she thumbed through the pages.

Her friend Camille had married a graphic artist and lived in an A-frame house on a mountain lake outside of Asheville. It was her phone number that Molly had given to her parents and Maeve. Besides her family, Camille was the only person who knew about Nola Wren. From the moment Molly boarded the Greyhound, she'd never spoken to a soul, except for her own in the pages of the journal, about the baby she'd left behind.

In Seattle, she had worked in a coffee shop, dated a guy who looked like one of her grandfather's dead Irish poets—wire-rimmed glasses, sweeping bangs, blank eyes. She was convinced he would kill her for no good reason. One night, they were supposed to go to a grunge bar with friends, but instead he drove her deep into the woods. He stopped the car in the middle of the road. "Get out," he said, not meanly, and she did, though later she wondered if this was a kind of death wish to go along with whatever scheme your killer had dreamed up. But he'd only wanted to show her the dam, how the river somersaulted over and swirled with starlight, he said, like a Van Gogh and he'd pronounced the *gh* like an *f* and she knew that would be their last date because she hadn't wanted to die—not then, not at all—and she'd felt so close to dying there. She would replay it for weeks, how the shove would feel on the receiving end, what shock her face would register, what thoughts she might have while flailing in the indigo air, whether she would live and then die or simply die.

In San Francisco, she got high on ecstasy and picked up a guy on New Year's Eve with luscious rock-star hair who told her he'd enlisted in the marines. She woke up in an apartment in Oakland, and it was 1994. When he suggested dim sum, she rubbed bar soap along her eyelids to remove smeared mascara then slipped back into the sparkly dress she'd gone out in the night before. "Wok of shame," she'd joked. In the daylight and sober, she knew for certain he wasn't going into the marines, but that was okay. She'd told him she was an accountant and that her name was Summer. They got Chinese food. It was easier to pretend they weren't both liars. He walked her to the BART station, and she kissed him on the cheek.

"Keep your head low, Marine."

"Good luck with the numbers, Summer."

She taped her fortune into her journal.

Your deeds today will be your memories tomorrow.

She'd written about her fear that her body gave her away, that anyone could tell she'd carried a baby and would wonder where that baby had gone. Alone, she would stare at it in the mirror, from the front and side, remember the way her waist disappeared, how her breasts had colonized the rest of her. Now, her stomach was flat, though her hips remained wider, a door jammed open. She'd managed to empty herself out and that had been satisfying, like she'd decluttered a hoarder's squalid house. She wondered how her face had changed, what strangers might see there, whether her family or Leo would even recognize her. Nola Wren wouldn't remember her at all.

In Santa Monica, that emptiness started to take a new shape. She wrote less about herself and more about Nola Wren and what she must be like now, notes from brief phone calls that helped Molly glean a picture of her baby, her little girl. She would see kids at the beach and imagine Nola Wren building sandcastles. She wrote her thoughts down, careful not to fantasize too much, to be practical. She wrote down something Yarrow said to her when she left the hippie house. "One day happiness will sneak up on you, Molly. Don't be surprised."

Her last night there, she'd stood alone on the pier at the end of a long shift serving umbrella drinks at a beach bar. She'd been in Southern California only a few months and marveled how every day seemed the same. Endless summer. The roller coaster was still, the night wind off the ocean lifted sand into swirls around her. She could not get much further away from her past unless she dove off the pier into the Pacific. She could remember a time when she might have welcomed that, but not anymore. She'd grown tired of following a sinking sun.

She went down to the beach, sat in the sand facing west, and thought about sunrise over the Atlantic. At first light, she stripped to her underwear and swam out into the surf. She was alive. She had survived her own self, and that was enough for now. When she left the beach, she'd felt a shift, like that headwind she'd been facing down for so long could be at her back. It was time to turn around. On the sidewalk, a beach bum, shirtless and shoeless, sat on a surfboard that had seen better days. His hair was twisted into salted locs. "Hey, babe," he said. "I dig that jacket. Used to have one just like it." He smiled at Molly, hand out. Molly reached into the pocket where she'd shoved bills from the tip jar the night before. "You know what, man? Here," she said, taking the jacket off her back. "Why don't you take this? I don't need it anymore."

With that weight off her, it had been a breeze to finally pawn the last piece of her broken past that she'd clung to: Sideny's flawless diamond bracelet. She was done shouldering blame for what Charlie Grant did to her. She was more than her flaws.

It took her a while, but once she'd made it to Birmingham, Camille pressured her to come up to the lake. "You're super close. We'll smoke weed and watch the Perseids."

She caught a train to Charlotte and the bus to Asheville, where Camille and her husband, Floyd, picked her up.

After dinner—Camille made her own cheesy lasagna now—they'd carried blankets down to the dock. Rimmed with dark pines and darker hills, the slick lake twinkled like star soup, as if it were the source of the light and some great hand had dipped a ladle in, flung galaxies across a black bowl hung upside down. Molly tilted her head, plotting where she ended and the world began. Constellation lines became animated, and Molly saw her own—the place she left behind, her stops along the way, a sail on a heeling boat.

Floyd spread the blankets, and the three of them had lain side-by-side on their backs. The air around them fizzed and crackled as meteors ripped the atmosphere. "Holy shit," Molly gasped. She felt Camille's hand cup hers. She gripped it in alliance as they shouted, "There!" and "There!" each time a star shot past.

"I get letters from Henry. We're buds," Camille whispered. "He and Leo are in Boston now. They work for the same law firm."

Molly turned her head. They were almost mouth-to-mouth. She missed her friend, missed knowing someone by their breath.

"He deserves to know, Moll. You never even gave him a chance. He didn't do anything wrong. You said it yourself. You can't keep running."

ର

After midnight, they went back to the house. Floyd had made up the pull-out sofa, and Molly collapsed face-first into it, then rolled over. Camille sat on the edge.

"I'm glad you're here. You can stay as long as you want. Floyd doesn't care."

"When I was a teenager, my grandfather died, and the last thing he said to me was, 'Go and love.' I was so mad at him for dying. I mean, I was mad at everything. He was always quoting Yeats—it drove my mom nuts. I didn't know that was from a Yeats poem until recently."

"The go and love thing?"

"Yeah. Something about a brown penny. 'I am too young. I am too old.' Something like that," Molly said. "Go and love is way different from love and go. I got so twisted up."

The living room ceiling was popcorned and sprinkled with glitter. Molly blurred her eyes. "I feel like I'm covered in stardust."

"Joni Mitchell said we're all stardust," Camille said.

Molly remembered that night when she was little, when she and Maeve lit sparklers with their mom. For weeks and weeks after she pushed Conor O'Kane over the railing, she'd scrubbed her hands raw, trying to get the feeling of him off her. She'd grabbed the sparkler that night, after it had burned out, seared it into her hand. She'd told her mother that she had seen the ghosts and they scared her, and her mother promised that she'd sent them away and that they wouldn't bother her anymore.

But that was never true. Not for Molly. It didn't matter whether it made sense. Right or wrong, fair or not. She'd never let herself forget. She was beginning to understand that it was in her nature somehow to inflict wounds on herself. She had to untwist herself, set things right.

"I might need to get myself back home," she said. "You know, go and love."

Camille had pressed a piece of paper into her hand then.

As the train pulled into South Station, Molly grazed her finger one last time over the toothy edges where she'd taped that paper down. She could close the journal. She'd stared at the number enough to know it by heart.

Molly checked out of her motel room early, left her bags in a locker at the train station, and made her way to the Public Garden to scope out the post on the bridge where he said they could meet, near the George Washington statue. To kill time, she fell in with a group of tourists and wandered paths through manicured flower beds and dripping willows, past the brass duck family she remembered from a children's book. Another thing she'd missed. She'd never once read to Nola Wren.

On Boylston, she leaned against a wrought iron fence and dug out her journal. She flipped through the pages to one that had a photo booth square of her and Leo taped in it. Black and white and timeless, her head thrown back in laughter, Leo in profile, holding an ice cream cone in his hand. It was the last one in the strip, but she knew the moment, Leo playfully threatening to shove it into her mouth. She put the journal back in her bag and joined the line that formed at the ice cream truck. Two women in front of her chatted, their arms resting on fancy European strollers, Bermuda shorts pressed, hair smooth as hide. Little pink hands poked out of the seats, reaching for each other, babbles coming from under the elaborate canopies. Molly's mind raced along a familiar path. She would buy Nola Wren an ice cream. She would hold her daughter's hand. She would be walking. And talking. She would not recognize her own mother. *Me,* Molly thought. *She won't recognize me.*

She ordered a twist cone and took it back through the gate, her head tilted, tongue mopping the edges to keep it from dripping. When she looked up, he was there, black hair slicked into place, his suit blue as that mountain lake, blue as the Perseid sky. His eyebrows crinkled, his mouth fell slack. "Molly?"

She wanted to throw herself into him, to touch that spot behind his ear. God, she wanted to smell him again. But she stood there in a sundress and sandals, like a girl on vacation, holding an ice cream cone in one hand, balancing her shoulder bag with the other. She couldn't hug him. She couldn't move. "Leo!" She bobbled the ice cream, and it splatted against her wrist, then fell on the ground. "Shit."

He took the cone from her hand and lobbed it into a garbage can. "Let me get you another one. I was headed that way myself. Thought I had time before . . . well. Hi."

"No, no, it's okay." What did it matter? She wiped her hand on her dress seam. She was already a mess. "Hi. It's so good to see you. You look great. Love the suit."

They hugged awkwardly, neither sure how close to get, whether to linger. Molly breathed him in, tried to create a memory for when he was gone.

"Should we sit?" Leo asked.

Guitar music from a busker on the bridge glided along the water with the swan boats. They took an open bench, sat in silence for a long moment. "Your hair's shorter."

Molly touched it awkwardly, like she was straightening a wig. "Yeah." She steepled her hands, held them to her lips, then pressed them along with her sundress between her thighs. "Leo, listen. I have to spit this out before I lose my nerve."

"Okay."

She pivoted so she could face him. "So, like I told you on the phone, Camille told me you and Henry were living in Boston. She gave me your address. I walked by your apartment yesterday. And your work." She squeezed her eyes closed, embarrassed. "Yesterday. And the day before. And the day before that." She opened them to see his expression.

"Seriously?" He shrugged, shook his head. "You should have called right away."

Molly nodded. Her knees and feet jiggled with energy. "I hoped I could, you know, bump into you. I thought it would be easier."

He bent to her hanging head. "What's going on? I mean, I haven't heard from you in, what? Almost three years? You made it pretty clear that we were done. And suddenly you have to find me and it's here, in Boston."

Those bright blue eyes. Maybe if Nola Wren had looked like Molly, she would have felt like Molly's too. Instead, she had been a constant reminder of Molly's failures. She put a hand on Leo's arm, sat up straight. "I'm so sorry for the way I left. It was unfair to you and selfish of me. I let you think I was, you know, a fun-loving party girl, but I'm actually a pretty scared person. I didn't want you to know that. I've been scared for a really long time. I'm still scared."

"Were you afraid of me?" He looked genuinely hurt.

"No! Not ever. Not for one minute." She could tell him, she could, about Conor O'Kane, about her hands and the way his body disappeared but left a mark on the rug, how he haunted her. She could tell him about Glenda, the way she'd seen through Molly straight to the brokenness in her, how she'd marked her. She could tell him how she was a soiled home-wrecker and thief. She could tell him all those things about her that were awful, that made her into the person she was when she met him, the person who kept his child from him, who then went and abandoned her anyway.

"Then what?"

You are more than your flaws. She thought of her grandfather sitting in the big chair by the stone fireplace at the cove house, weaving his stories. She wished she had his gift.

"Do you remember that first night at The Wren, and I told you about my magic carpet, when I was a kid? How I would pretend I was somewhere else, someone, some when? I wish I had a magic carpet right now, and I could go back and get this right. I did not know, I swear, when you left for law school. I thought I was doing you a favor. I didn't think . . . I guess I didn't think I was good enough for you, and I didn't want you to figure it out on your own."

"Molly. That's ridiculous."

"Hold on. There's more." Her teeth ached, and her ears rang. "Leo, I was pregnant. When you left, I was pregnant, and I didn't know it yet."

He threaded his fingers on top of his head, blew out breath after breath. "You could have told me. I would have—" He shook his head. "I don't know what I would have done, honestly. I'm sorry you had to go through that alone."

"I had the baby, Leo. A little girl."

It was like they were locked in a soundproof booth, all the noise, the laughter, dogs barking, horns honking, cabbies shouting, sirens, whistles, motors racing. All the sounds of the city were sucked up, suspended in some motionless, airless space.

Leo stiffened as he turned to her. The look he gave her was the worst she could imagine. He was horrified. "What? Where is she?" He looked around like he suspected a nanny lurked nearby, holding the hand of a black-haired child in a blue dress.

Molly, crying now, was unable to answer that question, not fully. Because the truth was that Molly didn't know their child either. "I left her with my family. In Maine. She's in Maine."

Leo covered his face, bent at the waist. Sobbing broke through.

Molly clenched as months of unwept tears fell and fell. She dropped her shoulders. Let them fall. What had she done? She placed a hand on Leo's bent back, apologized over and over.

He sat up, his face red, eyes swollen. "What's her name?" He asked like he needed to know so he could search for her, his daughter gone missing.

Molly had never told anyone the significance. It was a reminder of what was good. That was all. "Nola Wren. Her name's Nola Wren."

Leo closed his eyes. "Molly. Jesus. Nola? Like New Orleans. And The Wren? Why wouldn't you tell me? I mean obviously you cared, or you wouldn't have named her that. Seriously. What the fuck? How could you?"

"I thought about naming her Doria, but then I thought 'What if we get back together?' I mean, I know that isn't possible, but Doria Doria would be a crazy name."

"You know I'm not talking about the name."

"I'm sorry. I know. There are reasons, but there's no excuse, you know? And I'm sorry to spring this on you now." She held up her hands. "I don't need anything. I don't want anything. And I know it's completely fucked up and I'm sorry. I am so sorry. You have no idea. But I had to tell you. Before I went back."

Leo checked his watch. "I have a meeting, and I can't miss it. Fuck." He was trembling, biting at his lip, flexing his hands. "Can I see her? I mean, I have a million questions and no time to ask them. Why didn't you bring her? No, no. That would have been stupid. Yeah, I wouldn't have done that." He shifted and paced in front of the bench. "Are you with someone? Is that it? Does he know the baby isn't his?" He threw his head back. "Fuck. Is she okay? Like, healthy?"

Molly could see scenarios washing over him, drenching him in fear and possibility. She stood, took his arm, and stared him down until he was calmer. *Don't look back. Don't look ahead. Be in this moment.* "She's perfect. She's fine. There's no one else. But there is something I need to explain."

How could she tell him about her years away, what it was to sink so low. She remembered seeing palm trees for the first time, daybreak by the pier in Santa Monica, fishermen throwing lines into the surf, the stillness of the sleeping roller coaster. "Have you ever been to California?"

CHAPTER TWENTY-NINE

1995: Mid-Coast Maine

Maeve tossed a rubber duck into the blow-up pool, and Nola Wren pounced on it, splashing water onto the grass. The crunch of tires on fresh peastone made her look up. Her father's truck pulled in next to Maeve's car. They'd said they were taking a weekend off from grandparenting. She did an inventory, tried to follow everyone's advice and not jump to tragedy.

When Molly first left, Maeve was genuinely afraid for her sister, convinced she'd had some sort of breakdown, that she might harm herself. "Stop imagining the worst possible scenario. Life is much more mundane," Wendy said. "Think dull thoughts." But the weekend stretched into weeks and then months, and then it was winter and it was enough to worry about keeping the driveway plowed and the cars running and getting the kids to school and the baby over to her parents' place. That first winter had been a game of musical chairs—who slept where, who picked up whom. Maeve worried someone would accidentally leave Nola Wren in a car, pictured her freezing in the darkness while the rest of them sat by a fire, certain she was in the other house. More than once, Maeve had called her parents when Nola Wren was there to make sure she was safe. "That child is the most accounted for, most cared for child on earth, Maeve. You worry too much," her mother said. Even two years later, Maeve's disgust at Molly's behavior reared. Dylan and Opal were growing like weeds, both strong and capable, but she worried about them every day, worried when they were with Sam, worried when they were on their own. She couldn't imagine how Molly could be so selfish. The only grace Maeve could give Molly was by reminding herself that her sister didn't even know her own child, couldn't know how perfect she was, how a child can complete a circle you didn't even know was missing a piece. Nola Wren had become that for Maeve and Wendy.

Her mom got out of the truck, made a beeline for Nola Wren, who rolled herself around in the water.

"Look at you swimming!" Faye said.

"What's wrong, Mom? Why are you here?"

"Nola Wren, take Grandma in, and let's have some lemonade," Faye said, holding her arms out for the little girl.

"You're gonna get soaked, Mom. Let me get her." Maeve grabbed a towel and hoisted Nola Wren onto her hip. William came to her side, kissed the child who squirmed into his waiting arms like a dripping fish.

"There's Grandpa's girl!" He pushed her skyward, and she giggled, then collapsed onto his shoulder. He looked around. "No Wendy?"

"She's at the grocery. What's going on? You two are making me nervous," Maeve said. She expected her mother to tell her to relax in that way of hers, as if she didn't spend time on pins and needles, as if she didn't tense up and disappear into her own thoughts. Instead, her face softened, and Maeve instantly thought *cancer*.

"Let's go inside and talk," Faye said.

On the screen porch, Maeve sat dumbfounded by the news. "All of a sudden, and we're supposed to, what?" She stared at Nola Wren playing nearby in her plastic garden, crawling through the hole, opening and closing the gate, checking for mail in the red box. Maeve whispered, "Give her back? This is ludicrous. No. This is a goddamned nightmare!"

Of course, she knew that Molly was Nola Wren's mother, but Molly had also abandoned her. And Maeve and Wendy had talked. Maeve could adopt Nola Wren legally, forget this casual guardian business. They were raising her. Why not make it official? It had been a gift for her and Wendy, a child they could raise together who would be theirs. "She can't waltz back into our lives. It isn't right."

"Nola Wren is two. She'll adjust. Kids are resilient," Faye said through tight teeth.

"You don't actually believe that, Mom. I can see it in your eyes," Maeve said. "You're scared. You don't trust that Molly has changed any more than I do. And what about me and Wendy? We have poured ourselves into that little girl. We're the ones who love her. Oh, I want to scream, I'm so frustrated." Maeve flared her hands as if she could make sparks fly from them. "One: She's snotty. Two: Ir-re-sponsible. Three: Unemployed, I'm guessing. Four: Homeless."

Faye interrupted. "Maeve, she's not homeless. She'll stay with us until she's back on her feet. You girls always have a home with us. Always. Strike that from your list."

"So, does that mean she's taking—" She shook her head in disbelief. "Five!" she shouted, jutting out her chin. "And I'm sorry, but look at that whole nanny thing. No way she told us the whole story there. Five: To that point. She makes bad, bad decisions, Mom. Six: We all told her to tell Leo. Every one of us. Call Leo. If she had called"—her voice dropped back down to a whisper—"Nola Wren's father, maybe none of this would have happened, and we wouldn't be in this situation. Wendy is going to absolutely flip out."

"Maeve," William said. "Stop with the lists. You're not being fair. We have to accept things as they come, and your sister is coming home. Lord knows, no one made lists about you or Wendy."

Maeve shot her mother daggers at that one. She was pretty sure that Faye had made lists.

"We are more than a list of our flaws. We have to focus on what's right for our little girl here. That's what matters now."

"Dad, that's all we've done for two years."

As if on cue, Nola Wren, still in her strawberry swimsuit, climbed into William's lap and leaned sleepily into his chest, her hand drifting up to stroke the ruddy stubble.

"How much time do we have?" Maeve asked, slumping into her chair.

"Before she gets here? She said she'd be here Friday night, if that's what you mean."

Maeve stood, pulled a dozing Nola Wren from William's arms. "I need to get her out of this swimsuit and put her down for a nap. And for your information, I meant how much time do I have left to spend with this child who I have raised and loved. Molly will take her away from all of us. Maybe not Friday but soon. It's only a matter of time now. The clock's ticking. You better get used to the idea."

After bath and story time, Maeve and Wendy tucked in Nola Wren, snuggled her tight with her favorite stuffed bear. Maeve rubbed her back while Wendy sang a lullaby, her voice husky and off-key. Maeve could not grasp how it was possible she could lose something so dear. "I'm going to check the locks," Maeve said. Downstairs, Maeve peered through the glass panes on the new front door, half expecting to see her sister on the other side. She unbolted and bolted the lock again, then went to the kitchen to do the same at the back door, though she knew there was no lock that could keep her family safe now.

Later, Maeve sat up in bed, a novel propped on her knees. She couldn't concentrate. And she felt like a jerk. She wanted Molly to be happy, but why did her happiness have to come at Maeve's expense? Hadn't she sacrificed enough to hold this family together? To give Nola Wren the stability Molly couldn't? The kids were doing well, looking forward to school starting. They had friends, stayed out of trouble for the most part. At thirteen, Dylan was as laid back as his namesake

Bob. Like Sam, he was not easily fazed and, thankfully, not high strung like she was. Opal was hotheaded and too smart for her own good. Both kids were agile and confident, beautifully coordinated, outdoorsy, though neither was interested in basketball nor any organized sports, regardless of how hard she and Wendy tried to nudge them.

And now Nola Wren. Maeve's lips moved as the fight she was having in her head with her sister seeped out.

Wendy came into the bedroom, slipped off her pajama bottoms, and slid in next to Maeve, wearing only a T-shirt and underwear. "Your book's upside down."

Maeve startled, checked the cover. It wasn't. She pushed Wendy playfully, set the book on her side table. She tsked. How could this be happening? Nola Wren belonged to Maeve and Wendy. They had raised her, made a home for her. They were there when she took her first steps, when she said "Mom-ah" and "Mom-e." They'd gotten her through ear infections, croup. They'd bought the baby seats and the strollers while Molly was off doing whatever it was that she was doing. She'd had more sympathy early on, when Wendy figured that Molly's postpartum depression must have been severe, well beyond the "baby blues" that the moms' groups at her OB-GYN practice discussed. Surely she got over it, Maeve reasoned. Surely if she wanted to be Nola Wren's mother, she would have found her way back.

"I was thinking about the kids," Maeve said.

"I know. Me too." Wendy scooted down, turned on her side toward Maeve, who scooted and matched her there. "I'm really sad," Wendy said.

Maeve drew her into an embrace. "Me too, honey. Me too."

After Wendy fell asleep, Maeve tiptoed out of their bedroom. She rattled the gate at the top of the stairs to make sure it was secure, then peeked into the girls' room. The ocean-themed nightlight spun mermaids and dolphins and seashells along navy blue walls. They'd flipped all the rooms around, moved Dylan out of the big room into the smaller one so that Opal could share with Nola Wren. The kids fussed a little, fought a little. But they were the ones who took apart the crib. They were the ones who put the toddler bed together. Dylan, reminding Maeve of her father, shrugged it all off. "No big deal. There's room for all of us." Sam had shocked them with a rare joke about the fact that they would indeed need to paint Dylan's bedroom after all. While she watched Nola Wren sleep—legs and arms splayed like a sea star, ruby lips tapping together, popping invisible bubbles—Maeve tried to imagine a life without her, the shoes she wouldn't buy, the scrapes she wouldn't kiss and make better. She had already played out Nola Wren's first day of kindergarten, how she and Wendy would walk into the school proudly, how they would each hold her hand and explain that Nola Wren had two moms. But this beautiful child actually had three moms, and only one could determine her fate. And Maeve couldn't be that mom, no matter how much she wanted to be.

The next day, after Sam returned from the camping trip with the kids, they sat around the big table at the farmhouse. Opal, eight years old now, picked up Nola Wren and held her on her lap. "No one is taking my sister away from me," she said defiantly.

Faye let out of gust of air, pushed back from the table, and huffed into the kitchen.

"Mom," Maeve said. "You can't walk away. We have to talk this through."

A voice from the kitchen. "Give me a second, Maeve."

"Let your mother get squared away," William said. "And, sweetie?" he said to Opal. "This is going to be a tough one. The last thing we need is another fight on our hands. You're going to have to trust us that we're all thinking about what's best for Nola Wren."

Faye returned, wiping her eyes.

"Mom? You okay?"

"Fine. I'm fine."

Maeve looked around the table. Sam and the kids were grungy from camping and reeked of wood smoke and insect repellent. Dylan laid his arm on the table, rested his head there. Sam put his hand along the back of Dylan's chair. Opal sat next to Dylan, holding Nola Wren, who dropped a spoon into William's shirt pocket. Faye had her hand on top of William's. Wendy was next to Faye, turned slightly in her favor, her back toward Maeve but her chair scooted close. Maeve's instinct was to close the circle, make everyone hold hands or link arms to form a coven or tribe or wagon circle. But they weren't being raided. Molly was coming home, and that had to be a good thing. They would make room for her, but where would she fit in?

Wendy nudged her. Maeve realized she'd been staring at them all, lost in thought.

"It's going to be okay," her mother said, reading her mind. The pain in her voice was so pronounced, everyone turned. "If Molly's coming home, it's because she's trying to forgive herself. And we have to find it in ourselves to forgive her too. After that, we'll have to see."

"Are we done talking now?" Dylan droned, lifting the mood. "Seriously. I wanna go home and take a shower. I stink."

"You do," said Sam.

"You should talk."

"Okay," said Maeve. "So, we're agreed."

"Yeah, no one freak out when Aunt Molly gets here," said Opal. Nola Wren squirted out of her arms and ran around to Wendy.

"We have to get her home. We done?"

They were. William would pick up Molly, bring her back to the farmhouse on Friday night. There was no sense in trying to figure out what Molly's next move would be when they didn't understand where she'd been and what brought her home. Molly coming back was about Nola Wren, sure, Maeve told them, but it would affect everyone, regardless of whether she planned to stay. Until something changed, nothing would.

CHAPTER THIRTY

1995: Mid-Coast Maine

Faye crimped the crust on an apple pie while Nola Wren sucked on a sugar-coated slice that poked out of her mouth, dark hair up in pigtails that bobbed off the back of her head. Faye marveled at how the sweet smell of a blueberry pie fresh from the oven masked the nervous energy that vibrated through the house since Molly's call earlier in the week. The front door squeaked, and William's voice called out.

"In here," Faye responded. "Let's wash your hands," she said to Nola Wren. "Grandpa will read to you while I finish up."

Faye ran the child's tiny hands under the water, dried them with a dish towel, then the little girl stepped down from her stool dutifully. Her quiet nature sometimes worried Faye. She was wide eyed and observant—so like Molly when she was little—and sweet, especially with William. How he doted on her! But she had a fretful side, too, a twiglike furrow at the bridge of her little nose, as if she expected an alarm to go off. Faye knew it was nothing more than a trait, an expression of curiosity, though it caused her to wonder how much angst the child might have absorbed so early in her little life. They had all tried so hard.

And what would Molly even look like, how long might her hair be, what color even? She'd never said it aloud but, over the years, she'd worried about drugs and rapists and terrible things she heard on the news that happened to girls traveling alone. Would she be too thin? Anorexic even? She was never a great eater. So many worrisome thoughts! If Nola Wren's brow furrowed, she probably caught it from Faye.

Maeve had dropped Nola Wren off with Faye that morning. Her own flurry of activity since Molly's call had not yet subsided. Faye had tried to convince Maeve to slow down, to be reasonable. On the phone that morning, she'd asked, "Do you really think Molly's going to judge you? You think she's going to care whether you've cleaned under the couch? Try to put yourself in her shoes. She's nervous. She's the one who feels judged, Maeve. Not you."

"You're right," Maeve replied. "But also, tell me what you're doing, right this second. I'm guessing you're rolling out pie dough."

Faye laughed. It was true. She baked Molly's favorites, knowing she was never able to resist homemade pie. But weren't they all running around like they were preparing for a nor'easter? William had been in the barn of all places, tidying heaps of half-broken antiques, sweeping up shavings, hanging tools he'd left on the bench. Maeve was off to town now for more groceries as if a full cupboard equaled a happy home. Wendy had work until three and would be home soon after, she'd promised Maeve.

William peeked his head into the kitchen. "Smells good already!" he said. He was holding his right arm at an odd angle.

"What happened to your hand?"

"Ahh, I banged it on the bench." He dropped the newspaper he was holding on the table. Nola Wren grabbed his pant leg.

"I told her you'd read to her."

"Let me wash up. And I might shut my eyes for a bit before I head to the station."

"But you'll read to her first."

"Yes, dear," he said, shaking his hand out like it had been asleep. Faye touched his scruffy face. It was still electric for her, the whiskers on her palm. All these years later, and she loved him still, loved him more.

"You excited?" His eyes lit up. He'd talked of little else all week, Molly coming home.

"Very," Faye said. "And you are as happy as a leprechaun, William Sullivan. Now go get cleaned up."

He pointed at the paper. "Oh. I saw this in my pile. Is this that refugee program you talked about? Says here, 'Operation Shamrock.' The German girls? From the boat?"

Faye's mouth fell open, and the whole of the sea filled it. She tried to speak, but her throat clamped shut. William's name drowned on her tongue.

Too gleeful to register Faye's shock, he picked up his grandchild. "Your mommy is coming home! All will be right. You'll see." As he left the kitchen, he turned to Faye, his face dewy and gleaming. He smiled ear to ear, shore to shore, as broad as the horizon.

Pies in the oven, shears unstabbed on the table, Faye held the newspaper to her ear. German voices, jigs and lullabies, the Irish lilt of the girl singing children to sleep. Her knees gave out, and she sat herself in the chair. That Millay sonnet again, reminding her that she was her Irish father's daughter, the way poetry entered her head instead of her own thoughts.

> Call me in all things what I was before,
> A flutterer in the wind, a woman still;
> I tell you I am what I was and more.

She set the paper back down, peered into the faces there. Gisela. She was Gisela. She covered the face of the child she was with the tip of her finger. She did the same with Elisabeth's face. She stood briskly, the walls closing in as sure as birds blackened the sky. She grabbed her gathering basket. "I'm going to the garden," she shouted. "Back in a minute!" She turned the knob, halted. The newspaper. She snatched it from the table and tossed it into the basket.

In the barn, she switched on the light over William's workbench. A box was on the ground, a little haphazard, and two bundles wrapped in *The Irish Times* lay next to a stack of china. She pulled a weathered milking stool from under the bench and took the newspaper in both hands. She could read the story here, cry her tears here, decide what to do next here, away from eyes that she feared might see through her, accuse her. Somehow, after finding Hannie's letter to Jean all those years ago, and despite never having found the photograph, Elisabeth had become clearer in her mind, at least the girl that she had been, what with the endless tides of memories that had come and gone and come again. And this photo told the same story. Elisabeth, smiling and open, Gisela, furrowed and suspicious. *Ah, there's my granddaughter's furrow, there on a child's face.* Up until this moment, those girls were both so distant they could have been characters in a story. But now, she could almost taste the Irish air, soft and green on her tongue. She could almost feel her sister's hand in her own, how small. Time itself taunted her. *Come clean! Come clean!* The rough stool dug into the back of her legs. William was everywhere in this workshop. Had his face registered any doubt in her when he set the paper down? It had not. She was certain of that.

An image of Molly boarding a bus flashed in her mind. And then Maeve and Wendy. Yes, Wendy. William had been so understanding of Maeve, so forgiving of Molly. Surely, he would have that same grace for her. Surely, he would understand. It wasn't too late for the truth.

Her tears fell onto the newsprint—distorting, magnifying, obscuring. *We were only children, you see. We were only children.* Faye looked at her own face again, fuzzy in black and white, yet clear to her now in a way she could not begin to understand then. *I was so afraid.*

Back in the kitchen, she set the empty vegetable basket down. Her hands still shook despite the long minutes she'd spent in the barn, trying to gather herself. It did not have to be right now. This wasn't the time. But she would tell him. Once Molly was home and they could see the shape of their family again. She folded the newspaper over and set it on the table.

All was quiet in the living room. She looked in, and William was asleep on the couch, head back, mouth open, one arm loosely around Nola Wren, who fussed on his lap, *Miss Spider* in her hands. *Blueberries for Sal* lay spine up on the carpet next to a stuffed bear.

"Hush, now," she whispered, her arms out. "Let Grandpa sleep. He has to get our Molly soon." When the child reached for Faye, the book dropped onto William's leg. He didn't start.

What was it about his face, eyes closed beyond rest? Faye put Nola Wren down and shook her husband's shoulder lightly. "William . . ." He didn't stir. "William!" She spoke louder now, shook him more aggressively. Nothing. Nola Wren cried, and Faye bent to her, pressed the bear into her hands. She sat beside her husband, put her head to his chest, warm from where Nola Wren had cuddled. He was not breathing. "William!" she cried, black waves crashing inside her. "William. No, you can't. Oh!"

Nola Wren seemed to think it was a game and tugged at William's pants, laughing. Then she caught Faye's despair, amplifying it with uncharacteristic shouts. Faye ran past her to the telephone, dialed 911. "Please, hurry!" she begged. *Please, oh, dear God.* Faye pulled William, lifeless and heavy, into her arms. Nola Wren plopped on the floor, cried as if she understood.

Faye could hear paramedics arrive, the slamming of doors, knocking and shouting. But it was somewhere far away, in some other time where she wasn't. She held a colding body, but William—he was everywhere, the dust around her, a genie out of the bottle. She was behind the veil. She marveled at the grandeur of his spirit, breathed him into her lungs and bones, remembering a time they danced at the VFW hall. It was winter. In the corner of the wood-paneled hall, there was a Christmas tree with colored bulbs, light snow was falling outside. Yes, the Fireman's Ball. She'd worn a pretty dress, gold with white piping, her hair done up. So light on her feet! William twirled her until they were floating above all the other dancers and revelers. She threw her head back, joy and disbelief. She did not want to come back to earth. But then the dance hall disappeared, and she was in her living room with this slumped body, her grandchild cried out at her feet. If she moved, she feared he would fall over.

A hand on her shoulder, a face she didn't recognize, a ghost in a window, tapping on the glass with a delicate fingernail. Faye whispered into William's ear, deaf now to all sound. "Summer sang in me." Millay again.

And then, he was there, William, ten years then twenty years younger, leaning against the kitchen doorframe. Worn blue jeans, fur-lined slippers, down vest over a red flannel shirt she had not seen in a decade, hair the color of the setting sun. He held out his hands in that way of his, winked and gestured with his thumb toward the kitchen.

Syrupy smoke blackened the room.

In the oven, the pies burned.

PART THREE

1995–1996

CHAPTER THIRTY-ONE

1995: Mid-Coast Maine

Molly steps off the bus, wobbles to catch her footing. *I'm home. Am I home?* Pine and sea salt and low tide. Familiar yet foreign as the moon. She's terrified at how she has missed it all. Missed by way of longing, missed it like a deadline, like a train that's left the station. But relieved too. She has arrived, older but lighter than when she left. She scans the parking lot. Parents and friends and lovers wave and rush toward other passengers. No face is familiar. She doesn't see her dad's truck anywhere. She puts a dollar in the vending machine by the door of the station, presses the button, and a Coke bangs around the innards before dropping into the slot. She cracks it open, takes a swig, though she's jittery enough as it is. Fizz burns away the cotton on her tongue.

Leo tried to give her money for Nola Wren, but Molly refused it. She gave him the phone number at the farmhouse, promised he could meet their child whenever he was ready, though she's not convinced he will ever call. All she had asked was that he give her a little time to settle in, to get reacquainted, to figure out whether any of them—her parents, Maeve, Wendy, and, most of all, Nola Wren—would be able to forgive her. She was glad it was her father who'd answered when she called to say she was coming home. Unlike her mom and Maeve, he'd never slipped into judgment, though Molly knows she deserves their judgment and everything that's coming for her. She feels ready for it. As painful and heartbreaking and—Jesus, as soul-crushing—as leaving was, she'd never regretted it. Not once. She remembers putting Nola Wren into Maeve's arms, the relief, knowing she never should have been entrusted with something so precious and fragile in the first place. What worries her now is that coming back will somehow be wrong. She only hopes that it's not too late and her daughter will have her back in some way.

She looks through the grimy window at the big clock on the wall, trying not to get annoyed. Where is he? Minutes tick by until she's been standing outside for an hour. Despite herself, she plays out scenarios, all of them ending with her family deciding they didn't want her back after all. Another busload disembarks, and Molly tears up when three little kids run to greet an old man in a Red Sox hat. The parking lot empties again. She spots a pay phone. Give them fifteen more minutes. She leans against the building, puts her foot up like a dime-store cowboy.

A car, no headlights, turns down the street and heads in her direction.

Maeve spots Molly standing by the bus station. Her stomach, already sick from disbelief and sobbing, sinks. She feels terrible for one thousand reasons, not least of which is that, in the confusion—the utter, utter despair and confusion—no one left in time to meet Molly's bus. There'd been a flurry of whispered discussion between her, Wendy, and Sam. *Someone needs to go. Someone needs to stay with Nola Wren. Someone needs to stay with Mom.* Faye was so stunned, practically catatonic, that they'd discussed whether she needed to go to the hospital. Wendy was right. She was in shock. And that meant Wendy was the best person to stay with her. Maeve thought she should stay with Nola Wren, who kept bawling and bawling, though none of them could assume why except that everyone else was crying so why not.

That left Sam to pick up Molly. But that wouldn't be fair to either one of them. Maeve took the keys from him, drove as quickly as she thought she could manage. She'd stopped once—to gulp for air, to scream, to curse, to regather. Her first thought was that she didn't want to take care of Molly right now, but that had quickly been replaced by a new one. She couldn't get to Molly fast enough, Molly, the only other person who could possibly feel the same sorrow Maeve felt.

She turns off the ignition, and she and Molly catch each other's eyes through the windshield. There is affection, fear, sadness. *This is the worst day. This is the worst luck.* Maeve manages a smile she hopes will convey, beyond love, that she could not be more sorry for what comes next.

No one but the ghosts see these sisters tread lightly toward each other, the older with terrible news to break, the younger with a burden to unbear. The streetlight flickers on, a cone of illumination like a spotlight as they embrace. Maeve steps away first, careful not to take her hands off her sister. "You look really good, Pix," she says and means it. Her sister's face is full and clean. Her jawline and hair are their father's, and Maeve takes a breath at seeing him, like a mirage, there and gone.

"I'd say the same, but you look like you've been crying," Molly says.

Maeve can't do this in the car while she's driving, and she can't wait until they get back to the farmhouse. "I have to tell you something really, really bad."

They will agree later that it felt like they left their own skin, like, together and from some distance above, they watched death strike at them, collapse them into each other until they were on their knees, crying and grappling for a hold, there in an empty bus station parking lot.

It's almost sunrise, but Faye hasn't slept. It has been two weeks since Molly came home, since William's funeral, since her world cracked open. An eternity. Outside her window, a serenading robin joins the dawn chorus. Her sleeplessness is not the bird's fault. It is her own. She ruminated all night over something she saw the day before while aimlessly wandering the shops in town again, desperate to stay away from the sadness that cloaked the farmhouse.

In the bookstore, she had floated up and down rows of cookbooks and travel guides and thick studies of ancient history. She picked up novels idly, skimmed the back covers, set them back down. She was drawn to a gray book displayed on a rounder in the center of the store. Hardened eyes stared at her, daring her to speak. *Beyond the Front Line: Children of War in the 20th Century*. She lifted the heavy cover like it was sacred. She leafed page after glossy page, blurred blocks of text accompanying wrenching, saturated photos—children fleeing, starving, begging, injured, exhausted, shocked, bloodied. Some children brandished weapons, others confronted them. A child wept over a body. A wailing mother held a limp child. Children in concentration camps. Children wearing gas masks. Maimed children who managed to smile, children who would never laugh again, glassy-eyed children gripped with shock, children playing on mounds of cinder block while war waged around them. Vietnam, Ireland, Biafra, Germany, France, Belgium, Korea, Bolivia, Paraguay, Sierra Leone, Israel, Syria, Palestine, Iraq, Nigeria, Colombia, Afghanistan, Cambodia, Lebanon, Iran, Japan, the Philippines, Angola, Sudan, Bosnia, Rwanda. The list went on. Children playing in rubble, children picking through it for food. Men and their wars—wars for power, for money, for glory. War over territory. War over drugs. War over gods. For years, Faye had not understood war beyond what it had done to her family, how war killed her father first, then her mother, how it tore human beings apart. She had watched *Sophie's Choice* and *Schindler's List* with William, and the two of them had wept, though her tears had been soured with shame as if an entire nation's sins were her own.

She thumbed through the pages, past face after face, thinking she might see her own. She wondered what happened to the children who survived, what they made of the ruins of their lives. Did they grow up? Have families? Bury the past? Were their scars on the inside or outside? A bookseller, practically a child himself with his round glasses and skinny arms, glanced over Faye's shoulder. "I can't look at that one.

It's sickening. They're just kids." His melodic voice was pitched with disgust. "They didn't choose. They didn't have an ideology. War makes orphans and refugees and corpses. That's it. Unless you're an oligarch or warmonger, I guess. War makes rich men richer."

"Mm." She had nodded at the boy as he stooped to shelve a book. She brushed her hand reverently across the faces on the cover, traced the hollow cheeks of a hungry child, like dipping her fingertips into holy water. She found the old habit and crossed herself.

"It is sickening," she'd agreed, though the bookseller had gone.

She stares at her bedroom ceiling now, taps her holy fingers together. Shh, shh, shh, shh, shh. She remembers shushing Molly through her childhood nightmares, like she had been hushed, as if demons obey and will leave when told. She shifts into the slope of the mattress where springs bulge beneath the pad. She writhes so that they poke at her accusingly. How the body remembers! She flattens out stiffly, crosses her arms, feigns death. Early light streams through filmy curtains.

She gets out of bed. There is no need to dress because she still wears clothes from the day before when she was in the bookstore, when that book of war photography reduced her to a sad statistic. She puts on her slippers and goes downstairs to sit in the exact spot where William died. The funeral home gave her a paper bag with the clothes he arrived in, his personal effects. The bag is on the couch, though William will never be again. How had she not seen the way he held his arm? How had the strew of newspapers, the dropped box on his workbench not given her a clue? It was not like William to leave something undone, not like him to leave a mess.

If only she had stayed in the kitchen instead of escaping to the barn. If only she had not lingered there so long. It was like her father all over again. Had William cried out for her? Called her name? Had he uttered final words? And Nola Wren. That poor child abandoned on her dead grandfather's lap. And Molly, waiting, waiting for a father who would never come for her. It was too heartbreaking to replay, yet it was all she did and what she did. She had let him down, let them all down, in so many ways.

She'd used scissors to cut clean the story from *The Irish Times*, folded it neatly. She keeps it with her always now. She unfolds it again, presses it flat against her wrinkled slacks.

Around her, sheer cotton curtains flutter in the windows. Jays squawk from the next field over. Golden grass sways along the fence rail. *Dreamy.* The veil thinned when William passed, and now ghosts come and go at will. She is surrounded. All those spirits tell William about his bride. He knows the truth. It's the gift of death, finally seeing. *All is revealed.* She sets the clipping on the end table, covers her mouth with praying hands.

The house is too quiet. Faye doesn't know what to do with herself. Molly talked Maeve into letting her stay the night at the cove house so she could tuck Nola Wren in for sleep and wake up with her in the morning. Faye knows that when she stays there, she sleeps on the couch. This has been Molly's primary complaint. She is home, and yet there is no place for her.

She told Faye through tears, "I am trying so hard to stay, Mom. I need help, and no one is making room for me." She's right, the poor thing. Grief and ghosts take up all the space.

So, do something.

She slips on her muck boots and William's jacket, grabs his keys off the hook by the door. She takes the newspaper clipping off the table and slips it into her pocket. The stone blue sky is specked with morning stars, a dusting of distant pink. She thinks of Jean and the way she stood on the granite rocks looking over the cove, waving her arms side to side.

Do something.

She drives the empty roads, her hands on the places worn smooth by her husband. He is with her around every familiar bend and over every hill, along the stands of pine and empty fields. They lived their lives between two houses, two landscapes, for more than thirty-five years. The sky lightens as she arrives at Maeve's house. She closes the car door gently then makes her way toward the cove. She stands on Jean's rock, lifts her arms as the sun rises. First, she pushes aside fog that settles around boats and buoys. Then she sweeps away the little island and fishing boats and trawlers already out of the harbor's safety. She pushes Nova Scotia down to New York and Newfoundland up and out of the way to Greenland. She draws William's coat around her body, nuzzles for him on the collar, closes her eyes and opens them again, and she can see the cliffs of Ireland and Sheep's Head Peninsula and the gray-green water of Dunmanus Bay and Fiadh, standing on a stone, pointing directly back at Faye.

She will not be aware of it for hours, maybe even days, how she time-travels in that moment, how her clothes remake themselves into a girlish shape, never pregnant, sheep and goats in the old barn, bum on a wooden crate, sharp shears to cut lice out of little-girl hair, potatoes in a pot to boil, berries in a basket, fireside stories of faery mounds and children stolen and disappeared, eaten by witches or secreted into the never-grow-old land by leprechauns.

Faye can see Elisabeth's sleeping face as it was the night she snuck away to walk the path into another body, another life. She can see Jean and the bed where Fiadh's body lay, a shadow on a quilt. Faye sweeps her arm again, manifests the gritty floor under her bent knees, the rough of Jean's dress against her face. She can hear her own broken voice, pleading to become someone new. She tells them, though they don't understand, what Elisabeth doesn't know: There is no mother waiting for them, no Germany to take them back. She saw it happen. *Sie ist tot. Sie ist tot.*

"Take *me*."

Yes, Thomas and Jean had taken her. But she left Elisabeth first. She *left*. Like Molly left Nola Wren. To save a life. They were helpless children at the mercy of a world that had proven itself cruel. She and Elisabeth were not stronger together. They were twice as weak. If Molly was right to leave, if Nola Wren survived because of it, then maybe Faye had been right as well. Maybe Elisabeth survived because she left.

She holds up imaginary binoculars, though she knows there's only one way to see what she wants to see, to know what she can no longer bear not knowing. Elisabeth, or what's left of her, is out there somewhere.

And if Molly was healed and brave enough to return, maybe Faye could be brave too. Maybe Faye could heal.

She picks her way across the granite to the path back to the house. Sunrise banks off billowing clouds, pure and golden from having traveled across the wild ocean. It shimmers on the dew, gleams against east-facing windowpanes. The wind flutters leaves on the trees, blows needles from the boughs. *Der Wind, der Wind, das himmlische Kind.* Hansel and Gretel. Faye avoided it when the girls were little. "Mama is afraid of witches," she told them, making fun of herself. So many stories had witches in them, witches and foolish children. *I was the one who nibbled at the house. America fattened me up. Now she will eat me.*

At the front door, Faye lifts the mat, turns the spare key in the lock. Molly is curled up on the overstuffed couch. This house belongs to Maeve and her messy American family now, most signs of a German girl and her Irish parents gone, save for a row of books on the built-in, Thomas's beloved Irish writers that Maeve keeps for show. After today, Maeve will want to be rid of those, she imagines. She sits on the couch, shakes Molly gently. "Honey. Wake up."

Maeve wakes to the sound of a car door closing, eases out of bed so she won't rouse Wendy. At first, she fears it's Molly, sneaking out with Nola

Wren. She slips out of the bedroom into the open door across the hall, peeks in on Nola Wren and Opal. Sound asleep. She wants to crawl back under the covers with Wendy for another half hour of sleep but has an uneasy feeling. She goes to the window and sees a figure move across the dewy lawn to the back of the property. Her mother. Maeve has few memories of her grandmother Jean, but this is one: a somber woman standing on those rocks. It's a memory in silhouette, a shade, more gothic than it was in real life, but her grandmother radiated old country like a Grimm witch. And now it's her mother out there, swishing her arms elegantly, a summoner parting the sea or charming fish into nets. When her mother's arms drift down to her sides and she turns back to the house, Maeve steps into a pair of jeans, throws a sweatshirt on over her T-shirt, and heads downstairs.

From the landing, she sees her mother sitting on the couch next to Molly. Maeve rubs her eyes. It's too early for another confrontation. Yet here it is. "What's going on?"

Molly sits up. It takes her a moment to ground herself in yet another place that isn't her own. *I am in Maine. I'm in Maeve's house. My child is upstairs in Maeve's house.* And then a tugging inside reminds her. Sorrow. *I have lost my father. I have lost my child's father.* She pulls the blanket around her. *I will not lose my child.* "Be quiet! You'll wake the baby."

Maeve rolls her eyes dramatically to make a point. "She's not a baby anymore."

"And you don't need to be like that."

"Girls," Faye says. She reaches into William's coat pocket and pulls out the newspaper clipping, holding it between her fingers. It will come out now, not Fiadh's story that she told William all those years ago. Her own story. Her own consequences. She draws Molly into her, smells that spicy sharpness piping from the part of her hair. Faye would know her scent anywhere, both of her girls. "I love you so much, you know." She reaches out to Maeve, who takes her hand and squeezes. "Both of you."

"You're scaring us, Mom," Maeve says, pushing at Molly's legs to make room on the couch. "What are you doing here? I saw you out on the rocks."

Faye takes a breath like it's her final meal. "I've kept something from you both. And from Dad. It's eating me alive."

Molly tries to focus but flashes to her conversation with Leo, the truth-telling about Nola Wren and the fact that Molly had left her. "Abandoned her, you mean," Leo had said. She'd never thought he could be so angry. As bad as it was watching him seethe and storm off, she thought it was the reckoning she needed. But to find out about her dad. Had her leaving strained his heart? Had coming back killed him? She snaps herself out of the memory. "Mom . . . ?"

"Please, honey." Faye looks at a framed picture on the mantel, another remnant from when Thomas lived in this house. William and Faye with the girls when they were younger. Maeve wears bell-bottoms and a tight orange T-shirt, Molly, a short denim dress with a picnic-checked bow, both girls in rubber-soled sneakers. William wears jeans and a plaid shirt, Faye, a sleeveless green shell the color of canned peas, blue ankle-length pants, white sandals. There is nothing spectacular about any of them except that they are happy. It's spontaneous, and it was her father who had taken it with a camera William had gotten at a yard sale.

"Earth to Mom," Maeve says, snapping her fingers. She instantly regrets it. Wendy has chastised her over the last couple of weeks that she's too short with everyone and needs to settle down. "I'm sorry. I shouldn't be like that."

Faye points to the picture. "Pix, you must have been about seven or eight when that was taken. I was about that age when I came to America." She should start at the beginning she knows, but she thinks about a picture that used to be on the mantel, a long time ago, of her and Jean and Thomas. She was standing in front of her father in a dark coat and a furry hat of some sort. One hand was on her shoulder, and the other was around Jean's waist. They'd moved so many things out after Thomas died, making room so Maeve and Sam could build their own life together. Where was the photograph now? How could it have disappeared, something so rare? Perhaps all photographs eventually fade, first out of time and then out of memory.

"I didn't talk much."

Faye looks at her daughters, sees how much of both her and William are in each of them. Maeve definitely takes after her, the way her shoulders square, the slope of her bright eyes, her shiny brown hair. When anyone mentioned how Faye looked nothing like Thomas or Jean, her father had said that she was "the quiet part" of each of them. Molly is the spitting image of William, the thin lips, copper hair, and hazel eyes. This might hurt her more. "When I was a girl, there was an accident. The day before we left Ireland."

"We know," Maeve says, that new impatience in her voice. She softens. "A boating accident. It's why you don't like boats."

Of course, they know the story she told William that put them all on this course. "Yes, but—" She can't figure out where to start.

Thomas sits on the window seat across the room now, holding one of his books open to a worn page. His kind eyes crinkle downward. He's wearing the black suit he was buried in, the ugly quilt across his lap. She can almost hear his voice, the lilting one he used for reading aloud.

> Now that my ladder's gone
> I must lie down where all the ladders start
> In the foul rag and bone shop of the heart.

She left Elisabeth sleeping, climbed down a ladder she can never again ascend. She holds out the clipping. "Dad found this in his hoard of newspapers the day . . ." She can't say it. ". . . the day Molly came home."

Molly swings her legs around, and she and Maeve scoot in to get a closer look. "See here? These two girls? These are the German girls in the story about the boat. This is Elisabeth . . ." Faye's throat catches on the name, an odd pill of grief and love and regret lodged there. She points, holding the photo so her daughters can see. "And this girl, she was called Gisela."

"This girl," Faye says again. *Where all ladders start.* "This is me." Her voice pitches like a boat on a wave. "I am that German girl. That is me and my sister, before we were taken to live in the west of Ireland. See that headline? I was a refugee from war." She emphasizes the word "refugee." Had she ever thought of herself that way, as a victim of war? If William had lived, she could have taken him to that bookstore. She could have shown him what she once was. What war had done. He would have understood. *Imagine that. We were so close . . .*

Molly pulls back. Her stomach flips and flops. She can feel every drop of blood in her body. "What are you talking about? You're not making sense."

"I know. This is so difficult." How do you tell your children that your life has been a lie, built on another person's death, on grief, and that in living that lie, you've marked their lives as well? "The accident. With the boat." Faye shakes her head.

"Let me see that clipping," Maeve says, snatching it from her mother's hands. She scans it, lifts her head. "It says here these children were fostered all over Ireland after World War II. So, if this is you, how did you end up here?"

"My parents, your grandparents, Thomas and Jean. They were not my real parents."

"So, you're adopted?" Molly asks.

"Adopted? No, not exactly. More like . . ." Faye searches for the word. ". . . switched."

Maeve stands, though her knees quake. Her thoughts arrange themselves like bullet points. "Were you kidnapped? Did Grandpa and Grandma abduct you?" Maeve puts her hand to her mouth.

"Maeve, please. For once in your life, be patient. It wasn't that. Not really. They did have a daughter. Fiadh." Faye is out of her own body now, hearing herself say the thing she's feared most of her known life. "Fiadh drowned and . . . and somehow . . . they made the decision to bring me to America instead. Once we were on the ship, your grandmother realized what she'd done. But it was too late." She makes a mental note to show the letter from Hannie to the girls. "She had a friend back in Ireland, a woman named Hannie, who wrote to her and told her there would be fallout, tragic fallout, if they said anything. She told Thomas and Jean to stay away. And they did. I became Fiadh. And then Faye. And no one here was the wiser. It almost stopped mattering. And then I met your father. And Conor O'Kane showed up, and he knew I wasn't who I claimed to be." Her mouth clamps shut on the mention of the name they don't speak. Silence fills the room while that ghost takes up the seat by the window, his legs crossed, that smirk, as if he can't wait to hear what comes next.

"That's just great," Molly says, in disbelief. She raises her scarred hand as if to pause time. "So, now we get to talk about Conor O'Kane." She shakes her head. "Un. Real."

"I'm sorry, honey. I don't know why it's taken a lifetime to say these things. I was a quiet girl, after the war. I'd lost my family. My sister. I couldn't bear losing William or you girls." She tells them more, as much as she can recall in the moment, as much as she can bear.

"And Dad didn't know?" Maeve asks finally. "You never told him?"

Faye shakes her head slowly.

"How could you—"

"And what about Maeve and me? It never occurred to you that we had a right to know?" Molly has gone white with rage. "You're so goddamned selfish. Now I know where I get it from. I don't even know you!" Disordered thoughts of her grandfather and Leo and Nola Wren muddle with the darkness she'd swallowed and denied and endured since she was as little as the girls in the photograph. Could this revelation have put her own life on a different trajectory if she'd known sooner? How does that make sense? She puts her hand out to Maeve. "Give me that. I want to see it again."

"I'm trying to make this right!" Faye knows there is more, something deeper. "I—I want to go to Ireland and find out what happened to my sister! I don't want to wait for this reunion they're planning. I want to go now. Or as soon as possible."

Molly's whole body quivers. There is something about this. She looms over her mother slumped on the couch and drops the clipping on her lap. In her head, two images click together, sure as a buckle. "Let's go," she says. "You too, Maeve. Back home."

"We can't just leave." Maeve flares her eyes on the word "leave," a dig at Molly. "I have to get Nola Wren dressed. And Dylan and Opal have school." On cue, a toilet flushes upstairs.

"Get your wife to do it, Maeve," Molly says, her voice slick with contempt. She is sick of that holier-than-thou attitude. "We need to go back to the house. Now. I mean it. Mom, let's go. You can drive us. And bring that newspaper."

In an instant, Molly is on the front lawn, hands on her hips, gasping for air. *I should never have come back.* The sky darkens, and thunder rumbles overhead as Maeve and Faye join her. That ever-present shadow has caught up and is upon her now. She knows what she knows.

࿋

Back at the farmhouse, Molly sits on the floor in her old bedroom, which smells of fresh paint, though the color is the same yellow it has always been. Her back against the bed, she holds in her lap a vintage mahogany cigar box she bought at a thrift store when she was in junior high. She unhooks the metal clasp. The hinges move silently as she lifts. Inside, tamped blue velvet still reeks of wet smoke and banana peels. She removes relics one by one, lines them up on the braided rug.

Leo's played-out, gnarled mixtape; matching wristbands she and Nola Wren wore home from the hospital; a tattered patch of silk from Charlie's tie that she'd cut to shreds. She pauses, holds a purple plastic viewfinder to the light. Her and Leo, laughing at the beach. She sets it down, digs into the cigar box again. The key to her college dorm room.

The ink-stained layaway ticket for the leather jacket. A scorched silver wire she knows fits neatly against her thin scar. She feels crosscut and hewn, each relic like a growth ring of a tree, the core of who she is.

Beneath a popsicle stick and a paper doll, she finds what she came for. A creased photograph, black-and-white and face down, lines the bottom of the box. She pinches it carefully using fingers on both hands. Three boys and three girls in two rough rows. A brawny girl in loose pants and a tattered-looking blouse, dark hair in short braids, stands toughly between two boys, their features similar and so dark they look drawn on with a marker. Behind them on one side crouches another boy—light haired and beady eyed, with a jutting chin and underbite. On the low wall on the other side, two girls, identical haircuts and faces, identical smocks over dresses, one grinning, one squinting. They hold hands. Molly turns the photograph over. The words are faded, the handwriting different from what they teach in American schools.

Denis Jem Fiadh Con and the doicha girls

Sometimes, when Molly thinks about Conor O'Kane falling, he sprouts horns and hooves and crashes through the floor, through the cellar, through layers of dirt. Other times, the roof lifts off, and his black coat becomes oily feathers, and he never hits the ground. And sometimes, he flutters like propaganda dropped from a plane, weightlessly taking his time before he comes to rest untwisted and unbroken on the rug below.

She runs her fingers along the photograph's stained edge. Did it slip from his shirt pocket, follow him down when he fell? Was it in his hand all along? Like other relics in the box, Molly has never shown it to anyone. Before she had the cigar box, she'd pressed it deep between her mattresses along with the popsicle stick and the paper doll, beyond the reach of a mother making a bed. Once she'd put it in the box, it was left there to decay.

Maeve and Faye are at the door to her bedroom now. Maeve inches closer. "What is all this, Pix?"

Molly's legs splay like a dropped doll, her ruins assembled between them. Her jaws feel wired shut. She points at her mother. "You told me, 'Don't say a word.' You zipped my lips closed and never once asked if I was okay. Neither one of you did! And you know what? I was not okay. I'm still not okay."

She feels him on her hands, in the lifelines of her palms, in the tension of her wrists. None of it was ever what it seemed. "It's been fifteen years, but now it's okay to talk about Conor O'Kane? Do you have any idea—?" She gets up, hands the photo to her mother, who takes it as if it is on fire. "I found it under the table. After they took his body away."

It is Faye's turn to go white. "Honey . . ." Faye says. She stares at the picture. It's the one from Hannie's letter to Jean, she knows it. And there. A better likeness than the pixelated newspaper photo. Elisabeth, hopeful and happy, Faye next to her, suspicious of everything.

Had Jean given it to O'Kane, or did he swipe it when she wasn't looking? She imagines the two of them, Conor and Jean, bent like buzzards over roadkill, smoking and telling tales of Ireland and its green fields and heartbreaks. Jean was not a drinker, but maybe she became intoxicated by O'Kane, the wild indelible smell of him. How it came to be in Conor O'Kane's possession, she will never know. But she's glad for it now, glad to see the last of herself again.

Molly makes a humming sound, anger and regret and bitterness swarming her. Her hands clench. "You have no idea. Neither one of you." She juts her head toward her mother. "Look out there. Both of you. It was me! I pushed him over the railing. And then he died." She mimes the pushing motion, daring them to mount a challenge. "Mommy," Molly says, her voice tiny. "I killed that man."

"No, honey. No," Faye pleads. She flashes on Conor's final desperate breath. Yes, she hesitated but could not have saved him. His neck was broken. His lung was punctured. "It wasn't your fault. Forget about him." She tries to embrace her daughter, but Molly wiggles free.

Molly's brow tightens. "How convenient for you, Mom. To forget. What a goddamned luxury. Every day, he's been with me. Every night.

In every bed I've ever slept in. I have never once been able to . . . forget," she says, her fingers bracketing the word. "And Nola Wren! Mom. Look what happened to me. Look at me! I'm all tangled up in some kind of sick web. I can't take any more!" She pushes past Maeve and runs out of the room. Moments later, the back door slams.

"I'll go after her," Maeve says.

Faye steps around the scattered remnants of a whole life. She has never felt so lost, so alone. Thunder rumbles the windows, and a whip of lightning flashes the room. Tree branches scrape the side of the house. *If only William were here.* "Come back!" she sobs. "Oh, come back."

Maeve pulls the back of her shirt over her head and runs to the barn through sheets of rain. It's the only place Molly could have gone. She finds her on the floor in the old goat stall, a playhouse and hiding spot they'd both used when they were kids. She's soaking wet and shivering. Maeve wedges in next to her. "Maybe a tornado will lift up the barn and carry us away," she offers.

"Just my luck, it would drop on someone and kill them."

Maeve snorts, and the sisters sit quietly together—neither of them able to form a complete thought—and listen to the rain pelt the rafters. Molly taps her head against the barn wall. "Maeve. I miss Dad so much. It hurts so bad. Worse than anything. I can't believe I'm never going to see him again." She tries to gather herself, to stop the tears, but it's no use. "Why did he have to go and die? I don't understand."

Maeve shuts her eyes. She has cried so many tears already. She hugs Molly's knee, shakes her head. "God," she says. "I don't know." She rubs her eyes and cheeks, sniffles. "You should have seen him with Nola Wren, Pix. He was so cute. He loved her so much . . . and God, she adored him."

Molly rests her elbows on her knees, her head in her hands, and sobs. "He's everywhere in this barn and nowhere at all. Fuck, Maeve. What are we gonna do?" She lets out a laugh despite herself. "What a mess!"

"That night . . . Conor O'Kane," Maeve offers. "It was awful. You know Wendy and I had a thing in high school. You probably don't remember, but her prom date was killed in a car accident that night. Her mom figured out that Wendy was with me. That's why they moved away. Her parents would rather skip town than admit their daughter was gay."

"Why have we never talked about any of this?" Molly asks. "Why do we bury everything?"

Maeve points in the direction of the farmhouse. "Well, that might be a clue."

"Mom is not who we thought. Grandpa wasn't really my grandpa. And now, I guess we're German . . . ?" Molly says, incredulous.

"Guess so. C'mon. The rain's let up. We better get back and face the music before she starts baking pies again."

Sun streaks wetly through the open barn door. Storm clouds roll away behind spiky trees. Over the field, a rainbow appears, and then another. "Wow," Maeve says.

Molly takes Maeve's arm, stops her from heading in. "Maeve, I want Nola Wren to live here at the farmhouse. With me. I want her back."

"Pix—"

"No. Just. I don't mean right this second. We have all this . . . whatever it is we're supposed to do here. But I needed to say it so that you and Wendy know. I appreciate what you guys have done. But I'm her mother."

"I don't think you do. Appreciate it. I don't think you get it at all."

Faye waits for the girls in the kitchen. William's voice tells her they need time. He was better with them than she was, especially as they got older.

Something about their heat and passion, their fiery displays, frightened Faye, as if their outbursts might tempt her to show herself too. But now, she feels her walls crumbling. There's nothing to guard anymore. Nothing to lose. The letter from Hannie to Jean is on the table next to the photograph Molly stashed.

She tries again to explain it all. "I didn't save anything the way you did, Pix," she says. "But this is the story, right here."

"Did you fight them?" Maeve asks. "Grandma and Grandpa?"

"No. I told you. They didn't kidnap me. I left with them. They were going to take one of us, and I told them to take me." Faye's own words crush her.

"How could you leave like that?" Maeve asks. "Without even saying goodbye."

Faye steals a look at Molly.

Molly whistles. "Cut and run, right, Mom?"

Faye is more tired than she has ever been. Has she been pretending to sleep all these years? Sleep is upon her, dragging her down like a predator. "Please let's stop for now. We can talk—fight—more later, I promise. Right now, I have to close my eyes." She leaves her daughters as if she is not the one who flipped the table on them.

Molly reads Hannie's letter again. "'Grass covers ground now that should not be disturbed.' Hm. Do you think Mom really wants to go back to Ireland?"

"I don't know. Look. I'm sorry to leave you here—with her, with all this—but I have to get back," Maeve says. "Tell Mom I took the car. We'll bring it back later."

"With Nola Wren?"

Maeve holds up her hands, exhales all her breath. "Please. Can you just . . . ?"

Molly follows her into the foyer. "Wait," she says. "Do you remember if the police drew one of those tape outlines? Like on TV? I thought they did, but that doesn't make sense now. Didn't Daddy roll that rug up right away and get rid of it? He wouldn't have left a bloody rug. And I don't remember when this one showed up. The floor must have been bare for a while."

"God, I don't know. I was such a mess. I feel like I should be able to rationalize everything, put everything together and make it make sense. But we were kids, and Mom and Dad were freaking out, and, well, the body. I hardly remember the police even being here."

"That's where I found the photo," Molly says, pointing to a thick table leg. "It was dark. I wanted to see if the floor was still warm where he fell. I knew I killed him. It's sickening to say it, honestly."

Maeve pulls her in, gives her the last of her compassion even as her own grief rises. "It was an accident," she says softly, tightening her grip with each gentle word.

It is a mother's embrace, folded like rising dough. Molly slips her arms around Maeve's waist, exhales against her pillowy chest, and lets her sister love her again.

CHAPTER THIRTY-TWO

1995: Mid-Coast Maine

The moment Maeve turns the key in the ignition of Faye's car, it starts raining again. She flips on the wipers, puts the car in gear, and drives. The road clears and dissolves, clears and dissolves. Her mind is blank. She can't keep a thought in her head. The kids are at school by now, unaware of what they have lost, what they will lose. Thankfully it's Wendy's day off. Maeve still needs to call and let her own job know she can't come in.

The wipers rub the windshield, their swishing rhythm toggling her thoughts. Nola Wren and Molly on one side, her mother's secret on the other. Wendy on one side, Conor O'Kane on the other. Ireland, Maine. Back and forth.

She drives in the pouring rain. Past the house around the corner from the high school where the German boy Oskar lived with his host family. Past the ghost of the house where Wendy lived, the actual house consumed by fire and replaced by something cheap and dull. She drives in the circle of her life, around the town she's never left. She has fit herself into its shape and forced it on others—Dylan and Opal for certain, but Wendy and Sam too.

She likes to keep things straight. That's why she's made lists her whole life.

Things That Make Me Who I Am.

Nothing comes to mind.

She drives, feels the pain of losing her dad, the sting of what's to come. They will lose Nola Wren. Back and back she tumbles, like a cartoon character in a vortex. She thinks about ifs and thens. If she had known this, then she would have done that. She plays it out, but there's no going back, no stepping in the same river twice. She drives until she winds up at the cove house.

Home.

She remembers her grandfather, who is not her real grandfather after all. But what is that—to be real? Of course he was real. Velveteen, worn and loved. Yes, she loved him. Always reciting poems Maeve hardly understood, though she's beginning to understand now. Things do fall apart. The center cannot hold. She feels the flinging off, the falling away.

She rests her head on the steering wheel, but the bumps punch like brass knuckles. She bangs her head against it once, twice. Then Wendy is at the car door, Nola Wren with her. The rain has stopped, but drops trickle down the window, distorting and magnifying what matters.

Maeve gets out of the car, presses Nola Wren between her body and Wendy's as if she's preserving a plucked flower. She puts her head on Wendy's shoulder, her arm around her waist. "Let's go inside."

It's only noon, but Maeve feels she has been awake for days. When was the last time she was this tired? Probably when Nola Wren was a baby, in those horrible days after Molly left when they all realized she wasn't coming back. She sinks into the couch, throws her head back. "I don't know where to begin. This family. I swear."

"You okay? Where did you go? I saw that your mom was here, but then you all took off."

While Nola Wren eats peanut butter and jelly and grapes cut in two, Maeve tells Wendy about her mother and Conor O'Kane, about Germany and Ireland and refugee children and lost sisters and drowned friends and how crazy families are with their secrets, how they try to fool each other into thinking they are the best versions of themselves. She tells her about Molly and the picture she'd kept hidden all those years.

"I don't know how I was so blind to what she was going through. And before you say it, I know . . . you tried to tell me. I was so wrapped up in my own thoughts I didn't give her a second one. My mom." Maeve shakes her head. "That night, she said that Dad would be so disappointed if he knew I had been with you. But really it was her. Jesus, Wen! The guy died in our house! I mean, I must have noticed Molly acting weird after, but I was busy trying to be the perfect straight girl to make up for the fact that, you know, my *depravity* or whatever, was the reason he was in the house in the first place. But it wasn't because of me at all! It was because of Mom." The kitchen goes dark as rain pelts the windows, disappearing the lawn and rocks in fog. "God, it's gloomy!" Maeve says, her elbows on the table. She takes a bite of Nola Wren's sandwich. "This rain!" She groans. "I don't know what to do."

Wendy sits gobsmacked as Maeve recalls how their whole lives have been wrapped around her mother's deception, though she hesitates on that word. "Or was Mom kidnapped? I have no idea how to even think about this," Maeve says.

"Whew! That's a lot," Wendy says. "Talk about mayhem! And your dad never knew."

"He kept all those newspapers in the truck in case he needed them for his antiquing. I can only imagine him seeing that picture, thinking in that way of his—he was always so thoughtful—that

Mom would want to see it. Of course, she would. I wish I knew what he would have done if he'd found out. She says she was protecting him."

"Your dad? Protecting him from what?"

The rain stops, and a god ray of sunshine blazes through the kitchen window. Maeve lets it hit her full on, gathering herself in the sudden light. She laughs, wiping her eyes.

"What?" Wendy asks.

"My dad. He said I was like Scout from *To Kill a Mockingbird*. A ray of sunshine in pants. He was the empathetic one, like Atticus. I can just hear him. 'Imagine what it was like for her.' Blah, blah, blah. But it's true. Mom's kind of been in her own closet in a way."

Maybe her father knew something about Maeve after all. Maybe she tried too hard to be a sunbeam all these years, as if baking cookies and keeping house was what was expected of her. Even after Sam left and Wendy moved in, wasn't she still trying to fit into some accepted version of normal? Putting on a show for Dylan and Opal or her parents or neighbors and bosses, pretending like she and Wendy were some plain old married couple? If this was a house of cards, how could she continue to live in it while it collapsed around her?

Wendy wipes Nola Wren's mouth and hands. "NoNo, go play in the other room."

Maeve watches her run, free of grown-up problems and noise. They had tried clever monikers to distinguish each other—Mommy, Mama, Mom, Ma—but it had felt too contrived. They're just Wendy and Maeve, or "WindyMay" when she clumps them together. And now Molly is just Molly. Did Nola Wren have too many mothers or none at all? "Molly says she's ready to take Nola Wren to the farmhouse," Maeve whispers.

Wendy slams her soda can on the table. "Oh, come on!"

"No, she's determined. I saw it." Maeve pauses, tries to quiet her busy mind. Her head is peppered with thoughts and schemes and possibilities. Her eyes flick from side to side. "Remember how we stumbled down that path away from the kegger? We couldn't see our own hands in front of our faces. That's how I feel now. Completely blind. I have no idea what's next."

CHAPTER THIRTY-THREE

1996: Dublin, Ireland

From the back seat with Nola Wren, Faye listens to Maeve and Molly argue over the best route to Dublin from the airport. It has been push and pull for months.

In the aftermath of Faye's revelation, Molly had returned to that bar, the Salty Siren, in search of Glenda, determined to confess the truth about what happened the night Conor O'Kane died. But the bartender claimed he'd never heard of a Glenda and said people come and go. After that, the only solution for Molly was to go with Faye to Ireland so she could confess directly to any O'Kane at all. No one had been able to talk her out of it. That plan started rounds of bickering and negotiating and tears, battles over who would go with Faye and who would stay behind until the only solution was for Maeve and Molly to both go to Ireland and Nola Wren too. Their fates would be sealed or unsealed together.

Thankfully, there's no argument about who should drive. Molly knows she is a frantic driver—too close to the wheel, too many nervous glances over her shoulder, on and off the gas like she's playing a pedal organ. Maeve, though, is a natural, and it is when she looks most like William as far as Faye is concerned. Even here in Ireland, on the wrong side of the road, her right arm extends from the shoulder and drapes over the steering wheel, while her left hand rests easily on the stick shift. Nola Wren, glued to the window, watches cars and buildings and trees on the motorway. Faye watches with the same wonder.

Over decades of witnessing a changing America, Faye somehow believed that Ireland was only a rural place of hills and sheep and stone walls and craggy shores. The modern buildings and roadways, cars and lorries zipping around, shock her. Had she thought that time stood still here? Her only sense of an Irish city is the Belfast of news reports. She knows from William's clipping that she and Elisabeth got off the mail boat at the docks in Dublin, a memory so innate in her it is like a memory of sun on one's face. Dublin, though. It's a postcard, a colorized photo. She has no memory of this or any Dublin at all.

In the tiny hotel room, they stash their bags and wash up in the bathroom. The mattresses sag and the wallpaper is worn, but it's clean, which is all Faye hoped for. Molly stakes out the bed she will share with Nola Wren, leaving the one closest to the door for Maeve and Faye. Tight quarters to be sure. Nola Wren bounces on the bed now in her stocking feet, trying to touch the low ceiling out of her toddling reach.

It's not even noon, Dublin time. The idea of taking a quick nap is considered and rejected—there's no way they'll be able to sleep with Nola Wren awake. "We have to rally," Maeve says. "Get on local time." She takes out the guidebook. "Here. Let's walk to Saint Stephen's Green, stretch our legs, then grab lunch. Maybe afterward this little monster will be ready for a nap." She sweeps up Nola Wren, swings her around until giggles erupt.

Molly takes the child from Maeve. "Let's change your diaper, sweet girl." With that, chins drop, and Maeve and Faye set about fussing with their suitcases, knowing looks flickering between them as Molly struggles with the diaper bag. "You two can stop with the glances. I don't need you scrutinizing every move I make. Honestly, the judging! I've got this."

This terrible tug-of-war. Neither Maeve nor Molly seems able to let go—Molly trying to prove to everyone, herself included, that she is a capable mother, and Maeve, rubbing it in that Nola Wren still seeks her out despite the fact that the child lives full-time at the farmhouse with Molly and Faye now. "I wish . . ." Faye can't finish her thought. She doesn't know what she wishes for anymore. So many conversations, so many battles to get to where they are. They agreed they would start in Wicklow, at the center in Glencree. There they would look for information about Faye's sister. Maeve had suggested calling or writing ahead, but Faye said no. She wanted to go there in person even if they weren't able to find Elisabeth. Bad news would only keep her away. She wanted to retrace the last steps she took as a German girl. "Come what may," she told her daughters. From Glencree, they would head west to the village on Dunmanus Bay. She would know the fields and walls. She would know the sea. Then they would seek news of Hannie and Hugh and of the O'Kane family and their whereabouts.

"You wish what, Mom?" Maeve asks.

Faye shakes her head. "I wish I knew it was all going to be okay."

"It will be, Mom. Whatever happens. We'll get through this," Maeve says.

Faye hears William in her voice.

They enter the city park through black iron gates beneath a stone arch. The sounds of Dublin fall away in the green space, ducks and geese and swans lazing on the lagoon before them, gulls careening overhead. Friends sit on the grass together, couples push carriages. Nola Wren scrambles out of her stroller to scatter a flock of pigeons into a flurried whirl.

Maeve throws her arms up, dodges a stream of excrement. "Ew. Just what we need, to get shat on by a bunch of birds."

"Supposed to be good luck," Molly says.

"People only say that to make themselves feel special because a bird shit on them."

Despite the worry hanging over her, Faye recognizes that traveling with her daughters and granddaughter, sharing this space with them, is an adventure. The Irish accents remind her of Thomas and of William, sounds from the only sense of home she has ever known. She has been Irish most of her life. To be here now, in Ireland, preparing to relinquish her identity, feels like another betrayal. She hooks her arm into Maeve's, taking comfort there, as they follow Molly and Nola Wren along the winding path edged with low iron fencing. They pass through the open center, a Victorian garden of fountains and flower beds.

"I'm glad you're here," Faye says to Maeve. They watch Molly bend with Nola Wren to feed the ducks.

"Yeah," Maeve says. Faye hears that catch in her voice and stops.

"C'mon, let's sit down. What's wrong?" She wants to add "now" or "this time" but stops herself. Maeve doesn't need her judgment.

"My heart," Maeve says. "It feels like it's wrapped in thorns." She gestures with a nod. "After this trip is over, Molly will take her away somewhere. She can't stand being around us. I know I've made it hard on her. I got so used to feeling like I had to be the best mother and the best wife. To prove myself all the time. I didn't mean to make it into a competition with Nola Wren as the prize. I let myself think of her as mine. But she never was." Maeve rests her head on Faye's shoulder.

Faye touches Maeve's cheek. She knows it's all true. Molly chases after Nola Wren, who heads away from the open field toward a stand of trees and a fountain. "I don't know how to keep us together anymore," Faye says. That word. *Together.* It was so important to Elisabeth, it's one of the few German words Faye remembers. *Zusammen.* But it felt impossible to Faye even then, as if her old soul knew better. *Things fall apart,* she thinks.

"I was thinking about Grandpa, after you told us about, well, all of this," Maeve says. "Him and his Yeats. Things fall apart."

Faye smiles, stunned by the shared thought. *The ghosts are with us.*

"Maybe I've been kind of playing house, like make-believe. Same old, same old." Maeve says, touching her mother's sleeve. "If Molly hadn't come back . . ."

"But she did, Maeve."

"No. I know. What I'm trying to say is that this thing with Wendy is different. I'm different with her. When we go home, I want to do my life differently from here on out. I'm gay, Mom. I want to say that out loud so I can be that everywhere. I feel like I've been tiptoeing around, careful of revealing too much. Or maybe I'm just tired of trying to prove that I'm worthy even though I'm gay. It's not a flaw. It's who I am."

"I know I've made you feel that way. I'm really sorry, honey. I put my own worry about being outed—Is that the right word? Of being outed on you."

"Yeah, that's the right word, Mom. You're very cool now."

"Have you ever heard the saying, 'The barn's burned down, and now I can see the moon'?" Faye asks.

"No. But speaking of barns—" Maeve says, though Faye doesn't seem to register it.

"Basically, it means sometimes something wondrous is revealed after a catastrophe. We can only hope."

"I want to talk to you about an idea," Maeve says. "Wendy and I were thinking—"

"You guys!" Molly shouts, waving them toward her.

"Let's catch up with them," Faye says, pulling a reluctant Maeve to standing.

Molly points at a bronze statue of three women in a circular fountain where Nola Wren dips her hands. "Check it out. Maiden, mother, crone," Molly says.

"What?"

"Maiden, mother, crone," Molly repeats. "The three Fates? Spin, measure, cut?"

Maeve gives her a perplexed look.

"The three Fates. It's like, in all mythology. Women determine man's fate, the length of his life. The young girl unwinds the thread to spin it, the middle-aged woman measures it out, the old woman cuts the thread."

"It's us," Maeve says. "Nola Wren is youth, we're in the middle, and Mom's the crone."

"I'm not a crone!" Faye says.

Maeve spots a plaque laid in stone around the fountain. "Look," she says. "'With gratitude for the help given to German children by the Irish people after World War II.' Mom!"

A shiver of ghosts clacks up Faye's spine.

Maeve pages through the travel guide. "It says here the statue was dedicated in 1957. The sculptor was German. One plaque is in English and one in Irish."

Faye is spellbound by the statue, by memories sparking around her like fireflies. "It was here all along. If your father and I had come to Ireland, we would have seen it together. Proud as he was to be Irish, he was ashamed that Ireland stayed out of the war, ashamed for the way they played the whole the-enemy-of-my-enemy card. He couldn't understand it after all he'd seen the Germans do. I really felt like he hated the Germans. And I never wanted to be his enemy."

Molly picks up Nola Wren. "You and Dad were so in love it was ridiculous. There's no way he would ever have seen you as his enemy. You two made love look like it was supposed to be easy. I resented it, honestly."

"You resent everything," Maeve says.

Molly scoffs. "You're no picnic either. You're telling me you didn't worry Mom and Dad would be disappointed in you if they knew you were gay? Give me a break."

"Give me a break," Nola Wren says, mimicking Molly's words, down to the tone.

Molly shrugs. "I don't know, Mom. Maybe if you'd been honest, it would have been easier on me and Maeve to screw up. If we didn't think we had to be perfect."

"I never asked that of you," Faye says. "Perfection. Never."

"Maybe you didn't ask it. But Molly has a point. You two were hard to live up to. You both had such high standards. I didn't think you ever made mistakes. When Molly and I did something that you thought was wrong, you told us to hide it or pretend it never happened. It was like silencing us proved that the secret we kept really was something to be ashamed of. You were ashamed of your secrets, so you made us ashamed of ours."

"You know what?" Molly says nodding to the statue of the three women. "Maybe they're all Mom." She twirls her fingers in the air, winding imaginary yarn. "She unwound the thread, she measured it out, and she cut it. Fate sealed."

"That's a little much," Maeve says.

Molly purses her lip. "You're right. Sorry."

"It's okay," Faye says, disarming the attack. "I've put you through a lot." Faye considers the statue again. Three fates or one? One thread or three? "But, in my defense, I've been through a lot too. It's a miracle Elisabeth and I got out of Germany at all. I do wish I'd given your father the chance to decide about me for himself. You're right about that."

Maeve takes Faye's hand. "Dad loved you. Period. No matter what. He loved us all."

A throng of schoolgirls enters the park, knee socks and Mary Janes, plaid skirts and blue jackets and beanie hats, their voices joyous and young and hopeful. "You know what? We Sullivan women are survivors," Molly says, strapping Nola Wren into her stroller. "But I don't have energy to start crying again right now. Can we get lunch? I'm starving."

Faye watches her daughters walk down the path, side by side. She places her hand on the cool granite. It could have come from a quarry in the west, like stones she skipped with Fiadh and Elisabeth and those damned O'Kane boys. If Fiadh was cut short in childhood and Faye is the crone, would that mean Elisabeth was lost between youth and old age? Faye bundles her coat and follows her girls into the bustle of Dublin.

Molly lies awake, picturing everyone who has slept in this room over a hundred—maybe two hundred—years, bodies in this exact bed or the one next to it. Nola Wren curls up beside her, not quite touching but close enough that Molly feels her breath on her arm. In fact, the room is thick with breath, as if even the oxen and horses, the ladies and farmers on the fussy toile wallpaper are breathing too. Laughter and ruckus drift up from pubs below. Her thoughts collide like bodies on a dance floor. She will never sleep. She rolls over carefully.

"Maeve," she whispers. Her sister faces her, but her eyes remain closed. "Maeve!" More urgently this time. Maeve's mouth moves. Molly knows she's perturbed. "I know you're awake. Open your eyes."

Maeve's teeth flash in the streetlight. Her eyes flutter and roll. "What?"

"I can't sleep."

"Try harder."

A peal of laughter from the street below pings off the window.

Molly turns the digital clock so Maeve can see the red numbers. "It's only ten o'clock. Let's go down and get a beer."

"No! I'm asleep. I'm in my pajamas. This day has been long enough already."

"Please. One beer. A pint in Dublin while we're still pure Irish."

The pub is packed, but Molly manages to find two stools at the bar.

"You've always had it," Maeve says loudly, leaning in to talk in bar voice. She sips caramel foam off her pint of Guinness.

"What?"

"You know." Maeve waves around them, raises her eyebrows to the bartender, who Molly was able to hail with a glance. "It. The neon sign on your forehead that only guys can see." Maeve peers at Molly dramatically. "Nope. Couldn't tell you what it says, but it's there."

Molly takes a gulp of beer, wipes her mouth with the back of her hand. "Ah. Yeah. Maybe, Open for Business or Kick Me, I Like It or Will Fuck for Attention." She dots the last one with her hand like lights on a marquee.

"I didn't mean anything by it," Maeve says. "I don't have it, is all."

"Trust me. You don't want it." Molly clinks Maeve's glass. "I love Guinness. And it's even better here. I kind of think of it as the drink of my birthright. Like how we never thought we had to wear green on Saint Patrick's Day."

"Yeah, nothing to prove," Maeve adds.

"Well, I sure have something to prove now," Molly says. She drains her beer into her mouth like she's watering a shriveled plant. She knows it's the wrong time and the wrong place, but she says it anyway. "I'm really sorry, Maeve, for what I put you and Wendy through. I have this selfish, nasty, cruel streak, and I want to blame Mom for it. But that's not fair. We drew shit cards, is all. But I hope you can see that I'm better—that I'm *getting* better."

"We love her, you know. Nola Wren. Wendy and I love her. We think of her—"

"I honestly don't know how to repay you guys for taking care of her. But I won't give you my child. I know you understand that."

The lads in the corner strike up the music, and there's no more air for conversation. Maeve welcomes the interruption. She's not ready to hear what else Molly might have to say. "Let's finish our beers. Mom'll kill us if she wakes up and we're gone."

Nola Wren, alone in the next bed, cries out. The spot beside Faye is cool. Faye pushes the coverlet back, breaches the space between the beds, and climbs in with her granddaughter. "Shh, shh, shh, shh, shh." How could they leave like that? Didn't they think about how frightened Nola Wren would be? She's only a little girl. A little girl in a strange place. Faye cuddles her, remembers shivering with Elisabeth in beds they shared. *How could you leave her? Didn't you know she would be scared?*

The hotel room door creaks open, and light from the hallway fills the room for a moment, then disappears. Faye stirs at the girls whispering.

The movement wakes Nola Wren from shallow sleep, and she cries out again. Maeve sets her purse on a chair, steps into the bathroom, and closes the door. Faye returns to her own bed while Molly lies down with her child, wrapping her up in her arms. "Mama's here," she says. "Mama's here."

CHAPTER THIRTY-FOUR

1996: County Wicklow, Ireland

The Irish countryside moves past in a green current, narrow roads twisting higher into the Wicklow Mountains. They left noisy central Dublin early in the morning, drove through the suburbs and past the harbor and docks of Dún Loaghaire. Faye remembers little of it. Oranges. Chocolates. Children vomiting. A lifetime feigning this Irishness, donning it like a costume. She can't bring up O'Kane and risk sending everyone into another tizzy. But he is on her mind. Corrupter, meddler, pot-stirrer. His final breaths held no truth for her at all. In a way, he'd won out, upending them all.

Faye checks the map, gives Maeve turning instructions. They're close now, and the roads narrow even more. A tourist bus squeezes past, sending their little car into hedges trimmed within inches of the car door. "I think our transport bus was in an accident," Faye says, shaking her head. "Yes! When we arrived at the barracks, the bus had a gash in its side!" She feels the jolt, the fear they will slide down a mountain and die. Death always so close.

"We're here," Maeve says, pointing to a utilitarian sign that reads "The Glencree Center for Peace and Reconciliation."

They wind their way along the edge of a small cemetery, through granite block walls and open iron gates, past a stone church. A hardened barracks looms. Time folds over on itself, and though Faye wears jeans and a sweater, she feels the scratchy wool of an ill-fitting dress. Maeve parks the car, and Nola Wren clamors over the seat and out the passenger door with Faye. How strange, Nola Wren's hand in hers. The last time Faye was here, she was the child, her hand the one held by an adult. They walk to the church, and Faye stares up, tries to conjure the people who took her from here. They were kind, she knows that. Nola Wren tugs her hand. "Hold on, honey." Faye glances over her shoulder. She knows there is a lush fern grove and an emerald creek down the embankment. She half expects a passel of children to scurry over at the ringing of a bell. They are all around her.

Inside the church, Maeve gasps. "Wow." She gestures to a vestibule where a life-size statue of a seated and distraught Mary cradles the body of her crucified son. Jesus is plastered in brightly colored squares of paper, Post-It notes with prayers and confessions from visitors.

"Oh. Okay," Molly says, leaning in closer to read the requests. "Here's a good one: 'Please help Rosie to stop losing things.'" They each tilt their heads, read others out loud.

"Help John understand his sins and come back to me and the kids."

"Forgive me, Jesus and Mary and Our Father in Heaven."

Prayers for Maile and Tristan and Paula and Linda. Prayers from Heather and Grace and Kathleen and Aoife. A special request sticks an inch below a painted wound dripping with painted blood. "May my arthritis be cured and my health restored."

"I wonder what's in that one," Maeve says, pointing to a piece of wadded-up blue paper tucked into the hand of Jesus.

"Extra private," Molly says. "We probably don't want to know."

Nola Wren gives Molly a pink paper square with what appears to be a bunny drawn on it. "Put it on the man," she says.

Molly bares her teeth and stretches out her arm carefully, as if mother or son might grab her sinning wrist. "Here good?"

Nola Wren tucks her chin to her chest and smiles. "Yes."

Faye shakes her head. "If this was here, I sure don't remember it. But, then again, when were Post-It notes invented?" She sighs. "I'm old."

"You know what's wild?" Molly asks. "Look. Notice anything? It's mostly women. You can tell by the handwriting. Women asking for help and prayers, women confessing, women sending love up to heaven, women asking for love here on earth. It's the women looking for peace, women asking for grace. And there's Mary, cradling her son, after men—supposedly of God, by the way—vilified him, persecuted him, betrayed him, and nailed him to a cross. The women were there to clean up the mess. Literally. Like always."

"I sometimes feel bad we didn't raise you girls to be better Catholics."

"Don't worry, Mom. We're not mad," Maeve says.

All three of them think the same thought, that their own guilt is heavy enough.

"The truth is it all felt too small for me. Claustrophobic," Faye says.

"Plenty of phobias in the Catholic church," Maeve says.

"In all religions," Molly adds.

Faye wanders toward the altar and the girls follow. They take in the light streaming through stained glass, the muted way it makes the walnut pews shine. "I remember sitting in church with my parents, Thomas and Jean, and reciting the profession of faith. I knew all the words, but one day when I was a teenager—this is before I even met your father—I really heard the words I was saying and realized I didn't believe it at all. From that moment on, I looked for a way out. I've kept an image of a god that is so much larger than what these religions allow." She shrugs. "That helped me through a lot of hard times. I didn't need to feel seen in the eyes of some god. To me, the fact that I am so small and so inconsequential is proof enough that we're not even close to understanding the mysteries. I'd hate to think of a god capable of saving lives who doesn't. The one all those women are praying to for help." She glances over at Nola Wren, who is drawing more bunnies for Jesus. Faye blinks away welling tears. "I'm so sorry I let you all down. I didn't know how else to be, *who* else to be."

"You don't have to keep apologizing, Mom," Maeve says. "All three of us have been eaten up by secrets long enough. That's what this trip is about, right?"

"And I *love* that this place is about peace and reconciliation," Molly adds.

Faye wipes her eyes. "Thank you both. This would be impossible without you. I say we get out of here and find the office. The last thing we need is for one of us to burst into flames." She stares at the altar, taps her lips absentmindedly. "I think I might have bitten a priest in here."

In an office tucked away at the end of a long corridor, a balding man in a gray cardigan greets them. Faye steps forward. She rehearsed with the girls. *Give the least amount of information possible. If you start with something that smells fishy, alarm bells will sound, and what should be a simple task will become too complicated. You do not want to become a headline in* The Irish Times. She tells the man she was childhood friends with a girl who was fostered near Kilcrohane. "Elisabeth Sonntag. I'm hoping you might help me find her."

The man spins around to a filing cabinet and removes a list from a manila folder. "It's taken time to locate the children, you see. Some remained here in Ireland, and others, of course, returned to their families. Tell me again the girl's name." He puts on reading glasses and thumbs through pages of names. "We've put them in a spreadsheet, and then Janet comes in on Tuesdays to make updates and check the mail and such. Quite the undertaking."

Faye nods. She wants to rip the document out of his hands, search it for herself.

"I'm not finding it here," he says, thick fingers running two at a time down the pages. "Ah, hang on now. Let me look at something else." He spins and takes out another folder. In it is a single piece of paper. He removes his glasses and sits back in the office chair. "Well yes, there it is, I'm afraid. Your friend has sadly passed. Seems she never did make it back to Germany. Listed here that the parish in Kilcrohane buried her in 1947. Shame that. And so young."

Faye can see the man's mouth moving, his gestures, the sympathetic tilt of his head, but the room has gone quiet except for the reverb of the bell that has tolled. *Elisabeth is dead. Elisabeth is dead.* "Bit," she murmurs, recollecting her sister's nickname. "I called her Bit." The man behind the desk apologizes as Faye retreats.

Maeve thanks the man as Molly sweeps up Nola Wren. The three of them follow Faye into the hall. She is gone. She's not on the wide lawn or at the car either. "You check the church and cemetery. I'll follow that path she pointed out. Does that make sense?" Maeve asks, though nothing makes sense anymore.

The cemetery is empty. In the church, a man in black pants and a black shirt slips hymnals into a pew. Molly stares at Post-It Note Jesus, tries to imagine what her life would have looked like without her own sister. It was Maeve who went on her magic carpet journeys, Maeve who taught her how to jump rope, Maeve who played 45s on the record player on stormy afternoons. And after the night Conor O'Kane died, for a while, she'd even let Molly tag along with her and her friends. And Molly had kept hoping that, at any minute, Maeve would whisper in her ear or pull her aside and tell her she saw the ghost, too—accusing, taunting, laughing, hovering. She had been so angry when Maeve went off and married Sam, when she left her behind to deal with the dead on her own. Nola Wren taps her leg, and Molly looks down. Without Maeve . . . Molly shudders, remembering putting the baby in her sister's arms. "Your Molly needs a hug," she says, and the little girl wraps around her. Forgiveness is breathtaking, she thinks, whether it's requested or granted. "How about we each make one more?"

Prayer or wish? Which one, she isn't certain, though she doubts there's a big difference. Nola Wren draws a bunny and Molly, after careful thought, writes her note.

"Grant us peace."

Maeve finds Faye sitting beneath a stone bridge in a green gully. Next to her is a mossy grotto with a statue of Mary surrounded by petitions and photos and relics left for loved ones. "Mom?"

Faye turns to her but doesn't respond.

"Are you okay?" Her words are muffled by rock and river.

"The boys told scary stories down here about leprechauns stealing children and making them live under rocks. I was afraid all the time. Elisabeth tried to protect me. She could always see the bright side of things, and that felt so futile to me. So many bad things happened. It seemed impossible that anything good ever would again." Faye puts her hands behind her ears, rubs them down her neck. Her fingers are cold as death. "No matter what the weather was, it was cool down here. It feels like a grave now."

Maeve sits beside her. "It's beautiful."

"I could lie down right here and die, and by the end of the day I'd be turned to stone and covered with ferns and toadstools."

"I'm sorry, Mom. I know it's not the news you wanted."

"I waited too long," Faye says, and the tears fall. She thinks about Elisabeth, but she thinks about Conor O'Kane, too, and the night he died. How he fought for breath, his lungs surely collapsed, how his cold eyes pleaded for help or comfort. If he knew his life was ending, maybe all he wanted from her was kindness so he would not be alone. She gave him nothing. She wanted him gone and didn't give enough thought to how his dying might impact her daughters over the long run. She is furious too. Elisabeth died in Ireland. Why couldn't he have simply told her the truth? Why be cagey about it?

Maeve leans in, shoulder to shoulder. "It was so long ago. What could you have done?"

"I could have fought for her. She wanted to stay together. I could have fought for that."

"Maybe you were fighting to survive. We do that alone too often."

Faye stands, examines the photographs in plastic bags, the crucifixes and trinkets. "I wish I had something to leave. But all I have is the photograph. I won't leave that."

"You both left so much of yourselves here already. Isn't that enough?"

CHAPTER THIRTY-FIVE

1996: West Cork, Ireland

After a restless night in Cork, they rise early and head west. Nola Wren sits in the back seat with Faye, flipping through picture books quietly. Faye drinks her in, thinks about William's spirit passing right through her, wonders what part of him might cling to her still. The rolling countryside is the green of beard moss, and the day, misty as a ballad. At one point, Maeve misses a turn, and they wind up along the wild Atlantic coast unfurling into a churning sea.

"How much farther?" Faye asks.

Molly spins in her seat, shows Faye the map of where they are, near Skibbereen, and where they're heading, an *X* on a finger peninsula jutting into the Atlantic.

They make a turn and follow the Durrus River to where it flows into the bay near a vine-covered granary, long abandoned. The seacoast opens up along Sheep's Head. Faye shudders at the sight of the choppy water.

"Anything look familiar, Mom?"

How memory plays its tricks! Sponged ground beneath tiny toes, the way a skirt moves when the girl wearing it skips in a meadow, warm bread in open hands, a stone in that same palm, musty hay on a lumpy mattress, moonbeams shimmering like schooling fish on a calm bay, the sea smell in a girl's wet hair.

Faye shakes her head. It's too hard to describe.

"Let's pop into a pub and ask for directions," Molly says. "I don't see a cemetery on this map. I mean, that's the first stop, right? Pull over there," she says, pointing. "I can run in."

"No," Faye says. "I should do it."

"Let's all go," Maeve says. "We need to stretch anyway. Maybe they have sandwiches."

Two empty kegs sit in front of the pub, and the smell of braising meat hits them when they open the dark door. Inside, there are three tables, stools at a short bar, and men raising pints. There are no women, and Faye feels it when they enter. The barman asks if they're looking for a table. "Actually, we're hoping for directions," Faye says.

"Ah, Americans!" the barman says. "I can tell by the accent. Got a keen ear."

Faye smiles awkwardly. "Yes. We're looking for the cemetery."

"Oh, digging around the family tree, are ye? What's your name?"

Panic sets in. She glances over her shoulder at Maeve and Molly.

"Not meaning to ask you a hard question."

An old man in a thick sweater and wool cap turns on his barstool to watch the exchange. He cocks his head, and Faye can see that he's rolling his tongue over what teeth remain. He glowers at her as if he finds Americans in his pub offensive. "Well," she says. "My name is Faye Sullivan. These are my daughters and granddaughter."

"Lots of Sullivans here."

"No." Faye shakes her head. "No, I'm not looking for Sullivans. I had a different name before. I'm Fiadh Beatty." *I'm ten years old.* "I . . . I . . . grew up near here. My parents were Thomas and Jean. You're too young to remember them."

The old man sneers, hands his glass to the barman, who pulls the tap back for him. "No Beattys around here anymore, if that's who you're looking for. You lads know of Beattys?" The men at the table shake their heads. "Francis?" The man stares as he sucks foam off his beer. "Say your name was again?" His voice is made of salt and smoke.

"Faye Sullivan. But I was Fiadh Beatty."

"Dead Beattys from way back. Boys. They're out there."

Faye's voice shakes now. She doesn't dare bring up German girls who lived here once. "Out there. You mean the cemetery? Can you tell us how to get there?"

The barman flings a towel over his shoulder—two houses out of town, turn by the playground, stay left, a crown of trees, the hedgerow. "Can't miss it," he promises.

"You get that?" Maeve whispers to Molly. "I only understood half of what he said."

"Thanks for the help." Faye takes Nola Wren's hand and follows Maeve out the door. Molly, last to leave, stops suddenly, turns. "Do you know any O'Kanes by chance?"

The men at the table look at each other, then to the bar. The bartender's mouth opens, and he scratches his cheek with three fingers. The man in the sweater moves his head to the left, like a weathervane catching the slightest wind.

Faye pokes her head back in. "Pix . . ."

Molly's eyes widen, and she flashes a toothy smile. "Top of the morning to you then," she says wryly and heads out to the street with Faye.

"I thought the Irish were supposed to be all nice and friendly. That was the twilight zone. And what about Darby O'Gill in there? The way he stared was creepy."

"Maybe they're not used to strangers." Faye says, though her gut tells her it's something else. "Why'd you go back?"

"I asked about the O'Kanes," Molly says. "They all clammed up."

They pass through town and turn onto a narrower road. "Stay left," Molly says, checking the map against the directions they were given. Dew drips from branches shrouded in white mist.

The windows are down, and Faye undoes Nola Wren's seatbelt so she can spy the bubbling creek lined with tall grass. Sheep and shrubs dot the sloping countryside sectioned by stone walls. Ferns and vines form a thick border at the edge of the asphalt. "The plants are eating the road," Nola Wren whispers.

Faye has to agree. It seems it would take no time at all for signs of humans to be consumed by the wild greenness around them. They drive beneath a canopy of trees, past windowless stone farm buildings until the wall next to the road becomes more refined. The sea and a patch of blue sky appear. "This must be it."

"It's a burial ground, all right," Molly says. Maeve stops the car, and she and Molly turn in their seats. Beyond the iron gate is a tidy path that leads past limestone crosses and headstones to lichen-covered ruins of an old *cíll* and the white-blue bay beyond.

An eeriness sets in. Faye feels like she's passed into another realm, that it's possible she's dead. She wants to ask, "Is this goodbye?" She pushes the iron gate open and walks into the graveyard. If she is Fiadh Beatty, the bay where she drowned spreads out in front of her. Faye wanders along graves haunted by ground mist that moves with new life as the breeze picks up. Ancient letters and dates, names as familiar as home since so many families made their way to America. Coughlans and Dalys, Driscolls and McCarthys and Donovans and, yes, Sullivans. She looks around at the sea of stones. Where in this earth would they bury a German child?

"Mom! Come here!" Maeve shouts, waving her over.

Faye goes to where the girls stand. The stone is low and white, the engraving difficult to read. But the surname is clear. Beatty.

Maeve reads slowly, tracing each letter with her fingertips. "Erected by Thomas and Jean Beatty and daughter Fiadh . . . Oh, Mom! Okay.

In memory of sons . . . sons and brothers who departed this earth . . . John and . . . is that Patrick? I can't read the dates."

"She went crazy when they died, your grandmother. That was the story. They called her Batty Jean." Clumps of memory rise like peat. "Those O'Kane boys teased Fiadh with it. Taunted her until she threw rocks at them. I hardly talked then and didn't understand what anyone was saying half the time. I don't think your grandmother ever recovered from losing them. And then Fiadh. I wish I'd thought to bring flowers. Maybe we can come back later."

"It all makes me so sad," Molly says. "Just being here."

"I'm sad too," Nola Wren says, hugging Faye's leg.

"At least the fog is lifting," Maeve says. "See?"

In the distance, Carbery Island appears, a breaching whale. Faye exhales and time slips backward. She sees girls frolicking there before all was lost. *We foot it all the night, weaving olden dances, mingling hands and mingling glances, till the moon has taken flight.* She shakes her head in disbelief, the way her father's Yeats rings in her ears. She points toward the island. "I'm heading that way. Let me know if you see anything."

Before Molly can grab her, Nola Wren steals a handful of tiny yellow wildflowers from a nearby grave and chases after Faye. "Mom!"

Faye turns, waving that it's okay for the little girl to accompany her. She bends at the waist to accept the stolen flowers. "Careful," Faye says, showing Nola Wren how to tiptoe. "We're not meant to step on graves." Wind whistles through the headstones.

"What do you think's going through Mom's head right now?" Maeve asks. "I mean, it keeps hitting me. I try to imagine Mom as a little girl on a ship crossing the Atlantic with strangers who've basically kidnapped her. I still can't get my head around it."

"Yeah, imagine how hard that had to be, knowing that you asked to be taken and then your sister died. I mean, trust me, I get that she felt damned either way. A million times I thought I'd ruined Nola Wren by leaving her. But, honestly, Maeve. If I hadn't . . . I didn't know what else to do. Maybe that little German girl didn't either."

The sound of tires on gravel breaks the moment. Another car pulls up next to theirs. From the passenger seat, an old man emerges.

Molly's face twists with confusion. "Is that Darby O'Gill from the pub?"

The man scans the graveyard, then bends to talk to someone in the car before standing again. This time he closes the door and puts his hands on the roof. Another man emerges, and the two of them talk over the top.

"Was that guy in the pub too?" Maeve asks.

"I don't think so?"

"Are we trespassing or something?"

The men are together now, their attention focused on Faye and Nola Wren in the corner of the cemetery nearest the sea.

"I've got a bad feeling," Molly says. "I mentioned the O'Kanes, and everything got really weird. C'mon. Let's warn Mom. Be casual, though."

Molly and Maeve pick their way through scattered headstones, trying to balance hurrying with being cool but also not trodding all over the dead. Maeve glances over her shoulder and sees the second man open the back door of the car and lean in. "Shit. Do you think they have a gun?"

Molly looks. "Why would they have a gun?"

A third person gets out of the car just as they catch up with Faye. She is kneeling now, head in her hands. Nola Wren pats her shoulder, saying "There, there," over and over.

Maeve's mouth falls open at the sight of the enormous gray angel, delicate stone wings raised in glory in front of a Celtic cross. The angel is a child, her eyes downcast, wavy hair long and free. She clutches three wildflower stems to the bodice of an ankle-length peasant dress that ends at delicate bare feet. The angel seems not as old as the simpler block of dark stone from which she rises that bears an inscription: **HERE LIES A CHILD, ELISABETH, TAKEN LEAVE FROM THE WEEPING WORLD.** Nola Wren's flowers lay where they were irreverently dropped.

Molly puts her hand on her mother's shoulder. Faye struggles on weak legs to stand, and Maeve goes to the other side to help her.

"It's her," Faye says. "This is my Elisabeth. Oh, God. Oh, God." She cries a life's allotment of tears, tears for losing her mother and father, tears for war, tears for her failures as a sister and mother and wife. Tears gallop from her, wild ponies on a beach. "She swore. Together, always together. It was all she wanted, and I couldn't give it to her. God, how I let her down." Pain as searing as a stab wound punctures her belly. If this is the end of her life, she would not be surprised. It flashes in front of her. "What happened here? Oh, Elisabeth! What happened?" Her hands cup her mouth as she turns to her daughters, their arms open. The three women cling to one another tight as a root ball. Nola Wren plops down on the mound and plucks petals from the stolen flowers.

A gust comes off the water and captures the slip of paper Nola Wren pulls from the pocket of her blue wool coat—another drawing of a bunny she decided just then that she'd leave for the pretty angel. It skips away like a flat stone on a still pond. She runs after it, a rabbit herself, hopping between unruly graves and stones, unfazed by what lies beneath her feet.

Rock doves coo in the gorse as a figure passes through the first of two crumbling stone arches, disappears, then emerges through the second. It is a woman. She lifts her head, puts her hand up to shield her eyes from the white glare of lifting mist. The drawing flutters to rest at her feet. She picks it up and looks at the girl, who stops short and stares.

In the boneyard there are souls living and dead, but it is the living who for the briefest moment, think about the same thing—a rope to throw to save another person. Nola Wren looks back and sees two of her three moms with her grandmother. She looks at the woman holding her drawing of a rabbit, and surely that is her grandmother too. And that seems fine, so she goes to her to retrieve her rabbit and to hold this lady's hand.

The breeze warms. Three crows circle overhead, and the rope that was tossed is gathered, hand over hand, until all are within reach of each other.

"Is it you?" the woman says.

Faye steps forward, caught in a spotlight. Everything around her fades. What she sees is a ghost, and it is her. The woman looks like her, dresses like she does, cuts her hair in a similar style. It could be that the sun sets and rises before Faye can move. Stunned and tear-choked, her voice as weak as it was when she was a child. "Bit?"

"Yes! Yes! And you are my Gisela! Oh, that sounds strange! Francis told us he saw a fetch, and she talked and said the name Fiadh Beatty. We knew we had to come straight away." The woman's accent is Irish, but even her lilted voice is Faye's, though stronger, more spry. "I would know my sister anywhere!"

Faye brushes the woman's cheek, taps her hands along the woman's arms, making certain she is no figment. "You're real? How can you be real? The grave!" she says, throwing her arms around the woman until the two seem like one. Kisses and tears, on cheeks and foreheads, temples and hair.

The sound of Faye's voice, aching and plaintive, fills the graveyard. Maeve and Molly entwine arms, cling to each other.

Faye's cleaved heart races. "They told us in Glencree that you were dead! You're on the list of the dead! How are you here, alive? It says right there! 'Here lies Elisabeth'!"

The woman takes Faye's hands, turns them over and over, kissing them lightly. A thin memory, Mutti's lips on her head and hands before tucking her into bed. "This is Fiadh's grave. It's her body that's in there. Elisabeth is dead in name only. Dead but not buried. I'm right here."

Faye's head spins. "I don't understand." Conor O'Kane saunters up to her, laughs in her ear. *If I am dead, as dead I may well be.* How rotten, how *cruel*, to torture her that way.

"The name Elisabeth died the moment the Beattys concocted their plan. Old Father What's-His-Name filled in the death certificate with my name on it. But it was you they took."

Faye cringes. *I will be Fiadh in America.*

"Hannie was afraid to tell him he'd made a mistake. No one could tell us apart anyway except Fiadh, and she was gone. They called me Gisela, and no one was the wiser. Well, except the O'Kane boys. Hannie convinced Theresa to keep her mouth shut, that you don't go challenging a priest if you want to go to heaven. Theresa shut them up good." Her laugh is carefree and mesmerizing. "They didn't know it was Fiadh in there," she says, nodding to the angel. "They thought it was you. Or me. I suppose in some ways it was all of us." She takes Faye's arm protectively as if they are old friends. "Magnificent, isn't she?"

Faye, lifted from the ground, smells perfume blooming from stone flowers as she listens to her sister's long-lost voice. The air trembles with the idle beating of muscular wings. Diaphanous fabric brushes Faye's wrists.

"I feel her here. Fiadh. She was so clever and funny. Like her father. My father." Faye shakes her woozy head. "Ahh. I have so much to tell you. So many questions to ask you. I don't know where to begin except to say I'm so sorry, Bit."

"Call me Sela. Everyone does. I hated being called Gisela. It reminded me of you too much. Oh! I would throw such a fit. Hannie came up with the compromise. It suits me now."

Faye falters. She has so much to explain, so much to atone for.

"Such a miracle you're here. Fiadh Beatty of America! My imaginary friend!"

"She talks a lot," Nola Wren says, and it's like the house lights come on and the audience is invited onstage.

"And who have we here?" Sela asks.

"If we're doing introductions, I go by Faye now." *So much to tell.* "Faye Sullivan. These are my daughters, Maeve and Molly. And you've met Molly's daughter Nola Wren. Girls." Faye shakes her head. There is no denying it anymore. "This is my sister. My sister."

"Sela O'Kane. What an absolute delight to meet you all. Like a dream."

Molly's heart skips. "Did you say O'Kane?"

"Yes, that was my husband's father you saw in the pub today. You probably don't remember him. He fished us out of the drink. Can you believe it? I married Jem O'Kane."

Faye wills the girls not to react, to stand unmoving like ancient stones. "You've been here the whole time? You never left," Faye stammers. "I had no idea. I swear. And such incredible news. Jem O'Kane. He was the best of them for sure. If I'd known . . ." She curses the memory of Conor O'Kane. They have endured too much for it to end over that dead body.

ൠ

For Molly, seeing Jem O'Kane up close is to imagine what her life might have been if it had gone another way. A dead man alive after all. Her mother and Maeve seem equally shocked by the resemblance to his brother, given the way they eyeball each other and her. A shock of white hair under the cap he wears, summer-blue eyes, all lines in his face drawn up from grinning, dark lips visible through a ring of whiskers. He embraces each of them, saving Faye for last when his eyes fill with tears that could be an ocean. "Look at you! I see why my Da here made the call. I remember clear as day when you two urchins showed up."

Molly rubs her arms while the conversation whips between the past and loss and the all-too-present shock of reunion. Nola Wren pulls on her pant leg, begging to see the donkey braying in the pasture across the road. What Molly needs so desperately is quiet, to sort this out in a way and place that feels less . . . just less. That old urge to bolt. She would fly away if she could. A farmer rolls by on a green tractor, lifts a finger in greeting. She could jump behind him, tap his shoulder, tell him, "Drive, buddy!" Anywhere but here. "I don't want this to end, but Nola Wren needs some food and rest." She puts on her best smile, taps dry the last bit of kindness in her.

Maeve sees Molly losing her cool and awkwardly comes to her rescue. "Maybe everyone needs a little time to process what's happened here. I know I do. Mom . . . ?"

"Yes," Faye agrees. "I'm overwhelmed. I don't know what to do next . . ."

"I can't let you go!" Sela says. "Not again!" She insists they all come back to her cottage if they don't have other accommodations arranged. "While we get to know each other. Jem and I will drop Francis back at the pub, and you'll follow us."

"Best not bother arguing," Jem adds. "Sela always wins."

CHAPTER THIRTY-SIX

1996: West Cork, Ireland

Jem warned Maeve to watch for chickens and dogs and sheep, especially after they turn from the highway onto the two-track dirt road. Sure enough, as they approach the cottage, a tabby cat darts from a clutch of bluebells. Maeve slams on the brakes.

"Can you imagine if I killed one of their animals?"

"Just what we need, considering," Molly replies. It has taken her the bulk of the ride to calm down, to agree there will be time to bring up Conor O'Kane, but that the time is not now. "How you doing, Mom?"

Faye can hardly catch her breath. "Okay," she replies uncertainly. What would she have done if Conor had told her the truth? Faye briefly loses sight of the other car and fears that her sister might be the one to leave this time.

When Maeve rounds the last bend, Jem is out of the car waving his mitt hands like he's bringing in a plane. He is tall and broad with a head full of glowing hair and a belly ribbed like a pony keg. A spotted farm dog runs circles around him then jumps on Sela. Faye feels it again, that sense that she is not alive or, at the very least, that she is not awake. She tingles at the sight of her sister, this version of herself who became a true Irish woman. Her tongue goes numb.

"What a pleasure to have you here!" Jem says as they emerge from the car, faces red and puffed with emotion. A gray-and-white cat slinks out of the vine-cloaked shed and lumbers past their feet and around the corner. Nola Wren chases after it. "Go in, get settled. I can look after the little one. Nola Wren, right?"

Molly nods.

"Lovely name, lovely child."

Jem ambles away, a lightness about him despite his size.

"You think she'll listen to him?" Maeve asks.

Myrtle and hydrangeas and prickly heath bloom in a bobbled skirt around a peach-colored cottage tucked neatly in a dell between rolling hills. Gray stone faeries peek out from beneath massive rhubarb leaves, mischief-makers playing freeze tag. Nola Wren's laughter reaches around the corner, taps Molly playfully. "Yes. I think she will."

There is pot roast for dinner, carrots and potatoes, and the conversation turns from Jem's love of cooking to Faye and her life in Maine with William.

"You never told him the truth?" Sela asks. There is judgment in the way she says it, and Faye's hackles go up.

"I believed I was protecting him. And Thomas and Jean. They were my parents, and I'd grown to love . . ." Even now, Faye finds it hard to say she'd loved Jean. But Thomas. In that moment she wishes he was sitting next to her at this table. He could make them all understand. "Wouldn't you agree that some secrets are kept to protect the people you love? I don't think I should be judged for that. You lived your own sort of lie here, didn't you?"

Sela smiles tightly, forks a carrot into her mouth. "It's not judgment. And yes, we kept the truth about that girl in the grave hidden. I have no guilt about it."

Under the table Molly gives Maeve an I-can't-believe-this kick, and Maeve responds with a quick I-know tap on Molly's thigh. Wine flows, and Molly is quick to refill. Something about the conversation, the way her mother glosses over the most difficult parts of their lives, with still no mention of Conor O'Kane dying in their foyer. She swills more wine, shakes her head as events tick by, stories casually laced with facts about Germany and war that Molly and Maeve have only recently learned, things kept from their father. Maeve shoots her a warning glance as if she can see that Molly's fuse has been lit. It's the way Faye sugarcoats it that galls Molly.

"Did I tell you Maeve has two kids, Dylan and Opal?" Faye asks, clearly eager to change the subject.

That she completely skips over the worst of the years unglues Molly. Brave with wine, she clinks her glass with a fork. "Hang on, Mom," she says. "Before we go into how perfect Dylan and Opal are and what a great mother Maeve is—maybe we should tell your new family about our *other* secret."

"Pix!" Maeve hisses.

"Oh, don't worry. I'm not talking about the fact that you're gay and all of that." Molly flicks her wrist and takes a quick sip of wine.

Maeve scoffs in disbelief, sits back in her chair.

"Stop it, Molly," Faye says, adding apologies to the table.

"No, you stop. Look. I like you both. And your house? This place? Wow. It's a faery tale. So magical. And look at Nola Wren. She's in there asleep on the floor next to a cat! Do you have any idea how hard it is to get her to sleep? She loves it here. But it's like everyone is under a spell." Molly breathes through her mouth, hot as a dragon. She can't stop the eruption.

"Pix," Maeve warns. "Stop being an asshole." She grimaces a fake smile for the table.

Molly's eyes roll like flicked marbles. "First. Stop calling me Pix. I hate it. I'm not a pixie, and I haven't been since—well . . ." She sits up proper, shakes off years of pretending. She tastes guilt in her mouth as the words form there.

"I'm sorry," Faye says, knowing that the time is now.

"Jem. Mr. O'Kane," Molly says emphatically, the wine speaking volumes. "Your brother Conor was, well, something of a friend to my parents. But I don't think he was a very nice man. I didn't know him because I was little the night he died." She was wearing a red nightgown, with white rickrack around the cuffs and collar. She touches her wrist where the elastic dug in. "He came into our house and ran up the stairs and yelled at Maeve and my mom. And what I did, Mr. O'Kane . . ." Molly pulls her lips in and out of her mouth, wetting them to keep them from gluing shut. "What I did, was I got between him and Maeve, and I *shoved* him. As hard as I could." Molly gulps for air, and Faye is by her side, kneeling, telling her to breathe, rubbing her arm, but she is back there watching as he flies through the air, the bottom of his boots pointing at her, that look on his face. They are out of her, the words she was told to never speak. Molly sucks in air through her nose, inflates herself like a balloon, floats above the table. "I killed your brother. Sir." Trembling, she splashes wine into her glass then stands with a flourish. "I need air. You all, talk among yourselves."

Outside, a full moon turns the garden blue. Molly sinks onto an iron bench that faces it perfectly. She pushes up the sleeves of her sweater, admires the way her skin looks pasted in moon dust, more film than flesh. Leo said she was a goddess in the moonlight the night they broke into the garden pool. Some goddess you are, Molly Sullivan. Vengeful fury, more like it. She hears footsteps on the pebble path.

"May I?" Sela asks.

Rage shoots off Molly like heat vapors. Still, she makes room.

Sela sucks air in through her nose, holds it, lets it out loudly. "You know," she says. "It's in our nature to put our best foot forward. We do it in job interviews, when we go on dates, when we make new friends. We're so certain other people are judging us. Especially women. We're the worst." She pauses, like she's taking Molly's temperature, then tilts her head at the cottage. "I suppose Jem's telling them the story now about Con and what happened. You were right. He wasn't a nice person. Even when he was younger. He was a shit. The kind of kid who dropped boulders on frogs and pulled wings off butterflies. You know the type?"

"Yes, but that doesn't mean he needed to be dead."

"Molly, think about it. You were a very little girl. And you pushed a very grown man. He must have been plenty drunk if a tiny thing like you pushed him over. You probably could have blown on him, and he would have fallen. He'd been in a bad way for a long time. Trust me.

"He and his brother Denis ran around with a rough crowd. Con tried to rope Jem into their business—hijacking trucks—but Jem would have none of it. Denis was a bit slow. When we first came to live here, your mom thought Denis was the scary one, but he was a big lug, a bit short tempered like Conor, sure, but mostly just gullible. When the two of them got arrested, Conor put it all on Denis, and he went to jail. Got in a fistfight in there and took a bad blow to the head. Died in the cell. Theresa—that was their mother—she threw Conor out over it. Told him she never wanted to lay eyes on him again and never did. We heard he'd died in America. A letter came from some woman that said he fell down a flight of stairs. We never doubted he'd come to a bad end. You can't live the way he did—careless mouth, reckless behavior—and expect to die of old age. Con drew the short string a long time back. I know this doesn't take away your memory of what happened. But I hope it might give you some peace. What a terrible thing to go through, and at such a tender age."

"I see him sometimes."

"I bet you do."

"Falling. Sometimes he doesn't make it to the ground. Other times he crashes through."

The night is quiet in the pause, save for a sawing band of crickets. Sela sighs. "When your mom was taken away, I wasn't much older than you were when Con died. Your mom never talked much. And I talked enough for both of us, even before we came to Ireland. It might be in her nature not to dwell on hard things. Maybe you're a little like me. I play things over and over in my head, burn it in.

"I remember waking up that morning, and your mom was gone. I flew out of that house like I had no feet. I screamed for her and Hannie. I ran to Fiadh's house, but everything was gone. The bags, Thomas and Jean, and worst of all, my sister. I fell into the dirt, couldn't get up, couldn't move or talk. Hugh—he was the man who fostered us and eventually became my permanent guardian—he tried to pick me up, but I flailed and flailed. I knocked my head into the dirt until I bled. I yanked at my hair. I must have looked like a monster, growling and clawing. Everything bad was wrapped up inside me in a tight ball. I bet you know that feeling. She and I had lost so much, and I had been trying so hard to keep us together. I told myself we would be okay if we stayed together. I thought that would be enough. But the wheel was in motion."

Molly stays silent, so Sela continues.

"I thought I was dying. I think I wanted to die. It was days before I'd calmed down enough to even eat. The worst thing was feeling powerless. And you know what Hannie told me? She said I was protecting Gisela by letting her go, by giving her a mother who would love her. She said Jean had suffered so much and that losing Fiadh would kill her. She told me that Gisela—my sister, mind you—was a gift from God to Jean and Thomas. And that I was God's gift to her, that she and Hugh would love me and keep me if I wanted to stay here in Ireland.

"You know what I told her? I told her that was a load of horse shite. I said she and Batty Jean were kidnappers. I told her that if she didn't get Gisela back that I would tell the nuns at Glencree what they'd done, and God would have it in for them. Hannie slapped my face good and hard and told me what's between her and God was none of my business and to be grateful that Gisela didn't drown right there in the bay with Fiadh. She told me life isn't fair and that terrible things happen. She said—I'll never forget it: 'Suit yourself. Imagine her at the bottom of the ocean or the top of the Empire State Building. But she is gone, and that is that.' Then she slammed down the supper she'd brought me. It splashed all over the floor in a terrible mess. Took me another day before I cleaned it up and went downstairs."

"Hannie sounds like a jerk."

Sela laughs. "She was actually very kind and generous. No non-sense, for sure. She had a giant bosom. Jem loved hugs from Hannie Flanagan. All the boys did. What was best about her and what she taught me without trying was that there's no sense in looking back-ward. When I stopped beating myself up, I used my crazy imagi-nation to make up stories about Fiadh Beatty of America and the adventures she would have. In my mind, my sister went to America and had a wonderful life. And look! I was right!"

Molly empties the last drops of wine into her mouth. "Didn't you want to find her?"

"I've wondered about that, why I never made it my mission, especially since I was so bound and determined that we stay together. When we were girls in Germany, the building we lived in collapsed, and your mom and I were trapped in the rubble. I thought the slightest movement would make a beam fall and crush us. I didn't move or speak. I didn't even want to blink so I kept my eyes closed. And I think there was a point when I realized—after my sister was taken to America—that our lives had always been precarious. One wrong move from me might get her killed. So, I kind of get her not wanting to tell your dad or you girls the truth. It's probably hard for you and Maeve to understand, though maybe you will someday. I had Jem and my life here, and he knew everything there was to know about me. That was a luxury, I see now. I gave up your mother's ghost a long time ago. I was not one for being haunted."

"Nola Wren was right. You sure do talk."

Sela puts her arm around Molly's shoulder. "I know. You should try it. Let it all out. It feels great."

"Ha!" Molly says, wiping her eyes with the back of her hand. "That's not how we were raised. Keep quiet, keep quiet. Don't tell. Don't talk about anything. It was not wonderful."

Sela shrugs. "Sounds like fear. Your mom had it, and I'm guessing old Batty Jean didn't help that any. She probably passed it on to you two girls. What about Nola Wren? Will you pass it on to her?"

Molly scoffs. "I haven't had much of a chance."

"What do you mean?"

"Well, if you must know, Maeve's been raising her. I've been an absentee mom. And I'm not with Nola Wren's dad. He didn't know a thing about her until last September. This whole revelation about our mom is quite a twist. Here I was thinking that I was the most shit mom ever." Molly throws her head back, the words tumbling out of her. "God. And my dad. Yeah, I don't know what I'm passing on to Nola Wren. I don't know what's going to happen to us. I told Leo—that's her father—that I wish he could be in her life, but he was furious with me, as you can imagine. I've got amends to make. That's what all this is, at least for me."

"Oh, Molly. That makes me sad. I hope for both your sakes that you can get up off your knees. Otherwise, that little girl in there will catch it, too, and then what?" She lowers her voice. "Oh, look! A visitor." She bends silently to quiet them both. In the distance between the garden shed and greenhouse, a fox soaks in the moonlight.

"Hello, friend," Molly whispers. The vixen turns her head, regards them, then trots off blithely, three kits tumbling into formation behind her. "Do you think it's a sign?"

"Of what? A fox is just a fox. Not everything has to be a big mystery. C'mon. Enough now. Let's go inside and sober up."

"Sela?" Molly says. "I need to tell Jem's dad. About Conor."

"Oh, don't do that. Francis would not want to hear that name coming from you. Trust me. The Irish know how to hold a grudge, and

Francis holds one for Conor that your story would only make worse. And not because of anything you did, mind you, but because Conor was the kind of man who'd gotten himself into a jam such that one child had to protect another from him. Conor disgraced the old man in a thousand ways. I'm not sure Francis could stand any more. Jem and me are enough. Consider yourself confessed and forgiven if forgiveness is what you're looking for."

They walk toward the cottage, and Molly steals a glance over her shoulder. The path is moonlit and clear. The fox and her kits have moved on.

CHAPTER THIRTY-SEVEN

1996: West Cork, Ireland

Faye and Sela steal away from the cottage after breakfast, leaving Maeve and Molly behind with Jem to play with Nola Wren in the gardens and greenhouses and flower beds and to read and nap under the apple tree. The morning mist in the valley lifts by the time Faye and Sela reach the main road on the way to the village and bay where they were last together as sisters.

On the drive, Sela prattles on about her and Jem, their nieces and nephews—children of older O'Kane brothers Faye never even knew existed—off in Dublin and London. About Jem's brother Tim who died from pancreatic cancer—"an awful death," Sela reports—and how his widow Jennie lives with their daughter in Bantry. She talks about her love of American films, all kinds "except horror movies." She steers the car along narrow roads, her back and neck straight, and tells Faye she likes comedies and romances, action movies, dramas, adventures. She likes classics, too, especially the ones with that Jimmy Stewart, though she buys him better as a reporter than a cowboy. She loves movies set in the American west, the old south, in Los Angeles and New York City. She says she thinks she might be in love with Brad Pitt—though he's no Robert Redford—and wishes someone would remake *Butch Cassidy and the Sundance Kid* with him as Sundance. "He needs a buddy, though. Someone to be Butch." She tells Faye she imagined Fiadh Beatty the American woman who survives disasters, who stands up to bullies, fights aliens, who drives cars fast and drinks martinis dry. "It was better for me to think of you that way." In Sela's America, Fiadh wore sky-high heels and flowy dresses, overcame sadness and brutality, and got her man. "I went to the movies to see you," Sela says, smiling.

This back and forth—family history and stories, lives lived and losses suffered, the pregnancies Sela and Jem attempted and lost—is at once comforting and exhausting to Faye. "You're lucky to have children and grandchildren of your own," Sela offers. In the quiet between ideas of what to talk about next, Faye wonders how she and Sela will ever be able to make up time. After Molly dropped her bombshell about Conor O'Kane, she and Sela and Jem had talked and talked about it, so much that Faye's throat hurt and her head pounded. Still. To hear Sela talk was to relive her own life in comparison. She did not share every event with Sela but let herself put them in parallel. *When you lived in Dublin while Jem was in college, I worked for Aldo in the flower shop. When you were trying to have a baby, I lost one. The year you went to London was the year Molly was born.* Besides the day that Conor O'Kane arrived at her wedding, their lives never intersected. Yet they were always connected.

Sela veers off onto a narrow road, down an even more rutted lane that leads to the bay. "This is where we walked when Hannie and Hugh first brought us home. That farmhouse is where Hugh left the car. The Dalys still live here."

Faye shakes her head. None of it is familiar to her anymore.

Sela dodges puddles deep from the morning's rain. Sun dapples the bay, smooth and clear like it was that day three sneaky girls rowed out for a picnic. Faye touches her hip.

Houses pop up along the roadside, some new and fine, others little more than ruins. Beyond where the road ends is a cluster of vined chimneys, walls barely standing, thatched roofs long collapsed.

Sela turns off the car. "There they are, what's left of them. Francis sold the O'Kane land years ago and lives in town now. Walks to the pub every day and sits with Brian, Theresa's brother's youngest son. He's the barkeep you saw."

The cottages seem so small, so close together. The Beattys' cottage, Faye's parents' home with Fiadh, is nothing but a single wall and crumbled chimney. She and Sela stand in the doorway of what had been Hannie and Hugh's house. The interior is collapsed, the blue sky shining through a hole where two girls once slept. Faye remembers backing down a ladder that is gone now. *There was no way back to you once I went down.* "It doesn't seem possible that real people ever lived here."

"We did. You and I," Sela says, pointing. "Right up there by that cloud."

They squeeze past a cattle gate, trespass on the abandoned property. Faye stands on a low rock wall. "Good God, this is beautiful, isn't it?" Meandering lines of stone and brush divide the fields into paddocks. Her sister's voice is in her ear. *Das ist ein grünes Land.* No harm was supposed to befall them here in this green place. She had promised. Faye steps down, and the ground gives, bogged and mossy. "Was it always like this?"

"Yes, I suppose it was," Sela says. "Come on. Let's go down to the water."

They follow the green footpath between ivy vines and blackberry brambles. The buzzing air is lush with grass and manure and heather, bumblebees big enough for a faery harness. Faye follows Sela like a shadow. She has borrowed a pair of rubber boots so they are twins in this field, both in cream sweaters and blue denim, their hair in matched silvering bobs, though Sela wears a canvas gardening hat over hers. She stops at the top of a rise. "There's Carbery," she says, pointing to the island in the bay. "The accident happened about there. We'd have made it back if it was a day like today."

Faye tries to imagine three little girls rowing out on their own. Too vast, too far, too deep. "We had no business trying to take that boat across."

"We sure had fun, though."

"How can you say that? I almost drowned. Fiadh did. And then . . . someone should have stopped us," Faye says.

"Maybe," Sela says. "Over here." She leads Faye to the precipice, which overlooks a rock-lined green pool, clear as glass fishing floats. "We used to come here to swim when I was growing up. After."

After. Yes. "I never liked swimming. Or boating. After," Faye says. "Jean was nervous about water. Understandably. This reminds me of Maine, these rock formations, how craggy they are. Imagine Ireland floating across the Atlantic to Maine and docking like puzzle pieces. Then there wouldn't be this wild and green sea between us. We could walk to each other." She pauses. "I never imagined you were still here. Or maybe I did. I didn't know where you were."

"Somewhere along the line, I lost the fact that you went to Maine. I only remembered America. Like I said, it was fun to think of you there."

Faye prickles at the word. "Fun. You keep saying it. Was your childhood fun?"

"Was yours?"

"Are you angry with me?" Faye asks.

"You're the one who seems angry," Sela says. "And to answer your question, yes, my childhood was fun, eventually. This was my home." She spreads her arms open to the countryside and sea. "I tried to be two people for the longest time—the self I was inside, a girl who was Elisabeth, and also you, the sister I swore to protect, this girl everyone called Gisela, who I thought I had failed. We got separated, and I thought it was my fault. Maybe it was when Hannie told me she knew about Mutti and that I could stay here with her and Hugh. You kept telling me Mutti was dead. I didn't want to hear it. I thought if we believed, we could go home eventually—"

"But we didn't have a home."

"I know that, Faye! But I was foolish. Then you were gone, and the sun came up anyway. Every single day! It dawned on me that no one here expected anything of me. Hannie and Hugh were kind and good, but I didn't owe them anything."

"How liberating for you," Faye says.

"You *are* mad!"

Faye breathes in this place, tries to bring the memory back. Fish smells, seaweed and algae on the shore. She imagines it like she is watching it happen. She hits the gunwale, tumbles under water, churning in her own bubbles. She surfaces, choking. Elisabeth is on the boat, but it is Fiadh who jumps in, Fiadh who saves her. A seahorse. Not her sister. She is pulled onto a boat deck, taken ashore. The coughing. Her lungs ache. A crowd has gathered. "I'm not mad. But I think I was. I told William the story of the accident as if I was Fiadh. I told him about foolish German girls and how careless Fiadh was standing up like that. Do you remember that you coughed like you'd fallen overboard too? I thought I was going to drown, and you pretended you almost did. You didn't save me. You *couldn't* save me. Fiadh did. In so many ways."

"Do you want me to thank you for being the one the Beattys took? Is that it?" Sela's face collapses. "Are you trying to punish me? I did everything I could."

They are the same height, the same build. Faye suspects they even smell the same. But they are not the same person. They never were. "I know you did," she whispers. "And so did I." Faye wonders how she will ever stop crying. "I have to tell you something." She looks back at the remains of the cottages, crumbled by time and neglect. "It wasn't only Jean and Hannie who cooked up the plan. I think I was the one who put the idea of a switch into their heads in the first place. And then, when you went to sleep, I snuck out, and I told them to take me instead of you. That's why your name is on the death certificate. They planned to take you."

Sela pushes away, her face childlike with shock. "What?"

"We were trying to survive! All of it weighed on me! I was afraid to go back to Germany. And I couldn't stay here either. I felt so guilty. Fiadh's drowning. I could feel her on my hands!" Faye gasps then, Molly's words coming out of her own mouth, the burden of a death that they both carried. "We were only children. Too young for war."

"But didn't you wonder what leaving would do to me?"

"I knew you would never stop fighting. Yes, that I knew." Faye closes her eyes. "I'm sure I thought I was doing what was right, giving everyone some glimmer of hope in a hopeless, desperate situation. And I was drawn to Jean and her sadness, if you want to know the truth. Even before Fiadh died. Something in me needed to feel all her pain." Faye flashes on Molly, that leather jacket, and the day Thomas died. How like her Molly turned out to be. If only Faye had seen it sooner. "And I saw Thomas . . ." Faye's voice cracks then. "The way he held Fiadh that day, the gentleness in him, like our own father. I missed him so much. Vati was never cut out for such a brutal war."

"I was heartbroken without you," Sela says. "And this breaks my heart again. I did everything I could think of to keep us safe. Did you mean to betray me?"

"No! No! I know what you were trying to do. But that wasn't your job. I tried to make you understand. About Mutti. About our cousin and how he was hurting me. I was impulsive and selfish. But you were naïve." Faye takes the worn photograph out of her pocket. She's told Sela the story already, how all their secrets came to light. "Look at this again. We look so much alike. We still do. But we're not the same. You can see it in our expressions. Even then we looked at the world through different lenses. We had different survivor instincts. You wanted to fight. I wanted wings." She thinks of that war book again, the one with the children. "It was war that made these girls who they were, who we've become. I'm so sorry. Please, Elisabeth. Sela. Please forgive me."

Sela steps back from the edge and onto the path they'd walked. Her chest rises and falls, her breaths purposeful and deep. "Ask me again if my childhood was fun," she says.

Faye takes two steps toward her. "Was your childhood fun?" she whispers.

Sela's chin quivers as she struggles to speak. "I do not want to talk about this! I don't. I never did. This is not me. But the truth is that without you, I was not constantly reminded of Germany. Without you, I could stop pretending Mutti was alive. I know what you saw. I saw it, too, sister. I saw Mutti run toward us. I saw the truck hit her."

"But you said—"

"You were constantly telling me she was dead. I was trying to keep her alive for both of us, don't you understand? And, by the way, I knew what Herbert was doing to you. It was me who told Uncle to send us to the orphanage. I thought we would be safer there. I thought it was my job to be hopeful for you. That was stupid of me. But you made everything so hard! I've always looked for the bright side."

"And I've always lived in fear."

"Yes, and so because we were separated, I did have a good childhood. And I am a happy woman now, despite the sadness in my life. As I play things out in my head, I never would have forgiven the Beattys if they'd taken me, like I never forgave them for taking you. But it's what happened, isn't it? Us girls were not meant to stay together after all. Was it a boating accident or was it war that came between us? I don't know. I let you go a long time ago."

"If only Conor had told me the truth." Faye shakes her head, the disgust surfacing with a sudden image of Conor O'Kane splayed out on the floor.

"If he'd told you the truth, who knows if you would have had your life with William, if you'd have your girls and grandchildren. And from your telling it, your relationship with Thomas Beatty, your father, was quite lovely. How lucky for you, Faye! No, this is the way it went. There was no other way."

"Can you ever forgive me?" Faye asks.

Even in her floppy boots, Sela scrambles lithely onto the stone wall, tosses her hat onto the ground. "Forgive yourself," Sela replies.

"Sister. Forgive yourself." Arms out for balance, she places her feet like a tightrope walker and takes off in a prance.

Faye watches as her sister transforms into the child she was—barefoot, hair thick and brown, flax skirt flapping in the westerly wind. Faye hops on the wall, too, splays her arms, sets herself free. "Wait for me, Bit! Wait for me!"

The pub is full of locals who all know Jem and Sela, regulars for darts and games, good for a pint or two. Francis sits on his stool, tells familiar fishing tales. Sela and Faye arrive late, and Maeve waves them over, relief on her face. A band of brothers—one on accordion, two on guitar—performs songs everyone in the bar knows. The mood is playful and light.

When introductions were in order, before Sela and Faye even made it off the beach with their pockets full of shells, Jem had hesitated. How to retrace steps, untangle stories, dig up the dead and switch the bodies around? Wasn't his wife his wife? Sela would not want to start being someone else now. And Faye left behind that other name long ago, a name for an Irish girl who threw herself into Dunmanus Bay to save a drowning orphan.

Who is anyone if not themselves?

"This is Maeve and Molly and Nola Wren. Long-lost family from America!"

Hats and glasses tipped, hands rested on shoulders, brown beer flowed. By the time Faye walked in with Sela, friends were waiting for her.

"You must be Faye Sullivan!"

"You must be Faye Sullivan!"

"You must be Faye Sullivan!"

And she was. Of course, she was. She was Faye Sullivan and no one else.

Now, Nola Wren, belly full of fish and chips, dances with another child in front of the band in that wild way children do, no rhythm, all joy.

"She's been like this all day," Molly yells to Faye over the music. "She's so happy."

Faye holds Molly's face in her hands. Her little girl. William's pixie. Thomas's faithful one. She says each word plainly, speaks them with her eyes and touch as well. "I'm sorry for all the ways I hurt you." It's a start.

Molly tilts her head into her mother's hand, rests there. "It's all right, Mom. It is."

Back at the house, in a bed that is too small, on an ancient and sagging mattress, after deep conversation with Jem, Sela rests her hand on his heart until he falls asleep. She slips out of bed and walks down the hall.

In the guest bedroom under a heavy crocheted quilt, its needlework exquisite, Faye dreams of green pastures and William. She stirs as the cover lifts and a warm body curls into hers. A voice in her ear. *Du bist aber mutig. Ich verzeihe dir.* It is her sister. *You are very brave. I forgive you.*

Faye exhales. Her war is over.

Down the moonlit path, the vixen carries a limp rabbit to her kits. Beyond, in the guest cottage, up the stairs in the sleeping loft, Maeve snores on her right side, and Molly curls on her left. Between them, Nola Wren is wide awake, staring out the skylight at the moon like it's talking to her.

In the morning, Molly wakes before the alarm goes off. The spot between her and her sister is empty. She climbs out of bed, checks the cot where Nola Wren is supposed to sleep but never did. She is not there.

Molly rushes down the stairs into the empty sitting room. She runs out the door barefoot, heart racing. She thinks about her grandfather's stories of leprechauns and faeries stealing children away to the land of heart's desire where nobody gets old and grave and bitter of tongue or something like that. But his voice tells her all is well. The door is unlocked, the house quiet, though it smells of bread in the oven, which is heavenly. On a fringed rug near the simmering wood stove, the gray cat purrs on a pillow, and a little girl sleeps next to him, her eyelids fluttering as if she's whisked the cat away on a magic carpet. Molly's heart stops pounding. Outside the sliding doors, she spots Jem watering flowerpots, the sweeping spout of his brass can catching the first sunbeam.

She slides the door open, closes it gently.

"Good morning," she says.

An hour later, Maeve comes into the cottage fully dressed, sad to leave but eager to start the journey home. She misses Dylan and Opal. She misses Wendy. She misses Sam. She misses the cove house and the farmhouse and beers in her rocker on the porch with Wendy when the sun goes down. She doesn't miss the mosquitoes or the black flies or the way winter socks them in, but she also knows that no place is perfect. Sela and Faye assemble trays for their final breakfast together, their movements paired and fluid, an ease about them both. Molly and Jem sit on a bench outside the sliding glass door, watching Nola Wren circle the apple tree, laughing as if faeries dance with her. Sela says that the little girl has already helped feed the gray cat and that she and Jem checked on the barn swallows tucked in the rafters of the tool shed. Jem gestures off in the distance. Molly follows his glance and nods.

Maeve checks her watch, assures Faye that they're on time as long as they leave right after breakfast. It's a long drive back to Dublin, and Maeve doesn't want to get stuck in traffic or darkness. Molly is the one most likely to make them late, and Maeve doesn't want to be late. She slides the glass door open.

"Pix," she says, immediately regretting it. "Sorry. Molly. Ready to go after breakfast?"

The coffee in Molly's cup has gone cold, but that doesn't matter. She goes to Maeve, who has stepped out onto the patio, and squeezes her around the belly like she did when they were kids. Molly has been thinking about peace and reconciliation, about resilience and destruction, about the women who stuck prayers on Post-It Note Jesus, about confessionals and tribunals, and about whether a sin needs to be aired to be forgiven. She's been thinking about her mom and dad, about silence and the Silent Generation, and about her grandfather and Yeats and the Morrigan and shapeshifting and fate and Fates.

"You're a really good mom, Maeve. And a really good sister. I'm sorry I've been so ugly. I hope you'll forgive me. I can't imagine where I would be without you."

"You hug like Dad," Maeve says, and it sounds like forgiveness.

"Thanks, Maeve." Molly lets her sister go. "Can you get Mom and Sela?"

Maeve retreats into the cottage, returns with Sela and Faye, the gray cat sashaying wistfully behind them. Jackdaws quarrel with two magpies beyond the stone wall. The gray cat perks her ears then curls at Jem's feet.

"So?" Maeve asks. "What's up?"

"Bear with me," Molly says. She tells them again about her hands, how she has felt a dead man's body against them since she was a child. She tells them about fear and shame and that she doesn't want to live with either anymore. "I feel like I've been trying to one-up everyone on trauma, like mine's bigger, deeper, worse in every way." She rubs her hands down her arms, tugging at her own skin. "I apply my anger in coats—literally, sometimes," she says with a self-deprecating laugh. "I've lathered it on so thick I haven't been able to feel anything else.

Over the last couple of months, coming home, losing Dad, being here now—" Molly stops, takes in the expressions on the faces around her, the sweep of the valley as the mist clears, the waning moon in the light of day. "Yeah. That's it. Being. Here. Now. I swear I'm not trying to hurt any of you. Really, I'm following Nola Wren's lead. I want to do what's best for her."

As if on cue, Nola Wren runs to Molly, turns to face the others. Molly places her hands on her daughter's tiny shoulders. She knows she's the passenger now, and the magic carpet has brought her and Nola Wren to this green place.

"I called Leo last night, and I talked to Sela and Jem too. What I'm trying to say is I'm staying here. *We're* staying here, me and Nola Wren. Not forever. But for now. Kind of our own Operation Shamrock. The two of us need to recover in a place away from where all the bombs were dropped. And, Mom, I think Dad and Grandpa would be really happy about this. I know it's a big deal, but I'm asking you to trust me. I just want us all to be ourselves again."

The jackdaws flush and take to the sky.

CHAPTER THIRTY-EIGHT

Maine, America

In Maine, America, the mornings are chilly, but the days still warm up enough to shed jackets by afternoon. The leaves change from green to rust and crimson and gold. The house on the cove sits empty for the time being, cleared out and buttoned up for Molly and Nola Wren in case they decide to come back. Over the summer, Sam remarried, and Maeve and Wendy and the kids moved in with Faye. Settled now, they will spend the winter months modernizing the barn and making plans for goats and chickens and a farm stand to sell cut flowers and pottery and jam and fresh produce. Faye will sort through William's heaps of antiques, decide what they can sell and what to keep for displays. She will hand-letter and paint a rainbow-shaped sign that will read, **WINDY MAY FARM**. She feeds on the energy of ideas and feels young and useful.

At night, she falls asleep easily and dreams dreams without ghosts.

Faye discovered Jean's lost journal when she and Maeve emptied the bookshelves of the cove house. It is Jean's story of coming to America, bent with grief and regret. Jean paints a clear picture of how Hannie planned to keep Elisabeth and Gisela in Ireland all along. The nuns knew they had little to go back to in Germany and had told Hannie as much. Hannie thought of the girls as her own and loved them both. But Hannie loved Jean more and for longer and "selflessly" (Jean's word) gave away something that didn't belong to her. She gave away a person as if she could.

In her telling, Jean realized too late that what they'd done was not only a crime but a sin, a whip she beat herself with every day, a sin that prevented her from loving a child who could never replace her own. *At least the girl won't miss me when I'm dead,* she wrote, though she adds that she hadn't banked on Thomas loving the changeling. *It's true he's the bigger of the two of us.* There is a lofty holiness in her writing as if she believes this great sacrifice—denying Faye love so that she won't experience grief—not only honors Fiadh's memory but will assure Jean a spot in heaven.

And there, too, is Conor O'Kane, showing up in the journal on Faye's wedding day as in real life. Faye winces seeing his name, afraid he told Jean the truth about Elisabeth and that she'd kept it from Faye. Or worse, that Thomas had found the journal and had done the same. But there is no mention of Sela and Jem. Conor O'Kane, she wrote, was like her own boys, a proxy for all that she'd lost to God or the sea or to bad luck. With him, she could talk about Fiadh, about Ireland, about a life neither of them lived. The two of them come alive in the pages, smoking and smiling and scheming.

Jean's last entry: *It must be I am dead now, otherwise why read this account? I beg you pray for me and my sinner's soul that I be forgiven. I want to reach Heaven and see my children. This is my wish and my dream and my last hope spread here in ink.*

Though she doesn't believe, Faye sends up prayers for Jean and for Thomas, prayers that they have found each other again. He loved her, after all. She adds one for Hannie and Hugh, another for her friend Fiadh, none for the old priest who looked the other way, who should have known better than to do this to children.

Faye made photocopies of relevant pages and mailed them off to Sela.

It is our story, Faye wrote. *Yours and mine.*

On one crisp spring morning, Maeve and Wendy welcome three baby goats to the farm. Molly and Nola Wren board an airplane that flies over Fastnet Rock, the last land Faye glimpsed when she left Ireland. When their plane arrives in Boston, America, America the Beautiful, Leo will be waiting at the gate.

And on that same day, Faye receives a letter from Sela. "In some ways, we all went to our graves when Fiadh did. Jem and I thought it only right." With the letter is a photograph of a rough standing stone next to Fiadh's grave. Three names are chiseled around a triskelion spiral, no spaces between the letters, no beginning and no end. Faye traces the whirling maze onto the soft veins of her wrist like a tattoo, three circles connecting clockwise and counterclockwise, meeting and parting like contra dancers. Quietly, she casts the names like a silver net.

Fiadh. Gisela. Elisabeth.

They were children once, arms linked, weaving the ring, cracking the whip, laughing wildly and bravely together in the gray sedge and sea spray and fading light.

Acknowledgments

"A Drinking Song" by William Butler Yeats

Wine comes in at the mouth
And love comes in at the eye;
That's all we shall know for truth
Before we grow old and die.
I lift the glass to my mouth,
I look at you, and I sigh.

I first learned about Operation Shamrock on a trip to Ireland when I happened upon The Glencree Center for Peace and Reconciliation, where German children were housed while they awaited foster care. Thank you to Gisela and Reinhard Liedtke for giving us such a wonderful reason to visit Ireland and to Gisela for allowing me to commandeer her name. I'm grateful to Monica Brandis and her extensive work interviewing former children from Operation Shamrock, work that was supported in part by the German Embassy in Dublin and the Irish Embassy in Berlin. Thanks to Anna Schmidt for granting me access to her documentary of Operation Shamrock, *Irish Oranges*. I also consulted the memoir *From Cologne to Ballinlough* by Herbert Remmel, who was an Operation Shamrock child. The Maine Irish Heritage Center in Portland is a lovely resource, and I appreciate the time I spent there. Thank you, Edna St. Vincent Millay, William Butler Yeats, and Seamus Heaney for your poetry.

Writing *Westerly* ran in parallel with research into my ancestry, a journey that resulted in gaining Irish citizenship. Sláinte to my brother Kevin. I'm so glad we took that wild trip together. I was enriched by the work of The Irish Folklore Commission and their efforts to translate the written work of Irish schoolchildren into a searchable database of stories. Geraldine Powell was incredibly generous in helping me locate my ancestors' ruins near Kilcrohane. Her thesis, "Life in a West Cork Clachan," gave historical reference to the settlement type in rural Ireland. In Kilcrohane, the inimitable Noel McCarthy, to whom I'm related through my grandmother Anna Sullivan, provided a colorful account of my family history and a sense of place for *Westerly*. Also, a boy named Dylan Harrington popped out of a ditch with his little dog and helped me find the grave of my great grandfather. He reminded me to tread softly, and I wondered briefly if he was real or a spirit. My uncle Bill "Cowboy" Donovan, who art in heaven, passed on to me a letter sent to his mother, my grandmother "Hannie," from her aunt Mary. It's dated January 25, 1938, Gortnaclasha. Without that letter, I'm not sure *Westerly* would exist at all.

Huge thanks to my agents at Folio Literary, Margaret Sutherland Brown and Jenna Land Free, for their unwavering support and guidance through the publishing process and with the novel itself. I'm incredibly fortunate to have you both on my team. A ton of appreciation to Carmen Johnson and Laura Van der Veer at Little A for bringing *Westerly* to life so beautifully, and to Ronit Wegman for her thoughtful edits. Thanks also to Ali Castleman and Karah Nichols for ushering the novel through production; to Elsa, Cortni, and Brittany for their careful reads; and to Tree Abraham for spotting Rebecca Aldernet's gorgeous painting and suggesting it for the *Westerly* cover.

Many thanks to these fine people and places: the Sewanee Writers Conference and workshop leaders Tony Earley and Jill McCorkle; Pam Loring and The Salty Quill Writing Retreat for gin tonics, cold dunks, crackling fires, beautiful storytellers, the rugged Maine coast, and darkest of skies; Chris La Tray, the Freeflow Institute, my fellow rafting writers, and the storied Blackfoot River for reminding me I can be brave; Ben Shattuck, The Cuttyhunk Island Writers Residency, and that amazing cohort of writers with whom I shared the week and who have greatly enriched my life; Michelle Hoover, the GrubStreet Novel Incubator, and all the incubees for their camaraderie; and Anna Solomon, whose accountability workshop and introduction to the Pomodoro Method got me out of a ridiculous slump. Special thanks to Amy Berkower, Genevieve Gagne-Hawes, and Janet Rich Edwards, who read early drafts of *Westerly* and provided critical feedback; to Tess Callahan, William Dameron, and countless other writer friends for lending an ear and offering sage advice; and to Bettina Gentile for her help with the German language.

All the stars to my fellow Four Points Writers: Michele Ferrari, Jessie Manchester, and Kathy Sherbrooke. You embody everything good about this writing life. You're generous, loyal, tenacious, honest, vulnerable, inspiring, creative, bold, resilient, and the pillars that hold me up. I am the luckiest person to have you wingwomen on this journey with me. My appreciation for each of you is boundless.

Special and heartfelt thanks to the brilliant and wise Lissa Franz, who came through for me in the pinchiest of pinches as both a writer and friend; to Wanda Sigurdson and Pam Sohn for decades of friendship and the stories behind the story; and to Lynn Gallagher and Ann Horwitz, who are always up for popping the cork. Wishing peace and love to Joni Hudson and to all Mar's friends as you read between the lines.

To Wolfgang, Olivia, and Miles. I just love you all so much. Thanks for believing in me, for cheering me on, and for loving me back. To my mom and dad, as before, wish you'd lived to see the day. I think you would have liked this one.

About the Author

Photo © 2025 Traer Scott

Susan Donovan Bernhard is the author of *Winter Loon*, an Amazon bestseller and winner of the Boston Authors Club's Julia Ward Howe Prize for fiction. She is a Mass Cultural Council fellowship recipient, a GrubStreet Novel Incubator program graduate, and a Tennessee Williams Scholar to the Sewanee Writers' Conference. A dual citizen of the United States and Ireland, Susan was born and raised in the Bitterroot Valley of western Montana and graduated from the University of Maryland. She now lives and writes in Massachusetts.